Th... ...ver is a
ph... ...onable
reg... ...velvet
rib... ...made
of ... ...antly
sim...
mu...

"...

van...
Eng...

Lord Carro... ...her upper arms, but he
made no motion to release her. "I think you're forgetting
something."

"What?" Linnea gazed up at him uneasily.

"You forgot," he whispered, "to give me a kiss."

"I . . ." She stopped, unable to think of a reasonable excuse to avoid doing any such thing.

"We're married," he reminded.

"I am quite aware of that," she said tartly. "But this is
hardly the time—"

"—for embraces. You said that already." He smiled and
lowered his voice. "You have such a pretty mouth, sweetheart. What a shame not to use it for something more enjoyable than protests."

His cajoling tone, combined with the serenity of his expression, gave Linnea a provocative taste of her husband's
methods. And while she would have preferred to argue, capitulation seemed the quickest route to escape.

"Oh, very well." Closing her eyes, she raised her chin and
offered her lips with the air of a martyr.

Nothing happened.

After a few seconds, she reopened her eyes, and found
that he was gazing down at her with something suspiciously
like amusement. "Very good," he approved. "Joan of Arc
could not have done better."

She stared up at him in outrage.

"What a lot you have to learn," he went on, conversationally. "Kissing is not a penance, my dear. It is one of life's
sweetest pleasures . . ."

THE ROMANCES OF LORDS AND LADIES
IN JANIS LADEN'S REGENCIES

BEWITCHING MINX   (2532, $3.95)

From her first encounter with the Marquis of Penderleigh when he had mistaken her for a common trollop, Penelope had been incensed with the darkly handsome lord. Miss Penelope Larchmont was undoubtedly the most outspoken young lady Penderleigh had ever known, and the most tempting.

A NOBLE MISTRESS   (2169, $3.95)

Moriah Landon had always been a singularly practical young lady. So when her father lost the family estate over a game of picquet, she paid the winner, the notorious Viscount Roane, a visit. And when he suggested the means of payment—that she become Roane's mistress—she agreed without a blink of her eyes.

SAPPHIRE TEMPTATION   (3054, $3.95)

Lady Serena was commonly held to be an unusual young girl—outspoken when she should have been reticent, lively when she should have been demure. But there was one tradition she had not been allowed to break: a Wexley must marry a Gower. Richard Gower intended to teach his wife her duties—in every way.

SCOTTISH ROSE   (2750, $3.95)

The Duke of Milburne returned to Milburne Hall trusting that the new governess, Miss Rose Beacham, had instilled the fear of God into his harum-scarum brood of siblings. But she romped with the children, refused to be cowed by his stern admonitions, and was so pretty that he had the devil of a time keeping his hands off her.

The Rake And His Lady
Julie Caille

2/226

ZEBRA BOOKS
KENSINGTON PUBLISHING CORP.

*This book is dedicated to
the memory of
R. Gwendolyn Burns
with love*

Chapter One

The lumbering hackney coach that conveyed Miss Linnea Leyton to Brook Street was neither comfortable nor clean, but such considerations held no place in her thoughts. She was preoccupied with a personal matter, so preoccupied that it was several seconds after she paid off the jarvey before she realized he had given her the wrong change. And by then it was too late, for the coach had already started off, its ponderous job-horses leaving an aromatic donation at her feet.

Linnea glared after the hackney, her fine, straight nose quivering with outrage. Then she turned on her heel and marched up the shallow steps of the mansion where the woman she considered her closest friend—the Marchioness of Vale—resided.

She was admitted to the house by a tall, dour-faced butler, who led her up an elegant stairway to the drawing room. She was left alone for no more than a minute before light footsteps sounded.

"Linnea!" Amanda, Lady Vale, sailed across the carpet, her pretty features lit with pleasure and surprise. "How long have you been in London?"

"Three days." Linnea warmly embraced the other young woman, then accepted her invitation to sit. "I could not wait to see you again, though I suppose I should have waited for you to call first—"

"Oh, fustian. Don't you dare stand on ceremony with me. I thought we agreed that these stuffy social rules do not apply to us."

"So we did." Linnea's smile faded as she remembered the reason she had come. "At any rate, I had to talk to you. Something very disturbing has happened. In fact, it is intolerable," she amended in a low voice. "And though there seems to be no solution, I thought—I mean I hoped that if I could talk it over with someone, perhaps things would not seem so . . . so hopeless." She caught her underlip between her teeth and looked down, twisting the strings of her reticule.

"My gracious, this sounds serious." Amanda waved away the butler as he set a tray of refreshments upon a side table. "Wait a moment, Burke. A glass of sherry for us both, if you please. I think we shall be needing a little restorative."

Accepting the wine, Linnea tried to recall how much she had told her friend about her family. "When we met last year, did I ever mention that my mother was to inherit my Grandmother Northcliff's fortune? Because neither of her other daughters— my Aunt Bronsden and Aunt Gordon—needed it, as they had both married wealthy men?"

Amanda nodded. "Yes, I believe you did."

Linnea shut her teeth for a moment. "Well, Grandmama's changed her mind. For years she's been promising to leave her money to Mama, but now that her health is failing, she's made a new will and Papa is having apoplectic fits."

"A new will. In favor of whom?"

"That's the rub. Grandmama is being so infuriatingly eccentric. She says it's to go, every farthing of it, to the first of her granddaughters to marry. And if none of us are married at the time of her death,

8

the whole of it goes into a trust fund for her first female great-grandchild, who will not receive a penny until she reaches age eighteen."

Amanda's brow creased. "And by her grand-daughters, she means you and—?"

"My cousins, Iris Bronsden and Evangeline Gordon. Please understand that I don't begrudge it to either of them. What Grandmama chooses to do with her money is no concern of mine. It's only that Papa has been borrowing against the certainty of Grandmama's fortune for so long, I quite shudder to think of the consequences. Grandmama knows it, too. I think that's why she's doing it. She's fond of Mama, but she's always loathed Papa for the way—" Linnea broke off, quickly altering what she'd been about to say. "Papa claims she's lost her reason, but Dr. Willis says it's not so. Grandmama is not expected to live beyond another month. And then, as Papa says, the duns will be at our door."

"Oh dear." Amanda's face reflected her sympathy. "Linnea, I'm so sorry."

"That's why we're in London. We had no plans to come to town this year—mainly because we could not afford to—then Papa got wind of the new will. So here we are. Papa rented a house in Hartford Street—there wasn't much choice at this late date, and of course Grandmama will not permit us to reside with her because she detests my father."

Pausing, Linnea took a bracing sip of the sherry. "The instant we arrived, he dispatched Mama to visit Grandmama in Hill Street, but all Mama's pleading availed her nothing. So now Papa means to find me a husband." Undisguised bitterness crept into her tone. "Anyone will do, of course. He is quite desperate."

"Come now," said Amanda comfortingly. "I'm

sure your father could not be as heartless as you make him out."

Linnea shook her head. "You don't know him, Amanda. Nor my two cousins, for that matter. Evangeline is eighteen and a raving beauty. And Iris is also quite lovely, though a year older. I consider it quite likely that one or both of them will become betrothed very soon." She straightened her spine, a hollow twist of emotion fluttering in her breast. "And I'm past three-and-twenty with no suitors on the horizon."

Amanda frowned. "But since you are of age, your father cannot force you into a distasteful marriage. Nor would you be obliged to settle his debts."

Linnea's mouth curled ruefully. "Papa is not about to whistle sixty thousand pounds down the wind for such a paltry reason. I live under his roof, eat his food, and make use of his servants. I am as dependent upon him as I was when I was younger. And he knows it." Her low voice shook just a trifle. "The worst of it is, he's threatened to destroy my manuscript if I do not comply."

Amanda considered this with tightly pursed lips. "Then perhaps the best course of action *would* be to marry," she said slowly. "Think, Linnea. Once you have a husband to protect you, it will be his duty to deal with your father."

"But I don't want a husband," Linnea said fiercely. "Husbands are odious. They tell one what to do, and order one about and . . ." She bit her lip before she betrayed too much.

"Husbands don't have to be odious." Amanda patted her hand. "You must own that I have more experience in this matter than you."

Linnea studied her friend's face, noting the gentle amusement in the light silver eyes. She knew that

Amanda had married for love; she knew also that her husband, the Marquis of Vale, had been a scandalous rake before his marriage.

"Tell me," she said suddenly, "does he never order you around? Does he always consider your wishes? Is he sensitive to your needs?"

Sighing, Amanda picked up her glass. "John isn't perfect, Linnea. I don't pretend that. He can be excessively high-handed at times, even a trifle dictatorial. But he has never hurt me or shouted at me. And, yes, he is sensitive to my needs. Equally important, he has never been unfaithful to me. And I know he never will be."

Linnea bowed her head, awed by this simple statement of trust.

"And without a husband," Amanda went on, "you will never know the joy of being a mother. Little Jack is a source of constant delight to me and to his father." Emotion trembled her voice. "I could not imagine existence without the two of them, but if I ever lost one . . . at least I would have the other."

Linnea sat very still. In a flat voice, she asked, "But how does one go about finding a love like that?"

"I wish I could tell you," said Amanda regretfully. "How I wish John had an unmarried brother! I would love to have you for a sister-in-law."

For an instant Linnea allowed herself the luxury of imagining this, then resolutely pushed the fantasy aside. Three fruitless London Seasons weighed heavily upon her as she said, "He might have ten brothers, Amanda, and it would do no good. The truth is that . . . I don't attract men."

"What on earth do you mean?"

Linnea clenched her fingers, making sure it was the only outward sign of her distress. "Surely you

11

must know. I'm not pretty like you. And my character is too intense, to use Mama's word. She gave up on me years ago. She says I am plain and gauche and doomed to be a burden to them for the rest of their lives."

Amanda looked shocked. "She is wrong! Oh, I suppose 'pretty' is not quite the proper word. You are elegant—far moreso than I. You are taller, certainly, and that's to your advantage. Your hair is lovely—"

"But it's so red!"

"—like molten copper. Your mouth is wide, but your smile is charming. Your face has character, Linnea."

"Men do not look for character. They look for beau—" Linnea stopped abruptly, aware of a male presence in the doorway.

"I thought I heard voices," remarked the Marquis of Vale.

"John!" Amanda turned eagerly, her cheeks tinted a delicate pink. "Do join us. You remember Miss Leyton, do you not? We made her acquaintance at the lending library last year."

"Certainly." Amanda's husband moved into the room and bowed. "I'm delighted to see you again, Miss Leyton." He sat next to his wife and possessed himself of her hand, a completely natural gesture that was somehow made intimate by the look they exchanged. "Some men look for beauty," he informed Linnea, in rather a lazy voice. "But wise men look for women with character. Sadly, there are not a large number of wise men inhabiting the metropolis."

Amanda looked at him, her head tilted a little to one side. "Now John, I want you to think very carefully. Do you know of any very nice, eligible gentlemen in urgent need of a wife?"

"Nice ones, my love?" Amusement and tenderness chased each other across the marquis's handsome face. "No, I regret to say, I do not."

"Oh dear. Are you quite sure? Because—now this is confidential, of course—Linnea needs to find a husband as soon as possible."

While Amanda explained, Linnea strove to look unruffled. She stared down at her hands—the one part of herself she considered truly handsome—and wished fervently that she had sworn Amanda to secrecy. It was flustering to have a sophisticated man like the marquis know of her predicament, particularly when it seemed certain there was nothing anyone could do to help.

"You are in a difficult position, Miss Leyton," he commented at the end of his wife's speech. "Is there no gentleman to whom you could turn? Perhaps a past suitor who—forgive my indelicacy—hesitated to make you an offer for whatever reason. Now that your expectations have changed . . ."

"No, Lord Vale," Linnea said stoically. "There are no suitors, past or present. I've never had much interest in . . . in men." She finished her sherry in silence.

"A pity." His eyes swept over her in dispassionate assessment. "You're a well-looking woman."

"You see?" Amanda nodded in triumph. "John knows."

Linnea wriggled in embarrassment. "You are both . . . very kind," she murmured.

The marquis frowned, his thumb absently massaging his wife's palm. "That," he said dryly, "is akin to accusing me of mouthing platitudes, which I assure you is neither my intention, nor my custom. Would you care for a more detailed summary of your assets?" He crossed his legs, his eyes gleaming oddly.

"Now, John, don't embarrass her."

"I'm not in the least embarrassed," lied Linnea defiantly. "And I should like to hear what his lordship has to say. I'm sure he is well qualified to . . . to discuss the subject."

Oh, dear, that was a glaring gaffe. She should certainly not have alluded to his past reputation as a notorious rake. But a quivering muscle at the corner of the marquis's mouth was the only sign that he had noticed.

"Very well," he said softly. "You've an excellent figure, Miss Leyton, which you could accentuate with more stylish clothing. Your height and long neck give you an added elegance. My advice is to lower your necklines by at least two inches, and to leave off wearing white or pastels, which make you look insipid. Try green and blue instead, particularly the deeper shades. Certain hues of brown and yellow would become you as well. If you intend to ride, you might purchase a habit to match those sherry-colored eyes. As for your countenance . . ."

Linnea held herself rigidly, not quite daring to look the marquis in the eye.

"It has a serene, feminine quality," he continued. "You have good bone structure, and as Amanda says, character. I'll admit there is a certain obstinate quality about your chin, but your mouth is soft and well shaped. If it is your outward appearance that troubles you, I suggest you stop worrying."

"I wasn't actually worrying," she mumbled. "It is only that . . . my father is determined that I . . . well, I don't suppose it really matters. There is always Mr. Winterbottom."

"Mr. Winterbottom?" Lord Vale arched a brow.

"He works at a bank. I don't know where Papa

14

met him originally, but he's coming to dinner this evening. I've seen him twice before. He is short, fat, and seems very stupid." She gazed wistfully into her empty glass, wishing someone would offer her some more sherry. "His name is Baldwin," she added with an agonized shudder, "and he spits when he talks. Papa believes he will make me an offer."

Silence followed, a silence in which the marchioness sent her husband a pleading look.

The marquis's keen eyes fixed on Linnea. "Listen to me, Miss Leyton. No one can force you to marry the man, not in this day and age. You're past one-and-twenty, are you not? Then dig in your heels. In the meanwhile, I will endeavor to discover an unmarried gentleman who might answer the purpose. I can't promise anything, of course, but with the lure of your grandmother's money . . ."

Amanda squeezed her husband's hand. "Oh, John, thank you. And when we do find him, we'll ask him to dinner, won't we? And Linnea as well. We could ask Charles and Aimee, too, so it won't look so obvious."

The marquis raised his wife's hand to his lips. "My precious pea-goose, there is no way in the world we could make it look anything but obvious . . ."

Anthony Stanton, Viscount Carrock, had been summoned to Grosvenor Square that afternoon for what he knew was to be a raking-down by his grandsire, the Earl of Sayer. The old man had obviously heard about Anthony's latest scandal, which was barely twelve hours old. It was really no worse than any of his other scandals, he reflected, except that it involved a lady of good birth—though scarcely of good breeding.

The interview had been set for four o'clock, but Anthony arrived late. He was admitted into the house by a potbellied retainer (who greeted him with the affection of long acquaintance and the warning that his lordship was in a rare pucker) and ushered into the front parlor. Here, he was left to kick up his heels for some twenty minutes, a ploy which was too familiar to cast him into the fidgets. Never having been one to sit idly, Anthony used the interim to gaze out the window at a pair of comely females. The girl on the left, he noted, possessed particularly fine ankles . . .

Suddenly, the oak door crashed open, revealing the tall, slightly stooped figure of the old earl. "Well, Anthony?" he barked, in accents of highest displeasure.

As his grandfather stumped across the floor, Anthony said, in an amiable tone, "Well, sir? You're looking fit today."

Stopping short, the old man poked him with the tip of his cane. "Don't you try those tricks on me, you ramshackle boy! I'll not be beguiled by rascally smiles, so save 'em for that lot of witless females who languish after you." The cane prodded in a staccato motion that emphasized his next words: "What the devil do you mean by carrying on with Lindcastle's wife?"

Anthony shrugged. "Truth is, Grandpapa, if it had not been me, it would have been someone else. Susannah Lindcastle is—"

"—a lady," the earl cut in, thrusting his jaw out aggressively. "Confound it, Anthony, why can't you be satisfied with muslin from the lower class? Aye, you knew damned well I'd hear the tale from Lindcastle's uncle. Hang it, boy, the man's a close friend of mine, and straitlaced as the devil! Makes this

16

whole affair humiliating for me."

"Yes, I suppose it does," Anthony conceded, after a few more pokes with the cane. "I am sorry, Grandfather."

As it happened, he *was* sorry, for he disliked causing his grandfather distress; moreover, he did normally limit his amorous advances, not to women of the lower class, but to women of sophistication, women who understood the game of love and its complicated rules. Women, he reflected, who could never touch his emotions and who knew better than to expect commitment, fidelity or love. Women like Susannah Lindcastle.

He was about to explain this when his grandfather said: "Sorry! Ha! I'll wager you are. I imagine it was embarrassing to be caught practically *flagrante delicto* by the lady's husband."

"Actually, it was more embarrassing for Susannah," said Anthony coolly. "I still had my boots on. Though it did set me at a bit of a disadvantage, I admit."

The earl stared, then swore, long and fluently. "You're damned fortunate Lindcastle decided to hush up the story. Oh, it's gotten about, but the sordid details aren't generally known. Though I don't suppose you'd give a straw if they were!"

"Probably not," Anthony agreed.

This casual viewpoint seemed only to infuriate the earl, who turned very red and roared, "Damnation, that's just the sort of attitude I'd expect! But I won't put up with it! I'll have you show yourself worthy of the name Stanton! By God, I'll have you cease this disgraceful carousing and womanizing and lord knows what else." The old man paused, his breath huffing, his cheeks empurpled with emotion. "I want you settled down and wed."

17

"Wed?" Anthony lifted his brows. "To whom?"

"Thunder and turf, I don't know! If you'd show yourself willing, your poor widowed mother and I could put our heads together. Perhaps we'd come up with some names. Somewhere in London there's bound to be a girl desperate enough for a titled husband that she'd take you."

Anthony bowed, his smile a little strained. "I thank you for your concern, sir, but I don't fancy the wedded state."

"What's wrong with it? You're nine-and-twenty. It's high time you filled your nursery with heirs. Legitimate ones," the old man added scathingly. "Lord only knows how many baseborn brats you've fathered—"

"None." All traces of good humor vanished from Anthony's face. "None, Grandfather. You can think what you like about me, but not that."

"Oh, very proper," marveled the earl. "Well, then, you can be proper about this. Find yourself a respectable wife, one your mother and I will approve or—" He paced back and forth, then stopped, glaring ferociously from under his bushy brows.

"Or what?" Anthony inquired mildly.

"Sundridge is not an entailed estate. I'll leave it to your cousin Roland." Lord Sayer's voice was shaking and flat, but its obduracy was unmistakable. " 'Tis a heavy price I know, but . . . I swear to God I'll do it, Anthony, unless you obey me in this."

Anthony stood very still, momentarily deprived of speech. Sundridge was the haven of his childhood, the one place in the world he could go and find memories of his brother. It was his retreat, his refuge, his home. The mere idea of his smirking cousin Roland usurping his place as heir to the estate did something vile to Anthony's stomach.

"Very well, sir," he replied, after a stunned pause. "You leave me no choice. I will endeavor to find myself a wife as soon as possible."

"By the end of the Season," qualified Lord Sayer.

Anthony searched his grandfather's face. "Then Sundridge will be mine?"

"Aye, Sundridge will be yours." Looking weary, the old earl sank into a wingback chair. "That's the condition, Anthony. A decent, respectable girl, not some trollop from the streets. I don't care if she's wealthy, I don't care if she's as plain as a fence post, but she must be a girl of good birth, someone you can introduce into society without blushing."

"Anything else?" Beneath his drooping eyelids, Anthony's eyes gleamed dangerously. "Do you prefer blonde or brunette? Tall or short? Plump or scrawny in the bosom?"

Something akin to pain crossed Lord Sayer's face. "Damn you, Anthony, *don't*. You know I wouldn't force this on you if it weren't in your best interest. You could do what you liked if . . ." His voice trailed off as if he could not finish.

"If Roger were still alive. Yes, I'm well aware of it." Anthony swung away, staring blankly toward the fireplace. "If my brother were alive, it would be his responsibility to wed." His voice came out a monotone, but with a brittle, tired edge. "I'm sure you wish it were he who had lived. So do I, with all my heart. But it wasn't. And there's nothing either of us can do about it."

Without a backward glance, Anthony walked from the room, letting himself out the front door with scarcely a sound at all. His body rigid, he strode down the street with his teeth clenched so hard together that his jaw hurt.

Other things hurt too. His head, for one. And his

gut, where his grandfather had jabbed him with his cane. Anthony sighed, remembering how Susannah had promised that her husband would not be home for hours. She'd played on his sympathy, wept that she was lonely and unloved, that her husband never touched her, that his tastes were unnatural. That was when he'd allowed himself to feel pity for her. He should have known she was lying, that she had only done it to pay her husband back for some petty insult.

A lady.

Anthony kicked at a pebble, his expression dark and curiously savage for one with such an even temperament. He could use a real lady right now, he thought. Someone soft and gentle, who would gaze at him as though he were worth something. Ha, he'd give *that* long odds, he thought cynically. He had so few redeeming virtues, it would take a saint to identify them. And with his grandfather's ultimatum hanging like an ax over his head, he would have no time to search. He would never find her now, this paragon of his dreams that in all probability did not exist. He must find himself a wife, God help him, and a respectable one at that. And where the blazes was he to find such a girl?

Anthony decided to get drunk.

It was past four o'clock when Linnea arrived home. Hoping to avoid her parents, she slipped quietly up to her room, but she had scarcely taken off her bonnet before her mother came in.

"Where have you been?" Mrs. Leyton's normally attractive features looked pinched with displeasure. "You know you're not supposed to go out without your maid."

"I'm sorry, Mama," Linnea answered tightly. "I only went to visit a friend."

"A friend?" Her mother's eyes narrowed suspiciously. "What friend must you visit in so clandestine a manner?"

"There was nothing clandestine about it. I left Maria home because she was feeling poorly. There was no need to take her—"

"Where?"

"To Brook Street. I paid a call on Amanda."

"You mean Lady Vale?" Her mother's displeasure faded. "Well, why could you not say so, you foolish girl? But how did you go there? You did not walk, did you?"

"Of course not, Mama. I took a hack."

"A common hack!" moaned her mother, sinking into a chair. "Oh, Linnea, she will think you the veriest hurly-burly! 'Tis a marvelous piece of good fortune to call a marchioness your bosom-bow, but 'twill not last long if you do not conduct yourself with propriety."

"Lady Vale isn't like that," Linnea said quietly.

"No, I suppose not. Her origins are quite undistinguished, are they not? Still, her husband is of the first consequence, so her friendship can only add to yours. We must be sure to mention her at dinner. I make no doubt that Mr. Winterbottom will be impressed."

Linnea's chin raised to a stubborn angle. "He may be as impressed as he likes, but it will do him no good. I refuse to marry him." As she spoke the firm words she saw her mother's expression shift, first to anger, then desperation, then to a kind of cloying sweetness.

"Now, dear, we have been over all that. Your papa feels it would be a good match. You do not want to be a spinster, do you? Who will take care of you when you are old? No one, that's who. A husband offers security, Linnea, and that is something every woman must consider." Her mother shuddered. "And without your grandmother's fortune, we shall all of us be without a feather to fly with."

Linnea felt the weight of such responsibility blossom into full scale depression. "Is there *no* other way? Perhaps if we talked to Grandmama again, if we explained—"

"I tried." Mrs. Leyton's mouth twisted with agitation. "You know I tried, Linnea. But to no avail. She's determined on this course, and for no reason at all except to make my life even more miserable than it already is. If only Dr. Willis would sign a certificate saying she is mad."

"But if he feels she is not, it would be unethical for him to do so," Linnea pointed out. Frustration made her add, unwisely, "And it was wrong of Papa to extend himself so that he could not meet the payments on his debts."

"How dare you!" Surging to her feet, Mrs. Leyton dealt Linnea a stinging slap across the face. "Ungrateful child! How dare you criticize your father? You ought to be grateful to him for providing you with a roof over your head. By any right, your husband should have had the feeding and clothing of you these past years. What right have you to judge— you, whose only ambition is to write absurd stories! You ought to be flattered that Mr. Winterbottom is even willing to consider you."

Her cheek burning, Linnea stepped back, distancing herself physically as well as mentally. "I am flattered," she said tonelessly. "And I beg pardon, Mama, if I offended you."

Her mother drew in a ragged breath. "Think carefully," she warned, "before you come down to dinner this evening. Consider the life you might have as Mrs. Wlnterbottom with your grandmother's fortune at your disposal—"

"How much of it will Papa require?" Linnea asked carefully. "Do you have any notion how deeply he is in debt?"

" 'Tis none of my concern," her mother snapped. "Nor yours, I may add."

Linnea steeled herself not to react, not to shout that under the circumstances it was very much her concern. "Yes, of course," she replied. "We women are not clever enough to understand such things, are we?"

"Exactly so, Linnea," replied Mrs. Leyton coldly. "And I trust you will remember it. Wear your white satin with the pale yellow sash. It becomes you better than anything else you own."

"I've been told it makes me look insipid," Linnea could not resist saying.

Her mother's brows rose. "Nonsense, whoever told you that? Someone who knows nothing about women and what becomes them, I make no doubt. White makes you look young and innocent, which is exactly the picture you want to present to Mr. Winterbottom. You had better rouge your cheeks, though. You look positively pasty."

And with that, her mother swept from the room, leaving Linnea staring at the floor, her hands clenched into small fists. With a choked, bitter laugh, she whispered, "Yes, Mama, I'll be only too happy to look as painted and insipid as possible."

Chapter Two

Anthony chose the home of a certain young widow in which to become inebriated, largely because he could depend on finding his most disreputable acquaintances in this abode. He could also count on his welcome from the voluptuous Mrs. Brewster, who lovingly shooed him into her parlor and proceeded to offer him brandy, a back rub, and any other services he might require. With his most winsome smile, Anthony declined all but the brandy and settled back to survey his fellow guests. Here, among the debauched and despoiled, he was just another cock in the barnyard.

His grandfather would say he fit right in.

In one corner, for instance, Sir Gideon Buscot diverted himself with his current fashionable impure, Fifi Divine, who sat sprawled across his lap with her skirts hitched to her knees. Six feet away, Lord Philo Davis, fellow libertine, played piquet with Burton Winstock, while inches away, two painted opera dancers whispered and giggled. In the adjoining room, two effeminate young sons of the nobility huddled in rapt conversation upon a small settee; no barques of frailty at their feet, Anthony noted without surprise. There were others, too, whom he recognized—Uffington, Croxton, Sir Henry Neyle. Wild laughter emanated from the dining room, but Anthony wasn't interested in anything other than the brandy in his glass. He had things to ponder—wives, women, and the exact meaning of the word respectable. Did he know anyone to whom the adjective applied?

A second bottle of brandy later, he still hadn't come up with any course of action that would find him a respectable wife. He knew he could attend some of the Season's balls if he chose. There were hostesses aplenty who were only too eager to invite Viscount Carrock into their homes, even if he did have the reputation of the devil. On the other hand, he couldn't think of any who would introduce him to their daughters. His mouth curved wryly. Until this moment he had never fully appreciated the fact that popularity could have its disadvantages.

He had assimilated that popularity early on, beginning at the tender age of fourteen when one of the junior housemaids had crept into his bed to teach him the delights of shared bodily warmth. Not long after that, he had learned that his appreciation for the opposite sex was shared by his father, whom he had met one evening with an opera dancer on each arm. And so it was that hypocrisy was Anthony's first tutor, for while his father had been unfailingly courteous and considerate to his mother—who had worshiped her husband—he continued in his practice to deceive her regarding his mistresses. When questioned by his son, Anthony's father had sharply explained that theirs had been a marriage of convenience, and as such could not be expected to include fidelity—at least not on the part of the male.

Oddly, Anthony's twin brother Roger had not been of like mind regarding the delightfulness of females. Where Anthony considered them essential, Roger had thought them superfluous. Roger had found scholarly pursuits of far greater interest; and though he'd not been brilliant, he'd had the tenacity to do well at school. It had therefore seemed unfair that Anthony had succeeded almost without effort. While Roger had studied, Anthony had caroused and flirted and made love. While Roger had spent his evenings translating Homer, Anthony had gotten drunk, then passed his exams with flying colors.

In his third year at Oxford, guilt had finally driven Anthony to do poorly. It had seemed so confoundedly wrong for him to better Roger that he'd purposely failed an exam. Of course, Roger had known—and reproached him. Roger had always known him better than he knew himself, just as Anthony had understood Roger so well. Anthony broached his third bottle with a grimace of pain. Sweet Jesus, how he missed his twin . . .

"Evening, Carrock. Mind if I join you?"

Anthony glanced up to see Sir Gideon hovering over him.

"Not at all," he said politely. "Good evening, Fifi."

The girl clinging to the tails of Sir Gideon's coat sent him a coquettish smile.

Sir Gideon pulled over a chair, and with a casual wave of his hand directed Fifi to sit at his feet. "She's very pretty, isn't she?"

Anthony hazily considered Fifi's charms, which were as amply displayed as wares in a market stall.

"Very," he said, again with politeness.

Sir Gideon accepted a tumbler of whiskey from a servant and leaned back in his chair. "Forgive my curiosity, but do you currently have a female under your protection?"

Anthony pondered. "Not that I can recall," he said finally, "though I have been known to forget such details."

"Ah." Sir Gideon appeared to find this amusing. "Then I wonder if you might do me a favor, Carrock. I'm wishful to know the name of that little blonde filly I saw on your arm not two weeks ago. The one with the—"

The subsequent delineation was very vulgar, but accurate enough to jog Anthony's memory. "Peaches," he answered pensively. "I think that's the one you mean."

"Peaches." Sir Gideon murmured the word beneath his breath. "Appropriate. I wonder if you might give me her direction? In thanks, I will lend you my little Fifi for the night."

Rather taken aback, Anthony looked down at Fifi, who blew him a kiss and lisped, "You weel not be disappointed, *monseigneur*." Wriggling closer, she pressed against his leg, one hand creeping up to fondle his knee.

Anthony reached down to still her fingers. If there was one thing he was fastidious about, it was the process of selecting females he wished to bed. He did not like to have his hand forced, not by his grandfather, and not by Sir Gideon.

"I promise you, she's very talented," Sir Gideon assured quickly. "Aren't you, my chick? Would you like to tell the gentleman about your specialty?"

Fifi raised her face and made an "O" with her

lips, an action that was patently informative, but which also, unfortunately for Fifi, put Anthony in mind of a dead fish.

"I see." Arching a brow, Anthony tried not to laugh. " 'Tis a tempting offer, Buscot, but I've other plans for tonight. Will you owe me?" The query was a courtesy only, designed to spare the feelings of the ladybird at his feet, but Sir Gideon took it at face value.

"Certainly, dear fellow. In fact, I'll write out my vowel right now. Redeem it anytime you like . . . as long as you direct me to, er, Peaches, of course."

While Anthony searched his memory, Sir Gideon called for paper and ink, wrote out his debt, and signed with a flourish.

"Woodstock Street," Anthony said briefly. "Number ten, I believe." He shoved the vowel into his pocket.

Sir Gideon rose and bowed. "I am indebted to you, Carrock. Come along, Fifi."

Fifi uncoiled, her melting look focused on Anthony. *Au revoir,* she whispered sweetly.

When they were gone, Anthony sagged back in his chair. How Roger would have teased him about that little episode! Roger would have told him he was insane to be here at all. Roger would have said that a respectable woman was precisely what Anthony needed, that harlots like Fifi Divine were only going to cause trouble. Roger would have told him to go home and sober up.

But Anthony had seldom listened to Roger.

"Miss Leyton, will y-you do me the honor of . . . of . . ." Mr. Winterbottom paused, mopped his heated brow with a handkerchief, and tried again. Balanced precariously on his pudgy knees, he appeared as uncomfortable as Linnea. "M-Miss Leyton, will you do me the honor . . ."

Unable to endure another moment of this, Linnea forced herself to cut in. "No, Mr. Winterbottom, I am very sorry to disappoint you, but I cannot." There, the words were out and could not be retracted, no matter what the consequences might be.

"Eh?" Mr. Winterbottom looked up, his chubby face full of ludicrous chagrin. "You can't?"

Linnea shook her head, wishing she were not quite so repulsed by the man for he was really rather sweet. "I'm sorry," she said kindly. "And I am deeply honored by the offer. But I'm afraid we would not suit."

Huffing raggedly, Mr. Winterbottom struggled to his feet. "But . . . but . . . your father . . . he said . . . he promised . . ."

Linnea took a small step backward as a spray of spittle caught her in the face. "I am of age, Mr. Winterbottom. My father cannot promise my hand without my consent."

Her suitor appeared ready to explode; his face turned bright pink and his plump cheeks bulged with emotion. "It appears that I have been m-misled. Your father led me to believe that . . . that . . ."

"My father was mistaken," Linnea said with gentle firmness. "Believe me, Mr. Winterbottom, there is nothing personal in this. I simply have an aversion to being wed."

He blinked in confusion. "B-But I thought you were to inherit a mountain of blunt if . . . if . . ."

"If I wed." Linnea nodded. "That is perfectly true, sir. However, there are more important things than money. My, uh, principles forbid me to marry for such a reason."

"Ah." Enlightenment radiated from Mr. Winterbottom's countenance. "I understand." Then he frowned. "I-I think . . ."

"Perhaps it would be best if we returned to the drawing room," Linnea suggested with a sinking heart.

"Very well, Miss Leyton." Mr. Winterbottom bowed. "And let me say that it is an honor to have met such a highly principled lady as yourself."

"Thank you, Mr. Winterbottom." In a burst of self-preservation, she added, "I trust you will share those sentiments with my father."

True to her hopes, Mr. Winterbottom conveyed his respect for Linnea's principles to both of her parents, then took his leave with as much dignity as the situation allowed. Linnea, however, cherished no illusions that her father was anything but furious, and when he turned to her after their guest departed, his cheeks were positively vermilion.

"Principles!" he snarled, seizing her arm in a painful grip. "Damn your hide, I'll teach you what I think of your principles!" Swearing viciously, he dragged her down the hall to his study, ignoring his wife's wailing pleas not to be too harsh. Slamming the door in his wife's face, Mr. Leyton gave Linnea a shove that sent her to the floor.

Linnea lay on her side, her body frozen in a wave of pure panic. As if time stood still, she watched her father reach for his crop, which he kept in his study, and raise it over her head. As if spellbound, she watched it come down, down, until

30

the first crack of pain across her shoulders broke through the mist. Dimly, she heard her own cries as the crop came down again and again on her back.

When the blows finally ceased, her father stood over her, breathing heavily, his nostrils flared and his face contorted. "Damn it, where am I going to find another husband for you? Winterbottom was our best hope, you simpering bitch."

Linnea lay sobbing, her face buried in her arms, wishing she had the strength and the courage not to cry. But it hurt too much, and she was such a coward . . .

"Now get up," he panted, "and go to your room. And don't let me see your face again today."

Linnea dragged herself up, her body trembling, her vision clouded by tears. "Papa—"

"Get out!" he bellowed, his small eyes bulging with rage.

Legs not quite steady, Linnea stumbled from the room.

Outside, her mother huddled, still and pale, in the shadows. "I told you," she hissed. "I told you to consider carefully. And now look what you've accomplished, you little fool." As always, Mrs. Leyton's fear was too great to allow her room for compassion.

Linnea passed by with her teeth clamped shut. Perhaps she *had* been a fool to refuse Mr. Winterbottom, she thought dully. He might physically repel her, but she could have done worse. It would have been a means to escape her father. Climbing the stairs, she suddenly remembered Lord Vale's promise. What would she do if he did come up with a candidate? Would he be able to find anyone? For a few seconds she closed her eyes and prayed.

Let Lord Vale find someone, please. He doesn't have to be perfect. He just has to need, as I need. He has to need me.

"I beg your pardon," remarked Lord Vale, "but I see no occasion for such wild mirth." Despite the chortles of his closest friend, the marquis remained composed as he sauntered placidly along St. James's Street later that evening.

"It ain't mirth," denied Charles Perth with a grin. "I'm pleased as Punch for you, that's all." His head shook in mock despair. "Every once in a while, it still strikes me as odd to see you so domesticated."

"Domesticated." The marquis repeated the word thoughtfully. "Is that what I am?"

Charles nudged him with his elbow. "Well, look at you. Three years ago you were the wildest rake in London. Now you're a husband and father who won't look twice at any woman but his own wife. I'd say the wolf has been tamed."

The marquis smiled in the dark. "True enough. Are you reproaching me?"

"Lord, no." Charles's voice rang with hearty approval. "So now there's to be another one, eh? A girl this time, mayhap?"

"If God wills. Amanda is delighted, of course." The marquis's face relaxed into a sheepish grin. "And so am I."

They walked in companionable silence, mist curling around their feet as the sound of their steps echoed on the flagstoned walk. Ahead, the street

32

was empty, then suddenly a tall figure lurched out of Little Ryder Street, not a dozen feet in front of them. He was plainly a gentleman of birth, and he was just as plainly drunk.

"I say, ain't that Carrock?" asked Charles in a low voice. "Now there's a hell-for-leather 'un for you. From all the tales, it seems he's taken your place, Jack. They say he's wild as the north wind."

"So it would seem," the marquis murmured.

"Looks like he can barely walk. Should we give him a hand, d'you think?"

"That's what I like about you, Charles. You're such an altruist."

"Now really, Jack. There, I knew it! The fellow's fallen flat on his face." Charles hurried forward to assist the viscount to his feet. "I say, are you hurt?"

Vale followed, his sardonic gaze sweeping leisurely over the pair. "Rather up in the world, aren't you, Carrock?"

"As high as I can get," the man slurred, "and still make it home. Then it's one more bottle and I'm off to bed."

"I don't recommend it. Sleep is what you need."

Carrock laughed drunkenly. "Wrong. A *wife* is what I need. Sleep is what I *want*. Need and want aren't necessarily related."

"A wife?" repeated Charles in bewilderment. "No, no, you're too soused to know what you're saying. You live in Albemarle Street, don't you? Come along then, we'll walk with you. It ain't far."

"Don't want . . . to trouble you." The viscount's voice was indistinct. His eyes slid shut, his posture wavering as though he were about to topple.

Vale assessed the man through narrowed eyes.

33

"You're right, Charles, I think we'll have to help him. He'll never make it on his own."

With obvious effort, Carrock's eyes reopened. "How much . . . would you care . . . to wager on that?"

"Don't be a fool," replied the marquis brutally. "You're fortunate you weren't set upon by thieves. Recollect that you've only one life, my friend, and take better care of it."

Something in his tone must have penetrated the viscount's haze, for the man shot him a strange look. "Wise words," he murmured in a tired voice. "A pity I'm unlikely to heed them."

As they continued up St. James's Street, Vale cudgeled his mind to recall every scandalous piece of gossip he had ever heard about the fellow. His own past told him the stories probably had a basis in truth, but the knowledge that he too had trodden that path gave him a curious tolerance for the man.

"Tell me," he said at last, "just what makes you think you need a wife?"

"Sundridge," said Carrock, almost tripping over an uneven flagstone.

Both men steadied him. "I beg your pardon?" said Vale.

"I said Sundridge. Can you understand? My tongue's not working well at the moment."

"Yes, I understand. Sundridge is Lord Sayer's country seat, is it not?"

When Carrock did not answer, the marquis prodded, "You need a wife for Sundridge?"

"For m'grandfather." There was a long pause. "Won't leave me Sundridge unless I marry." Apparently, the subject rankled, for he continued with unrepressed passion, "And he bloody well knows that bastard Roland doesn't give a deuce for the place!"

"Ah," said the marquis, beginning to see. "If you don't marry, your grandfather plans to disinherit you."

"Aye." Carrock leaned heavily on his arm. "Can you credit it? M'grandfather thinks a wife will make me settle down."

Vale smiled. "It might," he said briefly. "How soon do you need one?"

"Soon as possible." Carrock made a sound that might have been a chuckle. "But she's got . . . to be respectable, and that cuts out every female I know."

"You could scarcely wish to wed one of your doxies."

"True enough, but respectable—? Oh, lord."

"Respectable doesn't have to mean dull, you know."

"Don't want . . . to be tied to apron strings."

Vale hesitated for only a moment. "Listen, Carrock, I think I might have the girl for you. I'll tell you about her tomorrow, when you're sober. Try to be up by noon, will you? I've appointments in the afternoon."

"What's . . . her name?" The viscount's knees sagged.

"Dash it, he's passed out," said Charles in exasperation. "Now we'll have to carry him."

"No, we won't," said the marquis. Reaching into his pocket, he turned and tossed a half-crown to each of a pair of young ruffians who had been stalking them for the past hundred yards. "Fetch us a hack," he said briefly, "and there'll be another, for each of you."

"Yes, guv'nor!" the two boys said in unison.

When Anthony woke, he hadn't the foggiest remembrance of how he had gotten home. Not that it mattered, he thought listlessly. All that mattered was that he *was* home, in bed, wearing his nightshirt, with the covers over him. Bless Billings, he was worth his wages, after all.

Knowing how he would feel when he moved, Anthony lay very still. He would simply lie here, he thought. Lie here until the call of nature forced him to stir . . .

His door opened. "Good morning, milord!" uttered an offensively cheerful voice. The floorboards creaked as Anthony's valet threw open the window curtains. " 'Tis a fine day, milord. Not a cloud in the sky. It reminds me of when I was a boy, back in—"

"Billings," said Anthony, in a low, ominous voice. "What in hades do you think you're doing?"

"Letting the light in, milord. 'Tis nearly noon, after all."

"And what has that to do with it?"

Billings looked innocent. "Why, 'tis time to arise, milord. You've a visitor below."

"Who?"

"A gentleman, milord."

"Send him away."

Billings shook his head. "Can't do that, milord."

"Damn it, why not?" He started to sit up, groaned, and fell back onto the pillows, swearing vividly.

" 'Tis Lord Vale, milord," put in Billings. "Him

36

that brought you home last night."

Anthony screwed open an eye. *"Vale* brought me home?"

"Aye, milord. He says you agreed to meet with him at noon."

Anthony swore under his breath. "I suppose I must owe him money." *What in the world had he done last night? Mayhap he had gone to some hell with Vale . . .* His imagination cranked to a stop at the notion. He and Vale had no more than a nodding acquaintance.

Billings, meanwhile, stood waiting, a patient expression on his broad face.

"Oh, very well," Anthony said resignedly. "Find me some clothes, will you? And a pot of the strongest coffee you can brew."

"I daresay you are wishing me at Jericho right now," remarked the marquis, declining the cup of coffee a servant offered.

"Not at all," said Anthony as civilly as possible. "Billings tells me I have you to thank for my arrival home last night."

"To be precise," said his visitor gravely, "you have Charles Perth to thank. But, yes, I had a hand in it as well."

Anthony sat back, observing the marquis uneasily. Why the devil did the fellow look at him like that? It was as though he knew a great deal about him, and found it mildly amusing.

"How much do I owe you?" he said abruptly. "It must be a great deal or you wouldn't be here. Or did I —" A nasty suspicion occurred to him. "I haven't met your wife, have I?"

37

He could have sworn the marquis's lips twitched. "No, I don't believe you've had that honor. As of yet," he added meditatively. "And no, you don't owe me a thing."

Anthony stared at him, feeling a trifle put out.

"You don't recall anything of our conversation last night?" asked the marquis softly.

"No." Anthony's lips pressed together to hide his irritation.

"Then I'll be frank. You confided your urgent need of a wife. You told me your reasons, which were understandable, if rather worldly. Don't be offended. I would do the same, if I were in your shoes."

Anthony eyed him with resentment. "Quite an admission from a man who never strays from his wife."

The marquis's eyes gleamed. "You didn't know me before I was married, Carrock. But that's neither here nor there. The reason I've come is that I may have a girl for you. She's respectable," he added calmly, "and she's attractive."

"Then what's wrong with her?" Anthony said grimly. "Is she breeding?"

The marquis's brows lifted haughtily. "Not to my knowledge. I would hardly have asked my wife's closest friend such a vulgar question." He paused. "But I think Amanda would have told me if it were so."

"Then why is she in desperate need of a husband?" Anthony smiled cynically. "She's obviously desperate or we wouldn't be having this conversation."

"Perhaps you misunderstand. I am here at my wife's behest, not Miss Leyton's." The marquis toyed with his quizzing glass. "Miss Leyton has the misfortune to find herself in a situation remarkably similar to yours. She is in need of a husband in order to inherit a certain sum of money, else it will go to someone else. I don't wish to go into it any more than that. If you are interested in meeting her, then I invite you to dine with us this evening. If not, then we can forget we ever had this conversation."

Anthony reached for his coffee. "I'm interested," he said shortly. "What does she look like? The truth, if you please."

"She's no antidote, if that's what you fear. Yet I think you would do better to judge for yourself. Beauty is in the eye of the beholder, as they say."

Anthony slumped in his chair. "That bad, eh? How big is the fortune?"

"Large enough," said Vale coolly, "to make it worth your while. Sixty thousand, I believe. But her father expects her to pay off his debts, the extent of which are entirely unknown to me. I think," he added in a careful voice, "that Miss Leyton would benefit from a husband who could deal with her family."

"I see." Anthony considered this and sighed. "I suppose I'd be willing to meet her . . ."

"Then shall we make it seven o'clock? Number forty-five, Brook Street." He paused. "Perhaps I should explain that Miss Leyton will also have to be persuaded. I rather fancy her to be a strong-willed young woman. She might be unwilling to consider you."

"Got a mind of her own, eh? That's some compensation." Despite his pounding head, Anthony smiled. "I suppose I should thank you."

The marquis rose. "Think nothing of it," he replied. "We've more in common than you imagine, Carrock. Which is why I will advise Linnea to keep an open mind. We humans have such an enormous capacity for growth."

And with this obscure utterance, Lord Vale took his leave.

Chapter Three

Linnea was relieved that Amanda had kept the size of her dinner party small, for it meant that there were fewer witnesses to her embarrassment. Not that Amanda's other two guests did anything to make her feel self-conscious—far from it. Charles and Aimee Perth were too kind and well-bred to make even an oblique reference to her situation, especially in front of Lord Carrock.

But though the situation had been handled with extreme tact, Linnea still felt ill at ease.

Thanks to her mother, she was wearing her usual white—silk, this time, with triple flounces and a pale blue sash tied beneath her breasts. The knot in her hair was elegant enough, but her mother had affixed such a profusion of ribbons and artificial flowers trailing out of it that she looked like a garden. Moreover, because of her pallor, Mrs. Leyton had insisted upon rubbing a generous amount of rouge into Linnea's cheeks, but Amanda, thankfully, had taken a handkerchief and removed most of it, promising that what was left gave Linnea a very pretty look. Certain that her friend was merely being polite, Linnea's distress only increased when her prospective suitor arrived late, which did not augur well for his interest in her as a bride, or indeed, as a living, breathing person whose feelings could be wounded.

And the meeting—what a disaster that had been!

Until she set eyes on Lord Carrock, Linnea had privately considered Lord Vale to be the handsomest man she had ever seen. But the viscount outshone even the marquis.

It wasn't fair, she thought resentfully. No living, breathing man deserved to possess such paralyzing masculine beauty. As if marble-perfect features, chestnut brown hair and delft blue eyes were not enough, nature had endowed the viscount with height, well-muscled legs, and a sensuously lean body that could have rivaled Michelangelo's David. As for his smile, it devastated. Its easy charm burned into her brain, muddled her thoughts, and made her knees turn to mush.

No, it simply wasn't fair.

Dipping her spoon into her Mulligatawny soup, Linnea cringed at the memory of their introduction. Perhaps because pudgy Mr. Winterbottom was so fresh in her mind, she had gawked at Lord Carrock like a complete idiot. Worse, when he had bowed over her hand, she had blushed and stammered like the greenest schoolgirl. Oh, he had spoken to her pleasantly enough, but she knew his first impression of her had been calamitous.

As she set down her spoon, she cast him a stealthy sidelong look. To her dismay, she discovered that he was watching her. In fact, it almost seemed as though those piercing blue eyes held a note of sympathy, but no doubt she was mistaken. After all, Amanda had warned her that Lord Carrock was a rake — and not a reformed one, by any means. No doubt that sort of person knew exactly how to make his victims melt like butter in the sun.

While cheerful conversation floated around her, Linnea shuddered inwardly. Amanda and Vale meant well, of course, but they had no way of knowing that Linnea's parents viewed this as her last and final opportunity to redeem herself. She dared not think what it would mean if she did not receive an offer from this man, nor did she dare to think what it would mean if she did. Either way, her future lay clouded in mist, a frightening journey she would as lief not face.

And how could she expect such a man to choose *her?* Amanda had explained that he was really quite wealthy, so Grandmama's fortune could be of no especial interest to him. He merely needed a bride so that he might inherit a certain estate, and surely he could find someone more interesting to wed, even if he did have a reprehensible reputation? And if he could not, that boded ill as well, for if he was really that wicked, what sort of a husband would he make?

Salmon and turbot followed the soup, followed by a host of other dishes and courses that Linnea barely tasted. The minutes crawled by until at last the dessert was reached — an impressive concoction provided by Messrs. Grange — and then it was time to leave the gentlemen to their port.

The moment the ladies reached the drawing room, Linnea turned to Amanda. "I shouldn't have come. This is not going to answer."

"Nonsense," the marchioness soothed. "Of course you're jittery, Linnea, but you haven't given

43

him a chance. You need time to become acquainted. After all, you've barely conversed with him except upon the most commonplace topics."

Aimee Perth pressed the back of her hand to her brow and pretended to swoon upon the sofa. "He is *fatally* handsome," she declared. "I swear if I were not so mad in love with Charles, I would be head over heels for Lord Carrock."

Linnea paced back and forth. "He was late," she pointed out, in an obstinate tone.

"True, but his apology was charming."

"I don't know what to say to him. He's too handsome. He makes me . . . terribly nervous. Every time he looks at me, I . . . I feel so strange. I can't explain it precisely . . ."

"Believe me, I understand." Amanda's lips curved oddly as she turned to Charles Perth's wife. "Listen, Aimee, when the gentlemen join us, I want you to say that you wish to play whist. And then I will say I do also, and you, Linnea, must say you don't care for the game. Then I'm sure Lord Carrock will do the polite thing and offer to sit out with you." Her pretty face solemn, Amanda went on persuasively, "And since it is a warm night, I shall suggest that he take you for a walk in the garden."

All Linnea's feelings rebelled at the proposed plan, but memories of her father's threats made her say, rather faintly, "But his reputation . . . are you certain it would be . . . seemly?" She very nearly said safe.

Amanda looked at her wisely. "Under the circumstances, I think so. Don't you, Aimee?"

Aimee Perth smiled conspiratorially. "Even if it

were not, no one but us need know . . . and we won't tell a soul."

Contrary to Linnea's hope, the gentlemen did not linger over their port, so that her respite ended before it had scarcely begun. As for Amanda's plan, it went off without a hitch (barring the insignificant detail that Linnea blushed too red to say her line), the only other deviation being that it was Vale rather than Amanda who suggested they explore the garden.

Lord Carrock's manners were nothing if not impeccable. "I would be honored," he said without the smallest hesitation. "Would you care to, Miss Leyton?" As it happened, he had his back to everyone else, so it was only Linnea who glimpsed the sudden devilry in his eyes.

"Yes, I . . . yes. That would be fine." The reply was automatic; Linnea's mind had completely ceased to function. Her one clear thought was that if Amanda had seen that expression, she would have revised her opinion concerning the seemliness of her scheme.

While a servant went to fetch her wrap, Linnea sat, silently watching as the others arranged the whist table and located a pack of playing cards. She knew she ought to be thinking of a means of escape, but outside of a swooning fit — which she had never had and could not possibly feign — what could she possibly do?

A cool, smooth weight fell upon her shoulders. "Your shawl, Miss Leyton."

Linnea looked up. Lord Carrock was gazing

down at her, his eyes as tranquil as a quiet sea. *Perhaps she had only imagined the hot blue flame of a moment before.* Unconvinced, she rose and accepted the arm he offered her. "Thank you," she said awkwardly.

They did not speak again until they reached the garden, located in the stretch of land between the house and the mews behind. In the lengthy April twilight it was possible to distinguish Amanda's plants—primroses, cowslips, violets, alyssum, masses of daffodils, and a few pied windflowers the marchioness had brought in from the wild. Enfolded in the seductive scent of foliage and flowers, Linnea had a sudden reckless desire to spill out all her troubles to the magnificent man at her side.

"Did they warn you about me?" Lord Carrock said lightly. "Is that why you look so frightened? There's no need, my dear. I won't bite—or at least not hard enough to do damage."

"That," she answered, in a voice that was almost steady, "is precisely the sort of remark I would expect a rake to make."

She saw him nod his approval. "Good, a flash of spirit. Perhaps we will deal well together after all."

As though the whole thing were settled, she thought indignantly. *As though he had taken one look at her and known she would never find anyone else . . .*

"You take too much for granted," she responded. "I doubt we shall deal together at all."

"Because I'm so wicked, you mean? But you're just what I need—a prim, respectable girl to teach me respectable ways. I can't claim I'll learn very well, but I might be persuaded to try." He reached

46

out, his strong fingers wrapping round her elbow to steer her toward the left. "Careful, now, you nearly trod on the violets. Stay on the path, there's a good girl. Would you care to sit down?"

"Where?" Linnea looked around, certain he was playing tricks until she saw the bench.

He laughed softly. "Certainly not among the daffodils. Only think what the little marchioness would think, to find her flowers crushed. You'd have to marry me then."

Linnea sank down upon the cold marble with an inward shiver. "I wish you would not joke about it."

He sat next to her, his lips curving into another of those heart-stopping smiles. "You prefer to lay our cards on the table? Very well, Linnea." His voice softened. "May I call you Linnea?"

Confusion washed through her at the sound of her name on his lips. She felt an urgent need for this to go slowly, yet it was as though all control over her own destiny was being wrested from her grasp.

"I would rather you did not," she said, making a vague motion with her hand.

"Very well, Miss Leyton. Without equivocation, my cards are as follows. I require a respectable wife to lend me countenance, and you appear admirably fit to fill that role. So tell me . . ." He paused for an instant. "Is it a position which interests you?"

She absorbed his question with curious dismay. Was this a marriage proposal or an interview? She felt like a butterfly trapped in a net, which was not the way a very sensitive young lady wished to feel in such a situation. "That's it?" she asked

47

desperately. "That's all you have to say?"

He gave a flat laugh. "I'm sorry, was I being unromantic? Did you wish me to swear eternal love? I can't, you know, for I scarcely know you. To be honest, I'm not that sort of fellow, but at least I'm truthful enough to own it."

A subtle nuance in his tone caught her attention. Perhaps she was mistaken, but it almost sounded like compassion, which he had no right to feel. How dared he feel sorry for her! Was there something about her that made him see her as an object of pity?

Flooding crimson, she snapped, "How pleasant to find you possess at least one virtue, Lord Carrock. I was beginning to fear you hadn't any." *How unreasonable she was being, how unladylike. If she wasn't careful, she would frighten her only suitor away . . .*

There was a short silence before he said, "I didn't think so either. How discerning of you to discover one so soon. I think I'm going to like being married to you." Again that quick smile, as mild and balmy as the soft night air.

Ridiculous tears pricked at her eyelids, but Linnea did not allow them to surface. "I have not agreed to marry you," she said stiffly, "nor do I recall receiving a formal offer to do so."

"Why do you wish to be formal? I should think a certain degree of informality would be more agreeable." With a fluid motion, his arm slipped around her waist. "There now, don't you feel like you've known me a long while? Why don't you pretend for a few moments"—every nerve in Linnea's body jumped as his lips brushed across

48

her cheek—"that we are lovers?"

She pulled herself free and scooted several inches down the bench. "Will you please try to be serious?" she said shakily.

"But I am serious, sweetheart. Wouldn't it make all this more enjoyable? But wait, we have not discussed *your* reasons for entering into this, have we?"

Something in his gentle, inscrutable gaze made her squirm with discomfort. "It is"—she moistened her lips—"rather difficult to explain."

"Try," he suggested, his tone like steel sheathed in velvet.

Recognizing that he was within his rights to require an explanation, Linnea tried to provide him with one. Omitting any mention of Mr. Winterbottom or her father's violent tendencies, she focused on her father's debts and her grandmother's eccentricity. As for the rest of it, she would have chopped off her hand rather than mention that she had been beaten that afternoon, or the consequences to herself should Lord Carrock fail to make her an offer.

He heard her out with the tiniest frown. "Is your grandmother fond of you?"

Linnea considered this. "With Grandmama, it is difficult to say. I do know she likes to be in control. It's been that way for as long as I can remember"

"Oh, I know that type well enough. So there's you and . . . Cousin Iris and Cousin—?"

"Evangeline." Linnea raised her chin. "And I know quite well what you're thinking, so there's no need to pretend."

49

He lifted a brow. "Do you really? Are you a mind reader?"

"Of course not. I only meant"—she paused, flustered by the way he looked at her—"that you are thinking that either Iris or Evangeline would serve your purpose equally well. And I may as well tell you that they are both younger and prettier than I."

"They must be very pretty then."

"I'm sure you'd prefer either one of them," she insisted, without pausing to consider that neither of her straitlaced aunts was at all likely to allow her daughter to wed a man of Lord Carrock's reputation.

"Are you?" The viscount's smile flickered. "Why? You don't know my tastes. Perhaps I like redheads."

She regarded him doubtfully, unsure whether he was joking or serious. "Your own hair has a bit of red in it," she said foolishly.

"So it does. Perhaps that accounts for my preference. A sort of narcissistic response."

"So?" she said nervously. "You're saying—?"

"I'm saying that I don't need to call on either of your cousins. Innocent young girls just out of the schoolroom wouldn't suit me at all, Miss Leyton, but thanks all the same. If I must marry, I want a woman of sense, a woman who won't expect more of me than what I can offer. So"—he reached for her hand—"is it a bargain?"

Linnea stared at the daffodils, wondering why he thought that description fit her. "Yes," she whispered.

"Good." He held her hand between both of his.

"Now I'd like to show you what I *can* offer. Come here."

It was neither request nor command, but it held a silky quality that froze her as nothing else could have done. When she did not move, it was he who closed the gap.

"Don't be afraid." The curve of his finger stroked her chin, then went up to brush across her lower lip. "We're going to seal our bargain with a kiss, that's all."

"We will do no such—"

The sentence was cut off by the viscount's mouth, which came to hers far more swiftly than she would have deemed possible. Swift he might be, but at the same time those expert lips were gentle, inflicting no pain, caressing hers with a cool expertise that accelerated her heart and tingled her flesh. Without the smallest use of force, he somehow managed to gather her closer, so that the heat of his body soaked right through the smooth white silk of her gown. Her eyes drifted shut. Pinpoints of light swirled beneath her lids as his lips trailed down her throat, then returned to hover a hairsbreadth above her mouth.

Then he was kissing her again, sweet shivery kisses that coaxed and warmed her all the way to her toes. Somehow—when, she didn't know—her hands fastened on his shoulders, though she could not have said whether she meant to push him away or urge him on. Dimly, she knew that she could stop him if she tried, yet the rational part of her brain had disconnected. She was too weak to resist, too weak and lonely and needy for . . . for something. *For love, for love.* Yet this had nothing to

51

do with love.

"Stop . . . stop it, oh, please!"

He released her at once. Vaguely, she had expected to have to fight him, so his instantaneous compliance made her blink.

"Why?" His voice sounded peculiar. "I thought you liked what we were doing."

She wiped a shaking hand across her mouth. "I did *not* give you permission to kiss me. Such conduct is disgraceful and . . . and inexcusable."

He drew back, eyeing her intently. "You've never been kissed before, have you?"

The fact that it was so obvious rankled deeply. "Of course I have!" she shot back. "Dozens of times, and by men far more worthy than you!"

She should have known that such an assertion would only land her in trouble.

"Is that so?" Once more he dragged her against his chest, so close the rush of his breath grazed her cheek. "Dozens?" he murmured against her ear. "In that case, I shall have to guard you well, for I don't intend to play the cuckold. How much experience have you acquired? Is it only kisses you've received? Or have they touched you here"—an overpowering faintness assailed her as he cupped her breast—"these dozens of men?"

Then, while her head was still spinning, he set her free and stood. "Never lie to me again, Linnea. As my wife, I will not require very much of you, but I will ask that."

She jumped to her feet, her hands fisted with indignation. "I will not marry you! You, sir, are no gentleman."

"Ah, but you knew that from the start. I'm Lord

Rakehell, remember?"

"I won't marry you! I dislike you intensely."

"Enough to break our bargain?" He sounded composed, yet she had the feeling he was provoked. "What of Papa's debts?" he challenged.

Linnea bit her lip and lowered her lashes. Her back ached, her bruises hurt, but she would not cry. She would not cry. It was all a ghastly nightmare, but this stupid wetness leaking from beneath her lids would go away. She would hold it back . . .

She felt him touch one of her curls. "Listen to me, Linnea. To please you, we'll do this the proper way. I'll call on your father tomorrow and beg permission to pay my addresses. Will you agree to that?"

Surprise brought Linnea's chin up. Her eyes locked with his, searched for some sign of emotion, of caring, but his expression remained unfathomable. *Make a decision, now, quickly, before it's too late.* And then, in a powerful jolt of self-awareness: *I want this man . . .*

Amazement nearly overwhelmed her as she drew a breath and nodded.

When he offered her his arm, she accepted it rather shyly. She glanced toward the house. "I suppose . . . they're wondering what we're doing out here for so long."

He made a low, amused sound. "I'm sure they can guess."

When Anthony finally set out for the Leyton residence, it was nearly the dinner hour of the following day. He had been out late the night before, for upon leaving the Vales' residence, he had met with some of his most harum-scarum friends, who had dragged him off to a bachelor party somewhere in Pall Mall. A copious supply of wine, women and bawdy songs had detained him until past five in the morning, when he had fallen onto his bed in an exhausted, inebriated heap.

As he made his way to Hartford Street, he regretted going to that party. It hadn't made him feel any better. It had only clouded his head, made him restless, made it difficult to think about anything but the imminent loss of his freedom.

Yet, oddly, the prospect of making his first honorable proposal did not feel like the death sentence he had always rated it. He pondered that discovery as he tooled his curricle around a corner. He supposed it was because Linnea was so different from what he had expected. In some mysterious way she had disarmed him, attracted him beyond the point of what was usual. Of course her lush body had been part of it — a large part — but it had been more than that. It had been her fragrance and taste, her shyness and desperate dignity. It had been the vulnerable, troubled expression in her eyes, a look that had filled him with the longing to hold her, to cover her with kisses, to make love to her until her eyes glazed with passion.

He had never seduced a respectable woman, but Linnea had forced him to revise his belief that they would be passive and dull. Judging from her response to his kiss, she had a fledgling sensuality he would enjoy nourishing. How ironic it would be if his own wife turned out to be as seductive as that little widow from last night. What the devil would be the purpose in going out?

The same purpose as always, he thought an instant later. *To escape. To run and hide and bury himself in insanity.*

Scowling fiercely, he flicked his whip over the horses' heads. Perhaps he was only rainbow-chasing. Perhaps marriage would be as bleak and lackluster as he feared. But at least he would have Sundridge, and that would be compensation enough.

Sundridge. Thirty-two rooms, each holding precious memories. It was more than just a fine house. It was a part of him, a part of his heritage, and it was worth any price.

He blocked all else from his mind until he stood on the steps outside her house. Then he thought about her—about her mouth, her breasts, her silly, defiant claim that she had kissed many men. He lifted the knocker and rapped once, and then again. And waited. After what seemed like far too long, the door eased open and a harassed-looking butler peered out.

"Yes, sir?"

Anthony presented his card. "Pray inform Mr. Leyton that Lord Carrock has called."

The butler's eyes widened as though with shock. "Uh . . . very good, my lord. If you will follow me?"

Anthony stepped into the hall, watching the man closely. What the devil was the matter with the fellow? His name might be a notorious one, but such a reaction seemed unwarranted.

Following the man toward the stairs, Anthony

heard the muffled roar of a male voice from somewhere in the house.

"This way, my lord." The butler set one foot on the steps.

Anthony stopped dead. "Where is Miss Leyton?"

"I . . . I really could not say, my lord. If you will follow me?"

Another distant shout reached Anthony's ears, harsh and grating in its anger. And then . . . was that Linnea he heard?

"Out with it, man. Where is she?"

The servant wavered miserably. "She is with her father, my lord. They are having a . . . a disagreement." His next words came tumbling out. "Pardon my boldness, my lord, but if you *are* here to offer for Miss Linnea, it might be fitting for you to interfere before things reach a—" He broke off at the next cry, for it was unmistakably female, though muted as though by thick doors. "That way," he quavered, pointing a finger.

Anthony cursed as he strode toward the rear of the house. His steps slowed as, for a moment, there were no sounds to follow. Then he caught the bellowed words, "That will teach you to make up sniveling lies about—"

He flung open the nearest door.

The sight that met his eyes angered him as nothing had done in years. Linnea lay sobbing on the floor, both hands pressed to her cheek, the curtain of her rich red hair spilled over her face. A large, thickset man stood over her, his face mottled, his bloodshot eyes turned in Anthony's direction. "Who the hell are you?" he snarled.

"Are you Mr. Leyton?"

"I ask the questions in this house." The man stepped over Linnea and approached Anthony, his eyes roving over the viscount's fashionable appearance. A hint of misgiving entered his expression, but before he could speak, Anthony's voice rang out cold and clear as the shot of a pistol.

"I happen to be Lord Carrock, and I should like to know what the devil you mean by striking my future wife."

The man's mouth gaped open. "You mean she was telling the truth? You want to marry her?"

Ignoring the question, Anthony walked past him and bent over Linnea. "Hush, sweetheart, he won't hurt you again. I'm here now." Pushing her hair aside, he removed her hands from her cheek and examined the damage. Then he glanced up, his eyes like blue shards of glacial ice. "If you'd broken her jaw, I'd have killed you."

The big man recovered from his shock. "Nay, my lord. I would never hurt my daughter like that. I merely thought to discipline her for telling lies."

"Lies?"

"I told him," Linnea whispered, "that you were coming to offer for me today, but when you didn't come, he thought . . . he thought . . ."

His mouth compressed, Anthony scooped Linnea up and set her in a wingback chair. Then he turned to her father.

"With or without your permission," he said coldly, "I plan to marry Linnea tomorrow, if I can procure a special license by then. If not, it will be the next day."

Mr. Leyton stirred uneasily. "Certainly, my lord. You're welcome to the minx. As one man to another, I trust you will make allowances for a father's natural anger. I was certain she had made up the tale, for you must admit it was unlikely."

"Unlikely?" repeated Anthony, with aristocratic hauteur.

"That she would attract you as a suitor," Mr. Leyton added hastily. "My dear daughter, can you ever forgive me? You, of all people, know the difficulties which beset me. My cursed temper has always been too quick, but"—a subtle note entered his voice—"you must tell his lordship that I seldom give rein to it."

"Give rein to it again," Anthony said through his teeth, "and you will rue the day you were born."

Mr. Leyton clenched and unclenched his hands, consternation clearly writ upon his face. "Go up to your room, Linnea. His lordship and I will discuss settlements."

Until now Linnea's face had been rigid as a mask, but her distress plainly increased with these words. In a halting voice, she said, "Lord Carrock, you must not feel constrained to marry me because of . . . of what you have witnessed. If, upon consideration, your wishes have changed . . ." She paused uncertainly.

"I may be late," Anthony answered brusquely, "but I am here to make you an honorable offer. Nothing has changed my mind about that, nor do I regret the promise that I made last night."

He had one clear view of those sherry-colored eyes before her gaze lowered, but in that instant he knew what it had cost her to say those words in front of her father. "In that case," she said softly, "I will leave you."

58

* * *

Linnea reached her room before she gave way to tears. Silly fool, to cry now, when it was over. To cry because Lord Carrock had been kind. She had to remember that he was only offering for her because of the estate he wished to inherit. That he seemed gentle was but an added bonus; perhaps it meant she would not have to live with the perpetual dread of displeasing him.

She swiped angrily at her tears. Her left cheek still tingled from the blow it had received; gingerly she ground her teeth, testing for further damage. No, thank heaven, there seemed to be no injury there.

The only true injury had been to her pride.

She had always striven to be strong, to disassociate herself from the unpleasantness of her family life, to rise above it. She had always tried to be someone who could fend for herself, a self-sufficient female able to rise above life's vicissitudes. Sometimes she succeeded; more often than not, she failed.

The air rushed from her lungs as she heaved a great, shuddering sigh. How pitiful she must have looked to him. Why, oh, why did he have to arrive just then? She would give anything to change that. Now he would view her as she must have appeared to him then—helpless, weak, cringing and spineless. She moaned and pressed her hands to her mouth.

And what was he doing right now, this future husband of hers? Promising to pay off her father's debts, which in time he would no doubt regret. A leaden ache grew in her chest. Was she mad to consider going through with this? If she were truly courageous, she would go down there and tell him the marriage would not work, and yet perhaps—another notion nagged at her—perhaps that was the coward's way out.

Confused, she went to her dressing table and sat down, her head propped on her hands. Her thoughts flashed back to the previous evening, and the words Amanda had spoken before they parted.

I like his smile, Linnea. I don't mean its charm, I mean its extraordinary sweetness and amiability. I cannot wait to see him fall in love with you! And he must do so, you know, because you are the sweetest girl in the world. I knew I could depend on John. Anyone with the least intuition can see that you and Lord Carrock are meant for each other.

It was just like Amanda to say such a thing—dear, innocent Amanda, who viewed everything with optimism because she had married for love.

But Linnea was not so naive. She knew what she was, and what she was not. She was not beautiful, accomplished, or remarkable in any way. Other than a flair for putting pen to paper, she possessed no virtues that set her apart from other women, nothing that distinguished her from the rest of creation. She had nothing to offer her husband except her body and her devotion—and the latter would likely be worth little to someone who called himself Lord Rakehell.

Tomorrow, she reflected with a shiver. Would she be married this time tomorrow? Would she be Lady Carrock? Would tomorrow night be her wedding night?

Without warning, the notion took on a terrifying new reality. *She did not know him.* He was a stranger, exotic and formidable and beautiful beyond her wildest dreams. With her own ears she had heard him threaten to kill her father if he abused her again. Was he capable of such violence? Outwardly, he seemed so gentle, but underneath he could be any kind of monster. As her fear of the unknown took root, she began to shake, and with the passing of each second the trembling took her further into its fold. She didn't know anything about him — what he liked to eat, where he spent his time, what he thought, what he dreamed. Why, she didn't even know his Christian name!

Coward, she thought bitterly. *Craven, lily-livered coward.*

Coward or not, somehow she would have to make him understand that until they knew each other better the marriage must be in name only. She raised her head and chewed the tip of her finger. Would he laugh when she suggested it? Would he grow angry? Would he demand his rights as a husband?

Seeking reassurance, she sought to remember his kindness, but instead it was the burning scorch of his lips that surged unbidden to her mind. He had not asked, she reminded herself. He had simply taken what he wanted.

Then her eyes slowly focused on her image in the mirror. Why was she worrying? She had never been beautiful, but right now she looked hideous. Her eyes were puffy, her nose was red, and her hair was in wild disarray. Her cheek had already started to swell, the beginnings of a bruise well in evidence. Experience told her that it would look even worse by tomorrow. No man in his right mind could wish to make love to a woman who appeared as she did. Especially not a man like Lord Carrock, she thought forlornly.

No doubt she would be perfectly safe.

Chapter Four

Rubbing her aching forehead, Linnea reread the lines of neat handwriting on the page she had just laboriously copied. The simple act of writing had calmed her, the scratch of quill upon paper being, in her mind, the most soothing sound in the world. She sprinkled sand over the ink with a small sigh. How unfortunate (Mama called it perverse) that she could not be satisfied with mere journal-writing, which was considered a fitting pastime for ladies of birth and breeding. According to her mother, proper young women did not seek to compose works of fiction, nor did they dream of having their efforts published.

But Linnea did.

Yes, despite her parents' derision, she had spent the better part of the last two years writing a novel. She was currently occupied with preparing the final version of *Miranda,* the story of a young girl's debut into the world and her observations thereof. It was also a love story, for during the course of the tale, the lively and fortuneless Miranda won the affection of the gallant Sir Gabriel Rhodes, who, on the very last page, offered his hand and heart to the girl he adored.

Linnea eyed the stack of nearly indecipherable pages which had yet to be transcribed so that someone other than herself could read them. Though it was past ten o'clock, the house was deathly still. She had no notion where her father was, but she knew her mother had gone calling on her aunts. Mama had wasted no time in rubbing her sisters' noses in the news of Linnea's betrothal.

A soft scratching sound heralded the arrival of one of the servants. "Visitors to see you, miss. Two gentlemen and a lady in the drawing room."

Heart thumping, Linnea rose and drew on a shawl, casting a self-conscious glance toward the mirror as she twitched the fringe into place. There was a faint discoloration along her jaw, but at least the ravages of last night's crying had been erased. Her nose had returned to its normal color, her hair was neatly arranged, and her eyes were no longer red.

As she suspected, it was Lord Carrock. He was accompanied by an elderly, gout-ridden gentleman with a cane and a handsome, willowy lady with a faded countenance. The lady proved to be Anthony's mother; the gentleman, Anthony's grandfather, Lord Sayer. Aware that it must appear singular for her to receive them alone, she explained, rather lamely, that her parents were from home.

"I should have thought," said Lady Carrock, rather coolly, "that they would have been expecting us to call." She clasped a vinaigrette to her bosom, and gazed accusingly at her prospective daughter-in-law.

Linnea knew this called for some kind of response, but before she could devise one, Lord Carrock came to her rescue.

"I am sure they have a hundred things to do, Mama," he said easily. "After all, there is a wedding to prepare for."

With a loud hrumph, Lord Sayer peered closely at Linnea. "I'm devilish pleased to make your acquaintance, Miss Leyton, but, dash it, are you certain you know what you're doing? I mean, if you need more time to think this thing over, you ought to say so. It won't hurt my grandson to wait."

Her stomach churning, Linnea darted another look at her betrothed, who arched a brow in response. "No, I . . . I mean, yes, I know quite well what I am doing." To conceal the fact that she did indeed have a number of doubts, she said stoutly, "I cannot imagine why you should think I would not."

Lord Sayer waved a hand. "Well, it's not so difficult for me to imagine," he said obscurely. "Never mind that. I only wanted to be sure he had not somehow, er, coerced you into agreement."

Determined to dispel that notion, Linnea raised her chin a small notch. "Surely, my lord, a gentleman's offer should not be perceived as anything but a compliment. I can assure you that coercion played no part in my decision."

"You see, she's my champion already." A faint smile touched the viscount's mouth as his eyes locked with hers. "And sensible, too. I like sensible women. We're going to deal well together, you and I."

"I trust so," Linnea agreed, and hoped fervently that it was true. "Have you, er, managed to obtain the license?"

Anthony patted his pocket. "The ceremony is scheduled for tomorrow morning at ten o'clock. I'm sorry, but today was out of the question—the archbishop was in a devilish mood. Are you familiar with

Grosvenor Chapel?"

Linnea replied that she was not.

"It's in South Audley Street. It's quite an attractive little church, though small and unpretentious." He gave her a quizzical look. "But perhaps you would have preferred St. George's?"

"Certainly not." Her parents probably would have, but that was hardly something she would mention. "It doesn't much matter where we are married—"

"—as long as the deed is done. I quite agree."

"Anthony should not have come," announced Lady Carrock suddenly. " 'Tis unlucky for a bride to see her future husband so near the wedding day. I told him so, but as always he would not listen."

Lord Carrock was obviously in a frivolous mood, for he countered by saying, "Ah, but to compensate I've arranged for a host of chimney sweeps to greet us on the way to the church. Only think how lucky *they* are! And it will be a Wednesday, you know, so that is to our advantage—at least according to my Aunt Allison."

Linnea looked at him, unable to follow his quick-silver mind.

He flashed her a small smile. "Don't you know it? Monday for wealth, Tuesday for health, Wednesday the best day of all..." Those bright blue eyes seemed to linger on her face for a moment before they shifted to Lord Sayer. "Well, sir? Will you bestow your blessing on our union?"

"Aye, that I will." Lord Sayer stared hard at Linnea. "So you're Margaret Northcliff's granddaughter, eh? You don't resemble her."

"Nevertheless, sir, she is my grandmother. My mother is her youngest daughter."

"I courted her, y'know, back when she was Margaret Ilford. She was a whimsical creature even then. Drove me mad, on occasion. Never knew what she saw in Northcliff." There was a long pause, then the earl cleared his throat in a no-nonsense fashion. "Anthony's told me about this fortune you are to inherit. Don't think I hold your reasons for marrying against you. Dash it, it's sensible! The only thing that isn't sensible is choosing my grandson, when I daresay there's any number of other fellows you could have. To be sure," he added hastily, "Anthony is a fine man. Dash it, *I* know that better than anyone—"

"Of course she must prefer Anthony," interrupted Lady Carrock with faint indignation. "Why should she not?"

Linnea wished they would not keep harping upon her preferences. "Would you care for some refreshments?" she said quickly. "I know it is a little early, but—"

"No, no, we only came to meet you," disclaimed Lord Sayer, "and your parents, if they were here." He sounded disapproving, and she wondered if Lord Carrock had confided the scene he had witnessed.

"They will be sorry to have missed you," said Linnea, quite truthfully. "I'm not certain how long they will be gone, but perhaps they will arrive while you are here."

She was, however, extremely relieved when another twenty minutes passed and neither parent put in an appearance. Exactly what sort of impression they would have made was beyond speculation, but to have expected it to be favorable seemed a trifle unrealistic.

When it came time for her guests to depart, the earl leaned heavily on his cane and shook her hand. "Miss Leyton, it has been a pleasure. I look forward to welcoming you into our family."

"No doubt," said Lady Carrock stiffly, "we shall meet your parents at the wedding. Do tell your mother that I am arranging for the wedding breakfast to be held in our house, after the ceremony."

Linnea thanked her, hoping she had made the right responses to all their various questions and remarks.

As for her future husband, his genial expression had quite vanished. In fact, his gaze was so steadfast and somber that she wondered if he was having regrets. But as the thought crossed her mind, he came over and raised her hand to his lips.

"Don't worry," he told her quietly. "Marriage may be a bit like the lottery, but you've nothing to fear from me."

"Your cousin Iris has volunteered to be your bridesmaid," Linnea's mother announced an hour later, "and I have accepted on your behalf. What will Lord Carrock do for a groomsman, I wonder?" She sniffed. "I trust he will not drag any of his disreputable friends to the wedding."

While Mrs. Leyton reported the reactions of the various members of the family to the news of her engagement, Linnea stood stiffly in her mother's white satin wedding dress. The fit was poor, but there was time to make alterations; the seamstress at her feet would take care of that.

"Iris had the good grace not to show how put-out she was, but Evangeline flew into such a tantrum that your Aunt Gordon had to banish her from the room. That little miss has not half your breeding, Linnea." Having suffered the slings and arrows of her sisters' snubs ever since her marriage to a man whose fortune had been derived from trade, Mrs. Leyton positively smirked as she added, "And though my sisters profess to be deeply shocked by your choice of husband, they have both agreed to grace the ceremony with their presence."

This was hardly joyous news to Linnea, who anticipated fending off an onslaught of condescending remarks. "Exactly what did you tell them?" she asked cautiously. "Regarding how this came about, I mean."

Mrs. Leyton sent the seamstress from the room before replying. "I told them you had met Lord Carrock at the home of your dear friend Lady Vale — which is true — and that his lordship was immediately taken with you. Of course, everyone knows it is a marriage of convenience on *your* side. Under the circumstances, we could scarcely make them think otherwise."

"I suppose not." Linnea fought off a ripple of vexation.

"I hope you will exercise good sense, Linnea. Lord Carrock is extremely attractive — even *I* am conscious of it, though he is young enough to be my son. A man like that is quite certain to have *other interests* in his life. Do you understand what I am saying?"

Linnea walked to the window and gazed out. "You mean he will have mistresses."

"Er, yes." Mrs. Leyton made a small, huffing sound. "You must not expect him to pay you much heed, nor should you make any indecorous demands. As his wife, you will naturally submit to him in all things, but it would be unwise to expect a great deal in return."

Linnea did not turn. "You're saying I should accept the other women in his life. Pretend not to know. Or care."

"Really, Linnea, there is no need to rephrase everything I say. If it is plain speech you want, then here it is. You are nowhere near pretty enough to hold the interest of a man like that, and if you accept that at the outset, you will be a great deal happier. At any rate," she went on quickly, "even if you were a beauty like Evangeline, I would tell you the same. A leopard does not change his spots."

Linnea traced her finger around a square of the window glass. "Is his reputation truly so shocking?"

"Good gracious, yes. So do not be getting any foolish romantical notions about him. Respect him, obey him, but do not allow your affections to be touched." With a touch of tartness, Mrs. Leyton added, "And it would not hurt to remember that you are not the first girl to sacrifice herself for her family, so do not, pray, be considering yourself a martyr. You are doing very well for yourself with this marriage, and if you think otherwise, you are very much mistaken. Not only has Lord Carrock agreed to settle your father's debts, but he has promised that any monies you inherit from your grandmother will be held for you and your children."

"Children?" Linnea stared blindly at the street below.

"Yes, children," repeated her mother impatiently. "Surely you have not overlooked the possibility that you may have them. You are not normally so slow-witted, Linnea. All men desire an heir, and your husband will be no different." A hint of melancholy entered her tone. "I wish I could have given your father more sons. He never quite recovered from the shock of Harry's death. Sons, replicas of themselves—that is what men want. Come now, let's have a look at you. 'Tis a pity we've no time to order a new gown, but this one should do well enough. By this time tomorrow, it will all be over."

Linnea looked up, suddenly feeling very cold and very nervous. "Do you really think this is the right thing for me to do?"

"Don't be foolish, Linnea. Of course it is." The statement was spoken without a spark of empathy, but Linnea tried once more.

"What if money were not a consideration? What if Grandmama were leaving you the money instead? Would you still wish me to marry this man?"

Mrs. Leyton's eyes slid away. "What a foolish question, Linnea. I refuse to encourage such nonsensical notions. Now let us take off the dress before you crumple it . . ."

"I know you don't like your cousin Roland above half," argued Anthony's grandfather, "but I ask that you accept him as your groomsman. Land sakes, boy, at least he's respectable. Look at that rackety set of hell-raisers you call friends. Black sheep, all of 'em. And it would please your aunt, which *ought* to weigh with you, even if it don't."

Anthony thought of his widowed aunt, Lady Allison Hallett. How such a warm, gentle woman could be mother to a cold fish like Roland was beyond him, but his grandfather did have a point.

He shoved his hands in his pockets and flashed the old man a good-natured grin. "Oh, very well, sir. To please Aunt Allison."

The earl gave a grunt that might have meant anything. "Another thing we've yet to discuss," he said.

"Where are you going to live?"

"What do you mean? I have a perfectly adequate house in Albemarle Street."

"Dash it, I know that! But is it a fit place to bring a bride?"

Anthony's lips curved humorlessly. "Of course it's fit. I don't keep a brothel, Grandpapa. Give me credit for a little discretion."

For a moment it seemed the earl would take umbrage, but in the end he only grumbled, "Well, you've chosen wisely, I'll give you that. Miss Leyton seems a well-bred, respectable girl. Still, 'tis a pity you must needs marry in such haste. 'Tis not at all what I had in mind."

"Nor I." Anthony wandered over to another chair and sat down, his smile faintly sardonic. "Recollect that you forced my hand."

"I gave you till the end of the Season, not the end of the day," snapped his grandfather. "People will gossip, y'know."

"Let them. I don't care."

"I know *you* don't. But what about Miss Leyton? Does she care?"

"There's nothing I can do about the gossip," Anthony said shortly. "Linnea must marry immediately in order to assure herself of that fortune. Not to mention . . ."

"Not to mention what?"

Anthony's jaw tensed. "I don't care to see her continue under that roof any longer than necessary."

The earl's eyes fixed on him. "D'you mind telling me why?"

His face hard with the memory, Anthony summarized the scene he had walked into at the Leyton residence. "I came within an ace of planting the bastard a facer," he added.

His grandfather surveyed him from under grizzled brows, but before he could say anything, Anthony's mother came into the room, followed by a handsome, rather sullen young man with dark hair and gray eyes.

"Here they are, Roland dear. So good of you to come. We do appreciate it, do we not, Anthony?"

Anthony stepped forward, kissed his mother's cheek, and greeted his cousin with a civility that bore no resemblance to enthusiasm.

Looking bored, Roland brushed lint from his sleeve, withdrew a snuffbox from his pocket, and flipped it open. "My aunt tells me felicitations are in order," he drawled, proffering it to Anthony.

"Indeed," said Anthony, accepting a pinch. "Are you offering them?"

"Can you doubt it?" Roland took snuff, then closed the box with a snap. "But why the haste, my dear coz? Isn't this a trifle sudden?"

Anthony smiled serenely. "I'm impatient for my bride. Would you care to be my groomsman?"

Roland looked at him with distaste, but Anthony knew he dared not refuse in front of their grandfather. "I suppose, if you wish it," he said ungraciously.

"Sporting of you." Strolling to the side-board, Anthony glanced over his shoulder. "Brandy?"

As Roland grudgingly accepted, Lady Carrock launched into a recital of the frantic arrangements she was making for the wedding breakfast, which she insisted on having, since "those Leytons" could not possibly afford to do the thing with style. She then progressed to the subject of the clergyman, complaining that Anthony ought at the very least to have engaged a bishop, since his grandfather was acquainted with any number of them.

As her voice droned on and on, Anthony glanced involuntarily toward the clock upon the mantelshelf. He did not normally pay much heed to the time, but tomorrow's prospect made him more conscious than usual of the seconds ticking by. If someone had suggested a week ago that he was about to relinquish his bachelorhood, he would have thought it a rare joke. Marriage had been years away, something he had no need to consider seriously. And though he knew his wild habits distressed his family, a week ago he would not have believed that his grandfather would go so far as to hold Sundridge over his head.

How quickly things could change.

Briefly, he wondered whether he should have called the earl's bluff, then dismissed the idea as cabbage-brained. Anthony knew better than anyone that the old earl had a streak of ruthlessness in his making, a ruthlessness he had exhibited on select occasions during his grandsons' formative years. Lord Sayer truly *would* have given Sundridge to Roland, Anthony told himself grimly.

He thought then of Linnea, with her flaming hair and soft sherry-colored eyes. An image of her formed in his mind, complete with details — the slope of her shoulders, the slender shape of her hands, the fine bones of her wrists. Oh, yes, he had noticed these things. And more. Much, much more . . .

Linnea gazed up at the diminutive church in which she was about to be married. Built of yellowish brick, with a porch of four columns and a small tower, it had a romantic quality that appealed to her.

She infinitely preferred it to the larger and more imposing St. George's Chapel, and silently applauded Lord Carrock's taste in choosing it.

She'd not had time to be nervous during the fuss and commotion of dressing for her wedding, but as she mounted the shallow steps, her stomach felt as if it were tied into knots. Behind her, Iris bade her to pause while she straightened the trailing wisp of gauze and lace affixed to the wreath of roses in Linnea's hair.

While Mrs. Leyton went to take her seat, they waited in the antechamber beneath the tower. Linnea was glad enough that her father had nothing to say, but her cousin's silence made her uncomfortable. "Wish me luck?" she asked Iris pleadingly.

Iris's lovely face relaxed into its first smile of the day. "Of course I wish you luck, Linnea. And for pity's sake, *smile*. You look as though you're headed for the guillotine." She moved closer, whispering, "I'm not as vexed with you as I should be, but don't ask me why, for I've no notion at all. Evangeline is furious though, so do not be surprised if she is not here." In a voice laden with dry amusement, she added, "She thought she would be the first of us to marry, so her nose is completely out of joint."

"I was afraid it would be." Linnea stared at the trembling flowers in her bouquet, deluged with last-minute panic. "Iris—"

But Iris hushed her as soft music drifted to their ears, as haunting and beautiful as the chapel itself.

"Come, daughter," said Mr. Leyton stiffly. "It is time."

Linnea's heart stopped and started. "I don't know whether I can do this," she murmured.

Iris gave her a prod. "Too late now," she said,

though her tone was not unkind. "Just be sure not to stumble walking up the aisle. It is bad luck, you know."

Iris's advice thrummed in Linnea's head as she slowly started up the nave toward the chancel. *Too late now, don't stumble, don't stumble, too late . . .* Dimly, she recognized faces. All her aunts and uncles had put in an appearance, and—her heart gave a glad little leap—Amanda, dearest Amanda had come, along with her husband. Heartened by the knowledge of her friend's presence, she dared to look past the guests in their pitch-pine pews to the two men waiting at the foot of the altar.

Her heart thudded against her rib cage. As tradition dictated, Lord Carrock faced the clergyman rather than the bride, but his groomsman, a dark-haired young man with a surly expression, stared quite openly at Linnea.

And then she reached the altar and Lord Carrock's smile banished the groomsman from her mind. Her pulse raced as once again it struck home that this exquisite man was to be her husband. And there was no disputing that, with his classical visage and tall, beautifully proportioned body, he was a man to make any female's heart beat faster.

Ninnyhammer, Linnea scolded herself. Those blue eyes might settle on her as warmly as though she were his ladylove, but that only meant he was an excellent actor. It meant nothing, she told herself fiercely. He was wedding her for convenience, not affection. She must not cherish any illusions on that score.

As the clergyman began, intoning the time-honored phrases that would bind them together, Linnea focused on the reredos behind the minister's head.

So much beauty and harmony. Her eyes rose to the magnificent traceried windows, and a curious languor stole through her limbs. *So much peace . . .*

"I, Anthony Richard, take thee, Linnea Margaret, to my wedded wife—"

Lord Carrock's golden voice wrapped round her like a caress.

"—to have and to hold from this day forward, for better for worse, for richer for poorer, in sickness and in health, till death us do part, according to God's holy ordinance; and thereto I plight thee my troth."

Linnea swallowed as he slipped the ring on her finger.

Now it was her turn. "I, Linnea Margaret . . ." Somehow her tongue twisted around the words, though her voice sounded woefully shaky.

And then he kissed her—a mere brush on the lips—and it was over.

It is done, she thought numbly, as they walked back up the aisle. She was legally bound to this tall, elegant stranger. In his power, for better or for worse.

High above, the bells in the tower of Grosvenor Chapel began to peal.

Chapter Five

Having survived the ceremony, Linnea faced the wedding breakfast with the knowledge that it could be an even greater ordeal. Other than Lord Carrock's grandfather, Lord and Lady Vale were the newlyweds' only allies; the remaining guests who gathered back at Lord Sayer's Grosvenor Square mansion were relations, each of whom, for one reason or another, disapproved of the marriage and saw no reason not to show it.

The first to strike was Linnea's Aunt Gordon, a strong-featured woman with iron gray hair and a blighting expression. "Well, young lady, I trust you are satisfied with yourself. I don't scruple to tell you that we are all deeply shocked by what will undoubtedly prove to be an excessively unfortunate alliance." She glanced across the Yellow Parlor toward Lord Carrock, making no effort to lower the volume of her voice. "None of us believed you to be a girl of such reprehensible whimsy. Your poor cousin Evangeline has suffered a severe shock to her nerves because of all this."

Behind Aunt Gordon, Linnea saw Amanda roll her eyes, which did more to revive her spirits than the glass of champagne in her hand. Bless Amanda, to make her want to laugh at such a moment.

"Pray convey my regards," she said, hoping her aunt would attribute the unsteadiness in her voice to remorse. "I am sorry my cousin is unwell."

"Small thanks to you," was the reproach. "I suppose you thought he was your last hope, as indeed he probably was. But I dare swear you will come to regret your impetuous action. Marriage to a man of libertine tendencies"—she paused dramatically—"can only be a chastening experience."

At this juncture, Iris's mother joined the attack. "I would have thought," Aunt Bronsden pointed out, "that a female of refinement would not stoop to such depths. I should not care to see my Iris wed to such a man, and certainly," she emphasized, "not in such unbecoming haste. Even if Lord Carrock were a man of impeccable morals it would cause talk, and as it is . . ." She shuddered delicately. "Have you considered what the Polite World will say?"

Involuntarily, Linnea glanced toward her husband, who was standing by the hearth, deep in conversation with the Marquis of Vale. "I have not the faintest interest in what they will say," she said defiantly. "And do not forget, dear aunts, that this marriage had my parents' consent and complete approval."

Both her aunts pursed their lips, but before either of them could speak, Amanda insinuated herself between aunts and niece and gave Linnea a warm hug. "Oh, Linnea, you look absolutely beautiful! I do wish you happy! The ceremony was so lovely I actually wept." The picture of innocence, she turned to Linnea's aunts, saying, "Were they not the handsomest couple you have ever seen?"

Aunt Bronsden and Aunt Gordon had no recourse but to agree, for neither would risk offending so notable a personage as the Marchioness of Vale. The aunts exchanged glances, then swept off in the direction of the groom's mother, no doubt with the intention of ingratiating themselves as fully as possible into her graces.

Linnea unclenched her teeth. "Thank you. You're an angel, Amanda. Now if only my uncles do not start, perhaps I can survive."

Amanda shook her head. "Don't pay them any heed. They only say such spiteful things because they're jealous."

"But are they right? Will everyone be talking and pointing at us?"

"The highest sticklers will gossip, but John and I will use what influence we have to see that people receive you kindly. The whole thing will soon blow over, you will see. Do you plan to stay in London?"

"Gracious, I don't know. Lord Carrock and I —" Linnea broke off with a hysterical little laugh. "Though I am married to him, I cannot bring myself to say his Christian name. I hardly know him, Amanda. I look at him and think 'he is my husband' and it has no meaning."

"It takes time. Come." Amanda took her hand and coaxed her toward the fireplace. "It is your husband's duty to protect you from the dragon-aunts. The more time you spend together, the faster you will become acquainted."

By this time their two husbands had been joined by the Earl of Sayer and the groomsman who had stared so rudely during the ceremony. Lord Sayer introduced him as her husband's cousin, Roland Hallett.

Mr. Hallett bowed. "Accept my felicitations, ma'am. I am charmed, I assure you." The words were respectful enough, but his eyes passed over her with insolence.

Linnea responded coolly, very conscious of her husband, whose gaze had been fastened on her face ever since she had started across the room. He appeared at ease, but she sensed a certain tension in his body, as though he found all this as trying as she.

Warmth flooded her cheeks as she addressed him with painful formality. "Would it be possible, my lord, to have a private word with you?"

"Of course." His mouth quirked into a small smile as he glanced at those who were gathered around them. "If you will excuse us?"

Taking her hand, he led her down a corridor to a small sitting room, shut the door, and locked it. "They're giving you a devilish time, aren't they?" He crossed his arms over his chest, his flawless features set in a benign expression. "Well, damn them all, I say. Let them cook their scandal broth. Where are you going? Come back here and tell me what you wish to say."

Linnea paused in her movement across the carpet. "I can do that very well from where I am."

"Probably, but that won't suit me, love. You're my wife now, remember? So come here and let me kiss you."

Swept with sudden shyness, she fingered a satin fold of her wedding gown. "I would prefer that you did not."

"Are you afraid of me?" He looked at her searchingly.

"Of course not. It's only that I don't want to go back out there looking—"

"—like you've been pawed." His face relaxed. "Under the circumstances, I quite agree. Only think what Auntie Gorgon would say."

"Aunt Gordon," Linnea corrected.

"Auntie Gorgon," he said relentlessly. "Come here."

"My lord—" Her eyes squeezed shut as, with a purposeful glint in his eye, he strode forward and took her in his arms.

"Linnea," he said softly, "open your eyes and look at me. You won't turn to stone, you little craven."

Her pride pricked, Linnea's eyes flew open; she stared up at him with a mutinous expression. "This is hardly the time for embraces," she said stiffly.

"Why not? We're alone and we're married."

"That is not the point." She pressed her hands to his chest in an effort to hold him off. "This is not why I came in here with you."

"Ah." One corner of his mouth curved up. "Sorry, my dear, but I can't help myself. Making advances toward women is an ingrained habit with me. Why don't you tell me what we *did* come in here for? Perhaps you'll distract me—though I doubt it."

"Well, I . . . um . . . merely wished to discover what . . . your plans are, regarding . . ."

"Mmmm? Regarding what?" Keeping one arm about her waist, he raised a hand and touched the curve of her jaw, very lightly, as one might touch an object of very great value and beauty. *Oh, yes, he knew exactly what to do to make himself agreeable . . .*

She took a deep breath. "Amanda asked me whether we meant to stay in London, and I was forced to say I did not know."

"You're asking whether I mean to take you on a honeymoon. To be frank, I hadn't thought of it. Do you desire one?"

"Not in the least. I only wished to be kept abreast of . . . of whatever it is you . . . we . . . mean to do."

"I suppose I could take you to Paris," he mused.

"That is quite unnecessary," she said firmly. "I don't expect you to take me anywhere."

Again, his lips curved. "No? How very modest you are. I've one place in particular I wish to take you, but we won't discuss that just now. Does it still hurt?"

"What?" Her gaze had been riveted on his cravat, but now she looked up into the blue depths of his eyes. "Oh, you mean . . ."

"This," he said quietly. Again, his finger traced along her jaw just where the bruise was located.

"Not very much," she admitted, vaguely surprised that he should ask. "It always looks worse than it feels." The welts on her back were another story, but she'd rather die than have him know about those.

"Always? Exactly how often does this occur?"

"If you don't mind, I'd rather not talk about it."

His eyes drilled her face, but he answered gently. "We won't, if it distresses you." A small pause. "I had meant to stay in London for the duration of the Season. Does that meet with your approval?"

"Of course. I daresay it will be very pleasant

now that I am—" *No longer under my father's roof.* She hesitated, not wishing to raise that subject again. "—now that I am married," she finished.

"Yes, you are 'my lady' now. Does it please you to be my viscountess?"

She hardly knew how to answer the question, nor could she discern what lay behind his facile expression. "I suppose so," she said cautiously.

"You sound unsure." He drew her infinitesimally closer, his voice like the murmur of a soft summer breeze. "Don't worry, I mean to employ all my talents to make certain that being my wife is worth any slights you'll have to endure."

Sensing his meaning, she said quickly, "That is quite unnecessary. Ours is a marriage of convenience, and as such does not require any . . . displays on your part. Rest assured, Lord Carrock, that I am not expecting you to live in my pocket, nor do I intend to plague you if you wish to . . . to live in someone else's."

"Reasonable of you," he remarked, "but I'm far too frivolous to live in anyone's pocket. Did your mother tell you to say that?"

Linnea's nervousness transformed, mysteriously, to anger. "I can think for myself," she flashed. "And I don't quite care for your flippancy, my lord. I don't appreciate being treated like a fool."

His brows snapped together. "Is that what I'm doing? I wasn't aware of it."

"I think we should rejoin the others," she retorted, with a wriggle intended to dislodge her from his grasp. When it achieved nothing, she added, with a hint of desperation, "We can continue this discussion on some other occasion."

His hands shifted to her upper arms, but he made no motion to release her. "I think you're forgetting something."

"What?" She gazed up at him uneasily.

"You forgot," he whispered, "to give me a kiss."

"I . . ." She stopped, unable to think of a reasonable excuse to avoid doing any such thing.

"We're married," he reminded.

"I am quite aware of that," she said tartly. "But this is hardly the time—"

"—for embraces. You said that already." He smiled and lowered his voice. "You have such a pretty mouth, sweetheart. What a shame not to use it for something more enjoyable than protests."

His cajoling tone, combined with the serenity of his expression, gave Linnea a provocative taste of her husband's methods. And while she would have preferred to argue, capitulation seemed the quickest route to escape.

"Oh, very well." Closing her eyes, she raised her chin and offered her lips with the air of a martyr.

Nothing happened.

After a few seconds, she reopened her eyes, and found that he was gazing down at her with something suspiciously like amusement. "Very good," he approved. "Joan of Arc could not have done better."

She stared up at him in outrage.

"What a lot you have to learn," he went on, conversationally. "Kissing is not a penance, my dear. It is one of life's sweetest pleasures."

"One you've no doubt explored to the fullest!" she snapped.

"No doubt," he agreed. "Which is the best reason why you should be guided by me in such matters." He released her with a sigh. "I think we had better take this up later when there's less chance of interruption."

Linnea stood still, contradictory emotions warring within her. "By the by," she said, to fill in the awkward moment, "your groomsman seems very odd. The way he looked at me, even during the ceremony . . . it was as though I had done something to offend him."

"Good old Roland," he said sardonically. "He's my heir, Linnea. His mother and my father were siblings, but Roland and I . . . well, we've never been close. And since I married to disoblige him, it is hardly surprising that he is disobliged. He would glower at any girl I took to wife."

"Oh," she said dubiously.

When they reentered the Yellow Parlor, she was acutely conscious of the penetrating looks bestowed upon them by her relatives; fortunately, however, not a hair on her head was out of place, so no one could speculate that her rakehell husband had treated her to lustful advances during the brief interval in which they had been alone. As this reflection passed through her head, Lord Carrock's head dipped close to her ear.

"It seems we have another guest," he murmured. "Someone you know, perhaps?"

Indeed, ensconced in a wingchair at the far end of the room, swathed to the chin in layer upon layer of pastel-colored shawls, sat a gaunt, grim-faced woman of approximately seventy years of age.

"My goodness, it's Grandmama," she informed him in a whisper. "I thought she was too ill to come."

Even as Linnea spoke, Margaret Northcliff's wheezy voice rang out. "Don't dawdle, child. Come along over here where I can see you. And bring that scapegrace you've married with you. I want a look at him."

When the newlyweds stood before her, Mrs. Northcliff raised a quizzing glass in one tremulous hand and inspected them from head to toe. "Willis told me I ought not to leave my bed, but he's an old woman," she said abruptly. "I never listen to doctors. Turn around," she added, her sunken blue eyes fixed on Anthony.

"Grandmama!" Linnea protested, quite scandalized.

Lord Carrock's expression did not visibly alter, but Linnea sensed his stunned reception to the directive. Still, amusement rippled his voice as he said, "Good afternoon, Mrs. Northcliff. I've heard a great deal about you."

"I've heard a great deal about *you,* and none of it good," the old woman shot back. "Now turn around. I want to see the rest of you."

"Grandmama, for pity's sake!"

But Viscount Carrock was more than a match for the Tyrant of the Leyton family. "Certainly," he said suavely. "Anything to please a lady." Linnea's tongue froze to the roof of her mouth as he reached back and flipped up the tail of his coat. With killing amiability, he added, "We missed you at the wedding. Shall I take this off? I promise there's no hump on my back, but you might like to be sure."

Linnea closed her eyes and waited fatalistically for the explosion, but to her amazement Margaret Northcliff only snorted.

"Good gad, you're a cool one, aren't you? Perhaps you'll do after all." There was a distinct note of approval in her voice; she was clearly pleased to have discovered a worthy opponent. "Ha!" She glanced at Lord Sayer. "He's better-looking than you were, Henry, and brassier than either of us. Linnea's going to have her hands full."

Completing his circle, Lord Carrock regarded the old woman with a lazy gleam. "Perhaps you'd care to examine my teeth."

"Devil take your teeth! I can see 'em every time you flash me one of those devil-may-care smiles. How old are you?"

"Old enough to know when I'm being put through my paces. But I beg you, ma'am, to spare my blushes any further. Has anyone offered you refreshment? There's plenty of it—my family has killed the fatted calf for the occasion."

The old lady stared austerely, but to Linnea's amazement, the corners of her mouth quivered. "Brandy, if you please. Willis forbids it, but I know it's good for me. And I didn't come to your wedding because I hate weddings. Never go to 'em. Funerals, either. When do we eat?"

This seemed a propitious moment to adjourn to the dining room, where an elegant and lengthy repast was to be served. Everyone drank to the newlyweds' health and happiness, and if Roland Hallett appeared to toast Iris rather than the wedded couple, Linnea pretended not to notice. The worst part seemed to be over, for neither of her aunts would dare to make disparaging remarks in the presence of their mother, whom they held in the greatest of awe. The meal passed without incident, and Linnea breathed a sigh of relief.

After the cutting of the brides-cake, Linnea's grandmother summoned her to a nearby room for a private interview. "Now then," began Mrs. Northcliff without preamble, "I want you to tell me the truth. Did they pressure you into this?"

"No, Grandmama, they did not."

The hooded eyes regarded her closely. "Don't lie to me, girl. My eyes aren't good, but I can see that mark on your face."

"I'm not lying," Linnea insisted. "Papa did wish me to marry. As you've guessed, he did his best to come up with a suitor, but I declined Mr. Winterbottom's offer. Papa became angry and . . . slapped me." It was close enough to the truth.

The blue-veined fingers clenched the arm of her chair. "Then, confound it, how and when did you meet Carrock? The fellow's a damned skirt-chaser, for land's sake, with more conquests than I have wrinkles! How the devil did you bring him up to scratch? No one told me a thing about this marriage until yesterday evening, I'll have you know!"

Again, Linnea settled for a part of the truth. "Lady Vale introduced us at a dinner party, er, two nights ago. He and I . . . got to talking and it seemed that . . . that we could . . . meet each other's needs because his grandfather required him to find a wife." She added, awkwardly, "So he proposed . . . and I accepted."

"He didn't compromise you?" the old lady demanded.

Linnea flushed. "Of course not, Grandmama. I would not have permitted that."

"I doubt he'd have asked your permission." A short silence followed. "Well, you've married a rogue, and a handsome one at that. How the devil are you going to manage him, have you thought of that?"

"My heavens, I don't mean to try."

"What?" The shrewd eyes sparked with outrage. "Good gad, and I thought you were the intelligent one of my granddaughters! Of course you'll have to manage him, little fool. You'll be miserable, else."

"Mama has already warned me that he will keep mistresses," Linnea began, only to be cut off by a furious oath.

"Your mother's a fool. My garters, Linnea, what makes you think she knows a thing about men? Look at that hellborn knave she married! I tried to talk her out of it, but did she listen to me? Of course not." She made a disgusted sound. "Fancied herself in love. Ha! I knew best all along. So you listen to me, girl, and you'll be better off."

"But, Grandmama," Linnea said patiently: "surely you realize that this is a marriage of convenience."

"All marriages are for someone's convenience," snapped the old lady. "If you're as clever as I think you are, you'll make sure it's your own." She smacked her lips together. "At any rate, you've beaten your cousins to the altar so you'll get my money, every penny of it. I'm glad it was you. Iris is a fool, and Evangeline's a twit."

"I wish you would leave it to Mama."

"More fool you," was the unsentimental reply. "Your father would only spend it, so why should I? If she wants for anything, I know you'll buy it for her." For a long moment Mrs. Northcliff appeared lost in thought. "Is he kind to you?" she said suddenly.

90

"You mean Lord Carrock? Yes, he, er, seems very kind. Gentle, even."

"He'd better be." The old lady's chin sank into her shawls. "I'm sick, y'know. I'm growing weaker every day. But until I get my notice to quit, I can still change my will."

"Yes, ma'am."

"Saucy chit. You keep the respect in your voice or I'll box your ears."

Linnea smiled faintly. "Inheriting your fortune was not my motive for marrying, Grandmama. You may change your will as many times as you like."

"And what *was* your motive?" inquired the old lady wrathfully.

Linnea looked down at her hands. "You know what it was."

"Your father." Mrs. Northcliff's shoulders sagged. "Well, you're a good girl, Linnea. Just try not to be a fool. That highbred husband of yours is going to need a skilled rider. He's a showy creature, but I've a notion he'll be a sweet-goer. Keep your hands on his reins, but keep 'em light, that's my advice."

"Lord Carrock is not a horse!" Linnea said with exasperation. "Which reminds me, Grandmama, I was never more shocked in my life than I was by your treatment of him. You were outrageous, you know."

"Of course I know, but you needn't sound so prissy. I don't have time or energy to waste, so I gave him a quick little test. He's self-possessed, I'll grant him that. And his hindquarters are as fine as I've seen."

"Grandmama!"

"Come, girl, why be priggish? Y'know, in my day, a man wore breeches, but these ridiculous pantaloons they wear nowadays . . ." She clucked her tongue in disapproval. "Well, they're indecent, but at least you know what you're getting."

Linnea bent down and kissed her grandmother's cheek. "I do love you, Grandmama," she whispered with laughter in her voice. "Even when you're being outrageous."

The old woman patted Linnea's hand and huddled further into her shawls. "Ring for a footman, will you?" she said pettishly. "I'm very tired. It's time I went home . . ."

Mrs. Northcliff departed immediately for the comforts of her Hill Street abode, but it was past three o'clock before the wedded couple were able to take their leave. Anthony handed Linnea into a private coach with the words, "I seldom use anything but a curricle here in town, but that won't do for today. Brides and grooms need their privacy, do they not?"

"I suppose some do," she replied evasively.

He settled into the squabs across from her, regarding her from under languid lids. "I've a hunch that's supposed to mean something, but I confess I'm at a loss."

"Something that seldom happens to you, I collect," she said dryly. Miranda would have come up with a far wittier response, but it was the best Linnea could do at the moment.

"True enough," he acknowledged, his mouth curving. "I suppose what you meant is that I won't try to make love to you *en route*. You are, in fact, quite right. There wouldn't be enough time."

Linnea pressed her lips together and stared out the window.

"Don't tease yourself about it," he added incorrigibly. "It's not because I don't want to."

She gritted her teeth.

"I promise to remedy the situation as soon as we arrive."

"I have the headache," she told him in a brittle tone.

"I see." He paused. "A real one?" He sounded detached, as though he had only a mild interest in whether she lied or not.

"Certainly a real one. I'm surprised you don't have one too, after that nerve-racking charade we just endured."

"Ah, but I don't suffer from afflictions of the nerves. Nothing bothers me." He gave her a clinical look. "Don't tell me you're one of these females who are forever swooning or sinking into a decline."

Linnea straightened her shoulders indignantly. "For your information, I never swoon, I don't sink into declines, and I am rarely ill! I am not such a poor creature, Lord Carrock!"

He laughed. "Thank the Lord. For a moment, you quite gave me pause. Honestly, dear, I am sorry about your headache, but I really must insist"—as he hesitated, her heart nearly stopped—"that you call me Anthony."

Relief rushed through her at this minor demand. "Well, of course I will when . . . when I am grown more used to you."

"And how long will that be?"

"I've no idea. Probably . . . a few weeks."

"Good God." He cocked an eyebrow. "You cannot be serious."

"It seems reasonable to me. *You* may be used to this sort of thing, but *I* am not."

"On the contrary, I am not at all used to 'this sort of thing', as you so decorously phrase it. I've never had a wife before. You have the honor of being my first, dear Linnea."

"Your first *wife,* perhaps, but—"

"Ah, I see. It disturbs you that there have been other women in my life. I'm sorry, love, but there's nothing to be done. If you wanted a saint, you shouldn't have married me." His dispassionate tone carried a hint of flippancy.

Linnea bit her lip, her innate honesty forcing her to say, in an uncertain tone, "No, I didn't want a saint," just as the coach rolled to a stop.

Without warning, her husband slid forward and captured her mittened hands. "Good," he murmured, his blue eyes locking with hers. She watched, mesmerized, as he brushed each quivering wrist with his lips. "Because you certainly didn't get one," he added softly.

Anthony's house in Albemarle Street was of average size. His income had allowed him to choose a dwelling that was larger than the typical bachelor establishment, but it was by no means as spacious as his grandfather's Grosvenor Square mansion. There were five bedrooms in all, the largest of which, naturally, he had adopted for his own use.

"But I'm giving it to you," he explained as he ushered Linnea in. "I'll be using the one next to it—when the occasion demands. Unfortunately, they are not attached."

With keen satisfaction, he saw the way her gaze flew to the bed.

"Thank you," she responded. "It is very nice. Now if you don't mind, I would like to lie down. My head really does hurt abominably."

Reluctant to leave, he glanced around, noting that, as per his instructions, his belongings had been replaced with hers. He took a step closer, observing the way she tensed as he drew near. "All your things appear to be here," he remarked.

"Yes," she said, a little breathlessly.

He watched her carefully, noting the stiffness in her slender shoulders. Was she afraid of him? If so, it was hard to tell. Her bearing was as rigidly correct as Margaret Northcliff's had been. She was certainly a proud little thing, he reflected with a twinge of admiration.

"If you like," he murmured, "I'll stay with you. I've a marvelous treatment for headaches. It's been handed down for generations."

"Yes, I'm sure you do," she said, with a wryness he found amusing, "but I think I'd prefer the conventional remedy."

He surveyed her with interest. Somehow he hadn't truly expected continued resistance, mainly because he did not quite believe in this so-called headache. But he could wait. He had patience. A short delay would only whet his desire.

"Very well, I won't plague you. Believe me, I want you ready and willing when the time comes."

He would have liked her to agree, but she merely turned away, saying, in rather a clipped voice, "Would you send for my maid? I know Mama sent Maria over, so she ought to be expecting the summons."

"I will, if you'll say my name. I've yet to hear it on your lips, Linnea. Except, of course, at the church, and that was mandatory."

She swung around. "Anthony. There, are you satisfied?"

"Satisfied?" His mouth curved ruefully. "No, I scarcely think that describes my present state of mind. But I'm pleased you can force it out. With a bit of practice, I daresay you'll find it's not so difficult."

She said nothing, only watched him with those wide, sherry-colored eyes. She looked so vulnerable standing there, so fragile and silent and lovely, that he was caught unawares by the sudden wave of possessiveness that plowed through him. At the same time, unaccountably, he longed to protect her, to shield her from all the little hurts that life could offer.

"I'll summon your maid," he said curtly. "Rest well. I'm going out."

Chapter Six

Linnea slept for over two hours in the large four-poster bed that had been her husband's. She awoke slowly, listening for sounds of Anthony, but all she heard was the distant rumble of carriage wheels on cobblestones. Unwilling to admit that her relief was mixed with disappointment, she threw back the covers and sat up, drawing a deep breath.

"This is my room now," she whispered aloud. "I am married, and this is my home." She had to admit it had a nice ring to it.

She had fallen asleep in her chemise, but her maid had left her dressing gown draped across the foot of the bed. Standing, she drew it on, observing her surroundings with far more curiosity than she had felt earlier. A handsome chamber, it was situated at the front of the house, overlooking Albemarle Street, and had clearly been decorated with deference to a masculine taste. Its most striking feature was the large Axminster carpet, but it was not this that drew her eye. Above the fireplace hung two portraits, which closer inspection revealed to be skillful depictions of Lord Carrock at a more youthful age.

Linnea studied them with fascination. In the picture on the left, her husband wore a dreamy expression, as though he were pondering some esoteric philosophy. In the other, he appeared to be contemplating some devilish mischief. How could they be so dissimilar? It was like looking at two opposite sides of a coin, she thought in amazement. And which side of the coin had she married?

The door opened suddenly. "I thought I heard you moving about in here."

Linnea spun around, her heart pounding as though she'd been caught stealing the crown jewels. Lord Carrock leaned against the jamb, his long legs braced apart in a negligent posture. "Feeling better?" he inquired.

"Yes, thank you." If only she were not so aware of him, she would be more able to collect her wits.

"I'm glad. Are you hungry?"

His smile was so friendly that, despite her state of dishabille, Linnea found herself smiling back. "Not very," she answered shyly. "But I would like something to drink."

"I've already sent for sherry. Unless you'd prefer something else? Perhaps ratafia?" He strolled forward, graceful and lean as a jungle cat, civilized as a prince. A simple shirt and breeches had replaced his elegant wedding attire, and his hair was ruffled, as though he too had been lying down.

"Ratafia," she repeated in surprise. "Do you really have it?"

"Only for you, love." He halted directly in front of her, his eyes glinting like sunlight on water. "Of course, there's an array of other choices available."

"Sherry would be fine," she said hastily. She backed up, bumped against an armchair, and fell into it.

"Careful." He gazed down at her in amusement.

"There's no need to be so skittish. I'm really a very nice fellow once you get to know me." He wandered over to pick up a poker and jab at the glowing coals in the grate.

"I thought," she said nervously, "that you meant to be out."

"I did go out. And I came back." He glanced up, then straightened and tossed down the poker. "But you were asleep, so I took a nap."

"Oh."

"So is your headache quite gone?" The question was light and casual, but the reason for his interest gleamed in his eyes.

"Oh, yes. More or less." She drew her lips into a tight smile.

"By that, I assume you mean it's subject to recall upon cue."

"I beg your pardon?"

He smiled. "Never mind. I think our sherry has arrived."

A servant set a silver tray upon the dressing table, bowed, and left. Lord Carrock poured the sherry into two cut-crystal goblets, and carried them over to Linnea. "Stand up," he said softly, "and we'll drink a toast."

Seeing no reason to argue, she rose to her feet and accepted one of the goblets.

He gazed down at her reflectively. "You're really quite lovely," he said. With his free hand, he smoothed back a strand of her hair. "Much lovelier than I had any right to expect."

"I'm . . . I'm happy you're pleased," she said faintly. Surprise at the compliment swirled inside her along with another emotion—a flutter of pure feminine satisfaction.

"And what of you?" he said quizzically.

Oh lord, what should she say? What did he expect of her? She looked up into his eyes and offered him a version of his own remark. "You're very handsome."

His low chuckle held a wealth of irony. "Thank you, but that wasn't what I meant. There's more to me than my pretty face."

"Well, there's more to me also." Indignation burned through her nervousness, submerging her softened attitude toward him. "But I don't know you, my lord. I know nothing about you, so how can I tell whether I am pleased or not?"

"True enough," he agreed. "It seems we have our work cut out for us."

"Yes, it does," she said, relieved that he understood. Perhaps this was not going to be as difficult as she feared.

"We'll start now," he murmured. "Shall we drink to our future as man and wife? It seems a good place to start."

Their eyes connected as the goblets clinked, then he raised his glass to his lips. Linnea watched the column of his throat as he drank, then she took a small sip from her own glass. She felt curiously lightheaded, as though she had already consumed a vast quantity of very potent wine.

Anthony, too, was conscious of a disruption of equilibrium, though his own had begun more than two hours before, when he had walked from this room the first time. He had done his best to shake it off, but it had dogged his footsteps as he prowled the streets, and followed him home with the persistence of an infatuated stray animal. Since Roger's death nothing had even come close to making Anthony care deeply about anything; he had thumbed his nose at all but the physical and superficial, and damned the consequences to himself and the rest of his family. Yet something about Linnea, some indefinable quality, triggered a startling response within him — every time he looked into her eyes he wanted to slay dragons in her honor. He didn't want it to be that way. He didn't like it at all. But there didn't seem to be anything he could do about it except wait for it to pass.

When her glass lowered, he took it from her hand. "Let's sit on the rug," he suggested, "right here, before the fire."

He saw her hesitate, but again she complied, arranging the skirt of her dressing-gown while he set down the goblets and disposed himself at her side.

"There, isn't this cozy?" Draping an arm around her shoulders, he drew her close against him. "Here we are, all alone," he murmured. "With no chaperon to plague us. Isn't it nice?"

"For you, perhaps."

"It could be for you also, if you'd give it a chance." His reply was amicable; he would not allow himself to take offense.

"I think . . . we are at cross-purposes on this matter."

"What matter, sweet?" Biding his time, he toyed with one of her curls, enjoying its incredible softness and color. "I thought you wished to know me better."

"I do, but . . . this is not what I meant."

"It's a good place to start," he said, and nuzzled into her neck.

Beneath the shadow of her hair, her skin was smooth and pale as moonlight, her scent as sweet as a Mediterranean rose. Feeling her tremble, he whispered words of reassurance as his lips rambled up and around the curve of her ear, then drifted across her cheek toward her mouth. He kissed her gently, tenderly, enveloped in the scent of roses and sherry and the inviting female fragrance of Linnea herself.

Her answering quiver assured him that she found it pleasurable, so when she turned her head and said, "Please don't," he decided to disregard it. Whether or not she wanted to admit it, she liked what he was doing; certainly the shivers running through her frame belied the tenuous protest.

He dipped a finger into his sherry, then stroked it along her lower lip. Her eyes fluttered shut as he bent and swept the sweet, shimmering wetness off with his tongue, subduing for the moment his desire to explore the rest of her—the soft curves and moist, secret places—in the same way.

Eyes tightly shut, she tipped back her head and made an agitated sound. "Please stop," she whispered. "I don't want this."

His breathing ragged, Anthony paused, but the bright fringe of her lashes still pressed submissively against her cheeks. With her head at that angle, the creamy expanse of her throat lay exposed to his gaze, and her breasts—they arched toward him, straining against her dressing gown, the contours of her nipples visible through the thin fabric . . .

Hunger coiled in his groin. His finger returned to her mouth, carrying more sherry to brush across that sensual lower lip. He had no intention of stopping, but for her sake he would try to go slowly.

"Of course you want this," he coaxed. His warm breath caressed her cheek as he kissed and licked the sherry away, lingering this time, waiting for an invitation to stay and explore.

When it was not forthcoming, he forgot his good

intentions. He forced her lips apart and plunged his tongue into her mouth in a devouring, intimate kiss that ignited the fire in his loins. His intention had been to seduce slowly and deliberately, but that had changed. He wanted her now, this moment, with an intensity that almost tore him apart.

"Oh, Linnea," he said huskily. "Lovely, beautiful Linnea, let me love you right now, here on the carpet." Fully aroused, aching with the need to touch her silken flesh, he slid a hand inside her dressing gown. White-hot desire jagged through him as he found her breast, covered only by the gauzy material of her chemise. "God, you're so soft, so deliciously warm—"

She rammed his chest with her fists. "I asked you to *stop!*"

Confused, he caught her wrist, his breath gusting from his lungs as he searched for some logical reason for her resistance. "What is it, Linnea? Do you have your menses? Is that the problem?"

"No," she choked out. "No, it's not that."

"Then what? Are you afraid? You mustn't be. I'm not going to hurt you." Seeking to fill her with the same fiery longing that inflamed him, he brushed his thumb down the valley between her breasts, then across to the taut, enticing peak of her nipple.

He heard her gasp, which pleased him.

He also saw her arm move . . . too late.

"Agh!" He reeled back, blinking indignantly as his best sherry dripped down his nose and onto his shirt front. Through the sting in his eyes he saw her clap both hands to her mouth in horror, and as his own hand lifted—only to wipe at his eyes—he saw her jerk back in an instinctive, frightened recoil.

The pathetic reflex banished much of his anger, so

that all he said was, "I think you owe me an explanation," instead of the string of frustrated curses that had hurtled through his head.

Clearly agitated, she jumped up and began ransacking drawers in the dressing table. "I-I'm terribly sorry," she said unsteadily. "I should not have done that, and I would not have, if you had paid the least amount of attention to me. Oh, where on earth are the handkerchiefs?"

"There is a stack of towels on the washstand," he remarked.

"Oh. Thank you." She snatched one up and returned to his side.

He held still, submitting to her ministrations as she dried him off. "Actually," he said, "I thought I was paying you a good deal of attention."

"Yes, but the wrong kind. Oh dear, what a monstrous way to begin a marriage!"

"Isn't it," he agreed. Rising to his feet, he settled in one of the armchairs and studied her curiously.

Linnea took the other chair, her expression contrite. "I should have made it clear—before this happened, I mean—that I wish this marriage to be . . . in name only." Her flush deepened; she bit her lip and looked down at her lap. "I realize that you have been used to . . . to going your own way, and I should not like you to think that I expect you to . . . to change."

"Go on," he said, expressionlessly.

She darted a glance at him. "You may be my husband, but you are little better than a stranger to me. I mean, we have only just met, after all! And I do not make a habit of . . . of granting liberties to gentlemen I do not know."

"And do you grant liberties to gentlemen you *do*

know?" It was an absurd question, but he felt a perverse desire to make this as difficult for her as it was for him.

"Of course not!" She frowned at him. "You may make a jest of it, but you cannot possibly believe that I could allow you to . . . do what it is you want to do."

"But I do," he said pensively. "You are my wife. You are mine to do with as I choose." Even to his own ears, the statement sounded pompous and arrogant. But according to law, it was true.

"Please try to understand," she pleaded. "I merely want to feel that I *know* you before we . . . before we . . .

"Consummate our vows." One corner of his mouth lifted, but it was not with amusement. "So in the meanwhile you are giving me permission to take my carnal desires elsewhere?"

She lowered her head and nodded.

"Understand this," he said, after a lengthy pause, "I have no intention of granting you the same freedom. I won't mince words, my dear. If you feel you must deny me my marital rights, you had damned well better not award them to someone else."

"Of course not!" Her head jerked up. "I resent your insinuation, Lord Carrock. You certainly need have no fear on that score."

"So." Anthony leaned back and regarded her with misgiving. "Am I to understand that this arrangement is to be temporary?"

To his surprise, her flash of temper faded as quickly as it began. "Well, I suppose so. I mean, you will surely be wanting an heir . . ." She gazed at the rug, clearly embarrassed.

"How very dutiful," he commented. "Very well,

then. I'll wait." Rising nimbly, he came to stand over her, watching the fluctuations in her mobile features. "But I won't wait forever."

Anthony was unaccustomed to having his advances spurned. It had been done, of course, by females who hoped such tricks would enhance their allure in his eyes, but inevitably they were disappointed by the results. That sort of game had never piqued his interest; he simply did not care enough to make the necessary effort to overcome their coy refusals.

And though he did not flatter himself that Linnea's rejection of him had been a game, he left his house a short while later with every intention of visiting an establishment called La Maison des Cygnes. His face devoid of expression, he strolled down the street, suppressing the seething mixture of his frustration, irritation and perplexity. It was a discomfiting experience to find himself in the ignominious predicament he had seen others endure from wives who, for one reason or another, disdained the men they had married. He had certainly never expected to find himself in a similar strait.

"Carrock?" called a voice. "Hullo, Carrock, is that you? What are you doing out and about? Thought you got shackled this morning."

Anthony swung around to find Charles Perth hurrying toward him, looking very natty in a snowy cravat and a waistcoat of watered silk. "I did," he answered briefly.

Mr. Perth reached him and stopped short, panting from the exertion. "Hang it, man, what are you doing alone? Where's that pretty little wife?"

Anthony did not normally confide his woes to virtual strangers, but his mood was black enough to make him say testily, "My pretty little wife doesn't desire my attentions. Have you tried La Maison des Cygnes? I've heard the girls are of a high caliber."

"Good lord, I don't go to such places! I'm married!" Charles Perth's expression reflected his shock and disapproval.

"Lucky you. To a lady who welcomes your embraces, I collect."

Perth blushed. "Of course she does . . . ahem. Sorry, Carrock, but you can't possibly go to such a place."

"And why not?"

"Because, dash it, it ain't right!"

"Tell that to my wife," he said shortly. "Perhaps it would influence her in my favor."

"Here now, we'd better talk this over." Looking distraught, Perth removed his hat and ran a hand through his unruly locks. He glanced around in a wild-eyed fashion. "Wish Jack were here. Hang it, he'd know what to say."

Marginally diverted by this well-meaning statement, Anthony kept his temper. "This is none of his concern, I'm afraid. Nor yours, may I add. Look, Perth, you're a good fellow, but I don't require your advice."

"That may be, but you're going to get it anyway. Let's go where we can talk. Are you a member of White's?"

"Yes, but I don't wish to go there. Come with me instead."

But Charles Perth proved to be of tenacious turn of mind. "Can't do that," he said stubbornly. "And I don't want to either. It's got to be White's."

The wind gusted suddenly, carrying some unidentifiable scent that brought back the memory of Roger, standing in almost exactly the same spot on the street. Anthony had been teasing him, trying to tempt him to some mischief that Roger had been resisting. Anthony had not been able to persuade him either . . .

"Oh, very well," he capitulated, as the sun scuttled behind a cloud. "Come on, then. White's it is."

Fifteen minutes later, they settled into comfortable wingchairs before a fire, two tumblers of brandy at hand.

"Now then," uttered Charles in an avuncular manner, "tell me what the trouble is."

"No trouble at all. I've simply got myself riveted to a lady who doesn't welcome my amorous advances."

Perth scratched his head. "Perhaps she ain't feeling well."

Anthony stared broodingly at the toes of his boots.

"Or perhaps . . . perhaps it's, er, the wrong time, if you take my meaning. Ladies don't like to, uh, well, *you* know."

Anthony nearly smiled at the other man's discomfiture. "Yes, as it happens, I do know. I'm fairly experienced where women are concerned — at least I thought I was until now. But that's not it either."

Perth gazed into his brandy with an air of fascination. "What reason did she give?"

"She doesn't know me well enough."

Perth looked up. "Well, there you have it then. What's so hard to understand about that?"

Anthony felt a surge of irrational anger. "Damn it, I'm her husband. This is our wedding day. People marry all the time without knowing each other well.

If she had given me the least chance, I'd have shown her . . ." He broke off with a curse.

Perth sat in bovine silence. "I know what it is," he said at length. "It's because you're such a dashed good-looking fellow. Jack had the same problem. Women always throwing themselves at him—spoiled him, y'see. Didn't know quite what to do when one of 'em didn't."

"I know very well what to do," Anthony objected. "But it didn't work. I was very gentle, very persuasive, not frightening at all, and what did she do? She threw a glass of sherry in my face! And it's not as though she's just out of the schoolroom." He knew her age had nothing to do with it, but he needed to justify his sense of ill use.

"Well, she's still a lady, Carrock. Give her a few days. I'll wager she'll come about."

"Now there's an idea. Shall we wager on it?"

"Good Gad, no!" A tiny spasm crossed Perth's face. "Tried that once, with Jack and Amanda. Thought it would do some good, but it didn't. Trouble, that's all it got us. Jack nearly lost Amanda because of it."

Anthony leaned back, hooking his fingers behind his neck. "What about you?" he asked. "Did your wife welcome you into her bed?"

Perth reddened. "Oh, well, that was different. Aimee and I married for love, and in any case, known her all my life. Cousins, y'see."

"Oh." Anthony sighed. "What it boils down to, I suppose, is that I shall have to woo her. I fear I'm ill prepared for it." His companion looked so skeptical that he added, with a short laugh, "I see you've heard about my latest scandal. Well, Susannah Lindcastle is not a lady, Perth, she's a strumpet dressed as a lady. And strumpets don't need to be wooed." He thought of that golden-haired sylph, who had offered herself every bit as brazenly as Sir Gideon's Fifi Divine.

Roger would have told him that laziness was his problem. Roger would have said that he'd forgotten how to toil for what he wanted. Everything came too easily and meant too little. Especially women . . .

"Aha, look who's here."

Anthony sat up, half expecting to see Lord Lindcastle bearing down upon him, but it was only Vale. As elegant and urbane as Anthony himself, the marquis sauntered toward them, his dark brows raised in sardonic inquiry.

"Am I interrupting?" he drawled.

"Not at all." Anthony stood and cordially shook hands. "Join us, won't you? Perth has been advising me on the hows and wherefores of the female sex. Your contribution should prove enlivening."

"I wouldn't think such a Don Juan would require advice."

Charles Perth coughed politely. "He's a lot like you, Jack. Before Amanda, I mean. Different problems though."

"Problems? Already?" Again the dark brows arched, but Anthony had a suspicion that Vale wasn't as surprised as he pretended.

Perth coughed again. "He was headed for La Maison des Cygnes. Stopped him, of course."

"Oh, of course. Charles to the rescue, as always." Sighing audibly, Vale dragged over a third chair and listened while Perth outlined the situation. Then he leveled his quizzing glass at Anthony. "Charles has a habit of embroiling himself in the affairs of others—for the best of motives, I might add."

110

"And you?"

"Oh, I prefer noninvolvement. It's none of my affair what you do. But I think"—the words seemed carefully measured—"that in this case Charles was right to interfere. La Maison des Cygnes is not the solution."

Anthony bit back a rude retort. "I disagree," he said crossly. "What the devil does it matter? Linnea would be delighted. It's what she told me to do."

Vale lowered his quizzing glass. "Lady Vale and I met your wife nearly a year ago," he said slowly. "Amanda has made a number of female acquaintances since we married, but of them all, I venture to say that Lady Carrock is the only one for whom she has felt a strong affinity. For that to happen, your Linnea would have to be an intelligent, virtuous, independently minded woman such as Amanda herself. Not a doxy," he added dryly, "like Susannah Lindcastle."

"So? I already know my wife is a lady."

"So a lady deserves better treatment. If nothing else, think how the tongues will wag if it becomes known that you went to La Maison des Cygnes on your wedding day."

"Damn it, a place like that has to be discreet—"

"Does it?" Vale cut in. "We all know the Regent goes there, do we not? I could name you a host of others."

"Certainly not you," Anthony shot back. "You're too pious for that."

Vale gazed at him, as though weighing his answer. "I love my wife, Carrock. I haven't desired another woman since the day I met her, but before that I had mistresses. Charles will tell you I had far too many of them, and the last nearly ruined my life." He paused. "Before Amanda, I thought all women were alike. She taught me differently. She taught me the value of love and constancy. Because of her, I respect the sanctity of my marriage vows."

Anthony eyed the other man, unable to shake the feeling that Roger hovered behind Vale's shoulder, nodding agreement with everything the marquis said. "Amazing," he remarked, a trifle sourly. "So what do you suggest I do?"

Vale's tone was not unsympathetic. "A little patience would not come amiss. Patience and . . . abstinence."

"I was afraid you were going to say that."

"I think he ought to court her," put in Perth helpfully. "Bring her flowers, that sort of thing. He's a handsome fellow, ain't he? She won't resist him for long."

Anthony's spirits buoyed. Yes, he had rushed his fences with Linnea, but the damage was not irreparable. Where women were concerned, he was no untutored greenhead, so why was he behaving like one?

He slapped the arms of his chair. "You're right, Perth. A little charm, a few attentions, that sort of thing. I'll give it a go." Reaching for his brandy, he felt a primitive rush of anticipation.

"One more thing," said Vale quietly.

"Yes?"

Vale glanced at Perth. "What do you think, Charles? Is a wager in order?"

"Confound it, Jack, you know how you feel about wagers!"

"Still," mused Vale, "under the circumstances . . ."

"What's the wager?" Anthony saw Charles Perth close his eyes.

Vale said, "I'll wager five hundred pounds that you

cannot remain faithful to your wife for the first three months of your marriage."

Anthony debated. The wager was obviously intended to force him to toe the mark, but monasticism was hardly a role to which he was suited. If Linnea continued to deny him, what was he to do? He was a sensual man, a man for whom physical touching was a necessity of life. Moreover, he was accustomed to doing what he pleased, with whatever woman appealed to him at the moment. Yet it rankled that these two men obviously thought he could not do it.

"A paltry sum," he said finally. "What odds do you offer?"

"Five to one."

It was tempting. Surely he could conform for that length of time, and how long could Linnea possibly hold out?

"Done," he said. "But keep it out of the betting-book, if you please. I've created enough scandals for one week. Now if you gentlemen will excuse me? I've a wife waiting for me at home."

A wife he fully intended to pursue as he had never yet pursued . . .

Chapter Seven

"So this is where you live." Iris glanced around the parlor where she and Linnea were seated, her hazel eyes alight with curiosity. Her blond curls framed a heart-shaped face whose features were nearly perfect, and her morning dress of twilled French silk displayed her petite, feminine frame to exquisite advantage. She leaned forward. "Tell me," she said in hushed tones, "what is it like to be married to a rake?"

Linnea wondered whether to take exception to the question, but decided against it. "Gracious, Iris, how should I know? I've only been married a day."

Iris smoothed her skirt. "Mama doesn't know I'm here. She thinks I'm walking in Green Park with my maid." Her pretty lips curved. "She thinks I'll be ravished if I set foot in this house."

Inexplicably, Linnea found herself bristling in defense of her husband. "That's utter nonsense. Lord Carrock is a gentleman."

"Yes, well, rakes like a different sort of female, do they not? I've seen them in the parks, have you? *Those* kinds of women, I mean?"

"I'm sure I couldn't say." Linnea searched her mind for a topic to divert her cousin. "Have you heard anything about Evangeline's come-out ball? When is it to be?"

"In three weeks, I believe. I daresay you'll be receiving an invitation, even though she is still very peeved." Iris paused. "I wonder if we shall see much of Mr. Hallett this Season? He seems a most intriguing man."

Linnea thought of her husband's groomsman and shivered. "Oh, I don't know, Iris. I thought him rather unpleasant. He made no effort to be sociable."

Iris smiled a shade smugly. "He was sociable to me."

"Indeed." Linnea reached for her teacup. "Well, I very much doubt he has anything proper in mind. I would beware of him, if I were you."

"Well, you're not me, are you?" Iris tossed her golden curls, her expression a little irritable. "I certainly find him more to my taste than Captain Theale."

"Captain Theale?" Linnea sipped her tea.

"Lord Poole's second son. He was in one of the Hussar regiments — or was it the Light Dragoons? Whatever the case, he resigned his commission, so I never saw him wearing regimentals. Not that it signifies. I have not the least interest in the man." She hesitated briefly, then gave a heartless-sounding laugh. "He was forever staring at me last Season, but only once asked me to dance. And even then he stepped on my toes."

"Perhaps you made him nervous," Linnea suggested. She tried to remember a Captain Theale,

115

but Iris's admirers had been too numerous to recall any particular face.

"If so, it says little for his courage."

Linnea debated whether to argue the point, but something in her cousin's face discouraged her from doing so. Instead she said, "You had two offers last Season, I believe," knowing Iris would prefer to talk about her conquests.

But Iris's sigh sounded melancholy. "Yes, but neither gentleman had a title. And to be quite frank, I doubt whether either of them would have offered for me if Papa were not quite so rich."

"What of this Captain Theale?" Linnea asked curiously. "Do you think he will try to court you this Season?"

"Court me?" Iris's hand went to her chest, her dainty fingers splayed. "Only if he can do so whilst I dance with someone else. And even if he went so far as to propose, I cannot envisage being married to a man with so little conversation. I would rather wed someone romantic, someone like . . . oh, Mr. Hallett, for instance."

"I don't know how you say such a thing. You are not even acquainted with the man."

"And who are you to talk? How many hours did you know Lord Carrock before you married him? And where is he, by the by? Do not tell me he has deserted you already!"

Linnea was too used to her cousin to be annoyed. "Anthony has gone out," she said calmly.

It was the first time she had said his name without her tongue tripping over it. In itself, this was a small victory, but it was by no means the only one.

Since yesterday, her situation appeared to have

improved. Her wedding day might live on in her memory as a day she would never wish to repeat, but last night had been better. Lord Carrock had returned after an absence of little more than an hour in an altogether different mood from when he'd left. In fact, he had stunned her by presenting her with a dozen roses, something no one had ever given her before. He had apologized for his behavior, supped with her, and kept her entertained for the remainder of the evening with a game of backgammon. She had lost, of course—she was not very good at games—but he had made it surprisingly enjoyable. And when it had come time for them to retire, he had bidden her good night, kissed her on the cheek and gone off to his own room without any attempt to force his attentions on her.

Iris looked pensive. "Well, if *I* had been married only yesterday, I would not take kindly to being abandoned so soon. Though I suppose you are glad enough since yours is a marriage of convenience."

"True, but that does not mean we dislike each other. In fact, those roses over there are from him. We happen to find each other's company quite . . . quite pleasant."

"Indeed." Iris eyed the bouquet with interest. "How prodigiously romantic of him. I am sure Captain Theale would never do such a thing, though perhaps Mr. Hallett . . ." Her voice trailed into thoughtful silence.

Eager to steer the conversation into other channels, Linnea commented upon her cousin's gown, whereupon Iris embarked upon a detailed summary

117

of each and every gown she had purchased for the London Season. "Your own dress is two Seasons out of style," she finished critically, "but that can't signify now that you are rich. I know! I shall take you shopping myself, right this instant."

Linnea glanced down at her dress. "Oh, but I couldn't . . ."

"Why not? You've married a wealthy man, Linnea, and when Grandmama dies, you will be even wealthier. Of course, we shall have to go into mourning then, so you may as well enjoy it while it lasts."

Linnea thought longingly of her unfinished manuscript, buried deep in her wardrobe beneath an old paisley shawl. "I do have a few things to attend to," she began.

"Goodness, what else could you possibly have to do? You don't want people to think Lord Carrock married a dowdy, do you?" Iris set down her teacup with a little clink. "They'll be enough gossip without that."

"What of your mother?" Linnea asked. "I thought I was *persona non grata* at the moment."

"Oh, she'll come around. Whether she likes it or not, you're a personage now. She cannot forbid me to see you. Only think what a scandal *that* would create."

"I see," Linnea said dryly. She glanced toward the window, where a blaze of sunshine proclaimed the day to be a fine one. She did need clothes; there was certainly no disputing that. "Very well, Iris. Let me go and change, and then we'll go."

She was in the process of donning her best walking dress when Lord Carrock ambled into her room. Fortunately, she was decently covered—Maria had only a few fastenings left to secure—but the invasion flustered her.

"Ah, there you are," he said casually. "I've come to take you for a drive."

He had been absent since breakfast, and had given her no reason to think he would desire her company at any time during the day, so the request took her quite unawares.

"I'm very well, thank you, but—oh, how lovely!"

The nosegay of violets which had suddenly swept out from behind his back came as an even greater surprise. He presented them with one of his searing smiles. "For you, love. I couldn't resist."

Linnea buried her nose in their blossoms, inhaling the heavenly scent. "Thank you, my lord. You are very kind. But I'm afraid I've already made plans to go out with my cousin Iris." Wishing she had not made that promise, she dismissed her maid and turned to face him. "Forgive me, but in the future I would take it kindly if you could knock before entering. It . . . it quite discomposes me otherwise."

Lord Carrock's smile faded slightly. "Very well, I shall, if you insist. Where are you and Iris going?"

"Shopping. Iris thinks I look dowdy."

"She's wrong." He came forward and took her hand, and the spicy scent of his shaving lotion wafted her way. "But as the new Lady Carrock, it's quite true that you ought to be rigged out to the nines." He surveyed her consideringly. "I think I ought to escort you. I know precisely what you should buy, and from whom."

Several objections swept through Linnea's head,

the foremost being that Iris might not appreciate his company. On the other hand, it would not do to encourage her relatives to avoid her husband, which could only make things more awkward than they already were. Nor could she quite subdue the spurt of pleasure that the prospect of his company produced.

Still, she answered cautiously. "Well, Iris may not like it, but I don't mind if you come. Though I fear you will be bored."

"I won't be bored, but why won't Iris like it? Does she dislike me?"

"As to that, I'm sure I could not say, but her mother fears you will ravish her." Startled by her own flippancy, Linnea shot him a swift look, but to her relief he was grinning, albeit a shade wickedly. She smiled back, taking simple pleasure in the shared moment.

He touched her arm. "Tell her it's too early in the day. I only ravish virtuous females between the hours of ten and midnight." Then his grin faded to seriousness. "I'm prepared to make a go of this marriage," he added softly. "Are you?"

"Yes, of course I am. I would not have you think otherwise, my lord."

"Anthony," he reminded her.

"Anthony." A surge of shyness made her look down, only to find her gaze settled on her husband's long legs. Encased in buff pantaloons, the contours of his thighs suggested strength, as though he had spent a lot of time in the saddle. He was slender without being sparse, able-bodied without being brawny; he also radiated virility—a virility that made her senses stand up and do pirouettes. And for an instant, she could not help but wonder how he would feel, pressed against her, without the barrier of clothing . . .

"Iris is waiting below," she said quickly. "Will you stay or come with us?"

"I'll come. I think you could benefit from my advice." He walked to the wardrobe and opened it, perusing her gowns with a critical air. "Has no one ever told you that emerald or sapphire would suit you far better than all these white and pastels?"

So much for his claim that he did not find her dowdy. He obviously thought she had no taste at all.

Mildly nettled, she lifted her chin and said, "Why, yes, as a matter of fact. Someone was kind enough to point that out to me quite recently. He also suggested yellow. And brown, to match my eyes."

She had not intended to provoke him, but to her surprise he swung around with a frown. "He? Who the devil would be impudent enough to tell you that?"

It was ridiculous to suppose he could be jealous, foolish to believe he might care. Still, it was an irresistible fancy. Imagine a man as handsome and sophisticated as Lord Carrock giving a brass farthing whether another man had given her advice. The very notion was like a balm to her fragile feminine ego.

" 'Twas merely a friend," she said casually. "Someone whose opinion I value."

"I see." His glance raked her. "Do I know him?"

"I've no idea."

"What's his name?"

His persistence betrayed him. Oh, yes, he definitely did not care for the idea that his wife might have a friend among his own sex. How very typical of a man, she thought. Not that she had known a great many of them, but she had always been a keen observer—it was where she obtained the fodder for her novel. She had long ago perceived that the majority of the members of the male sex—like her father—upheld a double standard. They could do whatever they liked, but their wives and daughters must not deviate from a strict set of rules.

And although Linnea was a very quiet, introverted sort of girl, she had an independent, rebellious streak. Already, she had had an incontrovertible taste of her husband's way of thinking. *I have no intention of granting you the same freedom,* he had said. Not, of course, that she had the least desire to break her marriage vows, but she certainly did not want to encourage him to believe he could limit her other activities. Whether this show of interest was attributable to jealousy (and really, it seemed most unlikely), there was her career as a novelist to consider.

"His name, Linnea."

Linnea reached for her bonnet. She did not want to tell him the truth, that it was only Lord Vale who had given her advice. The feminine side of her rather favored the idea of an unmarried admirer—it appealed to her romantic side.

"His name is . . . is Gabriel," she said recklessly. "He does not move in your circles, so I very much doubt that you know him." *Indeed, how could he when Sir Gabriel Rhodes was a fictional character in her book?*

Tying the ribands beneath her chin, she gave her husband an innocent smile. "Come, my lord, we had better hurry. I have already kept poor Iris waiting far too long."

Iris Bronsden was a young woman who turned heads and knew it. Anthony had noticed her the day of the wedding, and he noticed her even more today, not because of her beauty but because of the way she looked at him, as though he were a cross between a cannibal and a heathen deity.

Happily, she accepted his escort without visible signs of hysteria, and even graciously invited him to ride in her carriage when he offered his own for the excursion. He wondered what Iris's mother would say when she found out; whatever it was, he hoped she would not say it to Linnea. Then, rather irritably, he wondered who Gabriel was. Obviously not Linnea's suitor, since she'd needed Anthony to fill that role. A friend, she had said. A male friend who knew Linnea well enough to offer advice on her dress? The way she had hesitated to reveal the name suggested a guilty conscience, but he could not doubt her virtue. He could swear she was as pure as morning rain.

"I have never purchased anything from this Mme Seraphine," Iris stated, as the carriage drew to a halt at the establishment he had selected. "I had wished to take Linnea to Mme Giselle's." Iris eyed the portal of Mme Seraphine's with suspicion.

"I prefer Mme Seraphine," Anthony said, as the footman let down the steps. He naturally did not confide that Mme Seraphine had a niece who had

123

once lived under his protection, or that because he had treated the girl with excessive generosity, Madame took extra pains with any orders he placed. "Mme Giselle has an irritating voice," he added, an explanation that seemed to appease Iris.

The ensuing hour progressed much as he desired. A discreet woman, Madame did not so much as blink when he introduced Linnea as his viscountess. She raved over the coppery shade of Linnea's hair, said nothing about the gown that Linnea arrived in, and nodded earnestly while he explained that as his wife, Linnea was to be garbed in the first style of elegance. Quick to recognize Linnea's potential, Madame listened to his ideas, offered a few of her own, and accorded Linnea the respect she would have given a duchess.

"Gracious," said Iris, upon viewing Linnea draped in a length of pomona green silk. "I must say it becomes you. Your mama would never have let you wear such a color, but I like it."

"Yes, it is lovely," Linnea said softly.

Thinking she seemed subdued, Anthony eyed her carefully, but it was not until Madame briefly exited the room that he realized the problem.

"Surely," Linnea whispered in his ear, "we are being too extravagant. I cannot possibly *need* so many gowns, can I? And some of them are so dashing, I know I shall feel very self-conscious. Mama never encouraged me to wear such low necklines. Indeed, I am afraid I shall"—her voice lowered even further, as if with great embarrassment—"pop right out of them if I breathe too hard."

At once Anthony sought to reassure her, faintly

amused and also surprised by her fears. Linnea was rapidly proving herself unique, he reflected. The women he'd outfitted in the past had always tried to wangle more out of him, not less. As for the necklines, they were really no lower than anyone else's, he explained, very patiently. *And she certainly had the bosom for such a style,* he thought.

"Lord Carrock is right," contributed Iris. "Your Mama has always dressed you too conservatively, Linnea. As for extravagance, that is a great piece of nonsense. Wait and see. Before the Season is half over you will be saying you haven't a stitch to wear."

Though the remark was meant to support Anthony, he could not help reflecting how glad he was that it had not been Miss Bronsden he had married. He did not dislike Iris; in many ways he found her attractive. And yet he had several times wished that she were elsewhere.

Deciding to entrust the remainder of the shopping to the ladies, he handed them into the carriage. "I'll instruct the coachman to take you to Botibol's," he told Linnea. "You won't need me—your cousin can assist you with any choices that need be made. Miss Bronsden, if I may ask a favor? Do not let Linnea buy less than she requires. She needs a good many bonnets, as well as all the other fripperies—stockings, shoes, parasols and the like." He sent Iris his most winsome smile. "I know I can depend upon your excellent taste."

While Iris preened, Linnea's expression conveyed her opinion of his tactics. "You may be sorry," she warned him demurely. "I am sorely tempted to take you at your word."

Something passed between them as their eyes connected. "Do," he said, smiling a little. "I can afford it."

Linnea watched her husband walk away with a pang of regret. She had been enjoying his company more than she had expected and certainly far more than could be wise. *Take care,* she warned herself. *Remember why he married you.*

"What an admirable man," Iris remarked enviously. "Only conceive of one's husband saying such a thing! I cannot imagine my father giving such a carte blanche, nor either of my uncles, for that matter. You must take advantage of it while it lasts."

Linnea gazed out at the passing shops, unable to forget the debts her husband had been forced to discharge in order to win her hand. "I have no intention of squandering Lord Carrock's money," she said firmly.

Iris rolled her eyes. "Well, if you mean to nip farthings, I wash my hands of you. His lordship expressly requested that you spend his money and I quite fail to see why you should not do so. It is a wife's duty to please her husband, after all."

Reminded of her failure to do so in one respect, Linnea shifted restlessly. "Nevertheless, I shall buy only those items that are necessary."

Her cousin readily acceded to this, though it soon proved that Iris's definition of "necessary" did not tally with Linnea's. After an hour of constant debate on the subject, Linnea wearily suggested they finish the shopping another day.

"Would you care to go to Gunter's?" she asked, knowing it was one of Iris's favorite haunts. Iris agreed with alacrity, and the barouche set off.

Berkeley Square contained many fashionable town residences, but it also harbored a number of shops. Among these, Messrs. Gunter had proven one of the most successful. Its ice cream and pastries attracted the nobility from far and wide, who not only ate there on fine days such as this one, but hired them to cater their weddings and dinner parties. The two cousins headed toward the wrought-iron tables set up under the shade of the plane trees, and a waiter scurried over.

Minutes later, Iris sank her small teeth into a sugar plum. "Ummm, I could eat a hundred of these."

"So could I." Linnea bit into her apricot tart, then sipped cautiously at her pekoe tea. Starlings quarreled in a nearby treetop and a lazy breeze tickled her curls. How pleasant this was, she reflected. All in all, Iris was good company. As for Anthony . . .

A shadow fell across the table. "Good day, ladies," drawled a voice. "What a pleasant surprise to meet you here." Though the brim of her bonnet hid the speaker from her view, Linnea knew who it was.

She forced a perfunctory smile and looked up. "Good day, Mr. Hallett."

"Lady Carrock." A mocking bow. "And Miss Bronsden, is it not?"

Since the man was holding a confectionery, Linnea supposed it would have been rude not to have invited him to sit down. Still, she gritted her teeth as Iris smiled and begged him to do so in a tone that suggested he would be doing them a large favor.

He accepted with a catlike smile. "I own I am surprised to see *you* here, Lady Carrock, only one day after your marriage. Tut, tut. All alone, without the benefit of your new husband's escort? What can my cousin be thinking of?"

"I am scarcely alone, Mr. Hallett," Linnea said coolly. "My cousin bears me company, in case you had not noticed."

Mr. Hallett murmured an insincere-sounding apology and bit into his cream puff, whereupon Iris fluttered her lashes and commenced a flirtation.

Linnea looked away. She couldn't bear to watch Iris make a fool of herself so instead she examined the people at the surrounding tables. One very handsome lady in particular caught her eye. A buxom, fashionably dressed blonde, she was talking rapidly to another, much plainer lady who bore a look of pained resignation upon her face.

"You would do much better to ignore her," Mr. Hallett said softly.

Linnea started as she realized the comment was addressed to her. "I beg your pardon?"

He nodded toward the blonde. "She does not know who you are as of yet, but she soon will. As soon as the announcement of your marriage appears in the papers, everyone will know who you are. She'll be furious, of course."

Iris peered around. "Who on earth are you speaking of?"

"Lady Lindcastle," he said with a smirk. "She is

a particular friend of my cousin's. To say more would be indiscreet, but I'm sure Lady Carrock understands."

Torn between the desire to deliver a scathing setdown and an overwhelming urge to demand an explanation, Linnea retorted, "Well, I do not, Mr. Hallett. And I find your hints to be exceedingly ill bred."

"Do you, ma'am? I beg pardon. I will say no more upon the subject." Something malicious glinted in his eyes. "I would not for the world wish to distress you."

Resisting the impulse to stare at the woman, Linnea silently finished her tart. Mr. Hallett's insinuation was clear, even to an unworldly person like herself. He had wanted her to know that the blonde was her husband's mistress, she thought dejectedly.

Suddenly unable to bear another moment of the man's company, she sprang to her feet. "I am sorry, Iris, but I have suddenly remembered an appointment. Good day, Mr. Hallett."

"So soon?" protested Mr. Hallett, as though they had been having a wonderful time.

Iris dusted her fingers and eyed Linnea, but fortunately asked no questions. Instead, she offered Mr. Hallett her hand with the majesty of a princess. "Until we meet again, sir."

Mr. Hallett jumped up and, with an ingratiating smile, begged leave to call upon Iris in her home. Iris blushingly gave her consent.

"I hope you know what you are doing," Linnea said, once they were back inside the carriage.

"Why, whatever do you mean?"

"I mean I do not trust him, Iris."

Iris smiled. "He is very mysterious, is he not?"

"He is obnoxious," Linnea muttered.

"Really, Linnea! I can understand your resentment, but you must not hold Mr. Hallett accountable for any misconduct of your husband's. Oh, yes, I understood, and while I admit he should not have said what he did, I'm sure it was done out of kindness. He was merely trying to warn you."

"*Real* gentlemen do not make reference to such things, Iris. I don't think you should encourage him. Recollect the size of your dowry, then compare it with the probable size of Mr. Hallett's income."

Iris appeared ready to make an explosive remark, but instead she pursed her lips in a manner reminiscent of her mother. "That is the disagreeable part of having money," she said. "One can never be completely sure, can one? About a suitor, I mean."

"Oh, I think one could. I am sure there are honorable men who would not care about your money—though I doubt Mr. Hallett is one of them."

Iris shook her head. "Perhaps, but it must always be a factor. Why, even you married for money, Linnea. And you are the last person I should have expected to do so."

"I did not marry entirely for money," Linnea corrected. "There were other factors involved."

"Duty, you mean? Yes, I had almost forgotten about your Papa's debts. Why do men do such things, do you think?"

Linnea shrugged, and the two cousins lapsed into a brooding silence that lasted until they bade one another farewell back in Albemarle Street.

Linnea ascended to her bedchamber determined to put the unpleasant episode with Mr. Hallett from her mind. And the best way to do that, she decided, was to bury herself in work on her story. Ringing for tea, she dragged her manuscript from the depths of the wardrobe and regarded it with satisfaction.

There was now a desk in the room, an elegant *escritoire* which until this morning had made its home in the ground floor sitting room. Anthony had had no objection to its relocation, for she had explained, during breakfast, that she preferred to sort invitations and pursue correspondence in the privacy of her room. Naturally, he had no notion of the true use she would make of it.

And she had no intention of telling him.

Anthony dined with her that evening, and afterward invited her to sit with him in the drawing room. All through dinner he had seemed in a restless mood, as though he could not bear to stay in one place for so long. She supposed that he was used to filling his time with all manner of wild activities, though her imagination fell short at what some of them might be. Or was it her, she wondered uneasily. Perhaps she bored him. He had been trying very hard to be nice to her, bringing her flowers and such, and she appreciated that. But perhaps he longed to be out with his friends—or in with his mistress.

Keeping such thoughts to herself, Linnea waited with her hands folded while he poured them each some sherry. She watched him silently, studying his flawless profile and the elegant, graceful way he held himself. Without intending to, she pictured him with the blonde, Lady Lindcastle, but pushed that image away, quickly, before it could crystalize in her brain.

"So," he said as he came over to where she sat, "shall we play backgammon again? Or would you prefer piquet?"

"Neither," she said quietly. "Could we not simply sit and talk?"

"Talk." His lips quirked as he put the glass in her hand. "What a novel idea. I wonder how many husbands and wives actually talk to each other? We may be the only ones in London."

"I wish you would not speak like that."

"Like what?"

"Like . . . oh, I don't know. As though you were trying to show me how little you care about everything."

He looked at her, his eyes cool and intense. "But that's exactly it, my dear. I don't care. That's the key to being entirely content."

"Surely you cannot believe that," she protested.

"Oh, can I not?" He raised his glass to his mouth and drank half its contents in one swallow. "I assure you I do."

"But . . . why?"

He met her eyes and looked away, immediately. "I had a brother once. A twin brother called Roger."

Her mouth opened and shut. *Of course, the twin portraits. How could she have been so blind?*

"What happened?" she asked timidly.

132

"I killed him," he answered, his voice as emotionless as a stone.

Linnea simply stared at him; it was all she could do to contain her shock.

"I shot him." He paused. "We were attacked by highwaymen. They robbed us of our purses and threatened us with pistols. All we had to do," he added, staring downward, "was allow them to escape, but that was not good enough for me. I was angered by their effrontery and determined to defy them." He paused again, as if tormented by some image from the past. "Roger was a peace-loving soul. It was I who was the hot-blooded, impulsive one. That was nearly five years ago." He gave her a quick glance, as though to see if she were properly horrified, then returned his gaze to the carpet.

"But how did it happen, Anthony? I don't understand."

"Damn it, do I have to spell it out? I murdered my brother. It was unintentional, but the end result was the same. You have married a murderer, my dear. A rich and titled one, but a murderer all the same. There are those who will be only too happy to tell you so." There was a roughness to his tone, a ferocity that sent an involuntary shiver down her spine.

"But no one could blame you for an accident," she objected.

"No?" He smiled grimly. "At the time there were those who did not cherish so charitable an opinion. Roger was the elder twin, you see. He was the heir, not I. And his death changed that."

Linnea absorbed this with a frown. "I see. And

so because of this tragedy, you have simply given up caring."

"Don't think I sit around wallowing in self-pity. My life has gone on, though I don't deserve that it should. I've contrived to have a jolly time of it these past few years." He rose and wandered to the window, staring down at the street below. "You wished to talk, Linnea. I suggest that you do so. Tell me more about yourself."

She sat very still, trying to think what to say. "There's really not much to tell," she said uncomfortably.

He slanted her a look over his shoulder. "Very well, I'll ask the questions. Tell me how it is that you reached the age of three-and-twenty without becoming someone's wife."

Linnea flushed. "No one offered for me. That should be obvious." It was a slight prevarication, but Mr. Winterbottom really wasn't worth mentioning.

"I don't see why not," he said. "Have they been hiding you away in a tower?"

Linnea considered evading the question, but decided against it—after all, it was she who insisted they become better acquainted.

"When I was eighteen," she said steadily, *"my* brother died. Harry had been ill for a long time, and it was not unexpected. But we naturally went into mourning until the following year." Her voice faltered with remembered emotion, but she controlled it and went on. "The following year, believe it or not, I contracted mumps, which was most unpleasant as you can imagine. I was ill for most of April and May, and by then it was too late to go to

134

London. The year I turned twenty, my parents brought me to town, and my Aunt Bronsden presented me. Needless to say, I did not take, although . . ."

"Although?" he prodded.

"Although I did receive an improper proposal," she confided with a small smile. "I never told anyone about it."

Her husband's brows snapped together. "Did you, by God? Who the devil dared to do that?"

"He was a half-pay officer with a most attractive face. I don't recall his name and it really doesn't signify now. I wasn't in love with him, if that's what you're wondering."

He studied her face. "And then?"

"And then we went back to my father's estate in Surrey until the next year. That was the Season Mama persuaded my Aunt Gordon to undertake the problem of presenting me. Aunt Gordon is very good *ton,* you see, and has the entree into many establishments that are closed to my mother." Her lips curved. "But I'm afraid I failed Aunt Gordon, for no eligible suitor became enamored of my charms. She was most vexed with me."

A slight smile curved his lips. "Poor Linnea. You've had a rough time of it, I think."

"When I was twenty-two," she continued, "we tried again. That was the year of Iris's come-out, so of course my Aunt Bronsden could not be expected to take me on. And Aunt Gordon had quite washed her hands of me, so it was left to Mama to try to fire me off. All her schemes failed miserably, although I did make Lady Vale's acquaintance, which was my only saving grace. That was worth all the rest of it," she added reflectively.

"She is your friend," he stated.

"Very much so. She is like a sister to me."

"And yet," he said rather dryly, "she introduced you to me."

Linnea looked down at her wine glass. "Amanda did what she thought was best." The atmosphere of camaraderie between them emboldened her to add, "She believed we were well-suited."

"Perhaps we are," he said evenly. "At least *you* suit *me.*"

An absurd pleasure stole through her at the compliment, but before it could take root, he turned back to the window. "Had it been my choice," he went on, "I would have put off marriage as long as possible. But what's done is done. One makes the best of one's lot."

Linnea swallowed hard; something fluttered in her throat. "Of course," she said hollowly. "That is the sensible thing."

Silence followed. She studied her cuticles; he gazed at the street. Then, without warning, he swiveled. "Linnea," he said, in a voice that was oddly hoarse. "Come to bed with me tonight. Let me make love to you."

Her heart slammed against her rib cage. "Please, you promised not to . . . to importune me on this matter."

"Is that what I'm doing? I thought I was asking." He gazed at her, his eyes intense with some dark and restless emotion. "But I don't mean to beg," he added bitterly. "I never have and I never will."

And with these words, he left her alone.

Chapter Eight

Linnea did not leave her house on the morning that the announcement of her marriage appeared in the newspapers; instead she chose to spend the entire day shut in her room with her manuscript. The following day, however, brought a visit from Anthony's mother, who insisted that Linnea accompany her on a round of morning calls.

"Behave as though the marriage was the most ordinary thing in the world," Linnea's mother-in-law advised her in patrician accents, "and you may depend upon it that Society will do the same. After all, my dear, it is not as though you *eloped,* like that dreadful Chalfont girl last year."

Taking this as a sign that the Dowager Lady Carrock had decided to accept her, Linnea pinned a smile on her lips and did as she was told.

As was to be expected, the proclamation of the notorious Anthony Stanton's marriage to an obscure female of unimpressive birth had precipitated an avalanche of speculation. To give credit where it was due, Anthony's mother knew what she was doing, for in extending the umbrella of her respectability over her daughter-in-law's head, she shielded Linnea from what might otherwise have been a difficult time.

And Linnea acquitted herself well; her quiet dignity struck exactly the right note with the imposing London matrons. Afterward, Linnea's mama-in-law complimented her on her conduct, adding, with an air of satisfaction, "On the whole, I feel we have brushed through the business tolerably well. In fact you have made so excellent an impression it may do Anthony some good also. We will pay some more calls tomorrow, but I fancy the worst part is over."

So it was that, although the gossip continued to rumble, its general intensity ebbed. Invitations flooded in, but to Linnea's disappointment, Anthony expressed only a mild interest in guiding her through the morass of social demands. His advice was to accept those invitations which suited her; he would escort her where she liked as long as she gave him adequate notice.

She tried to be content with this. She told herself she had no right to feel forlorn or lonely or depressed. After all, she had rejected him, and he was still being nice to her. Every day he brought her flowers and other gifts — including a lovely pair of diamond earrings. Why couldn't she be satisfied with that?

There was a reason. She desperately wanted to know her husband, really know him as a person, but it wasn't happening. When he was absent — which was often — he did not tell her where he went; when in her company, he was attentive and warm, but the topics they discussed were light and frivolous. He allowed her no second glimpse of his pain, nor did he again treat her as a confidante. Like a turtle, he had retreated into his shell after one quick peep at the world outside.

One afternoon, when she was feeling particularly

blue-deviled by his absence, Linnea decided to pay a call on Amanda. To her surprise, when she arrived in Brook Street she was ushered, not to the drawing room as was the usual practice, but on up to the second floor and into Amanda's private chambers. She found the young marchioness reclining upon a handsome, silk-striped day bed, sipping green tea and leafing through a novel.

"Amanda!" Stopping short, Linnea scanned the other woman's face for signs of suffering. "No one told me you were ill."

Amanda tossed down her book and shifted to a more upright position. "I'm not ill—at least, not exactly. I am merely in a delicate situation. I only found out a few days ago, when—oh dear, I hate to say it, but I emptied the contents of my stomach. John insists that I rest every day."

"Oh, Amanda, how splendid! I am so happy for you." Linnea took the chair next to the day bed and kissed her friend's cheek.

"Thank you. I was most vilely ill with little Jack, but so far this time does not seem so bad. Still, it has been enough to prevent me from coming to see you, and I do apologize."

"There is no need. Actually, my mother-in-law and I paid *you* a call a few days ago, but were informed that you were not at home. Now I understand why."

Amanda laughed. "Yes, I'm afraid Burke has been refusing callers. But never fear," she added lightly. "I shall soon be back to normal. Do pour yourself some tea, if you like. It's very soothing to the system."

Consumed with curiosity about this most mysterious, fascinating part of womanhood, Linnea reached

139

for the pot. "Tell me," she said slowly, "what is it like?"

"What is what like? Being with child?"

"Yes, that and"—a betraying flush rose in Linnea's cheeks "and the part that leads to it."

"Good gracious, you mean you and Lord Carrock haven't . . ."

"No." Linnea shook her head. "I told him I was not ready."

"I see," said Amanda. "Well, all I can tell you about lovemaking is how it is for me. Of course, it has to be the right man, but for me it has always been quite wonderful."

"It is not . . . I mean, you never feel . . . embarrassed?"

"Not in the least, my dear. It is not like that, I promise you. To be frank, I enjoy it excessively, which John tells me contributes greatly to his own pleasure." Pink tinted the marchioness's cheeks as she added, a shade dreamily, "It is like nothing I can describe, Linnea. You simply have to experience it yourself."

"I suppose I shall," Linnea sighed. "Eventually."

Amanda's expression altered. "Oh dear, are things not going well? I do hope I haven't driven you into an unhappy marriage. I would feel dreadful if I thought—"

"Please don't concern yourself," Linnea said hastily. "You did not drive me into anything. I entered into the marriage of my own free will and"—she hesitated for a moment—"I cannot honestly say I regret it."

"I wish you could have had time for courtship."

"I suppose that can come after marriage as well as before," Linnea replied, with an optimism she did not feel. "He's been bringing me flowers. Every day, in fact. The house smells like paradise."

Amanda reached for her teacup with a tiny smile. "John used to do that too," she remarked. "For the entire first month of our marriage, he put a rosebud on my pillow every morning. He still does it sometimes, just to surprise me." She sipped her tea and added, "I am sure Lord Carrock realizes how lucky he is to have you for a bride. He is making an attempt to please you, Linnea, and that is a very good sign."

Thinking of her husband's frequent absences, Linnea was about to refute this when she realized it would only distress her friend. From somewhere she vaguely recalled that women in Amanda's condition were easily agitated, so she only said, "I suppose so. At least he has agreed that we should . . . take time to know each other before we . . . become intimate. I cannot say he was pleased about it, but he accepted it with, er, fair grace."

Amanda looked at her for a long moment, her silver eyes knowing. "Has he accepted your desire to be a novelist?"

"Not exactly." Linnea ran a finger along the thin edge of her teacup. "I haven't mentioned it."

"My goodness, why not? You told me it was a part of you, this burning need to write."

"It is also very private. I've never told anyone but you, Amanda."

"Well, you ought to tell Lord Carrock. One must open doors to one's husband, Linnea, that one keeps shut and barred to others."

Linnea pressed her lips together as memories of her parents' sneers slid through her mind. "I cannot tell him," she said stubbornly. "At any rate, it's none of his concern. He may be my husband, but that does not give him the right to take away what I have worked so hard upon." She ended with a vehemence that made the marchioness blink.

"Linnea, Linnea, why would he take it away? You're being unfair. Surely a man who takes the trouble to bring you flowers every day would not be so cruel."

Linnea dragged in a breath, knowing her friend's words made sense yet unable to rise above her own choking defensiveness. "Perhaps not, but I refuse to take the chance. Even my own mother doesn't understand and she's known me all my life. She thinks writing fiction is unseemly and useless. In fact, it embarrasses her so much she won't speak of it to anyone. And my father thinks I'm weak-minded. He only permitted me to write because it kept me out of his way. When I was younger, I wrote of princesses being rescued by handsome knights. I used to hide those stories because I knew, if either of my parents saw them, they'd be thrown into the fire. So how can I expect Lord Carrock to understand?" She curled her fingers into fists. *"If* it is published, *then* I may tell him about it. Afterward."

Amanda frowned, but wisely let this pass. "Have you contacted a publisher?"

Linnea nodded, relieved at the change in subject. "I sent a letter to Thomas Egerton in Whitehall, but I have yet to receive a reply." Her mouth curved ruefully. "You must realize that novels are not being well received at the moment. Everyone is sick of them—especially the reviewers, it seems. One critic has called it a 'worn out species of composition.' A few people even call Jane Austen's work nonsense, so I expect mine is total

142

rubbish. My parents are probably right."

"Oh, I cannot believe that," Amanda objected. "Fanny Burney has done very well. And look how well Maria Edgeworth's novels have sold, despite her propensity for long, moralizing paragraphs." She retrieved the book she had set aside. "In fact, I am reading her *Ormond* right now, and find it most entertaining. So what do these reviewers know?"

Catching her spirit, Linnea smiled. "And do not forget that every copy of *Sense and Sensibility* sold, so someone must be buying, even if it is not the critics. And it was even translated into French."

"Yours will be translated into a dozen languages," declared Amanda as she refilled her teacup.

Contentment pervaded Linnea during the ensuing hour. With Amanda, she felt comfortable enough to discuss anything, no matter how private. When Amanda returned to the subject of childbirth, Linnea did not hesitate to ask questions. And Amanda answered, which endeared her to Linnea, who had never had such closeness before, not with anyone.

When at last she rose to go, Amanda expressed the desire to take her for a drive in the park later that day.

"But do you feel well enough?" Linnea said doubtfully.

"I think so. If I find I do not, I will send a note around to your house and let you know."

"Very well." Linnea bent to kiss her friend's cheek. "Take care, Amanda."

She left the Brook Street house with her spirits revived, a spring in her step that had been lacking before. How marvelous to have a friend, a confidante with whom she could share her worries and dreams. Last year Amanda had been an agreeable acquaintance; this year their relationship had blossomed into something more enduring and substantial. And as their friendship had grown, Linnea had become increasingly awed by the marchioness's deep love and faith in her husband.

Linnea let out a small sigh. Perhaps someday she would regard Anthony in that light, but at present she could not envision it. He might be taking great pains to be pleasant, but she could hardly tell him the things she told Amanda. Then again, she had not told Amanda everything either. She thought of her father's brutality with a shudder. No, that was something she would never share with anyone. Nor would she confide her secret fear that Lord Carrock would, in time, prove as violent as her father.

Yet the fair weather made it easy to banish such unwholesome thoughts. High above, the sun bathed her with its healing rays, pouring over her like rich honey to sweeten her mood. And since she suddenly felt like walking in the sunshine, she directed her coachman to drive to Clarges Street, where her cousin Iris resided. Unlike Evangeline, who refused to expose her complexion to the rigors of the elements, Iris was a great walker.

Linnea found Iris and her mother in the drawing room, engaged in the genteel occupation of needlework. Iris looked bored to death, while Aunt Bronsden appeared to find nothing amiss with spending a beautiful day doing something so tedious.

"Good afternoon, Linnea," Aunt Bronsden greeted her in conciliatory tones. "You are looking uncommonly well today."

"Thank you," said Linnea. "I've come to see if Iris would care to walk in Green Park. It is too lovely to stay inside."

Iris put down her stitchery. "May I, Mama?" she asked eagerly. "Surely it is too late to expect more callers."

"If you wish," replied her mother with a glance toward the window. "Be sure and take a wrap, my dear. And a parasol. You know what the sun does to your complexion. Dear me, perhaps you should change into another gown. You would not want to risk soiling your new one. Then again, one never knows when one might encounter a gentleman admirer. And the dress becomes you most admirably. Gracious, what a dilemma. No, you had best leave it on. After all, my love, you are in your second Season, and we must be prepared for any eventuality. You may come across that delightful Mr. Osborne, or perhaps even Lord Mayhew, for I know he occasionally goes there with his sister. And we do want to encourage him, do we not? And then there is that handsome Captain Theale! Now be sure you do not exert yourselves," she implored, as the two girls edged toward the door. "Remember, a lady does not perspire!"

When they were finally free of Aunt Bronsden, Iris heaved a sigh of relief. "Thank goodness! I vow I am becoming quite fond of you, Linnea. The notion of being shut in there all afternoon was too dreary to contemplate."

Linnea smiled. "Doing stitchery no less. How could you bear it?"

"I could not," replied Iris frankly. "How Mama does fuss! What in the world does she think I will do to my dress? Roll on the ground in it? It is a very good thing she did not realize you were without your maid," she went on as they climbed into Linnea's carriage, "or we would have been obliged to hear

145

about that for twenty minutes. And why don't you have a maid with you? A lady should not be out alone, even if she is inside her carriage. It is really most singular of you."

Linnea sighed. "I know. If you had not agreed to accompany me, I would have gone home."

"Still, you must have a care for your reputation. Only think what the scandalmongers would say."

"Yes, Aunt Bronsden," Linnea teased.

Iris looked taken aback. "My heaven, I suppose I do sound like Mama, don't I? I shall have to be careful."

They accomplished the short distance to the park entrance in less than a minute. The carriage stopped, the footman let down the steps, and the girls climbed out and smoothed their skirts.

Linnea glanced at her cousin as they set off down one of the footpaths. "It sounds as though my aunt approves of Captain Theale," she remarked.

"Yes, he has managed to ingratiate himself with her quite thoroughly of late," said Iris darkly. "In fact, when he paid us a call yesterday, Mama positively fawned upon him."

"Then he must have some commendable qualities."

"Indeed, yes—Mama has discovered he has expectations! He is to inherit a fortune from some distant relative—a great-uncle, I think."

"Ah, that explains it. And does that weigh with you?"

Iris sniffed. "Not at all. I find him boorish. At any rate, I fully intend to marry a title. Lord Mayhew has been showing signs of interest. He is an earl, you know. And Mr. Osborne is heir to a barony. Captain Theale is heir to nothing—unless, of course, his brother does not marry, and that seems a remote possibility."

"I am beginning to think Captain Theale has done something more than step on your foot, Iris. Has he offended you in some way?"

Iris stopped suddenly. Her eyes had fixed on something in the distance, and a small gasp escaped her lips. "Oh, no, Linnea, it is he! I cannot believe my ill luck!"

Indeed, coming toward them on the footpath some thirty yards ahead, was a fashionably attired gentleman in his late twenties with a book in his hand.

"That is Captain Theale?"

"Yes," wailed Iris. "How I wish there were somewhere to hide!"

"Stay calm. Very likely he will only greet us and pass."

"Why in the world would he be walking alone? He is the strangest man of my acquaintance."

As Captain Theale's long stride carried him closer, Linnea studied him with interest. Tall and blond, with regular features set in a long, thin face, he fastened his eyes on Iris as a starving man might gaze at a feast.

"Miss Bronsden?" he asked, tucking the book under his arm. "It *is* you. I did not think I could be mistaken."

Iris presented a haughty exterior. "Good day, Captain. What a surprise to see you again so soon. Linnea, may I present Captain Theale? Captain Theale, this is my cousin, Lady Carrock."

Captain Theale bowed and smiled, revealing a furtive dimple. "I am pleased to make your acquaintance, ma'am."

Though she could not have said why, something

147

about the man appealed to Linnea. "And I am pleased to make yours, sir," she replied with a friendly nod. "My cousin has mentioned you."

"I hope in a favorable light," he said gravely.

Iris shifted her parasol from one hand to the other and blushed. "Are you here by yourself?" she asked uncertainly.

"Yes. I suppose you find that eccentric of me."

"No." Iris's blush deepened. "Well, perhaps, just a little."

With a sheepish grin, Captain Theale brought forth his book. "I came here to sit under the trees and read, but I'm afraid I drew a few stares."

Linnea's interest stirred as she glimpsed the title of his book. "You are reading *Mansfield Park?*"

"Yes. Have you read it?"

"Three times," she confessed. "I found it delightful, though I think, perhaps, that *Pride and Prejudice* is my favorite."

"I read that one twice," he confessed with a smile.

Iris primmed up her mouth. "If the two of you mean to discuss books, at least let us walk whilst you do so."

"If that is an invitation to join you, Miss Bronsden, I accept."

Sensing that Iris was not as averse to the captain's company as she pretended, Linnea seconded the invitation. "It is a pleasure to meet someone with such excellent taste in novels," she added warmly.

The captain fell in beside them, adjusting his long stride to match the women's shorter steps. In Linnea's eyes, he soon proved himself a charming conversationalist, for he was well read and well informed, with just the proper degree of respect for the truly great authors. It did not take long for her

148

to discover their shared interest in such novelists as Fielding, Smollett, and Scott, but since Iris maintained a frigid silence throughout, politeness soon forced them to change the topic.

"Do you go to Lady Besford's ball tomorrow evening, Miss Bronsden?" he inquired.

Iris kept her gaze focused on the footpath. "Perhaps. I do not recall which ball Mama wishes me to attend. We received invitations to three, I believe."

Her frosty tone would have discouraged most men, but the captain seemed made of sterner stuff. "Will you save me a dance?"

"How can I," she replied, "when you do not know which ball I am to attend?"

"Nevertheless, I would be gratified if you would do so," he answered quietly. "I shall endeavor to discover where you are."

Silence followed; Linnea gave Iris a nudge.

"Oh, very well," that young lady said, a shade pettishly.

"A waltz?" he persisted.

"La, sir, you ask a great deal! Everyone desires the waltz, you know."

Her admirer opened and shut his mouth. "I beg your pardon, Miss Bronsden. I should not have asked."

Linnea waited in vain for Iris to show pity, or for the captain to renew his efforts, but this did not occur.

"I am sure what Iris means," she interposed, "is that the waltz is extremely popular with all the young people and therefore the most difficult to save."

The captain gave a slight smile. "And is it popular with you, ma'am?"

Linnea thought of those few occasions when her

hand had been solicited. It had been a heady feeling, to whirl around the room with a gentleman's hand at her waist. "Yes, it is," she answered truthfully.

"Then perhaps I may partner *you*," he offered with gallantry.

"Thank you," she replied. "I should like that very much. But I do not plan to attend any balls in . . . in the near future."

What she did not add was that she had accepted scarcely any of the invitations that had been piling up on her desk. Sooner or later she knew she would be forced to — if only to justify the purchase of all those new gowns — but balls did not interest her just now, not when she knew how curious everyone was about the new Viscountess Carrock. If she had been more like Iris or Evangeline, she would no doubt have revelled in the attention, but her character was too contained to enjoy being whispered about. She hated the stares, and loathed the idea that there were people who believed she had married because she had been compromised. She would by far have preferred to have spent the first days of her marriage becoming acquainted with her husband, perhaps in the quiet of the country, instead of brazening it out under the eyes of the *ton*.

As these thoughts flitted through her head, they reached a point where the footpath split into two directions. Captain Theale used this as an opportunity to take his leave. "I shall look forward to renewing our acquaintance," he told Linnea with a bow. "Miss Bronsden" — his expression sobered as he turned to Iris — "perhaps I shall see you tomorrow evening."

"Perhaps."

"I shall look forward to it."

Iris twirled her parasol. "Good day, Captain Theale."

When he was gone, Linnea shook her head in exasperation. "How could you behave so abominably to that nice man? What has he done to warrant such treatment? You led me to expect someone boorish and ill bred, but Captain Theale is a delightful, sensible, sensitive gentleman. Not only that, he is handsome."

"Not as handsome as Mr. Hallett," Iris said sulkily.

"I thought you preferred Lord Mayhew and Mr. Osborne. For heaven's sake, Iris, why will you not tell me the truth?"

Iris lowered her parasol, struggling visibly for composure. "Promise you will not tell anyone?"

"Of course I promise."

"It's rather embarrassing."

"I will not tell a soul."

Iris continued walking, her gaze fixed straight ahead. "It was last year, during my first Season. I had seen Captain Theale and—yes, I admit it—I thought him very handsome and hoped he would seek an introduction to me."

"And?" prompted Linnea, when nothing more was forthcoming.

"And—oh, the long and short of it is that by pure chance I overheard him talking to one of his acquaintances." Iris stopped and bit her lip.

"Where did this occur?"

"At Lady Winwood's ball. I had gone to the ladies' retiring room, and was walking back down the corridor to rejoin Mama when I heard their voices. Captain Theale and the other gentleman were standing around the corner where they could not see me, but I

151

recognized his voice since I had heard him speak several times that evening."

"Well? What did he say?"

"They were talking about . . . women." Iris flushed. "Captain Theale's friend said something about a female—one presumes she was not a virtuous female—wearing a . . . a bust improver and how confounded he had been to discover it. He said he had expected that her . . . her breasts were truly as large as they seemed when she was clothed. He seemed most disillusioned."

"But that is hardly the captain's fault," Linnea pointed out, quelling an urge to laugh.

Iris flashed her an irritated look. "Then I heard Captain Theale say that he did not care for them either. He teased the other man, saying that *he* could often tell when a female was, as he phrased it, attempting to improve on nature's inadequacies."

"How very shocking. But I daresay gentlemen talk about all manner of shocking things when we females are not about."

"You do not understand," said Iris in a suffocated voice. "*I* was wearing one. All my gowns are designed so that I *must* wear them. Mama insists upon it because I am not very well developed and she says that bosoms are the main focus of the figure. And so when I was introduced to Captain Theale, I hardly knew which way to look."

Linnea sighed. "Well, I can see where you might have found it awkward, but you cannot know if he was telling the truth. Perhaps he only claimed such powers of discernment to impress his friend—though if so, I admit it does him little credit."

Iris was silent for a moment. "It is not the subject that they discussed which troubles me," she said glumly, "so much as the knowledge that Captain Theale prefers ladies who do not stoop to artifice. If he discovered that this is not all *me*,"—she patted her chest—"I am sure he would view me with contempt. He probably prefers large-bosomed women. Mama says most men do."

"You are making assumptions, Iris. At any rate, if he is truly so discerning, he has already divined your secret and regards it as unimportant."

"I am convinced he has not. Nor will he have the opportunity, for I refuse to consider him as a suitor. And I will not waltz with him either. Only think how closely he would hold me! I dare not risk it."

Since no argument Linnea put forth would sway Iris, she soon turned the conversation to other topics until the end of their walk. She returned Iris to Clarges Street and rode home, feeling sorry for her cousin as well as a little sleepy from the fresh air and exercise. And since Anthony was nowhere to be found, she went to her room and took a nap.

Sometime later she awoke to find him in her room. He was standing over her, watching her sleep, his face set in a brooding expression.

Highly disconcerted, she sat up quickly. "Did you wish to speak with me?"

"I'm sorry, I didn't mean to wake you. I came only to deliver this." He held out a note.

Absurdly conscious of him, Linnea strove for non-chalance as she unfolded it. "It's from Amanda," she said. "Oh, dear, she isn't feeling as well as she'd hoped. We shall have to change our plans."

"What were you planning?" He sat down on the edge of the bed.

"She offered to take me driving in Hyde Park. She thinks it will help to stifle the gossip if I am seen

153

with her." Linnea forced a shrug. "She says it is better to put on a bold face."

"My sentiments exactly." Looking relaxed, he lounged at his ease, one lock of chestnut brown hair flopping rakishly over his brow. "But I think a better strategy would be for you to go with me."

"With you?" She looked at him in surprise.

"Is it so inconceivable?" His hand moved to cover hers. *"I'll* take you for a drive in the park, smack at the peak of the fashionable hour. What do you say to that?"

Linnea stared down at his hand, feeling its warmth, sensing its strength. "I think it might be a good notion," she said slowly. "Thanks to your mother, most people have been kind, but there is still a great deal of talk."

"Then we'll do it," he said. He levered himself to his feet, then leaned down to kiss her cheek. "Which means you have one hour, my love, to make yourself ready. Lord and Lady Carrock are about to show the Polite World exactly what they think of it."

Chapter Nine

Linnea had always considered the *beau monde's* daily five-o'clock promenade in Hyde Park as something to be endured rather than enjoyed. She had driven there before — with her mother, with Aunt Bronsden and Iris, even with Aunt Gordon and Evangeline. However, on those occasions she had been mere Miss Leyton, a nobody, and so had failed to garner much notice. Nervously, she wondered whether being a viscountess would make it even more of an ordeal.

As if sensing her apprehension, Anthony gave her a low-voiced lecture as they entered the park. "Don't let it fluster you if people stare," he warned. "The gossips must have their food, after all. And with the hastiness of our marriage — frankly, some of them will be thinking the worst. But never fear," he added with perfect affability, "if anyone is uncivil, I'll throw a glass of sherry in their face."

Linnea laughed. "I hope you will not. And I really don't give a button what anyone thinks," she added proudly, if not quite truthfully.

He flashed her a grin. "That's my girl. Pluck to the backbone."

Suddenly, the whole world glowed. Colors burst

like melting rainbows upon a setting of such remarkable beauty that Linnea's breath caught in her throat. When was the last time she had met with praise? Her courage had always been called obstinacy, her dignity labelled wicked and prideful. Worthless, willful, contrary, ungrateful—these were the words which had been flung at her all her life.

That's my girl . . .

Her heart swelling with myriad emotions, she longed to turn to her husband and voice those emotions, to give them power. Instead, she simply looked at him, noting the perfection of his profile—the slightly arched nose, the high cheekbones, the firm, sculpted lips. Garbed in a dark blue coat and pale waistcoat, with pristine neckcloth, pale pantaloons and gleaming Hessians, he looked the very embodiment of indolent British manhood. Yet Linnea knew he was far more than that. Beneath the polished exterior lurked a complex man, a man of intelligence and wit and dangerous charm.

A man who admitted to killing his own brother.

Of course, not for a moment did she believe it was anything but an accident, but the knowledge that he considered himself responsible troubled her deeply. Whatever else he had done in his life, she thought, that was one burden he should not be forced to carry.

"My mother says you've made a good impression so far," he said suddenly. "I knew you would."

She placed the gloved tips of her fingers together and studied them. "I was not so sure. I was terribly nervous, but your mother helped me through it. She has been very kind."

He nodded. "She was against the marriage in the beginning, but I think you've changed her mind."

Linnea glanced up. "She seems to dote on you."

"I am all she has left," he said with a shrug. The hand he used for the reins tightened and relaxed. After a pause, he added, "It was hard for her to accept Roger's death. It took her a long time to forgive me."

While Linnea absorbed this, a high-pitched female voice intruded.

"Anthoneeee . . . oh, Anthoneeeeee!"

Linnea looked around to see a ripe-bodied woman of about forty waving madly from a nearby carriage. Anthony waved and smiled back, a response that had the woman simpering like an ecstatic puppy. "Can it be true?" she trilled across the intervening space. "Have you indeed dashed the hopes of every unattached lady in London, you wicked creature?"

"Indeed, Duchess, allow me to present my viscountess to you. Linnea, this is her grace, the Duchess of Weyland."

"Why, what a charming girl, Anthoneeee," chirped the duchess, cutting off Linnea's attempt to reply. "You must bring her to Weyland House, you naughty boy. You know how slighted I felt when you did not attend my last ball. Everyone else of consequence was there, you know!"

"Lady Carrock and I shall be delighted to attend the next, Duchess."

And so it went. Of the hundreds of barouches, phaetons, landaulets and curricles parading up and down the carriage road, it seemed that every other one contained a lady who, either by conversation, tone of voice or facial expression, betrayed her feminine appreciation for the handsome Lord Carrock. Some, like the duchess, conveyed that admiration

157

with flushed cheeks, sparkling eyes and flattery. Others gave themselves away with rapid speech and fluttering gestures. And with the most respectable and discreet, it was only a nuance, a mixture of top-lofty disapproval and reluctant fascination that Linnea picked up intuitively.

And resented.

Yes, after surmising that half the women in London were secretly in love with her husband, Linnea was suffering from an outrage more severe than anything she had ever experienced. By wedding Lord Carrock, she reflected sarcastically, it seemed she had inadvertently trespassed upon public property. True, the majority of the women greeted her with impeccable politeness, but there were definitely some inhospitable glances cast her way. Gritting her teeth, Linnea wondered exactly how many of them he had favored with more than just a smile.

She was profoundly thankful that they did not come across Lady Lindcastle, but as Anthony drove his curricle round near the Serpentine, she spied a familiar barouche. Her heart sank like a rock in a wishing well.

"Ah, here comes Auntie Gorgon," commented Anthony lazily. "And that lovely creature must be the infamous Evangeline, Gorgon-in-training."

Despite her crusty mood, Linnea choked back an involuntary laugh. "That, sir, is no way to speak about my relations. You ought to show more respect."

"If you dislike it, why are you giggling?"

"I am not giggling," she lied. "Giggling is ill bred."

He raised his eyebrows and cast her an amused glance. "You are trying to make me apologize, but I refuse. I know a giggle when I hear it." He bent his head, his beaver hat brushing the rim of her brand-new bonnet. "And a very engaging sound it is."

"Flirting will get you nowhere," she said with mock severity. "Pray attend to your horses before you drive us into the lake."

"Little vixen," he murmured.

By this time Aunt Gordon had seen them, and had commanded her groom to stop. "Good day, Linnea," she said, gazing down her arrogant nose at the newly wedded couple. "Lord Carrock, I believe you have not had the pleasure of my daughter's acquaintance. Pray allow me to present you to Miss Gordon."

Linnea watched her husband carefully as he and Evangeline exchanged greetings. Unlike most men, he did not gape moon-eyed at her cousin, who possessed curls as black as jet, flawless features, and violet eyes the size of pansies. In fact, as difficult as it was to credit, he seemed not at all impressed.

"Good day, Linnea," Evangeline added coldly. She cast Linnea's cerulean blue gown a disparaging look, opened her lovely mouth, then shut it again with a resounding snap.

This was when Anthony turned on his charm.

Later, Linnea would never quite recall exactly what he had said, but in less than three minutes he had both Aunt Gordon and Evangeline almost eating out of his hand. Subtle flattery, regret that Evangeline had been too "unwell" to attend the wedding, remarks concerning the multitude of beaux Evangeline was certain to acquire during her London Season—in retrospect it all merged together.

But as she sat brushing her hair before dinner, Linnea considered his motives. Had he only been trying to smooth over an awkward moment, as he had claimed? Or had he needed to win them over for some less admirable reason?

Frowning slightly, she turned to survey the two portraits above the fireplace. From the dreamy expression in Roger's eyes, it was easy to see that he had been of a nonviolent, sensitive, meditative nature. By comparison, the side of the coin she had married appeared almost devilish.

Linnea set down her brush with a sigh, feeling a trifle wistful.

The following morning she arose from her bed to be greeted by the news that Lord Carrock had gone out. *Out, out, he was always out,* she thought crossly.

Determined to conceal her chagrin from the servants, she did not inquire as to his whereabouts, but instead took a leisurely breakfast in her room while half-heartedly debating over which gown to wear. Choosing a jonquil-colored round dress of jaconet muslin, she completed her toilette, dismissed her maid, forced Anthony from her mind as best she could, and commenced work on her manuscript.

An hour later, a servant came to inform her that she had a caller. " 'Tis a gentleman, my lady. A Captain Theale."

Linnea put down her quill, reflecting that an interruption could not have come at a more welcome moment. Her hand was cramped from writing, and her neck ached from being bent over her work. Filled with pleasant anticipation. she descended to the drawing room to find Iris's would-be suitor pacing the floor.

"Lady Carrock," he said with a formal bow. "I hope you do not find it presumptuous of me to call."

Linnea smiled. "Not at all, Captain. I am very glad to see you again so soon."

"Under ordinary circumstances, I would not have presumed upon so short an acquaintance, but matters have come to such a pass . . ."

Seeing how distraught he was, she invited him to sit. "Have you finished your book yet?" she inquired, in an effort to set him at his ease.

"No, I have not," he replied. "I like to contend that since the author has taken the trouble to form such witty sentences, the least I can do is to savor every word." He grinned ruefully. "To translate, I read slowly."

"Yet such sentiments do you credit," Linnea said warmly. "Any author would be glad to know that you take pains to read so conscientiously. I am sure that *I* would be—" She broke off with a blush.

His gray eyes widened in amazement. "You, Lady Carrock? Do not tell me you are an authoress?"

His interest was so genuine that instead of the words of denial she meant to utter, Linnea found herself admitting, "An aspiring one, yes. But I beg you will mention it to no one."

"Certainly, if you do not wish it," he said seriously. "I am honored to be the recipient of your confidence. I am also extremely impressed."

Linnea thanked him a little self-consciously. "There is no saying that I will be able to find a publisher," she said quickly, "or at least one who is willing to pay the publishing costs. Possibly I might find one who would publish on commission, but that would mean I would have to assume those costs, which I fear would be rather steep."

"But they cannot be as great as that, can they? I mean, would not your husband—"

"Lord Carrock is unacquainted with my ambitions," she said quickly. Her cheeks burned as she added, "For . . . for personal reasons, I do not wish him to know." She could sense the captain's astonishment, though his delicacy forbade him to voice it aloud. "If my novel is published, I intend that it shall be done anonymously, just as Miss Austen did."

"But in her case, just as in Walter Scott's, the truth eventually got about," he pointed out.

"Very true. Yet it must still be my aim."

"I certainly hope you achieve it, ma'am. If there is anything I can do to assist you to your goal, I trust you will let me know." He cleared his throat and paused awkwardly. "Forgive me if I seem forward, ma'am, but in the light of your confidence, I wonder if I might make a confidence of my own."

"That depends on the nature of the confidence," Linnea responded, with a smile to take the sting from the warning.

Captain Theale settled his hands on his knees. "It concerns Miss Bronsden." He halted, clearly waiting for her encouragement.

"Please continue, sir."

"Thank you, ma'am. You apprehend, I believe, that I think very highly of your cousin."

"Yes, I received that impression yesterday."

"Pray believe that I am no fortune-hunter," he said earnestly. "I am as in love with Iris as any man could be without becoming an unintelligible Bedlamite. Yet thus far I have been unable to recommend myself to her by any means. My reason for coming here today was to solicit your opinion. Should I continue in my endeavors to woo her, do you think? If she has said aught to you in my favor, anything to make you think she does not view me with aversion, I hope you

162

will take pity and tell me." He smiled lopsidedly, his hands spread in appeal. "I am at your mercy, Lady Carrock."

Linnea studied him, her sympathies thoroughly aroused. "Oh dear, I do not know what to say."

"Then it is as I feared," he said despondently. "Her affections are otherwise engaged."

"Now, Captain, I did not say that." Linnea cudgeled her mind for some way to voice her support without betraying Iris's secret. "I do not think there is any one gentleman whom she favors," she said cautiously. "Nor do I think she dislikes you, although she may have given that impression."

"Then your advice is . . . ?"

"My advice, sir, is to persevere. I know not to what outcome your courtship may lead, but if your feelings for Iris are as strong as you claim, I should hate to see you give up so easily. Rest assured that I shall do what I can on your behalf." She paused, choosing her words with care. "Iris sometimes takes odd notions into her head. It is quite possible that in some way you have given her an erroneous opinion of your character." *Under the circumstances, it was as close a hint as she could give the poor man.*

Her visitor surged to his feet, his countenance lit with gratitude. "Ma'am," he said, as if deeply moved, "you have been very kind. If you are ever in need of any service, be it ever so trifling, please do not hesitate to call upon me."

And then, before she realized what he was about, he seized her hand and pressed it to his lips.

Anthony stood on the bank of the Serpentine, absently stroking the glossy flank of his dark bay thoroughbred. Whenever he woke early, it was his custom to exercise his mount in the park, though his well-trained groom knew to perform that service if his master did not appear in the mews by eight o'clock. A cool breeze ruffled Anthony's hair as he stared upwards at the trees. How long had it been since he'd viewed the sunrise without a damnable ache in his head?

Since his marriage, he had been deriving scant enjoyment from his late-night excursions, and so had been terminating them at an earlier hour. His mouth curved humorlessly as he considered the reason. Damn Vale and his bloody wager! Chastity did not suit him at all, particularly when his friends dragged him to disreputable places and threw him into the company of unvirtuous females who did everything in their power to entice him. If he were wise, he thought irritably, he would refuse to go; it was certainly what Roger would have advised.

His thoughts flew back to the respectable start of the previous evening, when he and Linnea had dined with his family in Grosvenor Square. All had gone well thanks to Roland's absence; his mother had been gracious, his grandfather congenial, and even his Aunt Allison had ventured a few remarks.

It pleased him how well Linnea fit in with his family. She had been dignified, well-bred and calm when conversing with his mother and aunt, while with his grandfather—Anthony grinned at the memory—she had been spirited, even a little pert. She had certainly made a conquest of the old man, he reflected with amusement. Then his grin died as he recalled how, upon their return to Albemarle Street, she had bidden him good night, gone to her room, and locked the door—as though she did not quite trust him not

164

to come in.

Which was why he had gone out.

Suddenly, he longed for the soul-soothing peace of Sundridge. God, how he wished he had taken Linnea there instead of wallowing in the absurdities of the London Season. On the other hand, after so quick a marriage, a hasty retreat could have been damning. For why would a rakehell like himself marry a respectable girl in so precipitous a fashion unless he had somehow compromised her? After all, no one but his family knew of his grandfather's threat to leave Sundridge to Roland—not even his mother. And very few knew of Mrs. Northcliff's eccentric demands, since Linnea's family had gone to some lengths to hush it up. Ironically, both families had erred, for the effect of so much discretion had been to exacerbate the scandal.

Anthony's mouth hardened. He hadn't expected to care about the whispers, but he did. It infuriated him that Linnea's good name should be questioned, but there was little that could be done except to keep putting on a bold face. And the truth was, no matter how the situation had been handled, there would still have been a few raised eyebrows. He had spent the last five years of his life ensuring that that would be so.

With a slight frown, he swung himself onto his horse, staring morosely at a family of tufted ducks skimming along the waters of the lake. High above, the rippling song of spotted redshanks mixed with the melancholy bark of a lone heron in flight. His eyes lifted to the slate gray bird, watching it glide to its nest with an odd jerk of his heart. *Oh, to be as free as that heron, relieved from the crushing burden he had carried for so long . . .*

Nudging his mount to a walk, Anthony thought of that long-ago night when he and Roger had been travelling down to Sundridge in the family coach. He hadn't been drunk, but he and Roger had been sharing a bottle of brandy, and Roger's share had been the smaller. Perhaps this accounted for the reason that neither of them had been alarmed when the shots rang out—after all, to be waylaid by highwaymen had seemed rather a lark at the time.

Anthony's lip curled with contempt at his own naiveté. What an ass he had been not to have realized the danger they were in. Trade restrictions had put the lower classes into intolerable economic hardship, and many had turned to desperate measures—though the gang that had held them up had in no way resembled misguided citizenry seeking to better their life. On the contrary, they had been a band of illiterate, brutal men who viewed all members of the privileged class as fair game for their cruelty.

Stand and deliver. He was still ashamed of how those words had fired his blood. To his more youthful heart, they had portended an adventure, a frolic, an escapade to remember.

Well, he remembered it—that desire had come true. For as long as he lived he would remember those moments when he had made the crazed decision to take on the masked figure pointing the horse pistol at his chest. Deep down, with the conviction of his own immortality that every human cherishes, he hadn't really believed the man would fire. And when the deafening roar had sounded, he'd actually believed, for a fraction of a heartbeat, that he had truly cheated death—until the truth had rammed its ugly fist into his face. *For it had been Roger on the ground, Roger with the splash of brilliant crimson on his shirtfront* . . .

He shut his eyes, blocking out the verdant green surroundings far better than the memories. How many times had he gone over this? How many times had he relived the agony—his own, his mother's, his grandfather's?

Yet as always, out of the need to retain his sanity, he pushed it aside, burying the knowledge of his guilt in a secret corner of his soul. Instead he thought of Linnea, lovely Linnea, and an odd urgency filled him. He wanted to see her. He needed to connect with her in some way, even if it were not in the physical manner he so desired.

As he headed back to the mews, his determination burned anew—determination to please her, to woo her, to conquer her in some elusive, elemental way.

But as he strode up the stairs to the first floor drawing room, an ardent declaration drifted to his ears: "—if you are ever in need of any service, be it ever so trifling, please do not hesitate to call upon me." He reached the doorway at exactly the instant that an unknown gentleman pressed his lips to his wife's hand.

"What have we here?" he said calmly.

Outwardly dispassionate, he watched Linnea jerk back her hand. "My lord!" Quite clearly, he saw the consternation in her eyes.

He walked forward and smiled, though it felt more like a baring of teeth. "I'm sorry, my dear, I didn't mean to startle you."

"My lord," she repeated, her voice breathless, "I . . . I do not think you have met Captain Theale. Captain, this is my husband, Lord Carrock." She pressed a hand to her breast, as if measuring the tempo of her pounding heart.

After the tiniest hesitation, Anthony extended his hand. "Captain," he said with a nod. "You're an army man?"

They shook hands, the captain answering, "Aye, I was with the 23rd Light Dragoons, but I sold out in '17."

For a few minutes the two men discussed the recent war with France, then the captain bowed and took his leave.

Anthony turned to Linnea, who gazed back at him with widened eyes. "It wasn't what you think," she said. "Captain Theale was merely paying me a social call."

His brows raised. "Did I suggest otherwise? What a suspicious husband you must think me. Come, let us sit. There is no occasion for us to be standing about in this stupid way."

He noticed she carefully chose a chair, rather than the settee he had indicated. Was she afraid to sit beside him? Vexed by the possibility, he examined her face. He cleared his throat, searching for some way to voice his displeasure without appearing to be a member of that absurd and much despised species, the jealous husband.

However, before he could do so, she turned the tables on him by saying, "I have been wondering where you were, my lord. I should very much like to know what you do with your time."

Taken aback and rather amused, he said, "I was out riding. You must honor me with your company some morning."

"I'd like that," she answered, and looked down at her hands. "I do have a riding habit, you know."

Abruptly, Anthony decided to drop the subject of Captain Theale.

"I shall buy you a mount then," he said. "I ought to have done so before—I wish you had reminded me." He looked at her, noting the fine texture of her skin and the delicate curve of her cheek. "Unless you already possess one I do not know about?"

She shook her head. "My father could not afford to keep riding horses in town. At least not for my mother or me."

"I shall see to it then." Aware that he had not yet answered her question about his doings, he added, "It has certainly not been my intention to abandon you. Is there somewhere you wish to go here in town? If so, I will be happy to escort you." Until this moment he had not realized how greatly he desired his wife's companionship.

"To own the truth," she said slowly, "there *are* places I wish to visit, though I fear they would bore you. In all my sojourns in London, I was never able to go to the British Museum or the Royal Academy of Arts. In particular," she added with growing enthusiasm, "I should like to see the Royal Library. They have hundreds of thousands of volumes, you know."

She sounded so much like Roger that Anthony stared. Then he threw back his head and laughed. "Lord save me, I have married a bluestocking," he uttered in mock dismay. "Most ladies ask to see the crown jewels, but mine wishes to look at books. Oh, the irony of it."

Linnea shot to her feet. "I am not *most ladies,*" she informed him in an offended tone. "I realize that your knowledge of my sex is extensive, but *some* of us are able to think beyond fashion and frivolity!"

Surprised, he regarded her heaving bosom with masculine admiration, wishing with all his heart that he could see it unveiled. "My dear, I was only teasing you. I will take you to any museum you please if you'll forgive me and sit down. Or shall we depart this instant?"

Linnea retook her seat, but her face retained its closed expression. "Actually," she replied, in a challenging tone, "I was intending to pay a call on my Grandmother Northcliff this afternoon. You may accompany me there, if you dare."

He regarded her quizzically. "By all means," he said. "Let us go and visit Grandmama. I only pray she won't eat us."

Chapter Ten

Mrs. Northcliff's health had failed considerably since the wedding. The comforting warmth of Anthony's hand was all that prevented Linnea from displaying her shock as she took in the sight of her dragonlike relative draped listlessly on a couch like a worn-out rag.

Miss Blainsworth, her grandmother's longtime friend and companion, hastened toward them. "Oh, Lady Carrock," she whispered, "and Lord Carrock. Bless you for coming. This is just the thing for dear Margaret, though I fear you cannot stay very long. She tires so easily."

"Quit that whispering, Blainsworth, and bring 'em over here. It's about time someone came to see me."

Linnea proceeded across the carpet and kissed her grandmother's cheek. "Good afternoon, Grandmama," she said softly.

"I see that scamp of a husband has you rigged out like a duchess — as well he should. I always told your mother she had you dressed wrong." Her eyes transferred to Anthony. "Well, young man? I trust you're behaving yourself now that you're married."

Anthony bowed. "I always behave myself," he

told her amiably. "Linnea will tell you I'm a reformed character."

"Hummf." The old lady struggled to sit upright,
overriding her companion's protests. "Oh, for
pity's sake, Blainsworth, let be. Why don't you go
and brew a tisane or something? Go on, shoo,
I've no need for you while my granddaughter is
with me."

Miss Blainsworth glanced apologetically at Linnea, and left the room.

"Sit down," ordered the old woman. "It hurts
my neck to look up."

"You ought to be nicer to Miss Blainsworth,
Grandmama," Linnea scolded gently. "Think how
dedicated she is to you."

"I am nice to her. I'm just having a devil of a
day, that's all. Dying isn't any fun, girl."

"Oh, Grandmama . . ." Linnea gazed helplessly
at the gray, pinched face, noting the sunken hol-
lows in the sagging, paper-thin flesh. "Please don't
say such things. You aren't dying."

"Of course I am, child, but don't fret about it.
I've had a good life. The tragedy is when the children die, not when old women like me kick the
bucket. So save your sympathy for those who need
it."

"Yes, of course, but . . . I never really thought
. . ." Linnea blinked rapidly as moisture seeped
into her eyes.

"Come, girl, that's enough. I refuse to listen to
any missish fiddle-faddle." With a slight grimace,
Mrs. Northcliff pointed a shaky finger. "Tell me
how you and this scapegrace are rubbing along
over there in Albemarle Street."

"Oh, er, everything is very well. Is it not, Anthony?"

"Indeed," he agreed. "We could not be happier."

"You'd better treat her well," threatened the old lady. "If you ever raise a hand to her, young man, I'll come back to haunt you."

"My dear ma'am," he answered mildly, "if I ever raise a hand to Linnea, you may come back and cut it off."

"Very well, I'll hold you to that. And you, Linnea. Are you being a dutiful wife?"

Conscious of her husband's ironic regard, Linnea's cheeks flamed. "D-Dutiful, Grandmama? Why, I . . . I trust so."

"A man needs a wife who'll see to his needs. You bear that in mind." The old lady gazed off into space, her attention drawn by some distant, pleasing memory. "My Richard was a real one for the petticoats in the beginning, but I took care of that." She heaved a wheezy, reminiscent sigh.

Linnea searched her mind for memories of her Grandfather Northcliff, but he had died when she was eight. "You were happy with my grandfather?"

"Lord, yes. We fought like lions at times, but it was splendid. Our courtship—what a time that was! He wouldn't take no for an answer." Her mouth flexed at the memory. "Once, he even challenged a man to a duel in my honor. I was terrified he'd be killed, but in the end we had thirty years together. And that blessed man never blamed me once for not giving him a son." There was a long pause, then, as though recollecting their presence, she cleared her throat and looked at Anthony. "Your grandfather once made me an offer, Carrock. Did he tell you?"

"No, ma'am, he did not."

"Well, 'tis true." As though she had suddenly run out of energy, the old lady's eyes slid shut. "Good thing . . . I turned him down . . . for we wouldn't have suited. . . ." Her mumble faded to silence.

"Grandmama?" Alarmed, Linnea leaped to her feet, but Anthony reached the couch first.

"She's only sleeping," he said quietly. He draped an arm around Linnea's shoulders. "Come, love."

Outside the room they found Miss Blainsworth, who had been waiting nearby rather than brewing tisanes.

"What does the doctor say?" Linnea asked.

Miss Blainsworth shook her head and sighed. "If we paid heed to him, my lady, she'd have been gone from us a month past. A fighter, that's what your grandmother is. Doctor Willis prescribed laudanum, but she refuses to take it except at night." She gave a slight, exasperated smile. "And she insists upon having her brandy, regardless of what he says."

"I suppose it cannot hurt," Linnea said with a sigh.

"No," agreed Miss Blainsworth, rather sadly. "It makes her happy, poor soul."

Linnea reentered the carriage with a heavy heart. Until today, she had not realized how fond she was of her grandmother. Here was a woman who had embraced life, who had married the man of her choice, lived and fought with him, given him three daughters and derived a deep, trium-

174

phant satisfaction from it all. By contrast, Linnea's own lot seemed lacking in dimension, void of the love which should have given it fullness.

Pain stung in her throat as self-pity and sorrow merged into one. At least her grandmother had been courted and chosen by a man who cherished her. At least her grandmother had loved and been loved—unlike Linnea, who had married in haste for all the wrong reasons, and had the rest of her life to regret it.

Illogically, her despondency grew when Anthony reached for her hand. "Don't look so sad, sweetheart. She's lived longer than most people. As she said, she's had her life."

Linnea turned her head away. In her present mood, it seemed a light dismissal of her grandmother's suffering. Even the endearment grated since she knew it meant nothing.

"You cannot understand," she mumbled. "She is not your grandmother."

"I see." He released her hand, which, bereft of warmth, went suddenly cold within its glove.

"I really doubt that you do." A lump in her throat, she stared resolutely at a speck of mud on the window glass.

"Then would you care to explain? I am capable of listening, you know."

She shook her head and closed her eyes, fighting to keep the tears at bay.

"I wish you would not play games with me," he said after a short silence. "I am losing patience, and that's something that seldom happens."

And what happens when it does? Will you keep your vow to Grandmama?

She opened her eyes and drew a breath. "Heaven forbid that should happen. I do apologize."

"Linnea . . ." He threw back his head and groaned, his head arched back against the cushions. "God deliver me from females! What in Satan's name have I done to deserve this?"

Torn with conflicting emotions, she pressed her lips together until she knew she had herself in hand. "Despite what we told Grandmama, our marriage is not a happy one. I know that sounds as though . . . I expect too much from you, but I assure you I do not. I am well aware that I have only myself to blame if you have . . . other interests."

His eyes stayed fixed on the ceiling. "Are you saying that you are ready to become my wife in truth?"

"No, that's not what I'm saying! Oh, I knew you would be unable to understand."

Frustration pounded inside her. Why had she even tried? Given the fact that she continued to disallow him into her bed, she would sound a fool to complain of his absences or her discomfiture at the way every woman in London ogled him. How ridiculous she would appear if she told him of her burgeoning desire to have him look at her the way Captain Theale looked at Iris, that she wanted him to yearn for her company and to stop leaving her alone all the time. Particularly since she had assured him of quite the opposite only a short time ago.

"Can Captain Theale understand?"

His abrupt question caught her off-guard.

4 FREE BOOKS

TO GET YOUR 4 FREE BOOKS WORTH $18.00 — MAIL IN THE FREE BOOK CERTIFICATE TODAY

Fill in the Free Book Certificate below, and we'll send your FREE BOOKS to you as soon as we receive it.

If the certificate is missing below, write to: Zebra Home Subscription Service, Inc., P.O. Box 5214, 120 Brighton Road, Clifton, New Jersey 07015-5214.

FREE BOOK CERTIFICATE
4 FREE BOOKS
ZEBRA HOME SUBSCRIPTION SERVICE, INC.

YES! Please start my subscription to Zebra Historical Romances and send me my first 4 books absolutely FREE. I understand that each month I may preview four new Zebra Historical Romances free for 10 days. If I'm not satisfied with them, I may return the four books within 10 days and owe nothing. Otherwise, I will pay the low preferred subscriber's price of just $3.75 each; a total of $15.00, *a savings off the publisher's price of $3.00*. I may return any shipment and I may cancel this subscription at any time. There is no obligation to buy any shipment and there are no shipping, handling or other hidden charges. Regardless of what I decide, the four free books are mine to keep.

NAME

ADDRESS _____ APT

CITY _____ STATE _____ ZIP

TELEPHONE ( )

SIGNATURE _____

(if under 18, parent or guardian must sign)

Terms, offer and prices subject to change without notice. Subscription subject to acceptance by Zebra Books. Zebra Books reserves the right to reject any order or cancel any subscription.

GET
FOUR
FREE
BOOKS

(AN $18.00 VALUE)

ZEBRA HOME SUBSCRIPTION
SERVICE, INC.
P.O. Box 5214
120 BRIGHTON ROAD
CLIFTON, NEW JERSEY 07015-5214

"Captain Theale? What has he to do with this?"

"Quite a lot, I should think. Unless you are in the habit of entertaining single gentlemen when I am from home? And," he added curtly, "of allowing them to slobber all over your hand."

"Captain Theale was not slobbering!" she protested, shocked by the description. "And how dare you make such sordid assumptions when you are out there making up to every pretty face you meet!"

Immediately she sensed his anger, though his expression remained bland. "Oh, not *every* one," he remarked. "That would be beyond even my capabilities." Placing a casual hand on her thigh, he leaned closer, his thumb stroking back and forth so that, beneath her gown and petticoat, her flesh tingled with virginal outrage. "Let me tell you something, Linnea. I know how to make a woman feel like a woman. What a pity you won't let me make you feel that way. I could give you pleasure you've never dreamed of . . . if you'd only let me. Surely a rake's wife ought at least to enjoy the benefits of his talent. After all," he added softly, "you know what they say about practice."

Linnea flushed hot with the realization that on some elemental level she wanted what he offered. "I don't need you to make me feel like a woman," she snapped. "Nor do I relish sharing you with half the females in London."

"No more than I relish sharing you with even one other man," he shot back. "Pray remember what I told you before we wed. Any children you bear—"

"—will be yours!" she finished furiously. "You

177

may rest easy on that score, my lord. *I* do not spread my favors around like . . . like . . ."—her breasts rose and fell as she searched for a fitting simile—"like dandelion seeds in the wind!" Teeth clamped together, she shoved his hand away just as the carriage slowed to a halt.

"Goodness, are we home already?" drawled her lord and master. "How time does fly when one is having fun."

Still seething, Linnea retired to her room and remained there for the rest of the afternoon. She was deeply humiliated by the knowledge that she had longed to succumb to her husband, and even more mortified by the suspicion that she might in some way have let him know it. To feel such desire under such circumstances was wrong, she told herself. Even if he wooed her with courtesy and tenderness, by any rights it ought to have been weeks before she felt such urges. Yet here she was, yearning for his touch, ready to toss her scruples to the four winds for the sake of a few minutes' pleasure.

She buried her head in her hands with a groan. She was beginning to think she should simply have accepted him from the start, before this had turned into such a contest of wills. Putting him off had somehow complicated the matter, perhaps blown it out of all logical proportion. Perhaps she had been making the proverbial mountain out of a molehill, she thought dolefully. And she had really made things difficult, for how could she yield to him now without her pride suffering?

Staring down at her manuscript, Linnea came to the gloomy conclusion that her heroine had far more sense than she did. Of course, Miranda had the advantage of being pursued by a man of high principles, she thought with a sigh. So why was it that poor, honorable Sir Gabriel Rhodes suddenly seemed lacking in some crucial area?

Glancing down at her brooch-watch, she decided to stop working since it was nearly dinnertime. She supposed she would be dining alone, she thought dismally.

Much to her surprise, however, she found Anthony reading a newspaper in the drawing room. She paused on the threshold, uncertain of her welcome. "My lord?" she ventured. "You are dining in?"

Immediately, he set aside his paper and stood, returning her gaze rather watchfully. "Yes, I thought I would. Do you mind?"

"No," she said quickly. "I mean . . . of course not. Not at all. It is your house, after all."

He approached her with a slight smile. "To be technical, I only lease it. I don't own any property outright." He reached past her and shut the door. "It's taken me several hours to admit it to myself, but I owe you an apology. I beg your pardon for the distress I caused you earlier. I behaved badly and I'm sorry."

Astonished, Linnea stammered, "Oh . . . no, no, it is I who must beg pardon. I was unforgivably rude and . . . and. . . ."

"Not *unforgivably*," he corrected.

"But I made you angry."

"Only a little. I seldom become truly angry." He

179

paced back and forth for a moment, then sighed. "Let's have our dinner. We can talk afterward."

The presence of the servants made intimate conversation impossible until after the meal, when Anthony led the way back to the drawing room. As he walked to the sideboard, her gaze was drawn to his hands as he lifted the decanter of sherry—strong, graceful hands as exquisitely formed as the rest of him. A shiver ran through her as she pictured those long, tapered fingers caressing her flesh.

"This time," he told her, "we'll drink to a better understanding of each other." Smiling in a way that made her limbs go watery, he handed her a glass. "I shall make a great effort to please you, if you will only tell me how. Yes?"

"I will try," she whispered.

"Now then," he said, after they both drank, "let us try this again. You are unhappy, and I am somehow responsible."

Linnea set down her glass. "I do not want to seem ungrateful," she began carefully. "I know you have been making an effort on my behalf." She plucked at her skirt, struggling for words to explain without betraying too much. "But what you must realize is that marriage to you has changed a great deal for me. For instance, all the invitations . . . I have yet to come to any decision regarding most of them. I've accepted two or three but" —she spread her hands helplessly— "there are so many it makes my head spin. If you would only look at them with me, it would make things easier. I want guidance from you, my lord. Guidance and support."

"And nothing else?"

"And . . . and . . . I would appreciate it very much if you could . . ." She stopped, flustered. Why was this so horribly difficult?

"Could what, Linnea?"

"You are absent so often," she finished painfully. "I have been lonely."

"But when I am here," he pointed out, "you are often locked in your room. What do you do in there all the time?"

Linnea hesitated, overwhelmed with an urge to confess her secret. But what would he say? Would he hoot and call her a bluestocking again? Or would he grimace and suggest that she find something more worthwhile to do with her time? She yearned to find out, yet at the same time she dreaded it. In the end, her inhibition proved too strong to surmount.

"Oh, I . . . I write letters," she said vaguely. "And I read. I have never been a social butterfly."

Anthony sighed. "No, obviously not. So what you are saying is that you wish me to be at your beck and call whenever you choose to emerge from your room, whenever that may be."

"No," she responded, a little sharply. "You must know that's not it. Why do you choose to misunderstand? What I am saying is that . . . it seems odd to me that you are never here. If you are not here, then where are you? What do you *do?* Or perhaps I've no right to ask, since ours is a marriage of convenience. Perhaps you feel it's none of my affair."

He leaned back and raked a hand through his hair. "Gad, you're a defensive little thing," he said mildly. "To be frank, when I entered into this marriage, I planned to continue as far as possible the style of life I lived as a bachelor. I won't deceive you on that score. However, that strategy no longer seems feasible."

"I know I promised not to interfere with you," she said unhappily, "and I did mean that, truly. But—"

"Sometimes," he interrupted, "I am with friends. Male friends," he added, "but more often than not we end up with females about us, though not respectable ones of course. Sometimes I go to Jackson's or Cribb's parlor. Sometimes I go riding. Sometimes I go to gaming houses, but I don't gamble much because unlike the majority of my friends, I don't care to be in debt."

"Oh," she said faintly.

"I drink," he went on, "but more out of boredom than thirst. Sometimes the world looks rosier when one is foxed . . . and sometimes it doesn't. Sometimes we travel out of town to attend a race or a prize fight, sometimes we go to the Vauxhall Garden masquerades." His lips twisted. "Day or night, the set of fellows I call my friends always have some spree or frolic planned, and since I've nothing better to do, I usually go along." He paused. "So tell me, does any of what I've said comfort you? I told you I was a frivolous, dissolute fellow."

"Well," said Linnea, determined to say something positive, "at least you are not a dandy."

Anthony looked at her for a moment, then threw back his head and laughed until she feared he would choke. "I wonder," he gasped, wiping his

182

eyes with his fingers, "if you might not be my salvation, after all. You know what they say about the love of a good woman—and you *are* a good woman, and a very nice one to boot. I'm devilish glad it was you I married, and not someone else."

"I'm glad too," she whispered.

She could see that threw him. All traces of laughter died from his face as he turned to look at her. "Are you?" he asked, scanning her intently. "Why should you be glad? I've caused you nothing but misery, it seems."

"On the contrary, you have been very kind to me. I only wonder if—"

"If what?" he prompted.

"If you might not be happier with a different set of friends." She looked down at her lap. "I realize you may not enter into my feelings on this matter, but it seems to me that they are a bad influence on you. Perhaps someone like Lord Vale, or that nice Mr. Perth . . ."

"So you would reform me completely?" He smiled, seemingly unfazed by her suggestion. "Roger would have liked you," he added reflectively. "He was always trying to reform me. You and he have a great deal in common."

"Tell me about Roger," she ventured.

Immediately, his face drained of expression, as though emotion of any kind was simply too painful. After a brief hesitation, he said, "My brother was my opposite, in almost every way. He didn't care much for females. He preferred solitude and academics." Anthony cleared his throat and looked away, toward the wall. "He wanted to write a book—a scholarly treatise upon the advantages of reform. I had no patience with such stuff, but . . . I loved him anyway."

"Of course you did," she said gently. "I loved my brother too."

"Ah, yes, Harry." He turned and looked at her. "Tell me about him."

Immediately, memories of her gallant little brother swept over Linnea. Even after all this time, it was difficult to speak of him without a tremendous tide of sadness catching her in its hold. "He was ill for most of his childhood. His lungs were weak. He had . . . these dreadful attacks where he"—she drew a deep breath and closed her eyes—"where he could not breathe properly. But he was always so good, so s-sweet. He . . . n-never complained . . ."

Anthony's arms came round her as her voice broke. "Shhh, love, forgive me. I didn't mean to make you cry."

Burrowing her face in his cravat, Linnea clung to him as she had refused to do earlier. "He was only twelve when he died. He was t-too young . . ."

"Don't think of it. Shut it from your mind." From somewhere, he produced a handkerchief. "Here, let me dry your cheeks. Come, sweetheart, you're ruining my neckcloth."

At once her head jerked up, but his smile was so tender that her heart turned over.

"Don't look so stricken, love. I was only teasing." He wiped her tears away, his blue eyes glinting in the candlelight. "One of us is always mopping up the other," he added lightly.

Linnea straightened, intending to pull away, but

his arm remained snug around her waist.

"Stay," he murmured. "Doesn't it feel good, to sit like this? We're human, Linnea, and humans need physical contact with one other." He brushed his lips over her hair. "You feel so soft. I like holding you against me. It makes me feel . . . happy."

Slowly, very slowly, Linnea relaxed in his embrace. "I like it too," she admitted, after a few seconds.

His hand paused in its light feathering of her arm, then moved to touch the side of her face. "Look at me."

Her head turned obediently.

"Beautiful Linnea," he whispered. "My wife, my redeemer."

She sighed as he entwined his fingers with hers and carried her hand up to press an open-mouthed kiss on her palm. Weakness pervaded her, spreading through her like potent wine as he took the pad of her thumb in his mouth. Through half-shut eyes, she watched him flick it with his tongue, her chest threatening to burst with the emotion it contained.

This is insane, she thought hazily. *He will think you're encouraging him . . .*

But resistance was impossible; she could not even think, much less protest. All reality melted away, leaving nothing but unbearable excitement in its wake. Somewhere in the distance she heard her own wobbly moan as he at last claimed her lips, passionately, his tongue driving deep into her mouth while his expert hands roved where they willed.

"My lovely, soft Linnea," he muttered, "so soft except right here"—he stroked the tip of her breast through the fabric of her gown—"where you're beautifully hard." Abandoning her lips, he bent to search out the nipple of her left breast, nipping it gently in a shocking, intimate action which made her gasp and arch as he suckled her through the muslin.

"Anthony . . ." She gasped his name and reached out blindly, not knowing what to do except that she must touch him. Her hand slid over the silken texture of his waistcoat, curling over its edges to rest just over his heart, which thudded madly under her fingertips. His warmth, his heat, enveloped her in a fog of yearning for a completeness she dared not envision.

Seconds later his weight shifted, and for a wordless moment she feared he was leaving her. Then his hands banded to her body as, with a strength that took her by surprise, he lifted her forward onto his length as he lay back on the sofa. "Kiss me," he said fiercely. "Kiss me as though you mean it. If it helps, pretend that you love me."

But I do, I do, she wanted to cry, not even knowing whether it was true. Acutely conscious of his arousal pressing into her belly, she gazed down at the minute stubble on his chin, aching to kiss it, and the mouth above it. *Do it,* tolled a voice in her head. *Forget your pride.*

Shyly, tentatively, she brought her mouth down to give him the kiss he demanded.

"Try again, little wife. I barely felt that."

Feeling adventurous, she obeyed, this time with parted lips.

"Better," he whispered. "Much better."

From then on, it grew both easier and sweeter. She might not be ready for lovemaking, but this kissing business was harmless enough. It was also pure heaven. It was like drifting on a cloud with the sun caressing your face. It was like—

Suddenly, she felt her gown start to slither up her legs. "What are you doing?" she asked in alarm.

"Unwrapping you."

As the cool air hit, she had a mortifying vision of how they would look to anyone who walked in. "Surely you do not wish to . . . to . . . I mean, you cannot possibly think to"—she flushed scarlet—"not *here!*"

"Why not?" He kissed the corner of her mouth.

"But . . . but we are in the drawing room! The servants—!" Panic rocketed through her as her gown reached midthigh.

"I'm sure they won't bother us." Obviously unconcerned, he slipped his hands beneath the muslin and fondled her hips. "I might have known you would wear drawers," he grumbled. "Damned unnecessary pieces of apparel."

Aghast, she squirmed away, shoving sideways with such force that she tumbled to the floor. "I might have known you would try this," she said accusingly. Panting a little, she yanked her gown back down to its proper position and glared at him.

He sat up, resting his elbows on his knees as he gazed at her with obvious bafflement. "Damn it, Linnea, what are you playing at? We both know what happened. Don't try to twist it into something else. If it's the location that troubles you, then fine. We'll go upstairs."

"No!" She scrambled to her feet, desperately quelling the part of her that longed to consent. "I cannot believe you would do this! I let you comfort me and you betray my trust by . . . by trying to seduce me!"

"On the contrary, I should call it a case of *you* seducing *me*."

"I was not!" Quivering with indignation, she crossed her arms under her breasts and tried to recall exactly what she had done. "I was merely letting you kiss me, that's all."

"That's *all?* My God, I can see I have to educate you." He rose in a fluid motion, his expression intensely sardonic. "When you kiss like that, Linnea, it's a great deal more than *letting*. In fact, it's a clear indication of encouragement. At least it is to a man." She retreated a step as he walked closer. "Last chance, my dear. I'm your husband and I want you. I want you tonight, right this minute. Not next week or next month or ten bloody years from now."

Linnea's resolve wavered. She swallowed hard as she remembered the unfamiliar, heady sensations that had been rippling through her body only moments before. She recalled what Amanda had said about lovemaking. She strove to gather her thoughts, to assimilate her choices, to assess the consequences that might result.

He wanted her, he said. Yet, unreasonable as it was, she wanted him to do more than desire her. She wanted him to love her. And she wanted his desire to derive from that love, as a seed springs from the nourishment of the soil. All at once that became dreadfully important, more important than anything else in her life.

"No," she whispered, as a tear trickled down her cheek. "Please, no. I'm sorry but . . . I cannot."

"Why?" His mouth clenched tight with displeasure.

"Because . . . oh, for a dozen reasons." And, turning, she fled the room, leaving her very frustrated husband alone.

Chapter Eleven

The following morning, Linnea descended to the breakfast room to find her husband already seated, drinking coffee. For the smallest instant, she froze, then forced herself to continue toward the table, wondering if her tightly knotted stomach could possibly accept food.

He rose and inclined his head, his handsome face aloof. "Good morning. Did you sleep well?"

"Fairly well, thank you." She waited while a footman pulled out her chair, then sat down, murmuring a quiet thank you.

There followed an awkward silence. Linnea accepted a cup of coffee from the footman, and sat looking at it unhappily.

Seconds ticked by.

Then Anthony, who had been spreading butter on his toast with the meticulousness of an artist, said casually, "I wrote a letter last night, formally applying for an appointment to visit the British Museum." His gaze shifted from his plate to her face. "That is how it is done, I have learned. It was necessary to name a preferred day and hour, so I chose tomorrow, at eleven o'clock. Is that acceptable to you?"

Rendered almost speechless with surprise, Linnea nervously fingered the handle of her cup. "Yes," she managed. "That would be fine."

"The application must be approved by the principal librarian. It is short notice, I grant, but I doubt we shall be denied." He smiled faintly, dusting crumbs from his fingers. "Even a courtesy title carries weight, I have found."

Their eyes met across the table. "I am very much obliged to you. It is kind of you to take the trouble."

"Not at all," he said languidly. "I have always meant to go there, and this affords me an opportunity."

"Good," she said. "Then I needn't feel guilty about it."

Anthony waved the footman from the room, then steepled his fingers, regarding her steadily over their tips. "You needn't feel guilty for anything," he replied. "As long as you never lie to me or deceive me."

She lowered her lashes. "I have already assured you that I would never do such a thing." Yet as she spoke, she thought of her manuscript, and her attempt to publish it without his knowledge. Would that, she wondered uneasily, rate as a deception?

"Then I shall say no more on the subject. After you eat, I will go over those invitations with you."

Again, she was surprised, though this time she managed to conceal it. Why should he be so agreeable after what had transpired between them?

"As you wish, my lord," she said with politeness.

"Last night," he said quietly, "you called me Anthony."

"Did I?" She blushed.

"I would ask that you continue. It seems," he added, "such a small request."

"As you wish . . . Anthony." She moistened her lips and studied her spoon as though it were the most fascinating object.

"You see, that was not so difficult, was it?"

What was going to prove far more difficult, she reflected as she finished her breakfast, was behaving as though last night's episode had not occurred.

A short while later, she brought the vast stack of invitations into the library and deposited them onto his desk.

"Good lord," he uttered. "No wonder you were overwhelmed. We appear to have grown quite popular since our marriage."

"*You* were already popular," she retorted, thinking of all those simpering females in the park.

"Ah, but that sort of popularity doesn't count, my love. Look at this"—he held up an envelope— "I never received an invitation from Countess Lieven before. And here's one from Lady Sandercock. Odd. The woman lives in dread that I'll seduce one of her daughters. I wouldn't, of course," he added cheerfully, "but it pleases her to think so."

Ignoring the remark, Linnea searched through the pile. "Here is one we'll have to attend," she said, drawing it out. "It's for Evangeline's come-out ball."

"Put it over here." He tapped the desk. "We'll start a yes pile."

Maintaining a flow of lighthearted banter, he

sorted the invitations into stacks—discarding some, retaining others, chuckling over a few. Then he drew out a calendar. "We cannot go to a ball every night—you'll be exhausted. How many should you care to attend per week, do you think?"

"Not very many, to own the truth. I am not a social creature, my . . . Anthony." She flushed slightly. "If I had my way, I'd choose to attend only those functions where the number of guests was small, such as an intimate dinner party given by my closest friends."

He lifted his brows. "Then we shan't accept very many. I've no wish to force you to do what will make you unhappy. I suppose I assumed that as a female, you would revel in such stuff."

"I revel in peace and quiet," she informed him in a low voice. "I prefer the company of those with whom I am familiar and therefore comfortable."

"Like my brother." Surveying her curiously, he lounged back in his chair and linked his fingers behind his neck. "Roger hated going to balls. He hated dancing as well. Do you hate dancing?"

"No." She hesitated. "If I am acquainted with my partner, or if the gentleman sets me at my ease, then I quite enjoy it. As long as I know he asks me because he wishes to, and not because he feels obligated. Which was often the case," she added candidly, "during my past London Seasons."

"My poor darling." He dropped his hands and picked up a small paperweight. "Well, if it is any consolation, I intend to squire you about from now on—and I don't feel a whit obligated. After all, it is not at all *comme il faut* for husbands to dance attendance on their wives."

"You needn't do that," she protested, uncertain why he should say such a thing. Did he mean it? Or was it only a frivolous promise, easily made and easily forgotten?

He leaned forward, his blue gaze pinioning her as effectively as if he had backed her against a wall. "Don't you hear what I am saying to you? I *know* I needn't do it. I'll do it because I want to, because I want to be with you. I want *your* company, Linnea, not some random harlot's."

"Oh." She blinked in surprise.

"The real question is," he paused, scrutinizing her closely, "do you want mine?"

It took her several seconds to decide what to say. "Of course I want your company," she answered finally. A delicate flush crept up her neck as she added, "If you want to give it. I'm not immune to your charm, Anthony. I find you attractive, just as all those other women do. I'm not willing to sacrifice my pride to gain your attention, but if you honestly wish for my companionship, I'll happily give it to you."

He rose and walked round the desk. "Give me your hand," he said, and when she did, he raised it to his lips. "From now on," he promised, "I'm going to be as devoted a husband as you could wish."

To prove his claim, he suggested they go riding together. He explained that while she had spent the previous afternoon in her room, he had gone out and purchased a mount for her—a Cleveland Bay mare with good clean lines and a tractable demeanor.

Fifteen minutes later, as Maria buttoned her into her brown velvet habit, Linnea found herself praying she would not disgrace herself. She was, she hoped, an adequate horsewoman, but she had never been the sort of girl who lived in the saddle. And though she liked horses and took pleasure in riding, she was by no means at home to a peg on a horse.

However, some of her fears were laid to rest when she discovered that the mare, Niobe, had already been exercised that morning.

"Well? What do you think?" Anthony asked as he lifted her into the saddle. He stepped back, gazing up at her with a rakish half smile.

It was Niobe he was inquiring about, but it was Anthony who drew her attention. Mesmerized, her gaze drifted over him, noting how well he looked in riding dress, how snugly his coat fit his broad shoulders, how the sunlight glinted his hair and brought out its chestnut highlights. For no reason at all, his sublime male beauty brought a lump to her throat.

"I think," she said unevenly, "that it was very kind of you to take such trouble—particularly when . . ." *When you must have been very miffed with me at the time* . . .

Anthony gave her a pat on the knee. "Let's not speak of that, *ma belle*. It's over and done with." Taking the reins from his groom, he swung himself onto his thoroughbred and nudged his animal forward.

Linnea followed, sitting her horse with rigid correctness, her mind focused on nothing beyond the need to hold her crop and reins at exactly the correct angle. When they reached the park, Anthony moved his horse abreast of hers.

"You've a nice seat," he said approvingly, "but there's no need to be so tense. Relax and enjoy yourself. Niobe won't throw you, I promise."

When they reached Rotten Row, Linnea followed his lead and urged Niobe into a canter. Ahead and all around, birds sang in the trees, a dozen different species all carolling their separate paeans to the skies. She breathed in the crisp air, savoring its fresh scent as she gradually caught the natural rhythm of the horse. Her heart soared. It felt good to ride with her husband on such a glorious day, to become one with the animal beneath her, to feel good about herself.

When they reached the Serpentine, Anthony turned to her and said, rather lazily, "Shall we dismount?"

Something in his tone caused a queer rush of pleasure to course through her. "If you wish," she replied.

"I wish," he said serenely. He slid from his mount, and lifted her from Niobe's back as easily as if she weighed nothing. As he slowly lowered her to the ground, something shifted inside her—a deep, primal thrill at his strength and masculinity.

For a long moment, they stood almost chest to chest. "You see what good ideas I have?" He gazed down at her with one of his odd smiles, then raised a hand to smooth a curl from her forehead. "One of these days, you'll begin to trust me," he added softly. "I look forward to that day." Before she realized what he was about, he bent to kiss her lips, lightly, a mere feather-touch of sensation that ended an instant later as he stepped away.

"I'll tether the horses, then we'll walk a little, hmmm?"

After the horses were seen to, she accepted his arm, allowing him to lead her a short way along the banks of the ornamental lake. Time passed, and in that time they seemed to reach a new plateau in their relationship. In a rambling monologue she did everything to encourage, Anthony told her more about himself — inconsequential things, like his fondness for treacle and the fact that he had named his racehorse Pollux because he had once had a pony named Castor. Spurred on by her curious questions, he told her more about his childhood, of his boyhood antics with Roger, of a stream they used to swim in and a tree they used to climb. He spoke with eloquence of Sundridge, describing it so clearly that she could see it in her mind — the long graveled drive flanked by oak trees, the Palladian splendor of the mansion. But his careful avoidance of the subject of his brother's death made it clear that it troubled him as deeply as her father's abuse had troubled her. And knowing how it felt to be hurt, Linnea longed to ease her husband's pain.

"Tell me more about the night your brother was killed," she said quietly.

The subsequent silence was broken only by the ceaseless chatter of birds and the distant sound of other people's horses cantering along the Row. "I thought I had told you enough," he answered. His voice lacked its previous animation.

"You told me little more than that you had been held up." She tightened her hold on his arm. "You

197

tried to make me believe you were responsible, but I cannot believe that."

"Why? Do you think me incapable of an error in judgment?"

"No." She hesitated. "But an error in judgment does not make you guilty, Anthony. You were not holding the pistol, were you?"

"No." He gave a deep sigh, not seeming to notice that she had used his Christian name. "No, I was not holding the pistol. But what I did was insane. I charged at the man who *was* holding it. There were only three of them, so I suppose I thought that a show of resistance would make them turn tail and run. I had it in my mind that they were cowards, that between my brother and myself and the coachman—who was a handy fellow with his fives—we ought to be able to capture them." His lips twisted. "Well, they *were* cowards, for the instant Roger fell, they were off like the devil was at their heels."

"Were they ever caught?"

"Yes, eventually they all were." He gazed out over the lake, giving her a view of his profile.

"You must not blame yourself," she told him.

"Then who am I to blame?" He spoke roughly, as though the words were dragged from him against his will. "Tell me the answer to that, Linnea. Am I to blame God for guiding that stray ball through my brother's heart? Do I blame the coachman for stopping the coach when he was threatened? Or do I blame Roger, for not having the sense to move when I had my fit of madness?"

They had come to a halt during this speech, and without thinking, Linnea laid a hand on his chest.

"You blame no one," she said, her head tilted back so she could look him in the eye. "You remember your brother as he was, and go on. What would he have said to all this? Do you think he would have wanted you to suffer these terrible self-recriminations?"

Anthony covered her hand, imprisoning it with his own. "No, he wouldn't. But that doesn't stop me from having them."

As Linnea bit her lip, searching for a suitable response, the sound of horses' hooves drew nearer than before. A moment later a quartet of riders entered the clearing, causing them to turn and move apart.

"Why, my gracious," purred a female voice. "Susannah, dear, only look who is here."

There were two gentlemen and two ladies—all of them very stylish and sophisticated in appearance. Linnea's stomach shivered as she recognized one of the women as Lady Lindcastle.

"What a surprise," gushed the blonde. Leaving her companions behind, she nudged her horse forward until she hovered over Anthony. At that moment she seemed everything that Linnea was not—full-bodied and poised, knowledgeable in the ways of the world. "Gracious, Anthony, can this be your new wife?" Her hard eyes skimmed over Linnea. "Will you introduce me?"

Anthony stood a little behind Linnea, his hand on her shoulder. "That, Susannah, is the question, is it not? I confess the answer escapes me at this moment."

Lady Lindcastle trilled a laugh. "Always the wit." She pointed her crop, a sly smile curving her lips. "Your husband and I are old friends, Lady Carrock. Do you dare to deny it, my lord?"

"That depends on how you define friendship. It's such an imprecise term."

"Alas, what a rogue! I vow you will have your work cut out for you, Lady Carrock, if you hope to keep pace with your husband's humors. Few ladies," she added with brittle emphasis, "have succeeded in doing so, I fear. In fact, I cannot think of a single one."

Linnea knew perfectly well that it was not Anthony's humors they were discussing. "Thank you for the warning," she replied, "but I do not anticipate any difficulty on that score."

"Ah, but you are a new bride," the other woman fairly oozed. "How I love new brides! They are always the most optimistic creatures." She put a hand to her breast, as though to show Linnea that even there she was superior. "Pray allow me to felicitate you both. She is a charming child, my lord. We are all *so* delighted"—she made the word sound offensive—"that you have found someone to . . . how shall I say it? Lend you an air of respectability?"

"Indeed, madam." Anthony's hand tightened on Linnea's shoulder. "I am a fortunate man."

Linnea dared not look to see his expression. After all, he might be sending signals with his eyes, telling his mistress to be careful not to betray too much to his unsuspecting little wife. Whatever the case, the blonde smiled back, a burning smile that revealed her sharp white teeth.

"Do call," she cooed, as she turned her mount around. "Lindcastle and I would be deeply honored." Kicking her horse, she rode over and rejoined her party, murmuring something that made them all laugh. A moment later they were off, thundering down the Row as though they owned it and the rest of the world.

Linnea moved away from Anthony. "I think we ought to head back," she said tightly. "It's nearly time for nuncheon and I must answer all those invitations this afternoon, as well as visit Grandmama again."

"Listen to me, Linnea. Lady Lindcastle and I are *not* friends, not in the way she was trying to make you think."

"Of course not. You are merely acquaintances. I understand perfectly." She walked to her horse, such an anger building within her that when he assisted her into the saddle, she could not prevent herself from lashing out, "Unfortunately for me, every woman we meet seems to feel she is your acquaintance, intimate or otherwise."

"Damn it, Linnea, that's not fair—"

"I know it," she cut in, nearly choking on her own words. "But just at the moment I do not feel like being fair. I may have married you, Anthony Stanton, but I can think of no reason on earth why I have to like your way of life!" She kicked Niobe's flank, sending the horse surging forward before Anthony had time to do more than open his mouth.

Anthony went out that evening. Still simmering from the injustice of Linnea's accusations, he took a hackney to Duke Street, near St. James's Square, and mounted the steps of a house occupied by a certain Sir Archibald Stanley.

A wild young blade in his late twenties, Sir Archibald had figured as one of Anthony's most prominent companions during the years since his brother's death. As it happened, Sir Archibald was at home when Anthony arrived, but his elegant mode of dress signaled his intent to seek diversion elsewhere.

"Well, if it isn't the happy bridegroom," drawled Sir Archibald when Anthony strode into his sitting room. "Where the deuce have you been hiding yourself?"

Anthony threw himself into a chair and accepted a glass of madeira. "I've been playing husband. And making a devilish mull of it too."

Sir Archibald snorted. "I'm not surprised. You're not cut from that sort of cloth—any more than I am. What surprises me is that you should waste the time. Such a strange fellow you are."

Unwilling to answer that, Anthony inquired into Sir Archibald's plans for the evening.

"Oh, I might take a look-in at Watier's or that new place in Pall Mall . . . you know the one?" Sir Archibald waved a languid hand.

"Mrs. Crabbe's?"

"That's it. I thought a little *rouge et noir* might relieve the tedium." Sir Archibald's deep sigh suggested this was a vain hope. "There's also a masquerade at Covent Garden," he added. "I believe Reggie and Gil intend to go. We could join them if you like."

Anthony looked up. "Yes, that might answer," he said abruptly. "Have you dined yet?"

In the end, they ate at Limmer's, where, between mouthfuls, Sir Archibald entertained Anthony with a witty (if rather ribald) account of his newest ladybird's charms. Anthony would normally have been amused, but on this occasion he found the narration in poor taste, particularly as Sir Archibald insisted on describing the indelicate details of their last encounter.

An hour and a half later, they departed for the opera house in Sir Archibald's coach. "Gil reserved a box for the evening," remarked Sir Archibald idly, "though I take leave to doubt he'll occupy it overlong. One pretty face, and he'll be off like a shot."

Anthony stared blindly out the window, his mind on one female face in particular. How dare Linnea behave as though he was sleeping with every woman in town! Aided by the quantity of wine he had imbibed, his self-righteous anger expanded to a full scale burn. The little vixen! Well, she could just go to the devil for all he cared. He had been constant to her since the day they had wed, but wager or no wager, he was done with that now.

"You're gloomier than a parson tonight," complained his companion. "What's wrong with you?"

"Nothing that cannot be mended," Anthony said grimly.

"Your wife, eh?" Sir Archibald gave him a knowing leer. "Poor Tony. Never mind, a nice bit o' muslin will restore your spirits. Nuptial shackles are only as heavy as you make them."

Anthony's gaze returned to the window, and his jaw hardened.

The Opera House was full of people of every order and state of inebriation, all of them, judging by the noise, having a jolly time of it. Sir Archibald had brought masks, and as Anthony tied his into place, he scanned the nearest females. Nothing to tempt him there, he thought critically.

They found Gil and Reggie without much difficulty, but from then on the evening went straight downhill. Under normal circumstances, Anthony could have found a dozen girls who would have taken his fancy, but tonight proved the exception. The first fair damsel to catch his eye irritated him with her coy giggles. The second was too thin, and the third too plump. The fourth, a dark-haired little beauty with luscious red lips, permitted him to escort her into the shadows and remove her mask, but for some unaccountable reason Anthony was disappointed by her compliance.

He kissed her anyway, telling himself not to be so hard to please, and she responded with all the enthusiasm a man could wish.

"Tell me your name," he urged as she slid her hands up to his shoulders and pressed herself wantonly against him.

"Blanche," she replied, smiling prettily. "And you, kind sir? What would you have me call you?"

"Tony," he murmured, backing her against the wall. She was truly a lovely creature—dainty and eager, ready to let him do whatever he wished. Why couldn't Linnea behave this way? For a long moment, he imagined he was home, and that it was Linnea in his arms . . . and on the heels of this fantasy came an arousal so intense he nearly groaned aloud.

He pushed hard against Blanche, wondering

whether she'd allow him to take his pleasure with her right here, quickly, so he need not be with her any longer than necessary. Even as the thought crossed his mind, he realized how selfish it was. He'd always taken his time with women, always been careful to bring them to fulfillment before he slaked his own lust.

"Where can we go?" he said softly. "I can't take you home with me."

"No matter," she whispered. "I can accommodate you. But we must come to an agreement first."

"Ah, of course. How much?"

Blanche stood on tiptoe and whispered into his ear, wriggling against his hardness with an expertise that told of experience.

And Anthony gently pushed her away.

It was not her price that gave him pause, nor was it that damnable wager he'd made with Vale. No, it was a plain, old-fashioned sense of what was right. Deep within him, in a corner of his heart he'd not known existed, he found he respected his marriage vows. But it was even more than that. Incredible as it seemed, he discovered that he desired no woman but his own wife. If he made love to the little highflier in his arms, it would be Linnea he saw beneath him, Linnea whose name he whispered.

And that revelation floored him.

"I'm sorry," he lied. "You're too expensive for me, sweetheart. I'm dodging the duns as it is."

Blanche stepped from his arms with a sigh. "I, too, am sorry," she said regretfully, "for I must leave you. You understand?"

"Of course."

When she was gone, he continued to stand in the shadows, feeling nonplussed and annoyed. What the devil was he to do now? Though the heat in his loins had been doused, his frustration had not. In fact, he felt like plunging his fist through the wall. Teeth gritted, he stalked back to the box, but since neither Gil nor Reggie were in sight, and Sir Archibald was fully occupied with a Cyprian of his own, Anthony decided to return to Albemarle Street.

It was past midnight when he arrived home. Billings greeted him without surprise, fussing over him like a mother hen while he pulled off Anthony's boots and hung up his clothes. When the valet held out his nightshirt, Anthony said dryly, "Thank you, I can manage. Take yourself off and get some sleep."

"Yes, milord." Billings bowed his way out.

Anthony donned his nightshirt and sat down, tapping the arm of the chair with his fingers. He didn't feel the least bit sleepy. A number of minutes passed before he picked up a candle and went to the door of Linnea's room.

All was quiet within.

He tried the knob and found it unlocked. Holding the candle aloft, he went in and walked over to the bed. Like that other time he had watched her sleep, a peculiar sensation gripped him as he gazed down at her. Strictly speaking, he knew she was not as beautiful as Blanche, but at that moment no other woman existed for him.

Her face was peaceful, her flame red hair spilled across the pillow like a blanket of fire. Yet although she appeared serene, the bedclothes were wildly twisted. Had she tossed and turned with the same restlessness that plagued him? If so, he hoped he was the cause of it. Whatever the case, only a portion of the sheet covered her, while her hiked-up nightdress exposed one shapely bare leg to his appreciative gaze. His heartbeat quickened when he saw how clearly the aureoles of her nipples showed through the semisheer fabric of her deceptively prim gown.

He swallowed hard, his imagination in full swing.

Suddenly, he was seized with a savage desire to rip off that nightdress and make love to her, to force her to his will if necessary. And for a mad, moonstruck instant he considered doing just that.

Then, firmly, he thrust the notion aside. The use of force against a woman had always been repugnant to him. He could never deal so with Linnea, no matter how long she denied him. Instead, he leaned over and pressed a gentle kiss to the rose-petal softness of her lips.

He must be patient. The time would come when she would give herself to him gladly, but until then he would have to wait.

Returning to his room, he snuffed out the candle and lay on his bed in the dark. He was very glad now that he had not broken his marriage vows. He had Vale to thank for that — Vale, and his own conscience.

He smiled wryly.

Roger would have been proud of him tonight.

Chapter Twelve

Rather to Linnea's surprise, the following day's excursion to the British Museum went very well. Upon their arrival in Great Russell Street, Linnea and Anthony were conducted through the various departments by an erudite little man with a nervous smile and an extensive knowledge of the museum's contents. And while the section of the museum which housed the Royal Library surpassed Linnea's expectations, such intriguing objects as the Rosetta Stone and Lord Elgin's Grecian marbles also gripped her interest.

As for Anthony, his shrewd questions to their guide took her quite by surprise. He might not spend his time with his nose buried in books, but he was not the frivolous ne'er-do-well he pretended. Everything seemed to interest him, from antique vases to law manuscripts, from David Garrick's original collection of plays to Captain James Cook's South Sea Islands souvenirs. She shook her head in amazement. Behind that rakish exterior lurked a man of considerable intellect, a man she would dearly love to see more of.

In the ensuing days, Anthony grew even more attentive. He took her riding and for drives in the park. He escorted her to the opera and accompanied her on visits to her grandmother. He took her to an exhibition at the Royal Academy of Arts and, as an added novelty, to a balloon ascension. Unfortunately, the more solicitous he grew, the more conscious she became of her failure to fulfill her duty as a wife.

On the evening of Evangeline's ball, Linnea chose a gown she knew Anthony particularly approved of. It was made of pistachio green *soie de Londres,* and luxuriously decorated with lace and flounces. It was an elegant dress, and she felt very elegant in it, though its bodice dipped even lower than the one she had worn to the opera. Still, she knew that Anthony would like it, and that was all that signified. With a curious thrill, she realized that tonight she would dance with her husband for the first time.

In truth it seemed almost absurd that this would be the first ball they attended when so many had already been given. She was a trifle nervous, mainly because of this fact, but the knowledge that Anthony would be at her side made things easier.

Squaring her shoulders, she went to search for him. She found him in the drawing room, gazing out the window with his hands clasped behind his back. He had not heard her approach, and for a long moment she studied him, quietly and with a sense of wonder. No matter what his faults were, no matter what he had done in his past, he was her husband. Other women might think they had a claim on him, but they were wrong. He was *hers*.

And she was glad.

Yet suddenly, unbidden and unwanted, a hodge-podge of memories flooded her mind—her father shouting, her mother weeping bitterly. *I should never have married him. He's an animal, Linnea, an animal* . . .

Shuddering, she shoved the disturbing memory away, but a tiny fragment of it remained to shadow her mood. "I am ready," she said softly.

He swung around. Slowly, lingeringly, his eyes trailed over her with masculine appreciation. "You look beautiful, Linnea. But something is missing."

Perplexed, she glanced down at her dress. "Missing—?"

Walking over, he pulled a small oblong box from his pocket and presented it. "For you, love. I realized I'd never bought you a wedding gift."

Linnea opened it with unsteady hands. "Oh, Anthony," she breathed, gazing down at a diamond filigree necklace so dainty it might have been fashioned by fairies. "It's exquisite. Will you help me to put it on?"

"I would be honored."

As he fastened the clasp at the nape of her neck, she noticed how gentle his hands were, how they brushed her skin oh so lightly. *This man would never hurt me,* she thought. Yet anger altered people, sometimes beyond recognition. Her father could actually be a pleasant, charming man when he was not in the grip of a fit of ill temper. And she had not yet seen Anthony in a true rage . . .

He turned her around to face him. "That looks better." Tracing the curve of the necklace with his finger, he smiled one of his throat-stopping smiles.

Linnea smiled back, feeling strangely embarrassed. "Thank you," she said. "I only wish I had something to give to you in return."

He cocked his head to the side. "I'd be perfectly willing to accept a kiss."

It seemed such a reasonable request that she could not deny him. With an odd flutter in her stomach, she placed her hands on his shoulders and raised her lips. She felt very shy, for it was the first time she had kissed him since the night he had accused her of seducing him.

Yet perhaps because she had relived that moment so many times in her mind, this kiss nearly shattered her self-control. It was only a light kiss, the merest brush of flesh upon flesh, yet it caught at her like a flame to dry tinder. She had to fight an overwhelming urge to surrender her scruples, to throw herself against him and beg him to take her upstairs and give her that education he'd mentioned.

Embarrassed, she wrenched from his embrace and spun away. "Goodness, look at the time," she babbled, with a brightness that hid the pandemonium within her. "I must have taken longer to dress than I meant. We had better go. The coachman grows so cross when we keep the horses waiting . . ."

There was a short pause before her husband replied, in a gently ironic tone, "Then by all means let us make haste. We would not wish to inconvenience the horses."

Evangeline's parents had spared no expense in launching their one and only daughter upon the *ton*. To facilitate the process, they had taken a house in Curzon Street—a handsome mansion boasting a large ballroom and an extravagant number of parlors and bedchambers. When the Carrocks arrived shortly after eight o'clock, Linnea's aunt and uncle greeted them with civility, if not with enthusiasm. As for Evangeline, she was too busy fluttering her eyelashes at Anthony to be spiteful to Linnea.

After they had gone through the receiving line, Linnea searched the crowd for a familiar face, which she found in the person of her cousin Iris. Her fingers tightened on Anthony's arm. "Will you escort me over to my cousin? She and my aunt are over there, standing next to that statue."

"Certainly, if that is your wish."

This proved easier said than done. Time and again their progress across the floor was impeded, a few times by gentlemen acquaintances who requested to sign Linnea's dance card, but more usually by ladies who gushed over her husband in a manner Linnea found highly irritating. Anthony had been strangely quiet since they'd left Albemarle Street, but under the flattering attentions of the female sex, she noted testily, he seemed to have revived. Thoroughly vexed, she resolved to keep him by her side until the dancing commenced; however, the moment they reached Iris, the Duchess of Weyland burst through the throng and dragged Anthony off to some distant corner to meet someone whose name Linnea was unable to catch.

By this time, Iris's mother had moved a short distance away, so that it was only Iris who witnessed the kidnapping. "It appears," she said dryly, "that her grace is fond of Lord Carrock."

"Every woman within a radius of five hundred miles is fond of Lord Carrock," Linnea said with a sigh. "I only wish I did not mind so much."

Iris's gaze lowered to the shimmering diamonds circling Linnea's neck, which were spilling out fiery shafts of color in every direction. "You are hardly the neglected wife, Linnea. That trifle around your neck must have cost a small fortune."

Linnea's face softened at the reminder. "Yes, he has been very good to me," she admitted. Reluctant to confide any more, she inquired whether Iris had seen or spoken with Captain Theale.

Iris flushed. "Indeed, he has been most attentive. I cannot understand it. The more I rebuff him, the more often he comes to call. The way things stand, he might as well pack up his clothes and move in with us."

"Such persistence would seem to indicate more than a superficial attachment," Linnea commented.

"Yes." Iris stared blankly at the milling crowd. "I keep wishing I had not overheard . . . what I did . . ." The corners of her mouth turned down. "He took Mama and me driving in the park yesterday. His manners are so beautiful. Mama believes he means to make me a declaration soon. She is urging me to encourage him."

"I urge you to encourage him also. Surely you do not wish to risk your happiness because of a conversation which was never meant for your ears."

Before either girl could say more, Roland Hallett appeared. "Miss Bronsden," he drawled, bowing deeply. "And Lady Carrock. Together, as always." His eyes drifted to the necklace about Linnea's throat.

Linnea watched him carefully as he flirted with Iris, observing how often his eyes returned to her diamonds. Finally, with a smile that made her skin crawl, he remarked, "That's a pretty trinket about your neck, Lady Carrock. A family heirloom, is it?"

"No," she said.

He gave her a cold-eyed smile. "Ah, then my cousin must have purchased it for you. I congratulate you. You appear to have earned his approbation."

His suggestive tone made her furious. "I am his wife, Mr. Hallett," she snapped.

"I need no reminder, ma'am. I trust you will allow me the honor of dancing with you this evening. And you, Miss Bronsden."

Iris relinquished her dance card so readily that Linnea longed to shake her, but courtesy demanded that she also yield her own. When he was gone, she discovered he had taken Iris's supper dance.

"What effrontery," she fumed.

"I shall be very pleased to have supper with him," Iris protested. "I like him, even if you do not."

Iris's mother chose this moment to rejoin them. "Good evening, Linnea. It is about time we saw you out in society." Waving an elegant ivory fan, she turned to her daughter. "Now do not be giving all your waltzes away, my love. Save at least one for Captain Theale." Her eyes darted anxiously over the crowd. "And where is the man? He promised he would be here."

"I've already told you, Mama, I will *not* waltz with him."

214

"Don't be ridiculous, child. Of course you can. Why do you keep saying such nonsensical things? I can see we must have another talk . . ."

It seemed a propitious moment for Linnea to excuse herself, which she had wanted to do ever since she had spied Amanda through an opening in the crowd several seconds before. Threading her way through what seemed like hundreds of people, she found Lord and Lady Vale standing near the rear of the ballroom with Charles and Aimee Perth.

Amanda greeted Linnea with an enthusiasm that drew a smile from her spouse. "One would think you had not seen each other for years, my love," the marquis teased.

"Indeed, it seems so," Amanda declared with laughing eyes. "You are looking very well, Linnea. That gown is exquisite."

"And so are the diamonds," added Aimee Perth rapturously.

Linnea smiled, real happiness bubbling inside her. She thanked both women, adding to Amanda, "You are looking better than the last time I saw you. You are feeling well?"

Amanda exchanged a glance with her husband. "Well enough in the evenings. It is the mornings that are troublesome." She laughed. "Sometimes I think John feels worse than I do out of pure sympathy."

For Linnea, the subsequent minutes were a pleasant change from balls of the past, where she had stood frozen and ill-at-ease. Both Amanda and Aimee treated her as though she was their dear, long-lost sibling, while their husbands complimented her on her appearance and reserved a place on her dance card. Yet there was a great ache inside her because Anthony was not at her side.

The announcement that the ladies and gentlemen were to take their places for the quadrille came all too soon. Linnea ruefully examined her dance card while the two men led their wives onto the floor. Of course, Anthony was nowhere to be seen; in fact he had not even had a chance to sign her card before the duchess had stolen him. Many of Linnea's dances had been taken, but there were still a few blank spots—including the first set. Feeling conspicuous, she was preparing to seek a place along the wall when a gentlemen appeared at her side.

"Would you do me the honor?" he asked with a low bow.

Linnea accepted with alacrity, not caring that they had not been introduced. At that instant all she cared about was that she should not be made to feel like a wallflower while her husband dallied with other women.

As the quadrille began, she smiled at the unknown gentleman, observing him with detachment. He was older than Anthony, with dark brown hair, sensual lips, and a dissipated countenance that might once have been handsome. Deep grooves etched the flesh on either side of his mouth, and something very jaded shone in his pale, world-weary eyes.

"You are Lady Carrock," he stated.

"Yes, sir, I am." When the movements of the dance again brought them together, she inquired his name.

"I am Sir Gideon Buscot." His eyes roved boldly

216

over her to settle on her cleavage. "Lord Carrock certainly has an eye for quality."

Startled, Linnea lifted her chin and challenged him with a stare intended to set him in his place. Instead, it seemed to amuse him.

"Perhaps I ought to have mentioned that I am acquainted with your husband."

"That seems to be universal," she said tartly.

He laughed as though she had said something witty. "Yes, he is a popular fellow. But I can see what lured him to wed."

The subtle, practiced flirtation continued until the end of the set, when Sir Gideon smiled mockingly. "You appear to have a keeper," he murmured, "whose displeasure I believe I have incurred."

Not comprehending, Linnea followed his gaze; then her breath caught in her throat. Anthony stood not five yards away, his arms folded casually across his chest, his aristocratic face set and pensive. It dawned on her that he must have been watching them, perhaps throughout the entire set.

Unfazed, Sir Gideon led Linnea over to her husband. "My dear fellow, how are you?" he drawled. "As you see, I have been making your wife's acquaintance. She is delightful in every way. Wherever did you find such a jewel?"

"Not," Anthony said calmly, "in the kind of place you frequent."

It was rude, but Sir Gideon only yawned. "One trusts not. Are you trying to warn me off?"

"She is my wife, Buscot. And a lady." Steel edged Anthony's voice as his hand curled around Linnea's elbow.

217

Sir Gideon gave a slight, bored shrug. "Then I surrender her to your care. My compliments, ma'am," he added, and strolled away.

Aware that the second set was forming, Linnea fumbled for her dance card, but quick fingers yanked it from her grasp before she could open it.

"I see that I shall have to monitor you more closely," Anthony remarked as he studied the card. "Buscot is a notorious philanderer, Linnea. Who introduced you?"

"No one, but—"

"No one?" His fine brows arched. "Then it was imprudent to have accepted him as your partner. I believed you to have better sense."

Nettled by the reproof, conscious that a good number of curious eyes watched them, Linnea's resentment welled. "Gracious, I don't see what it signifies. I married a notorious rake. Why shouldn't I dance with one if it pleases me?"

Drawing her closer, Anthony's grip tightened until his fingers felt fused to her arm. "Because I say so," he murmured into her ear. "And because it is a wife's duty to respect the wishes of her husband."

"And if I do not?" she asked tremulously.

"I will take steps to see that you do." Releasing her, he pulled a pencil from his pocket and scribbled his name next to the supper dance and one of the waltzes. Then he handed the card back to her and walked off without a backward glance.

Every muscle in his tall body rigid with displeasure, Anthony headed for the refreshment room, reflecting cynically that Buscot's presence at the gathering told him a great deal about Evangeline's mama. Disreputable Buscot might be, but he was also extremely wellborn, reasonably wealthy, and unwed—and that could outweigh much. Anthony himself had been invited to enough functions to know that if one's birth was good, a tendency toward profligacy did not mean that one was not received. Only the highest sticklers—and the patronesses of Almack's—failed to extend their hospitality to men such as Buscot . . . and himself.

His jaw clenched. Every time he thought he was making progress with Linnea, something happened to set it back. And now he had lost his temper and threatened her, and he knew she had resented it. But that was not the full sum of what was vexing him. That kiss they had exchanged after he had given her the necklace . . . why had she jerked away from him like that? All evening her action had chafed at him like a paper cut. Had she thought he was trying to buy her favors? Mulling the notion, he took a glass of champagne from a tray borne by a passing footman and stared down at it, but a trick of his senses made him see Linnea's face in the effervescent golden liquid.

All at once he had another vision—of himself, standing there mooning like a jealous lover because another man had dared to dance with his lady. The anomaly stung. Although he had desired many women in his life, he had never cared enough about a woman to object if another man chose to make her the recipient of his attentions.

Until now.

Cursing softly, Anthony tossed the champagne

down his throat as though it were water, then went to search for a partner for the third set.

His attention was drawn, not to the hopeful, languishing glances cast his way by females of youth and beauty, but to his Aunt Allison. A small, thin, unobtrusive woman, Lady Allison Hallett had hovered at the perimeter of his life for as long as he could remember. She had, as the saying went, tossed her bonnet over the windmill nearly twenty-seven years earlier for an untitled gentleman of moderate fortune, but upon the death of Joshua Hallett, she had moved back into her father's house, along with her twelve-year-old son, Roland. On social occasions she rarely uttered a word, but Anthony could remember many instances during his childhood when he had crept into her room to hear her fantastic tales of knights and dragons and fair maidens who needed rescuing. At the present moment, she looked so miserable and out of place that he felt compelled to go to her side.

"Good evening, Aunt," he said affably. "Would you care to dance?"

She looked rather startled. "No, dear. But thank you for asking."

"Shall I fetch you a chair?" He glanced around and spied one which had just been vacated by a young lady. "Aha, that will do nicely." He snitched it away without remorse, and settled her into it.

"So kind," she murmured, patting his arm. "You're always such a good boy. Are you happy in your marriage?"

"Of course," he said easily. "As happy as you were in yours."

"Ah." She smiled reminiscently. "I hope so, for

your sake." Then her smile faded. "I only wish Roland were more like his father. Joshua was content with a small manor house in the country, but my son longs for so much more." She colored suddenly, as though she had committed a faux pas.

"You mean he longs for the worldly goods which I, in due course, will inherit. I'm well aware of it, Aunt. There is no cause for you to be embarrassed."

She lowered her eyes, her fingers twisting together in her lap. "I am sorry, dear. I have never understood Roland. He is so restless, so . . . burning with ambition. Sometimes I fear for him," she added with a sigh. "I doubt he will ever find happiness."

Anthony touched her shoulder consolingly, his gaze wandering over the dancers until he found Linnea. How enchanting she looked—lovely as a wood nymph, graceful as sea foam, elegant as a queen. The soft folds of her gown complemented her shapely figure, its pale green color a fabulous foil to that crown of fiery curls. Even from where he stood, he could see the shining smile she gave her partner, Charles Perth.

"Well, if it isn't my dearest coz," drawled a familiar voice. "Dallying with my mama now, are you?"

"Hush Roland," admonished his mother. "Do not talk in that odious way. Why can you not be more like Anthony?"

Roland smiled nastily. "If I were any more like my cousin, Grandfather would cut off my allowance."

"That's probably true," agreed Anthony sardoni-

221

cally, "though I see no reason to distress my aunt by saying so. Are you in debt again?"

"Again?" Roland cocked an eyebrow. "Perpetually, dear coz. Unfortunately, my creditors aren't as lenient as yours—too bad for me."

"One must live within one's means," quavered Aunt Allison. "You must learn that, my son."

Over her head, Roland's flat marble eyes met Anthony's. "Gammon, Mama. Wherever did you get such an antiquated notion?"

The evening flowed by faster than Linnea expected, for each time she paused, thinking to rest her feet during a set for which she had no partner, some gentleman immediately presented himself for that office. Twice, she defied Anthony by accepting gentlemen who were wholly unknown to her, but defiance alone was not the object of her action. Perhaps it was insane to provoke her husband deliberately, but with the passing of each hour, it was becoming more and more imperative that she probe the hidden depths beneath Anthony's imperturbable facade. Despite his promise to her grandmother, Linnea knew that until she saw him roused to a full, blistering fury—a fury he was able to control—she would never quite trust him, never quite believe that he would not one day fly into a rage and strike her. She might be waving a red flag at a bull, but she had to know the worst, even if the worst was as bad as she feared.

Captain Theale arrived late, but sought her out almost at once in order to claim a dance and to give her the latest doleful report on his progress with Iris.

"I had hoped for either a waltz or the supper dance," he told her sadly, "but all her dances are taken. It is my own fault, of course, for being delayed, but it was unavoidable." Obviously downcast, he forced a lopsided smile. "But at least I have secured a waltz with *you,* Lady Carrock."

"Which is clearly not much of a consolation," Linnea teased, "but I shall dance with you nevertheless."

The captain, thinking he had offended, instantly began to beg pardon, but Linnea forestalled him with more teasing words. "Please," she finished on impulse, "call me Linnea. I know it is not quite proper, but . . . we are friends, are we not? And I hate to stand on ceremony with my friends."

Captain Theale hesitated, then smiled. "Only if you call *me* Gabriel," he said gallantly.

"Gabriel," she repeated in astonishment. She stared at him as a hazy yet daring plan leaped into her head. "What a . . . what an unusual name."

The captain gave her a peculiar glance. "Indeed," he said politely.

"Oh, I'm sorry. I didn't mean—" Linnea burst out laughing. "You must think me such a peagoose. It is only that I was thinking of something else." As the musicians struck up a waltz, she touched his arm. "Please, will you dance with me now?"

"Now?" He looked taken aback. "But the waltz you promised me is not for another hour."

Linnea's gaze strayed across the ballroom to Anthony, who had just taken his leave of a group of ladies and was heading in her direction. This was

223

his waltz, and what she was doing was bound to enrage him.

"I know, but my other partner has forgotten his promise," she lied, the color rising in her cheeks. "Please, Gabriel. I . . . I so love to waltz."

Clearly bewildered but willing to oblige, Captain Theale swept her into his arms and onto the floor amid the other dancers. From the corner of her eye, Linnea saw Anthony stop dead, but she dared not peek at him again. Instead, she pasted a dazzling smile on her face and recounted the history of the Rosetta Stone and its impact upon modern archeology to her slightly bemused partner.

When the waltz concluded, she thanked Captain Theale and scanned the crowd for Anthony, but he had returned to his gaggle of ladies across the ballroom and was standing with his back to her. Drat the man, she thought with vague disappointment. Not that she had wished him to create a scene in the middle of the ballroom, but now she would have to wait until the supper dance to learn his reaction—and her stomach was already shaking like a blancmanger.

From then on, time crawled by at a maddeningly slow pace. Linnea had ample opportunity to regret what she had done as she watched, surreptitiously, her husband flirt with the voluptuous brunette he was partnering in the minuet. As Linnea's own partner trod on her foot, she came to the lowering conclusion that she had been very foolish and rash. For days she had dreamed of the moment when Anthony would hold her in his arms and whirl her around the ballroom like a princess in a fairy tale. And she had stupidly thrown it away, she thought miserably. And for what? So she could discover how great a temper he had!

At last it came time for the supper dance, but Anthony did not appear. Linnea stumbled to the edge of the ballroom and collapsed onto a vacant bench, her pulse beating erratically. Until this moment it had never entered her mind that Anthony would pay her back in like coin.

The dance ended. Voices reverberated as the guests bunched into a line leading to the adjacent rooms where food was to be served. Linnea did not move. With every passing minute, the lump in her throat grew larger. Feeling forlorn and abandoned, she shut her eyes, preparing herself for the humiliation of being forsaken for the whole of the supper hour. Anthony would probably sup with that buxom, overblown brunette he'd found so alluring . . .

"Here, love, I hope I've brought you something you like."

Linnea's eyes flew open. So did her mouth. Before her, balancing two plates piled high with mouth-watering edibles, stood her husband, his expression as tranquil as ever. He pressed a plate into her hand and sat down next to her.

"How did you . . . ?" She stared dumbly, first at the food and then at her husband, whose eyes, she now noticed, held a curious gleam of mockery.

"I was first in line," he said blandly. "What an excellent notion to save us a seat. There are never enough tables at these affairs, and I dislike eating while I stand."

Shoulders rigid, Linnea settled her plate on her lap. "You are angry with me."

"Angry? Now what would I have to be angry about?" His voice held a definite thread of challenge.

"Because"—she moistened her lips—"I gave away your waltz."

"Ah, yes. I recall that, now that you mention it."

"So?"

He shrugged. "So I was annoyed. But I understand why you did it."

"You do?" she said nervously.

"Of course." He turned his head, his clear blue eyes examining her face. "It was your method of throwing down a gauntlet. You thought to prove that I may not tell you what to do. However, as your husband, I can and will do so if the situation warrants, particularly if you continue to behave in a childish fashion."

Stung, she retorted, "Well, if *I* was childish, then so were you! You left me sitting here during the whole of the supper dance—"

"So now you know how it feels," he said calmly.

Linnea flushed. "I'm sorry," she offered, her voice small.

"And so am I. Now be a good girl and eat your supper."

But as she picked up her fork, he went on, in a satirical tone she had never heard him use, "You danced with Edward Fortescue and Sir Henry Neyle. Fortescue is a well-known flirt, and Sir Henry is as much of a rake as Buscot. Correct me if I am wrong, but I don't believe you are acquainted with either one of them. No? I thought not." As Linnea stared down at her food, he went on, still with that light, cutting tone, "Since I have never adhered to the belief that women are incapable of rational thought, I ask that you use your brain for the purpose it was intended. Have a care, my love. Marrying a rake is one thing, but a public partiality for such company could endanger your reputation."

Hurt that he should think she would encourage such men, she said, "I have no partiality for rakes. Surely you, of all people, should know that."

"Yes, of course. How stupid of me." He rose, and favored her with an ironic bow. "Since your card is full, madam, I shall see you at the end of the evening."

Chapter Thirteen

After a night filled with shadowy, disturbing dreams, Linnea woke the next morning with a dreadful headache. It was early, but despite the hour and the throbbing pain, she threw back the bedclothes and got up. Headache or no, she had something she must do, something she was determined to carry out.

As fatigue crept through her limbs, she recalled the ball with a shudder. Images leaped into her brain, but she shoved them aside. She must put the ball from her mind and concentrate upon saving Iris.

While Maria buttoned her into her riding habit, Linnea reflected that if she could not achieve happiness for herself, the very least she could do was to help someone else achieve theirs. Iris and Gabriel Theale were meant for each other, and that was her only motive in meeting Captain Theale at so early an hour.

She picked up her crop and turned to her maid. "If his lordship should inquire for me, tell him that I have gone riding in the park." *After all, it was her duty to leave a message, even though Anthony would likely sleep the morning away.*

"Yes, milady." The girl bobbed a respectful curtsy. Linnea walked to the door, her ears attuned for the slightest sound from Anthony's room. She heard nothing.

"Tell him," she added, as an inspired afterthought, "that he is not to worry. I shall be with Captain Theale."

So much for pure motives, she thought wryly. Why not be honest and admit that she would be delighted if Anthony felt some small flicker of jealousy?

Yet the very notion was absurd, for to feel the effects of the green-eyed monster, wouldn't one have to love? And Anthony certainly did not love her! He merely wished to have a wife who, like Caesar's wife, was above reproach. He had made it very clear that it was her reputation and her virtue that concerned him, not the fear that she might fall in love with someone else.

Linnea left the house. As she had instructed, Anthony's groom had brought Niobe around, as well as a gray hack for himself. "She's a mite fresh," the groom warned as he assisted her into the saddle. "Are you sure you kin manage?"

Linnea patted the animal's withers. "Yes, thank you. Niobe and I are quite accustomed to one another by now, Mr. Mounce."

"Very well, milady. But I'll stay close by, gist in case."

Giving the man a nod, Linnea wished her headache would abate. Perhaps she should have taken time to drink some coffee, but she was already late and her plan could too easily fail. With a sigh, she recalled how she had again found herself in Iris's company for a brief moment near the end of last night's ball. Perhaps because Iris had just consumed two glasses of champagne, she had confided her in-

229

tention to meet Roland Hallett clandestinely in the park. When Linnea had tried to dissuade her, Iris had countered by pointing out, rather waspishly, that anyone who had waltzed *twice* with Captain Theale while ignoring her own husband ought not to lecture about what one should and shouldn't do. And what could Linnea say to that?

When she reached the entrance to Hyde Park, Captain Theale was waiting, his handsome face set in a resolute expression. Linnea greeted him, then addressed her groom. "Thank you, Mr. Mounce. You may return to the mews now. Captain Theale will see to my safety."

As the servant rode away, the captain asked, "Are you certain that was wise? I would not wish your husband to think I am meeting you clandestinely, Lady Car . . . I mean, uh, Linnea."

Startled, Linnea remembered that they were now on a first-name basis. "I am sure he will think no such thing," she said. "Now let us hurry and find Iris before Mr. Hallett ingratiates himself too thoroughly into her affections."

This was enough to spur the captain forward. "Indeed," he ground out. "If that churl dares to touch her, I shall" — his hands clenched into fists — "dash it, I shall rearrange the shape of his face!"

Linnea smiled to herself, thinking how much she would enjoy such a spectacle. If Roland Hallett were to behave in an ungentlemanly manner, then the captain could rush to the rescue! Then Iris would have to be kind to the captain.

As it happened, however, Iris was not being accosted by the wicked Roland Hallett when they came upon the couple ten minutes later. In fact, everything was surprisingly circumspect. Instead of struggling in Roland's embrace (as would have been ideal), Iris was sedately ensconced on her horse, chatting happily to her attentive escort. She had even brought a groom, who guarded the proprieties from a reasonably decorous distance behind the pair as they rode their horses along the grass.

Iris looked highly discomfited to see them. "Linnea . . . and Captain Theale! What in the world are you doing here?"

"The same as you, I trust," Linnea answered lightly. She nodded to Roland, who was mounted on a showy chestnut. "Good morning, Mr. Hallett. Are you acquainted with Captain Theale?"

The two men shook hands, though Linnea had the feeling that each would have preferred to start a bout of fisticuffs.

Iris kept looking back and forth between her would-be suitors and said, rather inanely, "What a pleasant morning for riding."

"Pleasant indeed," Roland drawled. "Yet not so pleasant that it lures Lord Carrock from his bed." His malicious gaze settled on Linnea. "You were wise to choose a substitute, Lady Carrock. Early morning rendezvous are not my cousin's style."

Linnea fought to keep her temper. "On the contrary, Anthony and I often ride at this hour, Mr. Hallett. Perhaps you do not know my husband as well as you think."

Roland studied her for a moment. "Perhaps not," he conceded, still with that irritating, oily smoothness. His gaze swept over to include the captain. "Won't you join us?" he added mockingly. "Miss Bronsden and I were about to shake the fidgets out of our horses."

Since joining them had been precisely her intention, Linnea accepted the invitation with pretended enthusiasm. The foursome, followed by the groom, took off down the Row, but by tacit agreement the two cousins soon dropped back behind the men.

"I suppose you came to spy on me," Iris said crossly.

"No, I came to be sure you were safe. I told you I do not trust Mr. Hallett." Linnea cast her pretty cousin a glance, noting how effortlessly Iris controlled her horse. "You escaped your house without difficulty?"

"No, everything went wrong. Mama woke earlier than I expected, and came into my room while I was putting on my habit. I was forced to tell her I was meeting Captain Theale. Otherwise she would never have allowed me to go."

"Oh, Iris. What if she discovers the truth?"

Iris grimaced. "She will not, unless you tell her. What I should like to know is when you and Captain Theale became such fast friends. Was it only last night, or have you been meeting him all along?"

Linnea could not be annoyed, for she heard the pain beneath her cousin's brittle tone. "We are no more than acquaintances," she answered gently, "and this is the first time we have gone riding. It means nothing, Iris. He is in love with *you,* as you ought to be aware."

"Then why are you with him? And where is *your* groom? You are being amazingly indiscreet, you know. What would Lord Carrock say?"

Linnea flushed slightly. "Anthony's opinion is of no consequence. I consider Captain Theale's protection to be quite adequate, which is more than I would say for Roland Hallett's."

"There is nothing wrong with Mr. Hallett. In fact,

he has been paying me the prettiest compliments I have ever received." Iris's gaze fixed on the two men, who had wheeled their horses and were heading back toward the women at a smart pace. "He rides well, does he not?"

"So does Captain Theale," Linnea pointed out.

Iris watched them silently, her pretty lips pursed as though her thoughts were troubled. "I would have danced with him last night if my card had not been full."

"You should have saved him a set."

"Well, I quite meant to," Iris said fretfully, "but he was so late! If he wished to partner me, he should have been there sooner."

"Oh, Iris, if you could only have seen how sad he was. I think he loves you very much."

Iris's expression fluctuated, but the two men arrived before she could speak.

"Sharing secrets, my little flower?" Roland teased Iris.

Linnea saw Captain Theale's mouth tighten as Iris blushed like a schoolgirl. "Yes, sir, we were," she chided, "so you must be gallant and refrain from asking what they were."

Roland looked ready to make some further remark, but something in the distance caught his attention. "Interesting," he murmured pensively. "It seems we are to have yet another addition to our party. Methinks the errant bridegroom is not as lenient as his wife perhaps believes."

Linnea's heart jerked spasmodically. She looked around, her poise disintegrating as her husband rode toward them across the grass. Like a centaur from a myth, he and his beautiful bay gelding functioned as a perfect unit — controlled, fluid, exquisitely graceful

233

as they sped over the ground. He reined in next to her with a tight-lipped smile. "I received your message." His glance, rapier-sharp, passed over her. "It was charmingly considerate of you not to wake me, my dear. Considerate, but unnecessary." Beneath his benevolence lurked a note that sent prickles down Linnea's spine.

"How . . . how good of you to come." Cursing the quaver in her voice, she managed a tremulous smile of her own.

"Not at all," he answered.

Beneath his cool exterior, Anthony was far from calm. Suspicion had erupted inside him since late the previous evening, suspicion that owed its origin to the discovery that Captain Theale was in fact Captain Gabriel Theale. Finding himself face to face with the man he now considered his rival, he decided to use the opportunity to prize out what he wished to know.

"Captain," he said, as pleasantly as he was able, "let us have a canter. Your black looks a good match to my bay."

Captain Theale looked a little surprised, but nonetheless spurred his horse forward upon the viscount's signal. One hundred yards down the Row, Anthony slowed his mount to a walk.

"I have a feeling," said the captain, falling in beside him, "that there is something you wish to say to me."

"Indeed there is. I should like to know exactly how well you know my wife."

The captain blinked. "Why . . . I am barely acquainted with her."

"Is that so." Anthony's lip curled. "I had the impression you had known her for some time."

"I cannot think why you should say so."

"Can you not? Perhaps it is because my wife mentioned you very shortly after our marriage." He cast the other man a distrustful glance. "She referred to you as Gabriel. She said you had given her advice upon her mode of dress."

"Her mode of dress?" Captain Theale sounded completely bewildered.

"The colors which suited her," Anthony added with a frown. "There is nothing wrong in that, of course. But just lately I have found her in your company too often for my liking."

The other man's long cheeks flushed. "Exactly what are you suggesting?" he demanded.

"I am suggesting," Anthony bit out, "that whatever it is you have in mind, you had better understand one thing. I will not play the oblivious husband."

Captain Theale halted his horse. "You insult me, Lord Carrock. I have no dishonorable intentions toward your wife, and I never gave her any advice. On the contrary, it is she who has given advice to me."

"Really?" Anthony casually fingered his crop. "What sort of advice?"

"That, sir, is none of your affair."

"Has no one ever told you that a good soldier knows when to retreat?"

"Has no one ever told *you* that a good husband does not ignore his wife? If Linnea does not confide in you, you have only yourself to blame."

Anthony's face darkened. "I do not ignore my wife," he snapped. "And I should like to know who gave you permission to use her Christian name?"

"She did. In deference to your wishes I shall certainly cease to do so, but I refuse to withdraw my

235

friendship entirely. Your wife, Lord Carrock, is a good woman, and I count myself honored to know her."

Anthony scowled. "I have no objection to an innocent friendship, nor is it my intention to keep my wife in chains. But if you ever lay a finger on her, if you touch her in any way, I shall personally see that you regret it." His eyes were hard as blue diamonds as he pointed the crop at the captain. "And that," he added, "is both a threat and a promise."

Captain Theale's mouth quivered with fury. "Again, Lord Carrock, you have insulted me unforgivably, but for her ladyship's sake and only for her sake, I shall disregard it on this occasion. However, if you ever dare speak to me in such a way again, I will not answer for the consequences."

"Nor will I, if the occasion demands," said Anthony grimly.

Linnea and her companions had been maintaining a bouncing trot while the other two cantered ahead. While Roland and Iris flirted, she watched her husband and Captain Theale with misgiving. From this distance, Anthony's face was unreadable, but something in Captain Theale's bearing made her uneasy. Puzzled, she let out a soft breath and glanced toward Iris, but all her cousin's attention was centered on Roland Hallett, who was paying Iris fulsome compliments upon her riding prowess. Feeling unsociable, her head still aching, Linnea returned her attention to Anthony, and allowed her mind to drift . . .

. . . until Iris's crow of delight sent a needle-sharp pain lancing through her skull. Wincing, she looked at Iris, who gazed back at her expectantly.

"Well?" said Iris, who had obviously just asked a question.

"I beg your pardon, Iris? I was not attending."

"I said shall we race?" said Iris impatiently. "It would be so amusing—your Niobe against my Gypsy." She patted her horse's withers. "My poor Gypsy has been pining for a gallop."

"We cannot gallop in Hyde Park. You know that as well as I."

"Pooh, who cares for these silly rules? There is nothing more exciting than a good gallop! Anyway, at this hour there is no one of any consequence around to see." When Iris darted a quick glance down the Row, Linnea realized she was staging this for Captain Theale's benefit.

Linnea sighed. "You know perfectly well that of the two of us, you are the better horsewoman. Why should I run a race to prove it? And what would your mother say if she found out?"

At that moment, finally, she saw Anthony rotate his horse and urge it into an easy canter back in her direction. Worried that he might have said something about the waltz, she examined the faces of the two men as their mounts carried them over the ground—her husband in the lead, the captain a little behind—but neither man's countenance betrayed a thing.

"Mama will never know," Iris was chirping, "and as for my being the better rider, that's fustian. You are simply being obstinate, Linnea."

"To be sure," Roland said smoothly, "you ride delightfully, Lady Carrock. I am sure the race would be a very close thing."

"What harm can it do?" wheedled Iris.

"What harm can what do?" queried Anthony as he

237

drew up. His thoroughbred danced sideways, then moved to walk beside Niobe.

"What harm is it to gallop in the park when there is no one about to see?" Iris said brightly. "It is not as though the patronesses of Almack's are lurking in the trees, for pity's sake. Anyone can see the place is deserted, save for a few children and governesses."

"I suppose that is true," he agreed distractedly.

"You see, Linnea? Lord Carrock has no objection to a race."

Anthony stiffened. "Wait a minute. *Whose* race?"

"Linnea's and mine. A short gallop to see whose horse is faster."

"Absolutely not," he said flatly. "Linnea is not a skilled enough rider."

If he had spoken these words in private, Linnea would probably have agreed with him, but this public testimony of her shortcomings too closely resembled the countless hurtful criticisms she had received from her family. For the space of a heartbeat, chagrin and hurt vied within her for the upper hand, then she straightened her spine and said, "Thank you, but I prefer to make my own decisions. I think a race would be fun. And as Iris says, there can be no harm in it."

"There can be a great deal of harm if you break your neck," Anthony countered, a straight, cool challenge in his eyes. "Don't you think you ought to reconsider?"

Linnea wet her lips. "No," she said baldly.

His answering look gave her another moment's pause, but she lifted her chin and glared back. Uncharacteristic defiance surged through her—a defiance spawned by a lifetime of constraints created not only by her parents, but by the mere fact of being female in a world created for the convenience of men. She did not care if he was angry, she reflected with a thudding heart. Indeed, was that not what she wanted?

Roland's eyes flicked maliciously from husband to wife. "Marriage is such a wonderful institution," he murmured.

"If I might offer my opinion, I don't think either of you should race," inserted Captain Theale with disapproval. "Miss Bronsden, such conduct is simply not proper. If you wish to gallop, you ought to go to Richmond Park."

But this admonition earned him nothing but scorn from the object of his affection, who promptly exclaimed, "Oh, you males are such hypocrites! You go out and have your own fun, then pompously take exception when we ladies wish to have ours! Well, Linnea and I won't stand for it! You are all tedious. Except for Mr. Hallett, of course." She fluttered her lashes at Roland. "Mr. Hallett, will you be so good as to choose a course for us?"

Roland smirked. "I would be delighted, Miss Bronsden."

Anthony maintained a frigid silence while Roland designated the edge of a certain group of beech trees as the finish line. Roland was to remain at the starting point, which was to be their present location, while Captain Theale was given the task of calling the winner at the other end. While they waited for the captain to take his place a quarter mile down the Row, Linnea carefully avoided her husband's eye.

Then she and Iris took their positions, their two horses aligned nose to nose. "On the count of three," intoned Roland, his arm raised. "One . . . two . . . *three!*" His arm slashed downward.

Niobe leaped forward as Linnea swatted her flank with the crop. The mare was strong and quality-bred; Linnea could feel the power in the motion of the sleek muscles, the stamina in the rhythmic, ground-covering stride. She drew in a breath, reveling in the sheer, mind-numbing speed. She had forgotten what it was like to gallop, to feel the breeze burrow into her hair, to soar free as a hawk on the wind. The trees passed in a blur; close by, Iris's Gypsy matched Niobe's gait, but as Linnea urged her animal on, it was not to win—she did not care about the contest—but for the exhilaration, the thrill. On this horse she did not feel vulnerable; she felt invincible, accomplished, endowed with a *force majeure*.

And then her heart almost stopped.

For just beyond Captain Theale, directly in the path of the horses, a tiny golden-haired boy toddled across the grass.

Euphoria gave way to panic. She had to stop the horse, had to warn Iris. Yet even as this went through her mind, Iris and Gypsy were no longer there. As if in slow motion, she saw the captain look around, saw him slide from his horse and run toward the child, but there was no more time. Acting on instinct, Linnea closed her eyes and gave one powerful yank on the reins . . .

Niobe reared up, her front legs pawing the air, a resentful whinny tearing from her throat.

Linnea hit the ground so hard every bone in her body felt broken. Stars whirled before her eyes as she tried and failed to draw a breath. Then the stars faded, replaced by Anthony, whose expression seemed more sober than she had ever seen it. Tears came to her eyes as more agonizing seconds passed.

Her lungs felt ready to explode from lack of air. Dimly, she realized that Anthony was repeating her name, that he had gripped her chin with his hand, that his face was inches from her own.

"Say something!" he demanded in an unloverlike tone.

Unable to obey, she rolled to her side and finally, thankfully, took in her first, tortured gulp of oxygen.

She heard him swear, softly and vividly, but his fingers stroked her shoulder with gentleness. "Easy now. You've had the wind knocked out of you. That's a girl . . . breathe slowly . . . that's it."

Gradually, Linnea's lungs recovered from the blow they had received. She lifted a hand and wiped at her eyes. "I'm all right," she said shakily.

"Are you certain?" His intense blue gaze raked her from head to toe.

Linnea wiggled all her parts experimentally, then pushed herself to a sitting position. "Really, I'm fine," she repeated in embarrassment.

"Praise God." With a strange mixture of relief and flippancy, he added, "You've no idea how lucky you are."

As he assisted her to her feet, she grew aware of the small crowd that had gathered around them—Iris, Captain Theale, Roland, and at least seven children and two nannies. The younger of the two nannies stepped nervously forward, the toddler clutched in her thin arms.

"Forgive me, madam. I thought the little one was right behind me. They do move so fast and I was busy with the others . . ." Fresh tears welled in her eyes, and her nose turned an even brighter shade of pink than it had been before.

241

Though Linnea's knees were still trembling, she took the time to reassure the woman, who clearly feared that her negligence would be reported to her employers. Then Anthony ordered the crowd to disperse and the nannies herded the children off.

Anthony glanced at Iris. "I'm going to take Linnea home," he said abruptly. "I'm sure one or both of these gentlemen will see you back to Clarges Street."

Iris nodded, looking subdued. "Linnea, I will call upon you later. "I'm so sorry this happened. It was all my fault."

"On the contrary, it was the nanny's fault," Roland said sharply. "The brat should have been better supervised."

"Still, if we had not been riding at such a mad pace . . ." Iris's voice drifted off. She seemed barely to notice that it was Captain Theale who helped her remount. The three rode off, Iris flanked by her two admirers.

Alone with her husband, Linnea stared down at the ground. Silence stretched between them; she could feel his gaze on her face. "I'm sorry," she said feebly. She reached up and straightened her bonnet, waiting for his reply.

"I imagine you are," he said, very dryly. "Can you ride, or shall I take you up in front of me?"

"I can ride." She shot him a look, then her eyes fell away from his. Her legs were horribly wobbly, but to accept the latter offer would have been a sure sign of weakness.

As he lifted her into the saddle, her gaze shifted to the children scampering along the banks of the Serpentine some fifty short yards away. Her face shadowed. If she had injured or killed that little boy . . . how could she have lived with herself?

As Anthony remounted his bay, she said, "He must have been hiding among the beech trees or Captain Theale would have seen him."

He slanted an unsmiling look at her. "I believe so."

"What did Iris do?" she asked, after an uncomfortable silence.

"She veered off to the right."

"I suppose that's what I should have done," she mumbled.

"What you bloody well should have done," he snapped, "was forego the race in the first place. Did it never occur to you that I could be right? I ought to turn you over my knee for that silly stunt! You risked your neck, Linnea, and for what?"

For a moment she could not answer; her headache, which had faded during the crisis, chose this moment to return in a pounding, staccato beat; at the same time a shaking took over her body, a trembling that nearly made her teeth chatter.

"I refuse to answer that," she quavered. "If I made an unwise decision, I will learn from it, but I will not be treated like a child, Lord Carrock."

She could feel him withdraw. She didn't even have to look at him to know that his face would hold the same lack of expression as when he spoke of his brother. Miserably, she fixed her gaze on the park's arched gateway and reminded herself that he was her husband in name only. What did it signify if he thought her childish? What did it matter if he did not love her?

And then the memory of those moments when she had lain upon the ground came back in a rush. Anthony's face as he bent over her—had it not been filled with real concern? She peeped sideways at him, noting the harsh set of his mouth. Perhaps, just perhaps, he cared for her a little . . .

"I suppose I gave you a scare," she ventured. "I said I was sorry and I meant it."

But her attempt to make peace was given a cool reception. "Do you have any notion, my love, how easy it is to break your neck? If not, pray allow me to enlighten you. When I was twenty, my father, who happened to be foxed at the time, took part in a curricle race. His curricle came too close to another and their wheels locked. He flew thirty feet into a wheat field and died instantly. Of course," he added brutally, "it doesn't always happen like that. Sometimes they linger for days or weeks. Sometimes they're only crippled or paralyzed."

His words increased the sickening tremble in her stomach. "You're trying to frighten me," she accused.

"Indeed I am. Am I succeeding?"

She lowered her chin. "Yes."

"Good. While I'm on a roll, let me tell you something else. From now on, you will not receive Captain Theale in our house, nor will you dance with him at any balls." In an implacable voice, he added, "I forbid you to have anything more to do with him."

Chapter Fourteen

Behind a screen in her bedchamber, Linnea sat in a tub of hot water, soothing the bruises which had resulted from her mishap. Until this moment she had not truly absorbed what had happened, but now, an hour after the incident, she shivered at the memory of her fall, and of the consequences that might have occurred. Tensely, she realized that Anthony was right.

She could have been killed.

As the shocking realization caught hold, she stared down at her knees, absently smoothing her hands over her calves. It was a frightening reflection—too frightening to dwell upon for very long—so instead her thoughts turned to Anthony's revelation about his father.

How dreadful to have lost both a father *and* a brother to cruel accidents. She had lost a dearly beloved brother herself, so she understood the pain of loss. But two of them—! For a moment she pictured what life would have been like without her own father, but could feel no emotion except the tight knot of resentment she'd always harbored. She and her mother would have been poorer, she thought bitterly, but almost certainly they would have been happier . . .

She frowned at a droplet of water on her wrist. It did no good to ponder old unhappiness when there were new problems to plague one. Everything she did seemed to go wrong, she reflected glumly. If she had not been so defensive and sensitive she would not have participated in the race, and if she had not been so impetuous, she would not have given away that waltz. In retrospect, the things she had done seemed so foolhardy that for a moment her sympathies were wholly with her husband.

On the other hand, she thought indignantly, he should have accepted her apology with more grace! He should not have taken that highhanded, insulting manner with her, or forbidden her to see Captain Theale. It was most unjust and unnecessary!

Then she sighed, long and deeply, and her resentment faded. Her lower lip caught between her teeth, she formed a cup with her hands and watched the water trickle through her fingers. Just so would her chance for marital happiness slip away if she did not do something soon. Why had Anthony never told her of his father's death? Why had she never thought to ask? She had been selfish, she decided — selfish and sharp-tongued and suspicious, quick to judge and quick to condemn. Of course, the knowledge of these failings did not banish them entirely, but it did give her pause.

Her gaze rose to the twin portraits above the fireplace. Two handsome young men, she mused, physically the same and yet poles apart, each bound inextricably to the other by the bonds of birth. Studying them, she grew convinced that the tragedy of their father's accident had driven them even closer, made them even more dependent on

246

one another. But while Roger was gone forever, Anthony was very much alive, very much in need of the comfort and peace of self-forgiveness.

She thought of the cutting things he had said to her, both last night and this morning, yet she could not remain angry with him, not when she knew how the guilt ate at his soul. *Who do I blame?* he had asked. And her heart ached for him. She ached for him, and for herself, and for what they could have together if only . . . if only . . .

If only that odious Lady Lindcastle had not come along and spoiled everything, she thought with a flash of anger. Perhaps she would have been able to comfort Anthony, to help him see that what happened was not his fault. Instead, she had suffered humiliation while that horrid woman had drawled out her innuendos and insinuations.

Slowly, Linnea lowered her head and wrapped her arms round her knees. Yes, despite the fact that Anthony did not love her, she yearned to make everything right for him, to ease his pain, to gather him into her arms.

Impossible.

She could not simply go to him and announce that she was ready to be the comfort and mainstay of his existence, not after what had transpired. She lacked both the courage and the confidence to survive the rejection she knew she would receive. Forlornly, she reflected that he probably depended on his mistress for comfort, though quite frankly she could not imagine a woman like Lady Lindcastle offering anything more than the pleasures of the body.

She frowned suddenly. What had Anthony said?

Lady Lindcastle and I are not friends, not in the way you think. Suppose he had spoken the truth? For a sweet, splendid instant, she allowed herself to hope, but this hope faded when it struck her that she was being naive. If Lady Lindcastle was not his mistress, that did not mean he did not have one.

Or several.

On the heels of this disquieting thought, she remembered Amanda. Her friend had reformed a dedicated rake with the power of her love—surely she would have some sage advice, some bits of wisdom to offer?

Recalling, however, that Amanda was frequently unwell at this hour of the day, Linnea decided she had better wait. In the interim, she could work on her manuscript; she had only the last chapter to edit and copy over, and then it would be complete, ready for the publisher to read—if he ever expressed the desire to do so, she reflected with a sigh.

Three hours later, she stood and stretched with weary satisfaction. It was done. The spirited Miranda had at last found happiness in the arms of Sir Gabriel Rhodes, and was destined to live long and happily. If only her own problems could be solved with the stroke of a pen . . .

She summoned her maid, who dutifully fussed over her mistress's hair and laid out a gown suitable for paying visits. As Linnea slipped her arms into the dress's long sleeves, she asked whether her husband was in.

"I believe his lordship is in the library, milady."

Linnea was not surprised. She had noticed that Anthony had been spending more and more time in that room lately. She had several times wondered what he did in there, but had never attempted to find out. The door was always solidly closed, and she had taken that as a sign she was unwelcome.

But when she went downstairs, she found herself pausing before the library door. *Do it,* she prodded herself.

Squaring her shoulders, she stepped forward and knocked.

"What is it?" The question was slightly curt, as though she had interrupted something important. Nevertheless, she edged open the door far enough to see that Anthony was at his desk, surrounded by papers. His brooding frown gave him the look of a fallen angel.

"Linnea." Other than a slight lessening of the crease in his brow, his face showed no expression as he rose and rounded the desk. He stopped an arm's length away and surveyed her clothes through narrowed eyes. "You are going out?"

"Yes, I'm . . . going to call on Amanda." Feeling awkward, she added in a rush, "I only wanted to let you know in case . . . in case you wondered where I was."

"Considerate of you. Or should I say dutiful?"

His ironic tone made her insides go cold. "I . . . I'm sorry I disturbed you," she said, backing away a step. "You're obviously busy."

"Not as busy as you," he mocked. "You, my love, are always locked in your room, always mysteriously occupied. What is it you do up there? Dream of your precious captain?"

For a handful of seconds she only gazed at him,

249

then she wheeled around and walked away. He did not come after her.

And she did not look back.

Amanda took one glance at Linnea's face and dropped the magazine she was reading. "Good gracious, Linnea, what is it? What has happened?"

Needing no further encouragement, Linnea sank onto the couch and spilled out everything. Amanda listened quietly, distress marring the usual serenity of her brow. At last, when Linnea paused to wipe her eyes and blow her nose, the marchioness said, very gently, "You're in love with him, aren't you?"

Linnea swiped at her eyes. "No. No, I only . . . oh, blast, I suppose I . . . I am." This seemed so tragic that more tears immediately poured from her eyes, so that she was obliged to accept a fresh handkerchief from Amanda, who slipped an arm around her shoulders until this second tempest had passed.

Then Amanda rose and fetched a small glass of brandy. "It is not the end of the world, my dear, though I know it seems so. Here, drink this. Then we will try to make some sense out of what you have told me."

Linnea choked as the fiery liquid burned a track down her throat. "Good grief," she said with a watery gasp, "do you drink this nasty stuff?"

"Only for medicinal purposes," Amanda answered with a small smile. "There, now at least you have some color in your cheeks. Do you feel better?"

Linnea heaved a sigh that felt dredged from her very soul. "Perhaps a little."

"Good." The marchioness gave her hand a comforting squeeze. "Now then, let us take this a step at a time. Your husband has forbidden you to receive Captain Theale."

"There is no reason to do so," Linnea insisted. "I have no more interest in Captain Theale than I do in . . . in the Prince Regent, for heaven's sake. But he *is* a friend, and I will not abandon him."

"It sounds to me as though Lord Carrock is jealous."

"I don't know about that." Linnea laced her fingers together and looked at them. "But he is certainly suspicious and dictatorial and . . . and possessive."

"Terrible faults indeed," Amanda commented, "but not uncommon in the male sex." She leaned closer and lowered her voice. "You have not yet given yourself to him, I collect?"

Linnea flushed and shook her head.

"That could be part of the problem. Men can grow terribly frustrated, and frustration brings out their temper."

"But if he has a mistress . . . would she not take care of . . . of that?"

"Tell me, why are you so certain he has a mistress?"

Linnea plucked at her skirt, hating herself for doubting him, yet unable to stop those doubts. "Because it makes sense," she said bleakly. "I mean, he is a rake, is he not? Even you warned me of his reputation right from the beginning. And I can think of no good reason why he should change. In any case, Roland Hallett said . . . at least, he more or less intimated . . . but I suppose I should not believe *him*."

"Roland Hallett?" Amanda looked confused.

"He was Anthony's groomsman, remember? He is also his heir until we . . . until we have a son of our own."

Immediately, Amanda's brow furrowed. "Which makes him a prime candidate for wishing to cause mischief between you and your husband," she said slowly. "I only hope . . ."

"You hope what?"

Amanda stared off into space, then shook her head as if to clear it of some peculiar thought. "Nothing. What I wish to say is that you must be realistic. I speak from experience, Linnea, so pay heed. My husband had mistresses before he knew me. Quite a number of them," she added, a little wryly. "And he is an extremely handsome man. Do you think they don't notice him now simply because he is married? Well, they do. You and I have exactly the same problem."

"But Lord Vale seems so devoted to you . . ."

"He *is* devoted. But I do not make the mistake of thinking that others would not like to take my place in his affections. That is not to say that they *could* do so. John's love for me is deep and true." She nodded in emphasis, her face reflecting the love and trust she had in her husband. "But sometimes, when a woman is looking at him in a certain way, I see it in her eyes. I know what she is thinking."

Linnea clasped her hands together. "Does it not

vex you? Does it not make you long to . . . to scratch her eyes out?"

To her surprise, Amanda laughed. "Sometimes," the marchioness admitted. "And sometimes, when some beautiful woman has been flirting outrageously with John, do you know what he does? He whispers in my ear how silly she is, and how he much prefers the lady he has married." She blushed a little. "And when we are home, alone, he shows me how passionate his preference is."

"But what would you do if he took a mistress?"

"Box his ears," said Amanda promptly. "No, I am jesting. I suppose I would ask him why. It's hard for me to say because I know he never would." She sighed. "Let us look at your situation. You love your husband, but you think he does not love you. Yet his behavior suggests that he cares for you. If he did not, would he have scolded you so for that race? Would he forbid you to receive Captain Theale?"

"I don't know," Linnea whispered. "I need your advice, Amanda. What should I do?"

The little marchioness considered for a moment. "I am no expert, Linnea, but my instinct says you should go to him"—she hesitated briefly—"whether he has a mistress or not. You've rejected him from the start of your marriage. His pride may keep him away from you forever. Unless you make the first move and offer him . . . your love."

Linnea was silent. Yes, that was what she needed to do, to offer Anthony her love. The need was there, burning inside her, clamoring to be free of the cage she had built for it. How long had she loved him? *From the first,* whispered a voice in her

253

head. *From the night she had met him, from the moment he had first seared her lips with his kiss . . .*

"Perhaps you are right," she said. "After all, I've nothing to lose."

Nothing but her hopes and dreams.

Linnea was stepping down from the carriage back in Albemarle Street when her eye chanced to fall upon a girl standing alone some twenty-odd yards further down the pavement. Perhaps because she had been thinking wistfully of bearing Anthony's children, she studied her for a moment, for the girl was noticeably large with child. Despite her swollen belly, she was a striking creature, a fragile, golden-haired doll whose intense dark eyes seemed to bore into Linnea. In fact, she stared so hard it almost seemed as though she wished to speak, but at that instant a second carriage drew up and distracted Linnea's attention.

The steps lowered and Iris climbed gracefully out. "You seem to have made a complete recovery," she observed. "I must say I am relieved, for I felt responsible." She heaved a melancholy sigh as they entered the house. "I only wish things were going as well for me."

She refused to elaborate until they were seated in the drawing room, where she plopped down upon the sofa and said, "You will never guess what has happened. First, Mama discovered it was Roland I went to meet in the park and gave me a horrid scolding. That nodcock of a groom, whom I had sworn to secrecy, blabbed to one of the kitchen

254

maids, and before half an hour was out, my mother's abigail had heard the story. And of *course*"—Iris rolled her eyes—"the talebearing henwit ran straight to Mama!"

"Oh dear," Linnea murmured.

"But that is not everything! You will never, ever guess what Captain Theale did! He went off to Brooks's, where my father practically lives, and interrupted Papa in the middle of a card game to beg leave to offer for my hand!"

Linnea smiled. "Ha, you see, I was right, Iris! He does love you."

"So of course Papa gave his permission and Captain Theale is coming this evening to speak to me, but"—Iris's voice lost its briskness—"I am not at all certain I will accept him."

"Oh, Iris," Linnea almost wailed. "Why not?"

Iris lifted her chin. "You know why, Linnea. At any rate"—her voice took on a brittle note—"I still believe I can do better for myself. After all, he may not inherit that fortune for years. I think I can bring Lord Mayhew up to scratch if I try hard enough. I rather fancy being a countess."

"The man loves you, Iris. All the titles and wealth in the world cannot buy that. And you care for him too. You know you do."

"Perhaps." Iris stared at her fingers, then she blurted out, "Do you know that people are saying Captain Theale is your lover?"

"What?" gasped Linnea. "Who told you that?"

"Mr. Hallett did. He thought he ought to warn me."

"And you believed him?" Linnea's voice trembled with indignation.

"Why should I not? Why should he lie?"

Recalling Amanda's comment, Linnea said vehemently, "Because he is Lord Carrock's heir, for one thing. I wouldn't put it past him to start the gossip himself in the hopes of—oh dear, forgive me if I shock you, but he might be trying to cause a rift between Anthony and myself so as to prevent"—the heat rose in her cheeks—"the conception of a son who could displace him."

Iris's eyes widened speculatively. "What a shocking thing to suggest."

"Perhaps, but it could be true. Mr. Hallett is oily and slick and cruel. And he clearly is no gentleman, for a gentleman would never repeat such sordid gossip to a lady, particularly not to one who is unmarried."

"That was not all he told me, Linnea, but I'm not sure I should tell you the rest."

"If it's to do with Anthony, I would rather not hear it."

"Of course not." Iris nodded with ingenuous relief. "And as his wife you would already know about it anyway. But one cannot help wondering what he sees in her. I mean, she is quite beautiful, but at the same time there is something one cannot quite like about her. I think she must be very full of herself, for she always wears such a superior smile."

"You mean Lady Lindcastle," said Linnea with resignation.

"Yes." Iris leaned closer. "Even Mama must know, for she always makes the most disparaging comments about her. According to Mama, the term 'lady' does not apply to Susannah Lindcastle."

Iris's blue eyes grew sympathetic. "Poor Linnea, I do feel for you most profoundly. Perhaps you are right about Lord Mayhew. I ought not to marry for a title, for only look what can happen when one does."

Suppressing her flailing emotions, Linnea changed the subject. "Have you paid Grandmama a visit lately?"

"Yes, Mama and I went yesterday." Iris's voice quavered. "I cannot quite believe it, Linnea. After all these years of imaginary illnesses, she really is dying. It . . . it makes me want to cry, and I didn't expect to feel this way at all, because Grandmama has always been so . . . so ornery."

"I know," Linnea said softly.

Iris sniffed, her nose turning a delicate shade of pink. "Evangeline has been quite horrid lately. All she says is that Grandmama had better wait until the end of the Season to die." She touched a finger to the corner of her eye, where a tiny teardrop had formed. "I am glad now that it is you and not Evangeline who will get Grandmama's money. I think Mama is, too."

Despite her wretched mood, Linnea cast her cousin a look of affection. "And I think Captain Theale has made a very fine choice, Iris."

Linnea spent the remainder of the afternoon wrestling with her decision to approach Anthony. She tried repeatedly to rehearse what she would say, even wrote it down on a piece of paper, but it was no use. It would have been easier if it had all been part of her novel, she reflected. Miranda would have thought of something desperately clever

257

to say, something that would have brought Sir Gabriel to his knees in a matter of moments. But after two hours of pacing her room, Linnea had yet to come up with a speech that suited her.

Perhaps this accounted for her acute nervousness as she paused by the door to Anthony's library. She had always known she was a coward; it had been the same during all the years she had lived at home—whenever her father had summoned her, her stomach had quivered so badly she'd felt nauseous. Her pride had been all that sustained her then, and it was her pride she relied on now.

Teeth clenched with determination, she tapped lightly on the sturdy oak door. No one answered. Glancing around, she spied a footman, who assured her that his lordship was indeed within. Puzzled and a little worried, she returned to the door, turned the knob, and stepped inside.

Anthony was not at his desk. Instead, he sprawled in a wingchair before the empty hearth, his long, muscular legs stretched out before him. He looked extremely disheveled, with his waistcoat unbuttoned, his cravat loosened, and his hair sticking out in odd directions.

"What do you want?" He barely glanced at her.

Resisting the urge to flee, Linnea shut the door and steeled herself to walk forward. "Anthony, we must talk."

"Must we?" He raised a tumbler to his mouth and drained it. "Why? Why now, for God's sake, when I'm three sheets to the wind?"

Linnea recognized the scent of brandy at the same time she spied the bottle on the floor. "You mean you're foxed," she said evenly.

His lips curved into a moody smile. "Clever girl. I knew there was a reason I married you. Sometimes I need to remind myself that there *was* a reason other than . . ." Breaking off, he reached down to refill his glass.

"Actually, it was about . . . our marriage that I wished to speak. Or rather"—she curled her fingers—"about us."

"Lord save us, you do choose your moments. This is my third bottle, m'love."

She opened and shut her mouth. "Oh. Well. I suppose this can wait."

"On the other hand," he went on with a laugh, "perhaps it's the best time to talk. This way you can be sure of receiving an absolutely frank answer." He leaned back, surveying her with a boldness that made her gaze shift to the paper-strewn desk.

"What, er, have you been doing?" she asked, thinking to progress to the matter by degrees. "Other than drinking, I mean."

"Going through Roger's notes. My mother didn't want them."

Ill-at-ease, she walked over and cast an eye over the top page of the nearest stack. What she saw surprised her. "Your brother was a radical?"

Anthony snorted. "He was a visionary. He dreamed of change, of a society where no one starves, where ordinary men can get a fair price for the fruit of their labors. He believed all people should be educated, regardless of rank or birth. He cared about them all, every man, woman, and child in our country." He looked at her with a sudden, penetrating fierceness. "If one of us had to die, it should have been me."

She glanced at him sharply. "Is that why you're drinking? You're trying to kill yourself?"

"No. I'm trying to kill the pain." He smiled suddenly, a lightning-swift change of mood that blew straight through her defenses. "Come here," he coaxed, his voice husky and golden warm. "Help me kill the pain, Linnea. You could do it, you know. You have it in your power."

"How, Anthony?" she asked steadily. "What can I do?"

Twin blue flames burned in his eyes as he assessed her slowly, from head to toe. "For a start," he suggested, "you could come and sit on my lap, and we could loosen that bodice a wee bit. Do you know how long I have wanted to see you naked? From the moment I met you, I've wanted to—"

"Please don't," she said, with quick dismay. "Please, Anthony, not now, not when you're drunk."

His short laugh had a bitter edge. "Just because I'm drunk doesn't mean I'm unable to function, y'know."

"That's not what I mean. I came here to talk to you, not to—"

"Not to have you make advances at me," he mimicked. He shoved a hand through his hair and set down his glass. "Very well, Linnea. What *did* you want to discuss? Our wonderful marriage? Or did you come to argue on behalf of your captain?"

"He is not *my* captain. And while we are on the subject, I would like to know what you said to him this morning."

"I told him to stay the bloody hell away from my

wife. What did you think, that I'd give him carte blanche to do as he wished?"

"There was no need to threaten him. I've told you I intend to keep my marriage vows. Unlike you."

Immediately, her heart sank. Her meaning had been that he had never made her a similar promise, but what came out sounded more like an accusation.

"Unlike me," he repeated slowly. "Would you care to clarify that remark?"

"I only meant . . ." She moistened her lips, racking her brain for a way to explain without sounding like a fishwife. Finally she said, "Do you or do you not . . . have a relationship with Lady Lindcastle?" Her heart beat wildly as she waited for his answer.

"I do not. I've already told you that."

"So you are telling me that you do not have a mistress?"

Please say it's true . . .

"If I did, would you believe me?" He rose to his feet, laughing harshly. "Of course you would not — you're far too discerning to be fooled by a seducer's lies."

Too crushed to answer, she simply stared at him.

"I never promised to be faithful to you, did I?" He sauntered closer and jerked up her chin, impaling her with his eyes. "Do you remember what Grandmama said? Men have needs, *ma belle*. And since you have neglected to see to mine, it should hardly surprise you that I go to other women."

Intensely aware of him, of his body, of his hands, she squeezed shut her eyes. "And if . . . if I

261

were to see to those needs?" she faltered. A vibrant, anticipatory shiver ran through her at the knowledge of what she was offering.

There followed a moment of heavy silence, then his hand fell away. "I wouldn't want to inconvenience you, sweetheart," he drawled. "In any case, you'd only be wishing I were dear Gabriel. And I wouldn't like that."

Stunned and affronted, her eyes flew open. "What an insufferable thing to say," she choked out. "What Captain Theale and I feel for one another is . . . is pure friendship. It is just like you to make it sound tawdry."

For a moment his face hovered over hers, chillingly beautiful except for his mouth, which seemed to mock her with its wicked twist. Then, to her consternation, as he shrugged and returned to his chair. "We should never have married. This marriage is a sham." He refilled his glass and downed it in a single gulp.

"Oh, Anthony," she said, in helpless misery.

"Leave me in peace, Linnea. Go away, before I do something I regret."

Defeat swept through her, defeat and an almost absurd, latent apprehension at what appeared to be a threat. "As you wish," she said sadly. "Forgive me for invading your sanctuary. I shall not do so again."

"Nor shall I invade yours," he murmured.

Chapter Fifteen

Sometime during the night the idea came to Linnea, an idea so fitting, so inspired, that she lay between wakefulness and sleep for what seemed like hours, her mind drifting with possibilities until at last she dozed again. At dawn she emerged from a slumber that had been riddled with dreams—hazy, bizarre dreams that left her feeling more disheartened than ever. Yet she forced herself to rise, determination driving her to disregard her exhaustion and fear of failure. Dressing quietly, she listened at Anthony's door to be certain he still slept, then she descended to the ground floor and entered his library.

Roger's notes.

That was what she had come to look at. But for the first few moments she sat behind that great mahogany desk, she could only gaze around, absorbing the essence of a room that was her husband's domain, breathing in the mingled scent of leather and lemon polish and books.

And brandy.

Unmistakably, it lingered on the air, recalling her to her purpose—to read through enough of Roger's writings to evaluate whether there might be sufficient fare for a book.

A book to be published in Roger's memory.

A book that might possibly provide the means to ease her husband's pain.

A cursory inspection revealed that the papers were not sorted into any order. Many of them were scribbled essays, some unfinished, others in draft form, many of them complete. They were fervent arguments, clearly springing from the heart of a man who cared passionately for the poor and unfortunate. Yet they were also the dreams of an idealist, she decided as she skimmed over treatises dealing with such topics as the principles of republicanism, the plight of chimney boys, and the advantages of a progressive income tax to provide for the aged and helpless. The writing style was literary and clear, full of wit, balanced and persuasive in content.

Impressed, Linnea sat back, chewing the tip of her finger. If Anthony agreed, perhaps Roger's work could be compiled into a publishable form. And perhaps, just perhaps, Anthony would be pleased enough to look at her with new eyes, pleased enough to give her a fragment of his heart.

At best, it was a gamble, but she clung to the belief that it was possible, that she had a sporting chance to save her marriage. Her plan might achieve nothing, might even arouse Anthony's hostility, but she had to try. Anything was better than doing nothing at all. Anything was better than yielding to defeat.

Hearing sounds that indicated that the servants

were about their morning tasks, she glanced at the clock. She had better leave. She didn't want Anthony to discover her here; she needed time to prepare what she would say to him, to think through her speech very carefully. Still, she felt the urge to linger for a few more moments, to drink in the masculine flavor of the room, to allow her eyes to wander over the walls, the books, the carpet. Then her gaze lowered to the desk itself, and for no reason at all she pulled open the drawer in front of her.

It was full of bills and receipts, notes and scraps of notes. She poked through them idly, without any particular interest other than a mild curiosity because they were Anthony's. Then, recalling the need to hurry, she started to close the drawer when a folded slip of paper caught in the crack. Without pausing to think, she tugged it out and opened it . . . and felt as though she'd just been punched in the stomach.

It was an IOU from Sir Gideon Buscot to Lord Carrock for "a night of erotic delight" with Sir Gideon's personal *fille de joie,* a woman bearing the preposterous name of Fifi Divine.

A carefully preserved IOU.

"To be redeemed at any time."

Linnea wanted to sob with impotent fury, weep with the knowledge that her plan was doomed to failure before she'd even begun. Her half-formed hopes for the future crumbled as a sick mass of despair gathered in her throat. What a fool she was—a gullible, starry-eyed, romantic idiot—to believe for one moment that she could win her husband's love. What could she offer Anthony when he had women like this Fifi Divine to pleasure him, when it was strumpets he wanted? Staring down at the IOU, she tortured herself with images of what someone with such a name would look like, what sophisticated pleasures she could provide.

Then, repulsed, she shoved the paper back into the drawer and stumbled from the room. Was this the sort of thing that men did frequently? Or was it only men like Anthony and Sir Gideon Buscot who traded women as though they were objects? Humiliation shivered inside her as she remembered how Anthony had warned Sir Gideon away from her. Perhaps he had thought Sir Gideon wished to negotiate a trade, she thought bitterly.

Reaching her bedchamber, she slammed shut the door and locked it, not caring if she woke every sleeping soul in London.

She is a lady. That was what he had told Sir Gideon. Illogical rage shot through her at what had seemed a compliment at the time. Apparently being a *lady* was a strike against her; *ladies* were not enough for men who preferred doxies in their beds.

"Linnea?" Anthony's voice, sharp with concern, came clearly through the door. "What's happening? What's wrong?"

Linnea drew in a shuddering breath. "Nothing." Her voice came out strained, peculiar. "Nothing that a divorce cannot mend," she added, more strongly.

The doorknob rattled. "What the devil are you talking about? Unlock this door at once."

"Go away." Swaying slightly, she clutched at the bedpost. "I don't want to talk to you, Anthony. Go away and leave me alone."

Silence greeted her statement; the only sound to reach her ears was her own thundering heart.

Then Anthony's footsteps retreated and there was more silence—a silence so complete it enclosed her like a tomb.

Already regretting her ill-considered words, Linnea collapsed onto the bed. With a low moan, she curled her fingers into the coverlet, bunching it into great clumps of fabric as she strove to control her sobs. *Come back,* she wanted to cry. *Come back, it doesn't matter. I love you no matter what.*

But of course, he was no longer there to hear.

This time, mercifully, she slept without dreams. When she again awoke, brilliant sunlight was splashing through her window with cheerful indifference to her woes. Rubbing her swollen eyes, she sat up, surprised to discover that a few hours of rest had revived her spirits sufficiently to enable her to face the day. Food helped further; by the time she finished her breakfast she could almost pretend that everything was normal, that nothing had transpired to rock her world to its very foundation.

Almost, but not quite.

Time had never passed so slowly as it did during the next few hours. He had left no word of where he was going or where he might be reached. He might be anywhere—out riding, playing cards in

267

some club, drinking himself to oblivion. He might be with Fifi Divine. He might even have left London, gone anywhere as long as it was far away from her.

With a tired sigh, she set aside the book of poetry she'd been trying to read and rested her chin on her hand. In the core of her heart, the last thing she desired was a divorce. She wanted to be his wife, even if it meant that her love would never be returned. It was devastating to feel so vulnerable, so open to potential hurt, but there was nothing she could do about it. She loved him, yearned for him with an unbearable hunger, for his love, for his smile, for his touch.

In the midst of these musings, Captain Theale arrived. Linnea frowned as she heard his voice in the downstairs hall, yet before she could decide what to do, the sound of footsteps told her that the butler had admitted him. Anthony had apparently neglected to tell the servants that this particular visitor was to be denied admittance.

The captain entered the drawing room wearing a very grave expression. "Lady Carrock," he said with a formality she did not correct, "I have come to inquire about your health. I trust you are suffering no ill effects from your fall?"

"I am perfectly well," she responded, smiling mechanically. There seemed nothing she could do but to invite him to sit down; after all, she could scarcely throw him out on his ear. And so she would explain to Anthony when he returned, for she had no intention of deceiving him on this matter.

He thanked her and accepted, perching in a chair some distance from her own. "I am glad," he said. "I must confess to feeling somehow responsible for what happened."

"Nonsense, Captain. It was not your decision, and I am not your responsibility."

"Nevertheless if it were not for me, you would not have been there."

"True, but I cannot allow you to blame yourself." Anxious to change the subject, she inquired, "How does it go on with my cousin? Has your suit prospered?"

His face shadowed. "Alas, no. Mr. Bronsden gave me permission to pay my addresses, but" — he hesitated, pain flitting across his face — "to my eternal regret, Miss Bronsden has refused my offer."

Linnea made an exasperated sound. "Forgive my inquisitiveness, Captain, but did she perchance give a reason?"

"She did not," he said steadily. "I can only assume that she could not find it in her heart to . . . to look upon me with affection."

"You must try again," she began, only to be cut off by a wry shake of the captain's head.

"Until now, ma'am, I have heeded your advice. But there comes a limit to a man's capacity to endure rejection. Without encouragement, a reason to hope . . ." He shook his head. "I cannot."

Linnea debated for a moment. "Captain," she said at length, "I believe I can offer you a reason."

He looked at her. "What is it?"

"It is a little difficult to explain. And I am betraying a confidence by telling you. But I honestly feel it is justified when your happiness — and Iris's — hinges on what I can only believe is a . . . a silly misunderstanding."

"A misunderstanding?" He looked utterly bewildered.

Linnea knew she was flushing. "This is a little awkward for me, but it concerns . . . bust improvers."

"Ma'am?" Her visitor's brows arched very high.

"Some women wear them," she explained in a flustered voice, "to . . . to increase the size of their — "

"I know what they are." The captain's voice shook just a trifle. "But what the dev . . . I mean, what do they have to do with Miss Bronsden?"

"Forgive me, Captain, but do you perhaps recall discussing the subject with another gentleman sometime last Season?" Searching her memory, Linnea added, "I believe it was at Lady Winwood's ball."

"Well . . ." Looking embarrassed, he rubbed the tip of his nose. "Frankly, Lady Carrock, I do, uh, have a vague remembrance that the subject came up. May I ask why?"

"Iris overheard you," Linnea said bluntly.

"Oh. I . . . I see." He frowned. "But if memory serves, we had not even been introduced at that time. Lady Winwood introduced us during the second half of the ball."

"That may be so," Linnea informed him, "but Iris was well aware who you were." She allowed that to sink in before she went on, "And the thing you must understand is that when a young lady's

270

mama insists she wear a bust improver, well, that young lady may feel very sensitive about it. And if she hears the object of her fancy make jesting remarks about women who use them . . ."

"You need say no more," said her visitor quietly. "I understand perfectly. I admit I did joke about them. I hope you do not think too poorly of me for doing so. It was insensitive and wrong of me, particularly in such a setting."

Before she could answer, a footman entered carrying a letter upon a silver salver. For a horrible, paralyzing instant she thought it was from Anthony, feared that he had written to say he was not coming back. Then her heart shifted again as she saw it was the long-awaited letter from the publisher.

Attempting nonchalance, she picked up the letter. "Please excuse me for a moment, Captain. This is something I must open now."

Her caller bowed his head as, with trembling fingers, she broke open the wafer and scanned the brief missive. Then she glanced up, elation surging through her.

"He wishes to see it," she said emotionally. "I know it means nothing, but I am so happy. It is the first step, you see."

"The first step?"

"I'm sorry, I'm making no sense. This letter is from Mr. Egerton, the publisher I contacted concerning my book. He wishes me to send the manuscript to his office as soon as it is convenient."

Immediately, the captain lost his morose look. "Congratulations, Lady Carrock. That is splendid!"

"Yes, it is. Thank you." Yet even as the pleasure throbbed through her she could not help thinking how different it would be if it were Anthony sitting there, Anthony smiling that soul-searing smile of his, congratulating her, saying how proud he was of her. Saying *that's my girl* . . .

You're chasing rainbows, whispered an insidious voice in her head. Even now he is probably with someone else, breathing tender love words into her ear, kissing her, murmuring easy flattery that sounds so beautiful and means nothing . . .

Squelching such thoughts before they became unbearable, Linnea drew a deep breath. "Captain Theale, you once said that if you could ever perform some service for me you would do so. I was wondering whether . . ." She stopped, nervously reconsidering what she was about to ask.

"Ma'am, I would be honored," he said at once. "What is it you wish me to do?"

She stole an involuntary glance toward the door. "I wonder if you would escort me to Whitehall. I should like to take my manuscript to Mr. Egerton at once, this very day."

This time she noticed the captain did hesitate, though only for an instant. "I understand your eagerness, Lady Carrock. And I am entirely at your disposal. We can leave this instant, if you like."

"You are very kind. I must go and change, but I promise I will not keep you waiting for long."

Leaving the sitting room, she issued orders for the carriage to be brought round, then proceeded upstairs. Perhaps she ought not to have asked for this favor, but she did not wish to go alone. And

272

taking her maid or a footman would simply not be the same as having the companionship of someone who understood her nervousness and excitement, someone who sympathized with her goal to become a published novelist. Captain Theale was a man who read novels, rather than scorning them. Moreover, he was a friend. And if Anthony did not like it, well, Anthony should have been here himself, she thought tautly. After all, if he had been here, perhaps she would have confided in him . . .

But the memory of that loathsome IOU ran like a current through her mind, setting her teeth on edge, making her push aside the guilt that was battering at her heart. She was doing nothing wrong, nor was she betraying her husband in any way. She was simply asking for another man's escort to a place she was a trifle anxious about visiting.

And that was all there was to it.

Despite an aching head, Anthony had been out riding since sunrise. He could always think best when he was riding, although his thoughts were frequently so cheerless that it felt more like a penance than a pleasure. Today, his reflections were even more unpalatable than usual, for Linnea's mention of divorce had shocked him severely.

Where the devil had he gone wrong?

He had tried to woo her, to charm her. He had repressed his natural urges and agreed to a marriage in name only. He had bent over backwards to take her to places of interest, given her the support and council she had desired. Most important of all,

273

he had been faithful to her. And what the bloody hell had he gotten in return?

Suspicion. Accusations. Rejection. And, to add soul-mangling injury to insult, the anguish of knowing she preferred another man to himself. Did she regret her marriage? Was she in love with Gabriel Theale? The possibility ate into him like acid, firing a jealousy so intense it burned its way into his brain.

When he had married, he hadn't expected this to happen. He'd desired her, of course, but he had never anticipated that he would come to care for her, to love her with a ferocity that left him dizzy. The walls he had erected around his heart were supposed to have protected him from this emotion, but somewhere along the line those walls had failed him. Somehow, despite the walls separating their bedchambers, Linnea's presence in his life had created doors where there had been no doors, carried light into a life that had been laden with darkness. She had made him vulnerable, destroyed his walls, then given him back the darkness.

And he dreaded the return of that darkness more than he had ever dreaded anything in his life. He wanted to run from it, to hide from it. He wanted the light.

Swept with desolation, he tipped back his head and stared upward at the clouds. He loved her, damn it! But, crazy as it sounded, he was afraid to tell her.

The irony of it nearly made him laugh. All his life he had been able to charm any woman he chose; even the ones he hadn't wanted had thrown themselves at him. And he hadn't appreciated it in the least, had taken them all completely for granted. Now his only desire was to win the heart of his own wife—and he didn't know how.

Restlessly, he thought of the previous evening, when he had spent hours sifting through piles of papers dealing with idealistic causes. Reading through his brother's work had awakened him to the purposelessness of his own life, the way he was wasting it, doing nothing to justify his existence here on earth. Perhaps it was because he had been drinking that he had felt so lost, or perhaps it was because he had yearned for Linnea's company. But as always her door had been locked.

Whatever the case, by the time she had made her appearance, he had been too foxed to be cautious. All his hurts had surfaced by then, all his guilt, all his rage. And so he had answered her with sarcasm, treated her with a churlish mockery that had really been aimed at himself. His worst mistake, of course, had been to allow her to believe he had a mistress, but the way she had accused him while defending her captain had provoked him beyond endurance.

And then she had offered what he had longed for so desperately—herself.

It had been the worst cut of all. He had been caught wholly off guard, electrified with surprise. But he had also seen how she had had to shut her eyes before she could make that offer, how she had shuddered visibly, as though the mere notion of lying naked in his arms was more than she could bear.

275

And so, his pride stung, he had turned her down.

Remembering, an anguished groan rose in his throat. He must have been insane. It had been the moment he'd been waiting for, his chance to teach her, to show her all that existed in his heart.

And now she wanted a divorce.

His jaw hardened. Well, he had absolutely no intention of giving her one. It was unthinkable, absurd. He had taken her for better or for worse; she was his wife, and he'd not give her up, not if she begged him on bended knees, not if she wept enough tears to fill an ocean. If she liked, they could have one of those polite aristocratic marriages like so many did, but he was not voluntarily going to lose the only woman he had ever loved.

That decision made, Anthony turned his bay homeward. He had no idea what he would say to her, but he was definitely going to say something. The important thing was that he must keep his temper. He would say nothing wounding or caustic the way he had last night. He would reassure her that they would be happy, that he was no ogre to be feared. Somehow he would convince her that divorce was out of the question, that he was not such a bad bargain after all.

Heading up Piccadilly, he tried to shut out his problems by concentrating on the external—the sounds and colors and odors of the street. He focused on the rhythm of his powerful bay gelding, the scent of the breeze, the warmth of the sun on his back. He disregarded acquaintances, even ignored the Duchess of Weyland as she waved madly

276

at him through the window of her vis-à-vis. Then he reached Albemarle Street and his whole body went rigid.

For straight ahead of him, rounding the corner not ten feet away, was his own carriage. And Linnea and Captain Theale were inside.

Mr. Egerton proved to be a spare, balding man with bushy gray eyebrows and a gruff, businesslike manner. "Of course Miss Austen's works have done very well for us," he explained to Linnea and Captain Theale after a preliminary polite exchange. "But we must be cautious. Book prices have risen to more than five shillings per volume, which is a great deal for most people to spend. Buyers are cautious, your ladyship. To be frank, most of our volumes of fiction sell to the circulating libraries."

Outwardly calm, Linnea perched on the edge of the chair before Mr. Egerton's desk.

"I understand," she said quietly. "And I am not expecting miracles. But I believe in my book."

The publisher inclined his head. "I am glad to hear it. But I'll warn you that a great deal of hackwork has been thrust onto the populace over the last decade or so. These days the public has an appetite for realism." As if sensing Linnea's dismay, his thin face took on a warmer expression. "But I do not mean to discourage you. There is always room for another good work of fiction."

"I am sure Lady Carrock's novel is not hackwork," inserted Captain Theale.

"I am sure it is not," Mr. Egerton said courte-

277

ously. "But I cannot promise to buy the copyright outright. It might be better if we published on commission. But of course that is something we can discuss later."

"After you have read it," added Linnea with a rueful smile.

"Exactly."

Linnea stood. "Thank you for taking the time to see us. You have been very kind."

She shook hands with the publisher and followed him to the door of his office, Captain Theale a little behind. Murmuring a dignified farewell, she stepped through to the outer office, which was currently unoccupied.

And that was when reality skewed into nightmare. For, occupying a chair not three feet from where she stood, sat Anthony, his long legs stretched out before him, his arms crossed in a leisurely posture.

"Hello, my dear," he drawled with horrid affability. "You did not expect to see me, did you?"

Chapter Sixteen

"My lord," Linnea faltered, shocked almost to the point of swooning. "How . . . how did you . . . ?"

"I followed you." Anthony's tone lost its cordial note as his icy gaze fixed on her escort. "Thank you, Captain. Your services are no longer required."

"Perhaps you misinterpret the situation. Lady Carrock requested that I—"

"Good day, Captain Theale."

Very conscious of Mr. Egerton's presence, Linnea gave the captain a shaky smile. "It's quite all right," she said, in what she hoped was a reassuring tone. "Lord Carrock will see me home."

As the captain bowed and stalked from the room, Anthony's hand closed round her elbow. "Pray excuse us," he added, with a glance at the publisher. Then, without any attempt at an explanation, he propelled her toward the door.

Outside, Linnea attempted to pull away. "Anthony, for heaven's sake, let go of me! How dare you treat me like this!"

To her dismay, he did not even look at her. Instead, his grip tightened as he marched her toward the carriage, whose steps had already been let down by a stone-faced footman. Under the pressure of those insistent fingers, she had no choice but to climb in. She sank onto the squabs and waited for him to follow, but he did not join her. A glance out the window revealed what she had overlooked in her distress—her husband had arrived on his bay thoroughbred. She glimpsed him now, as he swung astride the great horse, his Greek-god face as remote as Mount Olympus.

During the drive back to Albemarle Street, her consternation gave way to anger—anger at being followed, spied upon, treated so churlishly before the eyes of strangers. Moreover, she resented the boorish way her husband had dismissed poor Captain Theale.

Arriving at home, she descended from the carriage and whisked into the house and across the hall into Anthony's study. Hearing the door close behind her, she turned, ready to take him to task for what he had done.

Instead, she stopped stock-still, her throat closing on a wave of pure panic.

Since the night of Evangeline's ball, her fear that Anthony would strike her had gradually dissipated. For the first time in her life she had started to feel safe and secure, protected rather than threatened. Yet in one sickening flash, that was all gone, wiped away by the realization that she had finally done it. She had finally made her husband truly, savagely angry, as consumed by rage as her father had been the night she had turned down Mr. Winterbottom's offer. She could see the white-hot fury in his eyes, in the pinched look about his aristocratic nose, in his harsh, uneven breathing.

She also saw what he held in his hand.

"By God, madam," he grated, "you have gone too far this time."

As he started toward her, Linnea took an involuntary step backward, glancing wildly around in search of a weapon with which to defend herself.

Her action caused him to halt. Through a terrified haze, she watched the way he followed her gaze down to where his fingers curled around the riding crop. Something flickered in his eyes. "You think I'm going to hit you with this?" he said oddly.

Hating herself for showing fear, she only shook her head and took another betraying step backward. Slow, deep shudders rippled inside her, unreasoning and mindless and blind to all logic.

Swearing profanely, he hurled the crop away. "Stop looking at me like that! I'm not going to beat you, you little wretch. Though any other man would certainly do so—you're enough to try the bloody patience of a saint!" He covered the remaining distance between them and seized her shoulders. "Did I not forbid you to have anything more to do with that man? What the devil do you mean by disobeying me?"

Yes, he was furious. And yet, incredibly, he did not strike her. He did not throw her to the floor or shake her. He was not even gripping her hard enough to cause pain. His anger was intense, but controlled.

281

"Y-Yes," she stammered. "Yes, you did. But you have no right to forbid me to see a friend."

"On the contrary, I have every right! Any man has the right to prevent his wife from indulging in irresponsible clandestine behavior."

As her fear receded, she allowed a portion of her outrage to show. "Exactly when have you become so blameless you can judge what is irresponsible? You, who . . . who *dare* to admit you are unfaithful to me, have the gall to object because I choose to have an innocent *friendship* with a man who is — "

"Friendship," he mocked. His fingers tightened a little. "Can you honestly believe that any man would want only friendship from you? Are you really that naive?"

Linnea's mouth fell open with indignation. "What a tottyheaded thing to say! Captain Theale has no more interest in me than he has in . . . in Princess Caroline, for pity's sake! It just so happens that he has been in love with Iris for months! In fact, he proposed to her only yesterday but unfortunately she . . . she rejected him."

Not noticeably appeased, Anthony gave a rough laugh. "That doesn't surprise me in the least. Iris Bronsden has her sights set on bigger fish than your Gabriel. But I'm bloody well damned if I'll countenance his consoling himself with you!"

Infuriated anew, she cried, "He was not *consoling* himself with me! And even if he were, you have scarcely any right to complain when you associate with women like *Fifi Divine!*"

She could see she'd caught him off guard with

that one. "How the devil do you know about her?" he demanded.

"How I know does not signify. What matters is that I do know." Her voice trembled a little as she asked, "How many others are there, Anthony? Do they all have such ridiculous names?"

"There are no others!" He flung the words at her as he released her shoulders and turned away.

She wet her lips and stared at his back, confused and shaken and afraid to believe. "Then . . . then why did you say there were? Last night you admitted—"

"Well, I lied."

An anguished mass of hope and doubt writhed in her stomach. "You expect me to believe that? You must think me completely green, my lord. Green and utterly stupid."

He wheeled around. "Do you really want to know what I think of you?" Seizing her wrists, he slowly, inexorably, backed her against the bookshelves. "I think you are the most exasperating, maddening, infuriating woman in existence. But for some reason I can't get you out of my mind. Every time I'm near you, I want to do this . . ." And his mouth plunged down to claim hers.

Somewhere, in the depths of her mind, she expected it to be a punishing kiss. But it was not. Instead, it was highly sensual, infinitely erotic. His mouth moved over hers with searing hunger as he skillfully mingled his tongue with hers. Dimly, she noticed that though he maintained his imprisoning hold on her wrists, he was also gentle. Stunned, bemused, she found herself opening her lips more

283

fully, responding to his thrusting tongue as it emulated the rhythmic motions of lovemaking. There was no possibility of resistance, no possibility of mistaking his desire for anything but what it was — profound, virile, a potently masculine yearning to conquer, to possess and to vanquish.

At last he lifted his head, though his mouth hovered mere inches from her own. "There," he said in a raw, unfocused voice. "Does Theale make you feel like that?"

Why had she expected him to say something loverlike? Just when she had been ready to forgive him, a renewed spurt of fury made her snap out, "Why do you persist in saying such things? If I did not know better, I would think you were jealous."

"I am," he murmured, close to her ear. "I'm jealous as hell. You're all I think about, Linnea." He pressed his aroused lower body more snugly against her, his breath hot against her cheek. "Day and night. Every minute. Touching you, wanting you . . . how long have you known him?"

"Days," she gasped.

"That is not what you led me to believe. You said he was a close friend whose opinion you valued."

"Well, I . . . I lied," she admitted with a flush. "I had not even been introduced to him when I said that. In fact I took the name Gabriel from my—"

"From your what?"

"If you must know, I . . . I took it from my novel!" Every muscle in her body tensed with defiance.

284

"Your novel? What novel?" His grasp on her wrists loosened as he stared blankly down at her.

"The novel I've been writing. For two years."

"Good God, is that what you do when the door's locked?"

Linnea nodded, her heart plunging as his face changed from astonishment to wrath. "So that explains what you were doing in a publisher's office! I suppose it never occurred to you to confide in me?"

"I did not think . . . I would get a sympathetic response."

She winced as his expression darkened. Until this moment she had not realized how spurious her motive sounded. How could he believe her when he did not understand about the years of ridicule she had endured? Even to her own ears, her statement sounded flimsy, a weak excuse for deceit.

Her husband obviously thought so too, for sarcasm dripped from his tongue as he said, "Oh, really? Did you get a sympathetic response from Theale? Is that why you took *him* into your confidence?"

"Yes," she said with a broken sob. She freed herself with an abrupt twist. "And since you're so curious, let me tell you he was happy for me when Mr. Egerton asked to see my manuscript! *He* was here to escort me. *You* were not!"

Anthony's face took on a very still look. "That's all very well," he replied, his voice edged with a terrible new softness, "but he is not your husband, my dear. I am. And while I realize I am not your *beau ideal,* I'm going to remain your husband.

There will be no divorce. Nor will there be a book. I absolutely forbid you to publish anything."

"You . . . you cannot do that," she whispered.

"Oh, yes I can! I'll be damned if I'll let you publish a story with a character named after Theale. Bloody hell, Linnea, don't you know what people will say? Or don't you care?"

"I didn't name him after Captain Theale," she insisted desperately. "I didn't even know the man's name until the night of Evangeline's ball."

"Do you really think anyone will believe that?"

"Obviously you don't!" Hysteria bubbling within her, she darted over to the desk and yanked open the top drawer. "As for your claim of fidelity, my lord, I have a hard time believing it when I find priceless little gems like *this*"—she crumpled Sir Gideon's IOU and threw it in her husband's face—"lying around."

"What the devil—?"

Blinded by tears, she hastened toward the door.

"Linnea, come back!"

She did not turn around.

Despite the presence of the servants, Anthony's voice chased after her as she ran up the stairs.

"Linnea, this is nothing. It doesn't mean anything." A despairing note entered his voice as he shouted, "I never meant to redeem the cursed thing! I'd forgotten it was there. *Linnea!*"

She wept until she was exhausted. She felt drained, desolate, torn in half with emotion, yet when the tears finally ceased she saw a ray of hope, a shining star in the night black firmament of their marriage.

He had not hit her.

But he had not followed her up the stairs, either.

She sat up, mulling this over. Now that she was calmer, she could think more rationally. She could remember Amanda's advice. *Go to him,* the marchioness had advised. *His pride may keep him from you forever, forever, forever . . .*

Filled with a dogged new obstinacy, she jumped to her feet. "I will try again," she vowed through set teeth. "And again and again and again."

He was sitting in the same chair he had occupied the night before, but this time he was not drinking. He did not so much as move when she approached.

Daunted but determined, Linnea sank to her knees at his feet. "I'm sorry," she said softly.

His eyes shifted to her face. Then, as if he were very weary, he reached out and touched her hair. "For what?"

"For not believing you, for not confiding in you. For" — she made a convulsive gesture — "for everything."

"Are you sorry you married me?"

She shook her head. "No. Not that."

His hand stroked down to her shoulder and rested there. "Well, that's something at least." He paused. "Why didn't you tell me?"

"About . . . my book?"

"Yes."

"It's rather hard to explain." She drew a deep breath and placed her hand over his. "You see, all

287

my life my parents have belittled my desire to write. It may sound odd, but all that scorn did something to me, deep down, on the inside. They made me feel, well, shriveled, as though I were an aberration that no one could accept. They tried to make me feel as though I were doing something disgraceful. If they caught me writing, they would sneer and make derisive remarks."

"And you naturally assumed I would do the same." He sounded bitter.

"Well, you did call me a bluestocking," she reminded him in a small voice. "And you have never given me the impression that you were . . . were . . ." She floundered for a word that would not offend.

"Literary?" he supplied, rather wryly. "You are quite correct. I am not." He gathered up her hand and clasped it between both of his. "But that does not mean I'm incapable of understanding. I'm sorry I called you a bluestocking. I never intended to hurt you."

"I know," she whispered. Rallying her courage, she added, "And the reason I confided in Captain Theale was because he reads novels." Her eyes focused on the top button of his waistcoat as she related how she and Iris had come upon Captain Theale with a book tucked under his arm, and how later he had come to call only because she was Iris's cousin. "But even then," she added, "I only told him because of a silly slip of the tongue."

For a long moment he did not respond. "I be-

288

lieve you," he said finally. "So where does that leave us?"

The question loomed between them, a tentative bridge that had yet to be crossed by either of them.

Linnea clenched her free hand until the nails bit into her palms. This was the moment she'd been waiting for, a God-created opportunity to offer him her love. But how? Her pulse hammered madly as a veritable fountain of words spurted through her head. *Talk to me . . . touch me . . . tell me how you feel . . . do you still want me, do you care for me at all? . . . Can I really take away your pain? I love you.*

There came a rap on the door.

"What is it?" Anthony growled.

"An urgent message for milady, milord." A footman entered, and carried a folded sheet of paper over to Linnea.

Withdrawing her hand from her husband's grasp, Linnea scanned through the spidery handwriting. "It's from Miss Blainsworth," she said unevenly. "Grandmama has taken a turn for the worse. She wants me to come at once."

Hours later, Linnea sat by her grandmother's bedside, gazing helplessly down at the gaunt, sunken face that had once been accounted beautiful by her contemporaries. Now Mrs. Northcliff's eyes were glazed, and every breath rasped out of her as though it were her last.

"Dear Grandmama," Linnea murmured. "I wish I could do something to make this easier for you."

In the adjacent rooms, the relatives were gathered—Iris, Aunt Bronsden and Aunt Gordon, and Linnea's mother. Evangeline had been and gone, declaring that there was no point to being there—Grandmama would no doubt be alive the following morning. The men were downstairs, smoking and talking, perhaps even playing cards.

Except Anthony. Though he was not in the room at present, he had scarcely left Linnea's side since they'd arrived. He had seen that she ate and drank, urged her to rise and stretch her limbs every so often. But he had not asked her to leave. He had seemed to understand her need to be with her grandmother in these final hours of the old woman's life.

"How is she?" Iris paused in the doorway, then walked over to stand beside Linnea. In a low voice, she added, "I would not have believed she would last this long. Can you believe it is nearly midnight?"

"I know," Linnea said sadly.

"Why don't you try to get some rest? Miss Blainsworth has offered to take your place."

"I'd rather stay here."

Iris stifled a yawn. "Well, I'm going to lie down. I'm exhausted, both our mothers are asleep, and Aunt Gordon is snoring fit to wake the dead—oh dear, I should not have said that. I beg your pardon, Grandmama."

"Don't worry, Iris. If she heard you, she was amused."

"I doubt she can hear. Doctor Willis says her mind is completely gone."

Linnea stroked her grandmother's blue-veined

hand. "Grandmama never set much store by Doctor Willis."

Iris gazed down at their grandmother. "She really was a remarkable lady."

"She still is," Linnea said softly.

Anthony surveyed his sleeping wife with a tenderness that snatched at his heart. Urged by Miss Blainsworth, who tiptoed past him with a finger to her lips, he scooped Linnea gently into his arms and carried her down the corridor to one of the spare bedchambers.

As he laid Linnea down upon the cool sheets, he heard a clock strike somewhere in the distance. Three o'clock in the morning, he thought wearily. He should have insisted that Linnea retire long before this.

As his own fatigue crept over him, he gazed down at her face, entranced by some indefinable quality embodied in those quiet features. Then, with a sigh, he removed his boots and cravat and stretched out beside her, wrapping one arm around her waist so that their bodies touched.

Nestling close, he drank in her feminine, floral scent and rubbed his cheek against her silky copper hair. She smelled wonderful, felt wonderful. Certain that he had at last found heaven, Anthony kissed the soft skin beneath his wife's ear and closed his eyes.

And for the first time in years, he slept peacefully.

Just before dawn, a discreet tap upon the door jerked Linnea awake. To her amazement, she was lying on a bed with Anthony's arm slung over her waist and his warm breath stirring her curls. For a moment she simply lay there, too astounded and contented to move, but a second series of taps sounded too urgent to ignore. Easing herself out from under his arm, she rose and went to the door.

"She's awake," whispered Miss Blainsworth, "and asking for you, my lady." In response to Linnea's look, she added, "I think she's near the end, poor soul."

Linnea hurried to her grandmother's bedside. The old woman's eyes were focused on the ceiling and her lips moved soundlessly. Then her once-resonant voice wheezed out, rather more strongly than Linnea expected.

"I'm taking a long time to die."

"It's been hard to watch you suffer," Linnea answered quietly.

"Lord, child, I'm not suffering." The dull blue eyes shifted slowly to Linnea. "I've been here all the time, you know. Watching all of you—you and Iris and that rapscallion of yours and my fool daughters and those idiots they married."

"Now, Grandmama . . ."

"Don't you 'now Grandmama' me," said the old lady weakly. "You listen to me and don't interrupt. You're my favorite granddaughter so I'm going to warn you. I've changed my will again. A third of my money goes to you, a third to Iris, and the last third to Blainsworth. I made that will a week ago and it's the last one."

Love rippled through Linnea, love for the old woman whose eccentricity had created such upheaval in her life. "Don't think about money now," she chided tenderly. "We all love you, Grandmama. That's what is important."

"You all thought . . . I was touched in the upper works . . . when I made that other will. Don't argue with me, girl—I haven't the time for it." The old woman cleared her throat, but the wheezing would not go away. "Well, I'm not sorry I did it that way, because some good came out of it." There was a long pause before she continued, less distinctly, "Was a test of character. To see how they'd behave. Scurrying around like little mice, all trying to find the biggest slice of cheese." Her gaze started to come unfocused. "I know you had your reasons. About your father . . . you'll do what you can to help your mother, you understand? Once you get your own marriage in order . . . I know you and she don't rub along too well, but she's a good girl, my Rosalind. When she was a little girl, she used to bring me flowers . . ."

Linnea suddenly became aware that Anthony had come up behind her. "How is she?" he whispered.

"As well as can be expected," replied the old lady. "And her hearing still functions perfectly, thank you." For a short moment her eagle eye brightened as it fixed on him. "So, young fellow . . . are you still behaving yourself?"

Anthony's arms slipped around Linnea's waist, offering the warmth and solidity of his body. "I've been a virtual saint since my marriage."

"Hummf." The old lady's lips curved, and several seconds passed—seconds in which her strength ebbed almost visibly, like a rainbow whose colors were fading fast. "Tell your grandfather . . . that I loved him. I loved Northcliff too, of course. And Mary Lawrence was right for Henry. But tell him that . . . he always had a place in my heart."

"I will," Anthony assured her, with a gentleness that brought tears to Linnea's eyes.

"Know you will. You're . . . a good boy." Mrs. Northcliff's eyes slid shut.

And gradually, very gradually, her breathing stopped.

"She's gone," murmured Miss Blainsworth sorrowfully.

Linnea stared at her grandmother's face, denial heaving inside her. Then, with a sob, she turned into the welcoming comfort of Anthony's arms.

The next hour passed in a blur. The family was roused from their slumbers and given the news, but Anthony refused to allow Linnea to remain any longer. During the carriage ride back to Albemarle Street, he cradled her in his arms as though she were a baby. And she savored it, needed it, for fatigue had burrowed its way into every muscle and pore of her body. Never in her life had she been as tired as this, not even on the night that her brother had died. It was as though, by witnessing her grandmother's death, she had somehow been drained of some of her own vital life force.

Overriding her protests, Anthony insisted upon carrying her up to her room. "You're exhausted," he informed her as he mounted the stairs.

"But I'm too heavy for you," she murmured. snuggling against him.

"A fine opinion you have of my manly strength."

"But aren't you tired?"

"Very. I imagine we could both use some sleep."

Linnea's breath caught as she wondered whether he would ask to share her bed. Even though she had not had the leisure to absorb it at the time, it had been glorious to wake up beside him this morning. She had never realized how lonely a bed could be until the moment she had so briefly experienced the alternative.

Linnea's maid appeared just in time to open the door to her bedchamber. "I'll take care of her ladyship," Anthony told the girl as he settled Linnea onto the bed. "You won't be needed."

Maria bobbed a curtsy and withdrew, closing the door behind her.

He regarded her with an odd, half twist to his mouth. "Where is your nightdress?"

She gestured toward the wardrobe.

He located the garment and returned to her side. And then, with exquisite gentleness, he began to undress her.

Tremors throbbed through her as his hands brushed over her, caressing lightly as he undid buttons and loosened ties. Even half-conscious with weariness, she wanted him to love her, but she was too spent to say it.

When all that remained was her shift, she gazed up at him and waited hopefully. Aching for his touch, her breath quickened as he drew it up and over her head. Her heart did a queer little lurch at the way his eyes roved hungrily over her nakedness. Yet he did not touch her. He only looked.

Then, far too quickly, he reached for her nightgown. As he yanked it over her head, Linnea saw the tiny bead of perspiration on his temple and realized, with some age-old feminine instinct, that he was not rejecting her. He was simply being noble.

"Is there anything else you need?" he asked as he arranged the covers over her.

Yes, she wanted to cry. *You.*

Tell him . . .

She summoned her courage. "You," she croaked, blushing crimson. "Couldn't we . . . couldn't we sleep together, like we did last night?"

With a queer glimmer in his eyes, he sat down and took her hand. "It wouldn't be like last night, love. I'm not as tired as I was then."

"You mean . . ."

"I mean we wouldn't be sleeping," he explained with a hint of a smile. "And God knows you need your rest. Those dark circles under your eyes won't go away on their own."

Moved almost to the point of tears, Linnea gazed up at him, then a humiliating confession tumbled from her mouth. "I have to tell you something . . . about our wedding night. There was another reason why I didn't want to let you . . . make love to me."

"And what was that?" Ever so slightly, his brows pulled together.

"There were marks on my back," she said painfully. "I didn't want you to see them. They were made with a riding crop."

He looked away from her for a moment, his mouth clenched as if with scalding, impotent fury. "You should have told me."

"I couldn't," she said simply. "I didn't know you well enough. I didn't know that you weren't going to be like him. It took me a long time — until yesterday, in fact — to realize that I was . . . safe."

With a fierceness that took her quite by surprise, he dragged her up and into his arms. "You'll always be safe with me, do you hear me? I'll always protect you — with my life if need be. No one will ever hurt you again. I swear it."

Incongruously, something in his promise triggered the onslaught of tears she'd been trying to hold back. Weeks and months and years of pain gathered in a torrential emotional storm that spilled from her eyes and racked her body and drained what little energy she had left. While she cried, he held her close, rocking her, holding her, being everything she had ever wanted and needed. He murmured soft words while she hiccuped unintelligible words and buried her face in his shirt. Then at last it was over, replaced by a drowsiness so intense she felt as though she were sliding down an abyss . . .

"Rest well," he whispered as her swollen eyelids drooped shut. He kissed her on the mouth, once, twice, and then a third time.

"Anthony . . ." She was barely able to murmur his name before her mind tumbled away into darkness.

I love you.

Chapter Seventeen

Mrs. Northcliff was to be laid to rest beside her husband, who was buried in Gloucestershire, but a service was to be held in London for the many people who had known her. At breakfast on the day of the service, Anthony mentioned his desire to leave for Sundridge directly afterward.

"There will be no reason for us to stay on here," he remarked as he scanned the front page of *The Morning Post*.

"I suppose not," Linnea murmured with relief. She smoothed a hand over the black silk skirt of her mourning attire and tried not to look too happy about missing the rest of the Season.

"At any rate, we should reach there by dark. I wish we could get an earlier start, but it's not practical, what with the funeral being so late in the afternoon." He folded the newspaper and set it aside, regarding her with a small smile.

"We could wait until morning," she suggested.

He shook his head. "No, we'll go today. Sundridge will do us both more good than you can imagine. The sooner we arrive, the better it will be." His smile changed, heated in a way that made her pulse skitter. "I've waited a long time," he added softly, "to take you there. And take you I shall."

She searched his face, wondering if she understood him correctly. Was he aware of his double entendre?

"As you wish," she said, trying to look unruffled. "I will instruct my maid to pack."

"I'll go and tell her. I've a few things to do this morning, but you need do nothing but rest, *ma belle.*" He rose to his feet, gazing down at her with a look of tender amusement. Then he bent and kissed her on the mouth. "Save your strength for me," he whispered. "And finish your breakfast."

After he left the room, Linnea smiled to herself and reached for another slice of toast. Since the night of her grandmother's passing, he had been fussing over her. He insisted she rest during the better part of each day, hounded her if she did not eat enough to suit him, and intercepted visitors he believed would tire her. The only thing he had not done was make love to her, which was the one thing she wanted most desperately.

She had tried to make that clear to him in a perfectly ladylike way. She had provided him with opportunities. She had brushed against him as though by accident. She had made subtle, encouraging remarks. She had even offered to rub his shoulders, for pity's sake. But all to no avail. Instead of behaving in a manner even remotely resembling rakish, he had displayed a most exasperating obtuseness. The odd thing was that he was always caressing her—ruffling her hair, stroking her arm, touching her cheek. Really, it was most frustrating!

Still, as matters stood, they were closer than they had ever been before, and this comforted her. Having had so little harmony in her life, she treasured the peace which reigned between them as a sailor might prize the aftermath of a hurricane. Tranquility was of the greatest value, which was why she allowed several of her concerns to remain unsettled.

One of these was the matter of her manuscript, a subject she dared not bring up for fear she would find his sentiments regarding its publication unchanged. Another was the IOU, which, though it no longer seemed the threat it once had, continued to prick her with its long-reaching thorns. For the question that plagued her was this: what would prevent him from returning to his former ways?

He had claimed he had been faithful to her since their marriage, and she believed him. What she could not understand was why. After all, he had not been in love with her when they married. He had not promised fidelity. And she had spurned him, told him to go elsewhere.

So why? And more importantly, how long would it continue?

But fearing to destroy their newfound peace, she did not ask. For the present, it seemed enough that he was with her, fussing over her like a doting husband. And while he had never actually said that he loved her, it did seem as though he had come to care for her as a person. And that was something to be cherished.

The three days since Mrs. Northcliff's passing

had not been easy ones for Anthony. Even before the old lady's death, he had noticed that Linnea looked pale and thin. At the time, he had feared she was languishing for love of another man, but he no longer believed that.

He had had an illuminating talk with Captain Gabriel Theale, a conversation that had made him feel like a fool for the way he had behaved. His supposed rival had not only admitted to being in love with Iris Bronsden, but he had also confided his courtship troubles. Every time Anthony remembered that discussion, he wanted to laugh. Bust improvers! Good lord, the man had really put his foot in it. Unfortunately, he had been unable to tell the poor fellow what to do and so, in a flash of inspiration, he had referred him to the Marquis of Vale. "Vale is a genius at dealing with females," he'd assured Theale. "You've been introduced? Good. Tell him I sent you." Even now, Anthony's eyes lit with mischief as he envisioned what Vale's reaction might be.

His smile lingered as he entered his library and strolled over to his desk. Roger's notes and essays were all he had left of his brother, and he intended to box them up and take them to Sundridge. The portraits he didn't need—he had only to look in the mirror to see Roger's face. No, it was the essays that were precious. They represented the essence of what his brother had been.

Yet when he looked down at the papers, it was Linnea who occupied his thoughts. Every time he mulled over what she had told him, it did something queer to his insides. What a splendid, game

301

little creature she was. Ridicule had not stopped her from writing. Abuse had not shattered her spirit. Despite that bastard of a father, she had stubbornly persevered.

Suddenly, his mouth twisted. Was he any better? He, too, had put a spoke in her wheel by cruelly forbidding her to publish her story. Worse, he had not yet retracted those words, nor even apologized for them.

He frowned slightly. He still disliked the notion of his wife publishing a story featuring a hero named Gabriel. And even if she changed the character's name (which he would insist that she do), he didn't much care for the idea. He'd once read one of Mrs. Radcliffe's books — *The Mysteries of Udolpho* — and found it to be utter nonsense. It was all midnight castles and bleeding nuns and walking corpses. Ridiculous stuff!

On the other hand, he desperately wanted Linnea to love him. He ached for her love even more than he ached for her body. So he told himself that if it made her happy to write such twaddle, what the devil did it matter? He would tell her tonight that she could do as she wished.

Tonight.

Tonight he would make her his own. As a wave of desire streaked through him, he wondered how he had managed to resist her thus far. For the past three days, she had been tempting him in the most enchanting, delicious ways. He could almost laugh when he thought what a dullard she must think him. He had pretended not to understand, partly because he cared more for her health than for his need to possess her sexually, and partly because her alluring little ploys so delighted and charmed him that he did not want them to end. In fact, he broke out in a sweat just thinking about some of them.

But tonight, when they arrived at the ancestral home that meant so much to him, they were finally going to have their honeymoon. He was going to undress that sweet body and explore those luscious curves with his hands. He was going to kiss those beautiful lips, stroke every inch of that creamy body, and whisper every love word he knew into her ear. At last, at last . . .

His loins throbbed hotly as he imagined it. She would be shy at first, but her natural sensuality would overshadow that. She would be beautiful and responsive and eager to learn. And he would teach her everything he knew, give her more pleasure than she had ever imagined. And beyond that pleasure, he would give her his love, himself, which was something he had never given before, not to any woman. Somehow he would have to make her understand that. He must convince her that she was different from the others, that when he kissed her he was not thinking of anyone else.

Because there had never been anyone else.

Odd, how he had never realized that in all these years. He remembered how Roger had once tried to tell him what a meaningless existence he was leading. He also remembered how he had scoffed at Roger and called him a stuffy old man. A misguided saint. A prudish scholar.

But Roger had been right. God, how he wished

he could tell him. *You were right, old man. You were right.*

Linnea was fiercely glad when the funeral service ended. She had tried not to cry, but in the end she had done so, mainly from grief, but also out of anger at those around her. Of all her relations, only Iris had wept. Evangeline had sat, petulant and ethereal in her black mourning gown, unbending in her resentment toward the woman whose death made the termination of her London Season necessary. Neither Aunt Bronsden nor Aunt Gordon nor Linnea's mother had shed a tear. Her uncles and father had worn expressions of polite resignation. Only Anthony's grandfather, Lord Sayer, seemed genuinely distressed, for he had leaned heavily upon a stalwart footman and looked very tired and ill.

As for Anthony's mother and Aunt Allison, neither had had more than a passing acquaintance with Margaret Northcliff and had only attended out of respect for the family connection. Nonetheless, Linnea had several times noted Lady Allison Hallett dabbing at her eyes. Roland's mother obviously possessed the sensibility her son lacked.

At least Roland had not been present, and for that Linnea was extremely thankful. She did not care that his absence denoted a lack of respect; all that mattered was that he was out of her sight. Of course, she did not mention this to Anthony as they traveled back to Albemarle Street.

She glanced at him tenderly, her heart full of

love. He had been so kind and attentive, so understanding and sympathetic. Not at all like her father. It perplexed her now how she could ever have thought he would hurt her. She had wronged him so thoroughly she was ashamed.

She rested her head on his shoulder and closed her eyes, dreaming of the moment when he would show her Sundridge. Tonight, she thought with sudden determination. Tonight she would tell him that she loved him. And if he did not reciprocate, if he could not say that he loved her too, well, she would not make a fuss. She would love him anyway, give herself to him gladly and without regret. Eventually she would give him children—the heir he no doubt desired, and others, too, little girls and boys with chestnut hair and eyes as blue as a summer sky. And perhaps, someday, he would love her in return.

As this passed through her head, he kissed her brow. "Here we are, love. Now I want you to go into the house and rest until I come back. I won't be long."

"Tell your grandfather I said thank you," she reminded him as a footman opened the door and let down the steps. "And tell your mama and aunt that I shall miss them."

Despite the sadness of the occasion, Linnea entered the house with a spring in her step. Rest, she thought. No, she could not rest. It was wonderful to be pampered, but she was too excited, too jubilant. *Forgive me, Grandmama, for being happy on this of all days, but I know you would have understood. You see, he's taking me to Sundridge and I have such high hopes . . .*

Eager for Anthony's return, she entered the drawing room and rang for tea. She would not drink very much—it was never wise before a journey—but for the first time in days she was truly hungry. When the tray arrived, she selected a slice of pound cake and bit into it, savoring the rich, buttery taste. Anthony's cook had baked biscuits, too, but these were packed and ready for the journey into Kent.

Before she could eat any more, however, she heard the jangle of the front doorbell. Footsteps crossed the hall and the door opened. There were voices—a high-pitched female one raised in seeming protest against the objections of the male servant.

Growing curious, Linnea left the room and peered down the stairs, but the footman's broad body hid the caller from her view. "Who is it, John?"

The footman turned, his pugnacious jaw thrust out in lofty outrage. "There is a Young Person requesting to speak with you, my lady."

Linnea started down the stairs, then stopped in surprise. The caller was the lovely young pregnant girl she had seen on the street so many days before. "Who are you?" she asked.

The girl made an awkward curtsy. "The name's Dolly, milady. Dolly O'Malley. And I got something to tell yer ladyship that I think you ought to know."

Linnea studied the girl, taking in her delicate bone structure and bloated figure. "Let her in, John," she said quietly. "Send her up."

With evident reluctance, the footman stepped aside. "The kitchen's the place for the likes of her," he muttered.

Dolly's eyes widened as she stepped into the hall. "Coo," she breathed, walking past the trunks and valises waiting to be loaded into the coach. "Ain't this grand."

Linnea led the way to the drawing room and sat down, gesturing for Dolly to do the same. The girl obeyed, her gaze settling on the pound cake with such longing that Linnea offered a slice.

Immediately, Dolly reached out. "Thanks," she mumbled as she selected a piece and bit daintily into it.

Linnea waited for her to chew and swallow before saying, "Now what is it you wish to tell me?"

"Yer going on a journey, ain't you?" Those lovely dark eyes gained sudden intensity.

Linnea studied her. "Why should that concern you?"

"It just don't seem to me to be a good day fer travelin', that's all. Yer ladyship oughtn't to go."

"On the contrary, it is an excellent day for it. Now please oblige me by stating your business or I will have to send you on your way."

" 'Tis about . . . yer husband, milady."

Linnea stiffened. "What about him?"

Setting down the remainder of her cake, Dolly grew oddly sorrowful. "Yer a woman of the world, ain't you? You know wot men are—specially a gent like his lordship. Now me, I've got no choice but to humble meself." She spread her hands in an abject gesture. "I've got me unborn child to think of.

307

Happen yer ladyship knows what I mean?" Her gaze fell to Linnea's middle, as if to suggest that a child grew there.

Linnea was not about to satisfy her curiosity on that score. "I wish you would get to the point," she said tersely.

To her astonishment, Dolly dragged a handkerchief from her pocket and burst into tears. "I'm tryin' to, milady, only 'tis so hard to tell you."

Linnea watched her with distress. "Hush, now, do not cry. Tell me what the trouble is and perhaps I can help."

The girl shook her head. "Sometimes I have visions, milady. Visions that come true. One of 'em were about you. So I've come to warn you not to go with yer husband." With surprising strength, she clutched at Linnea's arm. "You mustn't go! You'ud be in terrible danger, milady, and yer child, if you be carryin' one!"

Linnea stared at her. "This is nonsense. I don't believe a word of it. And what in the world does it have to do with my husband?"

The girl's sobs stilled, and for a few seconds she did not speak. Then her head lifted. "He's the father of me child, milady," she whispered. "He seduced and abandoned me, and now he won't even give me money for the babe, though I've begged and begged."

"I don't believe you," Linnea said, her tone very flat.

"As I live and breathe, milady, 'tis Gawd's own truth. It weren't just once neither. He were after me again and again back last year when I was still a respectable housemaid. But of course a maid with a package like this"—she patted her belly—"ain't exactly welcome. Turned off without a character, I was."

Linnea searched the girl's eyes. "Why should I believe you? Any man could be the father."

"You want proof?" Dolly sniffed and blew her nose. "Well, 'tis only natural. How 'bout this? I seen that big ole scar he's got on his leg right here"—she touched her upper thigh—"from that accident he had when he was young. 'Tis a wicked-looking mark, milady. It fair made me want to cry every time I seen it."

Linnea felt as though a hand had closed around her throat. A scar? An accident? She didn't even know if the story was true.

"I'll give you money," she said curtly, "if you promise not to come back."

"Oh, I kin promise that. If I kin git to my auntie in Plymouth, I know she'd take care of me. Why, the very same thing happened to her when she was a girl, so I know she'd take me in. But that ain't why I came. The world's a frightful place, milady. There's no saying what people will do, and no hope of changin' most of 'em. I seen you afore. I been watchin' you, wonderin' if you carried his child. Then I started off having this vision, see? Over and over I've had it, like a flash of picture in me head. Don't go with him, milady—"

"Stay here," Linnea broke in, her voice strained. "I'll be back in a moment."

She hurried from the room, deliberately keeping her mind a blank. Money. She had quite a bit of it

309

packed in her smallest valise, which was still in her room in case she needed any of her toilet articles before their departure. Plunging into her bedchamber, she tore open the valise and found the banknotes — pin money she had never spent. Surely this would be enough to satisfy the girl — it would be a small fortune to someone who had worked as a housemaid.

Shoving her hair from her face, she rushed back down the stairs and into the drawing room, and stopped dead. The room was empty. The girl was gone — and so was the pound cake. She gazed around, clutching the money, staring at the chair which only moments before had been occupied by a startlingly beautiful, very *enceinte* young woman.

Why had she gone?

Upon inquiry, no light could be shed upon the mystery. The footman, John, had not seen the girl depart, nor had anyone else. Dolly had simply taken the cake and vanished. "Good riddance," opined the footman, shaking his head in disapproval.

Confused and heartsick, Linnea returned upstairs and restowed the money into the valise. No matter what, she would not breathe a word of this to Anthony. This was not the time to hurl recriminations at him, not now, not when all she wished to do was to make him happy.

After all, she'd known he had a past. She'd even had a hazy idea what sort of licentious things a rake might do. Yet Dolly's story had horrified and repelled her. On the other hand, it hardly coincided with what she knew of her husband. Anthony was not the sort of man to behave in such a heartless fashion. He was sensitive, warm and kind. And she certainly did not believe all this nonsense of visions. Perhaps the girl was mad.

But the tale nagged at her. Suppose he regarded women of the lower class—like Dolly—as fair game, exempt from the gentleness he extended to his own wife? No, Anthony was not like that. Yet that girl had described a scar upon his leg! The fact that Linnea had not seen the scar herself meant nothing. Dolly would hardly have dared mention it if it were not real. And if Dolly really had seen it, how else could she have done so, except in the way she had suggested?

Feeling unwell, Linnea went to the window and gazed down at the street, instinctively searching for some sign of her caller. But the street was empty. And Dolly O'Malley was nowhere to be seen.

Light drizzle fell from the sky. The gloomy weather matched Anthony's mood, for the entire afternoon had been tension-filled and cheerless. Under normal circumstances, he would have feasted his eyes on the Kentish scenery, but as he stared out the window of the lurching coach, he was too aware of Linnea.

Worry gnawed at him. This morning he could have sworn she had been anticipating the journey down to Sundridge with pleasure. Yet ever since they'd left London she had been oddly subdued, though she had assured him that nothing was wrong.

311

That was pure humbug. Obviously, something was bothering her, though he was damned if he knew what. Instinct told him it was something other than her grandmother's death. In dealing with that, she had turned to him for comfort, which he had given in full measure and would give again if she asked.

But this was different. Now she avoided his eye, turned away from him rather than toward him. And it hurt far more than he would have thought possible.

What had he done to displease her? He racked his brain, trying to recollect some inadvertent transgression. Or could it be nothing more than shyness over the night to come? No, no, that was doing it too brown. This was more than shyness, more than fatigue or sorrow or nervousness.

Silently, he cursed his decision to bring Billings and the maid along in the same carriage, for if they had been alone, he might have coaxed Linnea into confiding in him. Instead, they were prisoners of convention, forced to limit their conversation to inconsequential topics until they could be rid of their servants.

By the time they entered the lowland area where Sundridge was located, heavy storm clouds and gathering dusk shrouded what had once been a great forest area. As far as Anthony was concerned, the Kent Weald was the finest corner of England, and though many of the trees—ash, hazel, chestnut, and the ever-present oak—had been cut down, many patches of woodland remained to lend it a lush pastoral beauty. There was

312

but one fearsome memory attached to this setting, one tearing fissure to mar the perfect sylvan picture.

As the miles passed, he braced himself. His heart always hammered when they approached the copse of trees where Roger had been shot. It wasn't fear. It was a kind of taut animation, an uncontrolled flow of energy that coursed through his veins. It made him want to run and shout and drive his fist into something made of flesh and blood. No matter how much he tried to prepare himself, it was always like this — and it was worse when it was dark, like the night when those deadly masked figures had been waiting.

Gritting his teeth, he strove to control his breathing, to concentrate on reality, on the soothing motion of the carriage, on his consciousness of Linnea. He tried to think of the night ahead, of what making love to his wife for the first time would be like. But of course that did nothing to calm his heart.

When they neared the copse, he broke out in a sweat. He felt trapped, claustrophobic. Embarrassed, he tried to hide his reaction by turning his face toward the window. His pulse raced like a hound on the scent, just as it had on that long-ago night. Soon, he promised himself. Just a few more miles and they would be past that fatal site. *Soon, soon, soon . . .*

He watched the trees slide by, saw their silhouettes scrape against the darkening sky. He listened with affection to his valet's snores. Poor, old, faithful Billings, who had been with him for so long and put up with so much. How many nights had he waited up, while his master caroused and lusted and drank himself into oblivion?

Thanks to Linnea, he no longer sought such a state. Was he wiser than he used to be? His lip curled. He did not feel any wiser, but by falling in love he knew he had gained something precious. His love for Linnea filled a gaping crevice in his life, poured liniment over hurts he'd thought would never heal. She had done that for him. Pray God he could give something back, and help her to heal her own wounds. Pray God he could make her happy.

Pray.

He had not prayed since he was very young, but now, briefly, he prayed as he had never done before. Instinctively, he knew this was his final chance. Linnea was his last and best and only hope. He had to make his marriage work. He *loved* her. Didn't that count for something? Was he worthy of her? Had he done anything in his life to deserve her love? *Give me this chance, Lord. Give me her love and I'll do anything* . . . Damn, that sounded so inadequate. Frantically, he searched his mind for good deeds, anything he could use to justify his plea to the Supreme Being.

Ironically, when the shots rang out it took a full second for their significance to register. For a fantastical second, they seemed but an extension of his fragmented memories, perhaps even a cruel answer from God. Then, appalled, his body snapped to attention.

Those were real pistol shots.

Chapter Eighteen

"Stand to!" someone bellowed.

Icy coldness sluiced through Anthony. *Again. Holy Mother of Christ, how could it be happening again? There had been no highwaymen in these parts for the past five years.*

He heard Linnea gasp as the coach came to a jarring halt. "Good God, Anthony, what—?"

For the first time in their marriage, he treated her ungently. As any woman would, she reached for him in her fear, but he pushed her aside in his dive for the flintlock pistol under the seat.

Fool, fool, fool. There had been a time when he'd have kept it in his hand, loaded and primed, but like a bloody fool he had cured himself of that weakness . . .

Somehow he found the sleek weapon, cocked it, and brought it up just as the door crashed open. He felt rather than saw Linnea recoil as he pulled the trigger. The maid's screams vied lustily with the crashing report, and the stench of gunpowder filled the carriage. But as the man he had shot staggered backward, clutching his chest, the opposite window shattered. Glass sprayed everywhere. Anthony swiveled in time to see the muzzle of a pistol thrust against his wife's skull.

"Drop it," hissed a vicious voice. "Drop it, or I'll blow her brains all over your coat."

Anthony cast about for an alternative, but there was none. Not when there was a four-barrelled pistol at Linnea's head.

He let the pistol fall.

"That's right," crooned the voice in a gravelly whisper. "Now kick it out onto the ground, way out as far as you can. Good. Now put your hands on your head and climb out."

Anthony obeyed, ignoring the body of the man he had shot. Blood roared in his ears, heightening his senses so that he could hear and see and smell with extraordinary keenness. A part of his brain counted the number of opponents, measured the distance between himself and the man who was obviously the leader, noted the man's height and probable weight. "Leave my wife alone, damn you," he said harshly. "If it's money you want, we've plenty of it. You can take it all."

There were a few guffaws, but no one answered. Instead, someone jammed a pistol into his back.

Fists clenched, he watched Linnea as she disembarked. Head held high, her face betrayed nothing of her fear, even when she found herself surrounded by malignant masked figures. Unfortunately, both the coachman and the groom lay wounded, a sight which sent Linnea's maid, when she followed Linnea out of the coach, into hysterics.

"Shut her up," rasped the leader coldly.

One of the men struck Maria down with a single blow. She lay unmoving, sprawled like a broken toy,

316

but when Linnea attempted to go to her, the leader dragged her brutally back. Swearing, he dug the pistol so hard into her neck she cried out.

Despite the cold metal pressed against his spine, Anthony started forward. "I don't care who the bloody hell you are—you hurt her again and you'll answer to me."

"One more step," the man snarled, "and I'll do more than hurt her." He grabbed a handful of Linnea's hair and twisted it until she whimpered with pain.

Anthony gritted his teeth. Choked with impotent frustration, he raged inwardly while the blackguard ran a casual hand over Linnea's curves. Anthony's body vibrated with the need to plunge forward, to seize the man by the throat and throttle him. *God, how he hated to feel helpless.* But the knowledge of what could happen froze him. He felt charged with fear—fear for Linnea's life, fear that he would somehow make another fatal mistake. He dared not do anything that would endanger Linnea. If anything happened to her, he would go stark, raving insane . . .

One of the highwaymen had begun rifling through the interior of the carriage, while two others unstrapped the luggage and hurled it to the ground. Items of apparel scattered as they searched for money and jewels. The man who found Linnea's diamonds whooped with glee. "What a set o' sparklers!" he crowed, waving it high. "Soon as I clapped me glimms on this rattler, I knowed the swell was well breeched."

Covertly, Anthony glanced up and down the lonely stretch of country road. Surely the rogues were taking a dangerously long time to rob them. Though this route was little used except by those who lived locally, every passing second increased the chance that some other vehicle would come along. Even now, he could swear he heard hoofbeats beneath the gusting wind.

The other man must have had the same thought. "Stop mauling through that rubbish," he snapped. "Find what you want and take it." With sudden violence, he shoved Linnea to the ground. "Such a shame," he muttered, leveling his pistol at her head. "Such a bloody waste."

Anthony's muscles bunched. "What the devil does that mean?"

There *were* hoofbeats — he could feel the horses pounding over the turf. He fought the urge to turn and look. Why did no one else notice? He could count them, smell them. Their tempo matched the throbbing in his blood. He could see them in his mind — two geldings and a stallion. Their riders crouched low, demanding impossible speed. *He was already going mad*.

"It means," taunted his adversary, "that in a very few moments she will have outlived her usefulness. And so will you."

"Why?" *Distract him* . . .

"Because, that's why. Any more questions, fancy boy?"

Anthony's eyes narrowed as comprehension slammed into him. Only one person had ever called him that.

"No," he said curtly. *You just answered them*.

Now he knew who his adversary was, but he was still afraid. Linnea's life depended on his ability to move quickly, and he did not know if he could do it. He flexed his knees, his hands. All that signified was that he save Linnea. He wasn't afraid for himself. The only thing he feared was failure . . .

"Lope off, lope off!" roared one of the highwaymen suddenly. "Leave the gentry-cull, guv'nor! Someone's acomin'!"

The leader's head lifted. "Damn. Well, I'll have to make this short and sweet, then." He leaned down and put the pistol to Linnea's head. "I hope you're watching, fancy boy."

With the ferocity of a wolf, Anthony sprang. It felt so damned good to move at last, to stretch muscles that had cramped with tension. As he offered himself as a target, he saw Billings lunge for Linnea. A pistol exploded, but whether it was the one at his back or the one held at his wife's head, he didn't know.

Dimly, he heard Linnea scream, but for some strange reason he was lying on his back, staring up at the night sky. Something had knocked him down. More shots were being fired; horses whinnied and hooves thundered. Shouts reverberated through his brain.

Linnea.

Terrified that she had been killed or wounded, he struggled to sit up, but there was no need, for she was kneeling over him. Puzzled, he gazed up at her face, whose features he saw as clearly as if it were daylight. She was crying, he noted. Why was she crying? Despite the dark, he could see the individual teardrops rolling down her cheeks. He tried to lift up his arms to hold and comfort her, but they flopped helplessly at his sides. *Helpless again,* he thought ir-

319

ritably. He watched as she ripped off a section of her petticoat, not understanding why she was pressing the wadded fabric to his chest. Dizzily, he tried to focus on what she was saying.

"My God, my God, Anthony, can you hear me? Please answer me, darling."

It finally dawned on him that he had been shot.

And that was when he felt the pain. Sweet Jesus, how it hurt. Agony spiraled through him, gripping him mercilessly, shuddering through his body as he tried to draw a complete breath. "Linnea," he mumbled, through the nausea in his throat. "Not hurt?"

"No, I'm not hurt." Her voice sounded fragile, faraway. "Lord Vale is here. Mr. Perth has . . . has gone for help, and . . . Captain Theale chased after the highwaymen. One was shot, but the rest . . . ran away."

Anthony tried to turn his head. "Vale?" he said hazily.

"Lie still," came the marquis's voice. "You've been shot, but it's missed the heart. Charles has gone to find a doctor."

He closed his eyes, feeling the warm seep of his blood spilling from the hole in his body. "A mere . . . flea bite," he murmured. "Can't kill me."

He felt Linnea kiss his lips. "Of course not. You have to live because I love you. Do you hear me? I *love* you!"

He tried to smile, to kiss her back. "Love you too. With all my heart."

A curious rushing sound blotted out her reply. For what seemed like a long time he listened to it, wondering what it was. At first, he thought it was the wind, but that had disappeared. It had also grown darker. A blackness he had never known had gathered around him, enclosing him in a warm cocoon. The pain was gone. He wanted to tell Linnea because he knew she would be pleased, but to his utter confoundment he was looking down at her from above. He could see the top of her head, the coppery strands of her hair, the despairing slump of her shoulders. He could see Vale hunkered down beside . . . *his own body.*

Now that was devilish odd. He could see the blood on his clothes, on Linnea, on Vale. He could see his own face. Baffled, he listened to what they were saying. Linnea was sobbing, Vale was trying to soothe her. Anthony glanced around, saw the body of the highwayman he had killed. Linnea's maid, now sitting upright, sat weeping quietly into her handkerchief. Billings was tending to the wounded coachman, who had been shot in the shoulder.

Before he could assimilate more, Anthony felt himself moving away, through a pale gray mist. Frantically, he tried to call out to Linnea, to tell her once more that he loved her, but she did not lift her head. Gradually, the mist narrowed, and as it narrowed he seemed to accelerate through it like a ball through the barrel of a cannon. Far, far ahead, he could see a powerful light, a light so brilliant it would have outshone the sun. Somehow he knew it was the light that drew him forward, that the light offered something far more splendid than he had ever imagined. Yet as desperately as he wanted to go closer to the light, he also wanted to go back to Linnea.

And then, to his astonishment, he saw his brother. Roger was blocking his path, obstructing his progress toward the light. "You must go no farther," Roger told him.

Anthony gazed longingly toward the light, but Roger shook his head. "Not yet, Tony. You were brought here for another reason."

Suddenly the light and mist disappeared, replaced by a dark and lonely country road. The scene was so vivid he could hear the leaves rustle, smell the wind. It was the night he and Roger had been held up, his brother informed him. Fascinated, Anthony watched the highwaymen ride out of the trees to surround the coach. He saw himself climb out of the coach, swaggering a little from bravado and drink. He also saw Roger disembark and look around. The scene flashed by quickly, but he absorbed it all—the highwaymen's taunts, his own threats.

"Now watch," Roger instructed.

Whereas until now the scene had gone by with extraordinary swiftness, at this point it slowed to a crawl. Anthony saw his own furious lunge toward the man who held the pistol. The man fired, and Anthony watched the ball arc over his shoulder, fly past Roger, and sink into a tree. He could absorb all this, and at the same time take note that while it was happening another of the men was taking aim at Roger. Astounded, Anthony followed the progress of that ball as well, watched it drive into Roger's chest and knock him flat. The two shots, he realized, had been fired simultaneously.

"Let go of your guilt," Roger said gently. "You did your best, Tony. It was not your fault."

Then the scene faded and the radiant white light reappeared, filling everything. Bathed with wondrous feelings of peace and love, Anthony gazed at it with enthrallment. Roger was still there, but this time it was the light which spoke to him. *You must go back. It is not your time to come to me.*

Immediately, the tearing pain in his chest returned, yet it somehow seemed more bearable because he was back with Linnea. ". . . don't you dare die on me," she was sobbing. "I won't let you, do you hear? You listen to me, Anthony Stanton. You open your eyes right this minute!"

Anthony opened his eyes.

"He's alive!" she cried out, her hand flying to her mouth. "Oh, thank God, he's alive! Oh Anthony, Anthony . . ." Her voice shuddered and broke as she gazed down at him with intense joy.

Anthony stared up at her, taking in her beloved, grief-ravaged features with a sense of wonder. "Of course I'm alive," he whispered weakly. "It's not my time."

"I've never seen anything like it, milady, not in all my days." The wizened country doctor snapped shut his medical bag and wiped a hand through his thinning gray hair. "I would have placed his lordship's chances at nigh to zero, but his heartbeat is as steady now as it was an hour ago." He shook his grizzled head in bewilderment. "The ball passed clean through him and out the other side, and look at him! I'd say you didn't need me at all."

Linnea gazed down at her sleeping husband. Incredible, she thought, that only an hour had passed since they had transferred Anthony to this small country inn. Incredible, too, that even with all the jostling of being lifted into and out of the coach, the bleeding had not restarted. Granted, he looked nearly as pale as the bandages swathing his broad bare chest.

But he was alive.

Linnea opened her mouth to say that for a time she'd believed otherwise, that he had stopped breathing for what seemed like a number of minutes. But she hesitated to voice what she and Lord Vale had seen.

"I'll come by again in the morning," the doctor continued. "Mind you, I don't approve of your decision not to bleed him. When the fever sets in . . ."

"*If* fever sets in, I will reconsider," she said firmly.

Fever was not going to set in. She knew it beyond a shadow of a doubt. Anthony would live. By some miracle, they had been given a second chance.

Time proved her right. By the following afternoon, Anthony was awake and alert, though exceedingly weak. "Feel helpless as a damned baby," he grumbled, as Linnea plumped his pillow and tucked the bedclothes around him.

She smoothed back a lock of his hair. "You were severely wounded. It is natural that you should lose strength."

He grimaced. "Well, I don't intend to lie about in this inn for very long. Not with Sundridge a bare five miles away."

She smiled lovingly. "You must not be a rebellious patient."

"Little tyrant." Lips quirked, he wrapped his fingers around her wrist. "Come here."

"I *am* here, silly."

"Not relative to where I want you, you're not. I'm an injured man. I need a kiss from my wife."

"Oh, well, if that's all . . ." Blushing, Linnea leaned down and pressed her lips to his with an enthusiasm she hoped would convey the depth of her feelings. When she would have moved away, his hand came to rest upon her nape, trapping her there for another slow, lingering kiss.

"No, that's not *all*," he murmured. "But it will certainly do for a start." His eyes smiled into hers, but he released her with a sigh that told of the pain he was in. "I want to talk to Vale before the laudanum puts me to sleep. Where is he?"

"He's downstairs, with Mr. Perth and Captain Theale." As his eyes drifted shut, she rose to her feet. "I'll fetch him."

Reluctant to leave, Linnea glanced back when she reached the door, noting how relaxed he looked, how at peace. With his dark lashes pressed against his cheeks, he looked far too angelic to have done the things that Dolly had claimed. But last night, when they had undressed Anthony, she had seen the nasty, jagged scar on his upper thigh.

Dolly's prophecy had been haunting Linnea. It was almost as though the girl had known they were to have been held up, which seemed impossible. It must have been merely a strange coincidence. Yet Linnea's doubts remained as she straightened her shoulders and entered the parlor where the rescuers were gathered. All three men leaped to their feet.

"He wishes to speak with you," she told Vale.

"How is he?" put in Captain Theale.

Linnea fought past the block of emotion in her throat. "He . . . seems well, though very weak of course. The doctor remains astounded by his progress." She smiled feebly, suppressing the tears

325

that kept trying to steal out. What a watering pot she had become! "To own the truth, I think the man hoped a fever *had* set in, simply so he could have had the pleasure of saying he told me so."

"Confounded sawbones," said Charles Perth contemptuously. "No better than undertakers, most of 'em. Hang it, the fellow actually had the insolence to object when I pounded on his door! Tried to feed me some Banbury story about how busy he was. Busy, ha! Why, the frippery fellow was wearing his nightshirt!"

Vale and Linnea exchanged glances. "Do you accompany me?" the marquis asked gently.

She nodded, biting her lip. "If you don't mind." She suspected he knew quite well that she could hardly bear to leave her husband for an instant.

When they entered Anthony's room, the patient appeared to be asleep, but his eyes opened at the sound of footsteps. His gaze flew to Linnea first, in that hungry, intimate way that made her heart flipflop, then his face altered as he looked at Vale.

"It was Roland," he said flatly.

Linnea took a seat by the bed, stifling her surprise that he had known.

"Yes," said Vale. "You recognized him?"

Anthony's lips thinned to a grim curve. "Not at once. He disguised his voice too well. It was . . . something he said." His tone held a curious note as he added, "Did you catch him?"

"In a manner of speaking." Vale paused. "He was shot."

Anthony absorbed this in silence. "And?"

Linnea held her breath while the marquis answered, "He didn't make it." She thought of the body, lying close by in one of the adjacent bedrooms, its handsome, cruel face gone still and white — and serene as it had never been in life.

Displaying no visible sign of emotion, Anthony turned his face to the wall. "So. How the devil did you become embroiled in all this?"

The marquis took a seat. "Your aunt had begun to suspect something. After the funeral service, she went to your cousin's lodgings. Hallett's manservant would tell her nothing except that her son had gone out of town."

"Then how — ?"

"She searched his room. Your cousin kept a journal. Apparently he had written down enough to confirm her suspicions. She threatened the manservant with all manner of dire consequences if he did not confess what he knew."

"She *threatened* him? Timid little Aunt Allison?"

Vale smiled slightly. "That is what she told Lord Sayer. She returned to Grosvenor Square in hysterics, but managed to tell a lucid story. Sayer sent a servant around to your house, but you had already left."

Linnea reached out and took Anthony's hand as the marquis went on, "Your grandfather made the decision to take two of the footmen and go after you himself. Unfortunately, in the process of climbing onto his horse, he fell and broke his arm. Vital time was lost while the earl was carried into the house and attended by a physician."

Anthony's lips compressed to a tight line, but he said nothing.

"Your grandfather was desperate. He knew of your wife's close friendship with my wife. He knew . . . of me. So he sent urgent messages to my house

327

and all the men's clubs. They found me in White's. Theale and Perth were with me, and offered their services. We rode hard, hoping to overtake your carriage before anything occurred. Unfortunately, we were a few seconds too late."

"No matter," added Anthony with a grimace. "As you see, I had everything under control."

Vale regarded him steadily. "I've already sent a message to your grandfather. Is there anything else I can do?"

"Yes, you can satisfy my curiosity. Why would my grandfather think he could depend on you? Why not simply dispatch a servant?"

"He knew I would understand the urgency. You see, I also had a cousin who tried to murder me for my title and wealth. The story was hushed up, but one or two trustworthy people knew of it. Your grandfather and the Earl of Besford are close friends. Amanda was staying with the Besfords at the time that the attempt was made. In fact, she was with me when it happened. She saved my life."

"How brave of her," Linnea said, a shade wistfully. "I wish I were not such a coward."

Anthony squeezed her hand. "You're not a coward," he said with peculiar intensity. "You're the most courageous woman I've ever known."

She looked at him with surprise. "But I was terrified."

"Fear and courage are often partners," commented the marquis. "The one does not preclude the other. Only a fool would be unafraid when a loaded pistol is held to one's head."

"You stayed calm," Anthony emphasized. "If you

328

had behaved as your maid did, Roland might have killed you on the spot."

Linnea started. "Oh, Anthony, I quite forgot to tell you that Maria is unharmed. She recovered consciousness only a few minutes after—"

"I know. I saw her."

"You saw?" Linnea stared at him.

Anthony opened and shut his mouth. "Yes," he said finally. "I saw you all. I even saw . . . Roger."

Linnea's eyes widened.

"Perhaps I should leave," Vale said tactfully.

"You don't believe me?" Defiance edged Anthony's voice.

"Yes," the marquis replied, "as a matter of fact, I do."

"Why?"

"There are more things in heaven and earth, Horatio," quoted Amanda's husband softly. "Who am I to dispute what you saw? You stopped breathing. We thought you were gone. And now here you are. Alive."

Anthony's frown changed to a small, drowsy smile. "Alive. By heaven, that has a nice ring to it."

She sat by the bed while he slept. During the long hours of the night, she had stretched out beside him and tried to doze, but she would not do that now for fear of disturbing him.

Instead, she studied him, her weary eyes taking in every small detail—the elegant curve of his cheekbones, the shadowed stubble on his chin, the strong column of his neck. His beautifully-muscled shoulders and chest. If had not been for Roland's villainy, she would have known every inch of him by now. She

329

would have known what it was like to be loved by him. Instead, she had nearly been widowed.

Thank you, Lord, for sparing him.

Folding her arms under her breasts, she closed her eyes and repeated the phrase, over and over, until a sense of tranquility filtered through her seething tumult. Everything would be fine. Everything *was* fine. If only, if only . . .

Someone knocked softly on the door.

It was Lord Vale, and he was frowning. "I think you had better come down," he said pensively. "There's a young woman below who insists she must see you."

Linnea's insides clutched. Could it be—? As she moistened her lips, the marquis shot a glance over her shoulder at Anthony.

"I'll stay with him while you're gone. She's down in the parlor with Charles and Theale."

Linnea nodded. "Thank you." Certain it was Dolly, she descended the stairs with mixed feelings.

Flanked by Charles Perth and Captain Theale, the pregnant girl huddled in a chair near the hearth, her slender hands twisting in the folds of her skirt. "Yer ladyship," she said tearfully. Despite her ungainly figure, she rose and performed a clumsy curtsy. Her eyes were red-rimmed and swollen, her lovely face blotched and pale. "I have to speak t'you."

"Did you come to collect your money?" Linnea inquired, a shade coolly.

"No, milady, I came because . . . oh, God!" She shoved a shaking fist to her mouth. "Them two"— her eyes slid over to Perth and Theale—"they wouldn't tell me nothin', but I know yer ladyship will. He's dead, ain't he?"

330

"No, my husband is alive and well."

"Yer husband?" The girl sniffed and blinked. "Oh, I weren't talkin' about him, though I'm glad enough for yer sake." Her voice cracked. "It don't matter now, anyway."

Linnea stiffened, touched with a soft brush of suspicion. "Once again you are making no sense," she said curtly. "Whom do you think has died?"

Dolly's lips trembled. "Kin I sit down, please?"

Linnea inclined her head.

Dolly returned to the chair by the hearth and pulled out a crumpled handkerchief. "My Roland," she disclosed, mopping her eyes. "I knowed it was agoin' to happen. I warned him, just as I warned you. But he wouldn't listen. He never listened to me. He was always so full of plans, so sure his way was the only way . . ."

Linnea drew a deep breath. "Gentlemen, I think Miss O'Malley and I should talk alone."

The two men exchanged a look. "We'll be in the next room if you need us," replied Captain Theale, rather grimly.

When they were gone, Linnea took a seat. "Yes, I'm afraid Mr. Hallett has been killed." She paused. "How long have you known him?"

Dolly's face took on a hopeless expression. "He's been my protector fer five years, milady."

"I see. So you knew of his plans to murder my husband?"

Dolly buried her face in her hands and nodded. "He's been talkin' about it ever since the other 'un died, but I thought 'twas no more than talk. I never thought he'd do it. Then you fell off your horse, milady, and that drove him near wild. He kept sayin' as

331

how he wished you had broke yer neck. I know it sounds terrible, milady. I told him he ought not to say such terrible things. But he wanted yer husband's place so bad it fair ate him up. He thought if you was dead, his lordship would never wed again. And if there was no child—"

"I understand," Linnea said curtly. "So you lied to me. Roland is the father of your child, is he not?"

Again, the girl nodded. "I just didn't see the need to kill you too. He'ud get the title and money if yer husband was dead." She placed a protective hand over her belly. "I thought you wouldn't go with him if I told you that wicked tale. I didn't want you to be killed. I was afraid you might carry a babe, like me, and I don't hold with killin' children. I tried to find out, but yer wouldn't tell me. Roland, he didn't want to take no chances. He wanted you both dead. But I thought, if there weren't no child, or if there was and it were a girl child, there was no need. He should have been patient . . . waited to see . . ."

Linnea closed her eyes against a flood of horror and pity. "You loved him," she whispered numbly.

"Aye, milady, I did. He was manly and passionate and he treated me better'n any man I ever knowed. 'Twasn't his fault he wanted more than life saw fit to give him. Some of us are just like that. Like me. I wanted to be his wife, but I knew it'ud never be. Gentlemen like my Roland don't marry girls like me. He had to wed his own kind. I understood that. Sometimes he talked about some rich girl named Iris. But he always said he would keep me. He promised he would and he'd have stuck by his word if . . . if he'd lived." The pitiful statement faded to a sob that, despite everything, wrenched Linnea's heart.

332

"Dolly, if he had lived," she said quietly, "he would have hanged. If you had told me all of this the first time, perhaps this tragedy could have been averted."

"I c-couldn't," wept the girl. "I was afeared of what might happen. And he trusted me with his secrets, milady. How could I betray him? I *loved* him. All I could do was to try to warn you."

Linnea's mind whirled with what she had heard. "Tell me," she said slowly, "did Roland have anything to do with Roger Stanton's death?"

"You mean t'other 'un?" Dolly shook her head. "No, milady. That I know fer certain. It just give him the idea. It fed him, if you know what I mean."

"Yes. I think I understand." Linnea stood. "Do you want to see him?"

Dolly gulped. "Where is he?"

"Upstairs."

The next hour was highly unpleasant, but it passed. After Dolly finished weeping over the body of her dead lover, Linnea settled her into one of the inn's bedchambers and made sure she had something to eat. She then conferred with Vale, Perth and Captain Theale about the girl's fate. Like her, they were of the opinion that Dolly should not be turned over to a magistrate.

Drained of emotion, Linnea had a short conference with the innkeeper's wife before she returned to Anthony, who was still asleep. Billings rose as she entered and put a finger to her lips. "Thank you," she whispered quietly. "I'll stay with him now."

When the valet had gone, Linnea gazed with longing at the vacant half of the bed. She had had almost no sleep last night, and there really was plenty of room. For a moment she debated. Then she locked the door and walked around to the far side of the bed. Feeling almost light-headed with fatigue, she slipped off her shoes and removed her dress. Very, very slowly she pushed the bedclothes aside and sat down. Anthony didn't stir. She swung up her legs. No movement. She eased herself down and carefully drew up the covers.

There. She had not disturbed him in the least. With a soft, grateful sigh, she closed her eyes and, muscle by muscle, began to relax. And then a hand crept over her thigh . . .

She yelped.

"Good grief," came a complaining voice. "And here I thought I was finally making progress."

"I thought you were asleep!" She raised herself up on one elbow and peered at him indignantly.

"I was." A slow, slumberous smile curved her husband's lips. "Until a beautiful female crept into my bed and woke me."

"I was not creeping," she corrected. "And I am very sorry I disturbed you. How are you feeling?" She reached out and touched his brow, anxiously checking for signs of fever.

"Rotten. Far too weak to do what I want." His heavy-eyed gaze fell to her breasts, exposed by the gaping neckline of her shift. "Which is . . ."

Linnea's cheeks heated as he described what was on his mind. "Well, we cannot do any of that," she pointed out regretfully. "Not until you are much, much better."

"No, but we could think about it," he said in a wistful tone. "We could talk about it." He closed his eyes. "We could talk about . . . us."

"I'd like that," she answered, and for once felt no shyness.

He was quiet for a long moment, then his hand reached out until the tips of his fingers grazed her cheek. "What a fool I was to think that I could marry you and go on . . . living the way I had been."

Emboldened, she caught his arm and held it against her, pressing the back of his hand to her lips. "You're not a fool," she uttered fiercely. "You're human, that's all. I think you're perfect. You're brilliant, trustworthy, courageous, kind—"

With an unsteady chuckle, he covered her mouth with his fingers. "I don't know about all that, darling, but I swear I've been faithful to you." He paused, staring off into space. "At first, it was only because of a wager, but that didn't last long. I simply didn't want anyone else. I'm not sure, but I think I fell in love with you the first night we met. I know that when I came to offer for you, when I saw you on the floor, crying, it made me absolutely livid."

Linnea winced at the memory. "I was so humiliated that you saw that. I wanted to curl up and die."

"I wanted to strangle your father," he said, with a quiet savagery that even now sent a shiver down her spine.

"And I sensed that violence in you. That's why I was a little afraid of you. That's why it took me so long to trust you."

"God, I wish I'd known. Perhaps I could have said the right thing. I should have made more effort to understand you." His mouth twisted. "Instead all I could think of was seducing you. In fact, it's still all I can think of, lecherous sinner that I am."

Linnea smothered a giggle. "Tell me about the scar on your leg, oh lecherous sinner."

"Aha, so you *were* the one who undressed me. I've been wondering about that."

"I helped," she said primly. "I considered it my wifely duty."

"You did, eh? Well, you were certainly thorough. I'd like to know what you did with my drawers."

"I threw them out. Everything you wore was covered with blood." She shuddered in remembrance. "Except your boots, of course. I believe Billings saved those."

"I see." He slanted her a look from under his lashes. "So my scar bothered you. It's quite ugly, I know."

"It is not ugly and it didn't bother me a jot. I was only curious because . . ." Resting her head on the pillow, she proceeded to tell him about Dolly. "I'm so ashamed that I listened to her," she ended in a small voice. "Do you think you can ever forgive me?"

His silence unnerved her. She examined him nervously, wishing he would open his eyes and say something. How it must pain him to learn of her faithlessness, she thought guiltily. She had been wrong to tell him now. She should have waited until he was stronger before she confessed her perfidy. He had suffered so much and here she was, adding to his countless torments . . .

"I'll forgive you on one condition," he murmured. Opening his eyes, he sent her a drowsy, delicious smile. "You must promise that when I am well you will let me make love to you in the drawing room—"

"Anthony!"

"And in the front parlor—"

336

"Really, Anthony, do be serious."

"—and among the daffodils—"

"You're being ridiculous."

"—or wherever else I wish, at whatever time of the day or night I get the urge. Promise me that," he finished, "and I'll forgive you."

Linnea mulled this over. "What if we have guests?" she said finally.

"We shall excuse ourselves. Politely of course."

"I shall blush and give us away."

"Ah, then that obviates the need for excuses. I shall simply fling you over my shoulder and leer knowingly."

Since she was already blushing, Linnea thought it judicious to change the subject. "So how *did* you get that scar?"

"The horse I was riding refused to take a fence, and I went flying. A splintered rail drove into my leg."

"And you rebuked me for taking risks!"

He snorted. "It wasn't a risk. I'd taken scores of fences, and I knew the course. The horse was simply being obstinate."

"I suppose Roland was with you."

"Yes, but he had nothing to do with it. He wasn't born murderous, you know."

"Just ambitious." Linnea sighed. "How I feel for your poor, poor aunt."

"Let's talk about us," he mumbled. "My head's getting all fuzzy again, and there's something I want to tell you before I do something infamous like fall asleep while you're talking."

She laid a hand on his cheek, tracing her thumb across the rough, masculine stubble. "What is it?"

337

"About that book you wrote . . ."

Her fingers stilled.

"I have no objection to its being published. What I said to you before . . . it was wrong of me. I was too angry to care about your feelings or ambitions. I only wanted to wound you, to retaliate for what you had made me feel." A bitter chuckle dragged from his throat. "Do you think you can ever forgive me for that?"

Linnea studied him, a slow, feminine smile tilting the corners of her mouth. "I'll forgive you on one condition," she said demurely.

"Which is?"

"That you promise to behave yourself and rest so you can heal properly. And then, my dearest love, I promise I will gladly make love with you among the daffodils."

"And in the drawing room," he reminded her drowsily.

"As long as the door is locked."

"Don't like . . . locked doors."

Overwhelmed with love for him, she touched his hair, tenderly smoothing it back from his brow. "No, my darling. There will be no more locked doors between us. No more locks, no more walls, no more secrets."

The rake she had married heaved a sleepy sigh and entwined his fingers with hers.

Epilogue

One Year Later
Sundridge, Kent

"It says that *Miranda* is 'a salutary and superior work which is certain to have been written by a man,'" uttered Amanda incredulously. "Though it 'exemplifies a certain understanding of the female mind, the various personages and situations are too complex and the philosophy too astute to have been composed by a member of the fairer sex.'" Eyes flashing, the marchioness slapped down *The Quarterly Review*. "Of all the insults—!"

"I believe it is meant to be complimentary, my love," the Marquis of Vale said dryly. He glanced down at the sleeping infant at his arms. "At any rate, our own Miranda does not appear to have taken offense."

Linnea picked up the magazine and returned it to her friend. "Do read the rest, Amanda. It gets better, I promise." She snuggled closer to Anthony and gazed wistfully at Amanda's baby. How she longed to hear the vast rooms and corridors of Sundridge echo with her own children's voices.

Anthony draped his arm along the back of the

sofa and squeezed her shoulder. "At least you're guaranteed anonymity," he teased. "Or have you changed your mind? Is it fame you now desire?"

Linnea shook her head. "No," she said simply. "I only want people to read and enjoy it."

"Goodness," Amanda commented. "It says 'the deft construction of this sparkling'—now that sounds nicer!—'comedy of manners reminds the reader of another author whom time revealed to be a woman.' I'm sure he means Jane Austen! 'Be that as it may, *Miranda* is replete with wit, sense, and an admirable moral tone. The character of Sir George Rhodes is multi-faceted and skillfully etched, while that of the villainous Lord Edward . . .' "

While Amanda read, Linnea studied the faces of those around her. Iris positively glowed, a consequence of her upcoming marriage to Captain Theale. Linnea had never been able to discover exactly how their difficulties had been resolved; all Iris had been willing to say was that she and Gabriel had had a long talk and at the end of it they had kissed passionately. The captain must have acquitted himself well, for Iris had had every one of her gowns altered to fit her natural figure and had burned all her bust improvers.

Linnea's gaze shifted to Captain Theale. How glad she was that he had struck up such a close friendship with Anthony. Lord Vale and Mr. Perth were also good and loyal friends, but for some reason the ties between Captain Theale and her husband were especially strong. He and Iris would be leasing a nearby manor house after the wedding, so they would be seeing a great deal of each other in the future.

Lord Sayer was dozing contentedly on the sofa. He

had aged in the last year, but his gout had been troubling him less and his arm had healed nicely. As for Anthony's mother, she had declared herself inspired by her daughter-in-law and had taken up poetry-writing, something she had been longing to do for years. Her efforts were meritorious, which was fortunate since she had taken to reciting her verses to anyone who would listen. Even now, a sheet of paper rested in her lap as she patiently waited for Amanda to finish.

Yes, much had changed during these past months. Amanda had had her second baby—a healthy little girl named Miranda Emily. Aimee Perth was also in a delicate situation, which kept her husband twitching and clucking over her until (as Aimee had crossly put it only moments before) she was fit to go mad. And Lady Allison Hallett had chosen to emigrate to America, where she now made her home in Richmond, Virginia.

Dolly had gone with her. Lord Vale had made an honest effort to find the girl a husband, but Dolly would have none of any man he produced. Astonishingly, Roland's mother had taken a firm liking to the girl who was to bear her grandchild; shortly after the child was born, the two women had set sail, each of them determined to make a life for herself in the new world. Lord Sayer had provided them with funds, and according to the last letter he had received, all three of them were doing well.

All the highwaymen had been rounded up, and Linnea's diamond necklace had been recovered intact. Lord Sayer had hired Bow Street runners to track the rogues down, a feat they had accomplished in less than a week. None of the men had been killers, but their association with Roland Hallett had been enough to condemn each man to seven years' transportation.

As for Linnea's parents, her mother no longer resided with her father. It had taken repeated urgings from Linnea, but Mrs. Leyton had finally summoned the courage to leave her husband, and had taken up permanent residence with a cousin in Bath. As expected, Mr. Leyton had not been favorably disposed toward the plan, but Anthony's threats had convinced him to accept it, albeit with a lack of grace. This past winter Mrs. Leyton had spent a month at Sundridge, a period during which Linnea had striven to improve her relationship with her mother. Enough progress had been made so that they now corresponded on a regular basis.

While these thoughts were passing through her head, Linnea had been very conscious of Anthony's thumb lightly rubbing the curve of her shoulder. Knowing her husband well, she sent him an answering look. Their eyes linked for a brief moment, then Linnea returned her attention to Amanda before a blush could form on her cheeks.

"In any event, you must be pleased with the general tone of the review, Linnea, even if the reviewer does leap to silly conclusions regarding your gender. *Miranda* is wonderful. *I* certainly loved it," the marchioness added loyally, "and so did John."

"I could hardly put it down," inserted Aimee Perth. "I was so relieved when Miranda refused to elope with Lord Edward." She sighed, and pressed a delicate hand to her bosom. "And I adored Sir George. He was so honorable and romantic! In fact he reminded me of—"

342

"If I hear one word about that Lochinvar fellow . . ." warned her husband.

Aimee blinked. "Lochinvar? Why, Charles, I was going to say he reminded me of *you*."

"I am glad you enjoyed it," Linnea put in quickly, as Mr. Perth turned beet red. She shot a mischievous glance at her husband. "I am sure Anthony did not expect to do so."

"Untrue, my love. I was simply expecting it to be more—"

"Lurid," finished Linnea with mock sorrow.

"Bleeding nuns," Anthony explained serenely. "Moaning corpses. Ancient, decaying buildings filled with an evil atmosphere."

Everyone laughed.

Then, to Linnea's surprise, Anthony brought her hand to his lips and kissed it. "But if you had chosen to write that sort of story," he said tenderly, "I would have been equally proud of you."

Deeply moved, Linnea looked into his eyes, unable to speak for the emotion that tightened her throat.

"Are you going to write another?" inquired Captain Theale.

"Another?" Anthony arched a brow. "Has she not told you? She's halfway through a sequel already. The publisher practically begged her to write one."

Linnea found her voice. "Now, Anthony, you know that is an exaggeration—"

"No, I don't," he countered with an irrepressible grin. He looked at their guests. "She also has another project in mind." As he paused, Linnea knew he was thinking of Roger. "When my brother was alive, he did a great deal of writing . . ." He proceeded to summarize the themes of Roger's work,

343

and their decision to publish the essays in the form of a book.

Meanwhile, Lord Sayer had opened his eyes and was listening intently. "By George," he said, "that's a famous notion. Ha! Roger's radical notions may shake up the realm a bit, but with the way things stand now, I'd say it's in need of it." The old man's voice shook with an emotion that plainly embarrassed him, for his cheeks flushed and he cleared his throat several times.

Tears also glistened in the Dowager Lady Carrock's eyes. "Indeed, it is a splendid idea, Anthony. We should have thought of it years ago."

"You must give Linnea the credit, Mama. The idea was hers."

"Indeed I do thank her—for that, and for marrying you. Linnea, my child, you have made my son so very happy. For years I have worried about him, ever since . . ." She dabbed at her eyes and waved a hand. "And then you came along and worked your miracles on him. I vow I cannot thank you enough."

"There is no need to thank me, ma'am. I love your son very much and will do all in my power to see that he remains happy." Hoping to distract the dowager, who looked ready to burst into tears, Linnea added bracingly, "Would you care to read us your poem now? I am sure we would all love to hear it."

The dowager's face brightened. "Are you certain? I am not boring you, am I?"

"Anyone who is bored can leave now," Anthony said teasingly. "You see, Mama? No one is leaving. We are all agog to hear your latest creative effort."

"Oh, very well."

344

While Anthony's mother recited the love poem she had been laboring over for three weeks, Anthony's thumb began making wider and wider circles on Linnea's shoulder. Linnea did not look at him, though her body hummed with sensual awareness. In the last year Anthony had taught her much about lovemaking. She had learned of the wild, exhilarating heights that one could soar to; she had learned, too, of the soothing, shimmering beauty that came after, the endearments and the peace, the comfort and the warmth.

When he stopped touching her, she knew why. She understood it was because he was as affected as she, that for him there could be embarrassing consequences.

Later, she thought dreamily. Much later, when they could finally be alone, he would take her in his strong arms . . .

Everyone was clapping. Linnea joined in, feeling a little guilty because she had missed a portion of the poem.

Anthony stood. "Mama, that was positively inspiring," he said affably. "There is nothing in the world more motivating to a happily married couple than a good love poem."

The dowager beamed and blushed.

"In fact, I found it so inspiring," he continued, "that I find it necessary to go and meditate upon it. Linnea, I believe our guests can amuse themselves for a while."

Linnea looked up in surprise, then turned a vivid scarlet as her husband drew her to her feet.

"You once made me a promise," he said, a wicked sparkle in his eyes.

345

"Yes, but . . ." Words failed her as she stared up at him indignantly.

"Well, then? Did you not remark to me this very morning that the daffodils are in bloom?"

"Gracious, did I?" Her blush intensified as Aimee Perth giggled and said, "Oh, go along, Linnea. I'm sure Charles and I can contrive to occupy ourselves for a while."

Out of the corner of her eye, she saw Lord Vale reach for his wife's hand. "We ought to take Miranda up to Nanny," he remarked. "I suppose little Jack will still be napping?"

"Yes, I . . . I believe so." Amanda fanned herself as though the room had suddenly grown very hot.

Across the room, Iris and Gabriel exchanged soulful looks. "Perhaps a walk?" Iris suggested.

"Walk where you like," said Anthony. "Anywhere except in the maze."

"My goodness," said the dowager, staring at her poem with surprise. "I had no idea you would all like it so well. There was one place where the imagery did not seem quite right . . ." She shook her head, looking pensive. "I had better go and start another one. I'm obviously very good at this. Perhaps in the end I shall publish a volume."

"An excellent notion," agreed her son, a lazy smile curving his mouth. "And I've another one." In one smooth movement, he bent and, to Linnea's astonishment, hefted her tail-up over his shoulder. "Do excuse us," he added cheerfully. "Linnea and I will be occupied for a while, but we shall see you all at dinner."

Outraged, Linnea cuffed him in the back. "For pity's sake, Anthony, put me down! At once, do you

346

hear?" Her hair flopped down, and the pressure of his well-muscled shoulder against her lower torso made civilized speech nearly impossible.

As he started for the door, Linnea squeezed shut her eyes and tried not to imagine what she looked like with her derriere in the air. In her heart she knew her guests were unoffended, that each man and woman in her drawing room understood about love and need and passion. And even though she was highly embarrassed, on some primitive level she was also flattered and aroused.

He carried her all the way to the center of the maze, where a fountain spilled and sparkled, and a bed of daffodils thrived like sunshine. The moment he set her down, Linnea planted her fists on her hips. "Anthony Stanton! How could you do such a thing? I have never been so mortified in my life!"

Even before she finished the sentence, his arms were around her waist. He drew her closer, cradled her against him, pressed his mouth to her hair. "Were you, my heart?" he said thickly. "I am sorry, but you know how impatient I am. I've been thinking about doing this ever since you mentioned daffodils."

"So have I," she confessed in a whisper. She slid her arms around him and shivered. "But you really must cultivate a little more patience, my darling. Such rough-and-ready tactics are not fit for the drawing room." It was difficult to concentrate when he was raining kisses over her face, when the hot, familiar tension was driving all else from her mind.

Pulling away, he took her hand and led her toward the square of grass surrounded on three sides by flowers. "Little prude," he grumbled, pulling her down onto his lap. "No, I shouldn't call you that.

After all, you did live up to your promise regarding the drawing room."

"And the front parlor," she reminded, in a very prim tone. "And, if I remember correctly, numerous other rooms of the house. What the servants must think, I'm sure I don't know."

His soft laugh stirred her coppery curls. "Come now, you know we're always discreet. But I will admit that 'prude' is entirely the wrong word for you." His arms circled her, forcing her to straddle his thighs. "Come here, my lusty wench. Don't think I haven't guessed your secret."

"My secret?" Her lips parted in surprise.

He wiggled his brows. "Your secret desire to seduce me in the scullery. But I fear even I must draw the line at that."

Linnea smiled. "You silly man. *That* is not my secret."

"Oh?" He lay back onto the grass and drew her down onto his hard length. "You really do have a secret, then?" He caressed the rounded curves of her buttocks and eyed her speculatively.

"Why, yes." Oddly flustered, Linnea worked one of his shirt buttons in and out of its hole. "I thought you might have guessed . . . because you are so very clever . . ." Leaving the button undone, she transferred her efforts to his cravat. "I did not want to mention until . . . until I was sure . . . but it has been nearly three months now so—"

"Oh Linnea, oh love, are you telling me that—?"

She nodded shyly. "That you are to be a father."

"A father." She watched anxiously as he drew in a deep breath and shut his eyes. Then he hugged her, very hard. "No, I never guessed," he said shakily.

"Naturally, I had hoped. But all these months have gone by . . ."

Smiling to herself, Linnea tossed the cravat aside and lay her head on his chest. As always, she took simple pleasure in the strong, steady beat of his heart, which never failed to remind her that life was a precious gift. "I suppose it takes longer for some people," she remarked. "Frankly, I thought it would happen much sooner, considering . . ."

"Considering?"

"Considering how often we—" Lifting her head, she caught his lazy grin. "Wretch! You are trying to put me to the blush again."

"No, my beautiful wife, I'm trying to decide how to thank you. You have given me so much—love, hope, passion, a life worth living. And now a child too." His voice grated, raw with emotion. "God, I love you, Linnea."

"I love you too, Anthony. And if you really wish to thank me . . . ?"

"You know I do."

Her lashes lowered provocatively. "Daffodils," she whispered.

For the length of a heartbeat, the rake and his lady simply gazed at each other.

And then they smiled.

Author's Note

For those who are interested, several of the secondary characters in *The Rake And His Lady* figured as characters in Julie Caille's other Regency novels. Specifically, the Marquis of Vale and his marchioness, Amanda, were the hero and heroine of her first book, *The Scandalous Marquis*. Charles Perth also appeared in that book, as well as in her second, *Change of Heart,* where he lost his heart to Miss Aimee Farington.

Julie's other full-length Regencies include *An Impetuous Bride* and *A Valentine's Day Fancy.* Her short story "Journey's End" was included in Zebra's Mother's Day Collection, *A Mother's Heart,* published in May of '92.

Julie Caille welcomes letters from readers and invites you to write to her c/o Zebra Books, 475 Park Avenue South, New York, NY 10016. Thank you for your support.